JIM & MARTHA

A NOVEL ON ECO LIVING

JOEL SCHUELER

ISBN: 978-1-672323-41-3

London Oxford Press

Cover Design by Kingwood Creations

Book layout by ebooklaunch.com

JIM & MARTHA

Chapter One

S he hadn't seen an erection in thirty-five years. She was transferring galaxies, cross-dressing time. Her eyes were a mean white today on October 16th 2021. That was one Mrs McCall that lived down the road from Cherryblossom Street with her spindly black cat— the only thing she stroked. Today she left a present outside camp.

Meredith, the post-neoteric sappy extraordinaire galloped along giddily. Applied was just enough makeup to make it look as if she had smacked both sides of her face really hard.

'Martha!' she cried. 'Look what they've given us!' Meredith presented a carded oblong box with six handmade double chocolate chip muffins.

'That's nice of them,' said a far less enthusiastic Martha, taking an attack from the sun in her eyes with distinction. Of her personality, Martha was like an orange, each segment a characteristic to which she could, from all the segments that made her, interchange like the wind its course.

'It's unmarked, no note on it or anything. Some-one must have feeling, a generosity.' Meredith paused. 'You alright?'

'Yeah fine,' said Martha unconvincingly, though she liked that she was asked. Indeed it sometimes felt as though Meredith could systematically pick at parts of Martha's brain, contacting intricate ramblings of thought and make sense of them. By this way at least, the two had telepathic connectivity. Meredith presented herself as if to say: I'll be your plate, load it up, there's not much on it. Get an all-you-can-eat buffet if you like. Martha loved how if she ever got too high, Meredith could ground her in an instant like a cat from a fall; the nib to her pen.

#

Jim had financially soiled himself. Forty-six hours earlier and he realised just how bad things had got. His voice about four thousand cigarettes deeper than this time last year, Jim, the one whose papers were creased and food-stained, the one for whom time felt easy. To look to the next path to adapt to lies a path of odd circumstance or serendipitous creation. Sucking and hissing and crowing and belching went the old door as Jim heard his girl.

'Come on Martha, sort your bags please.'

'I am.'

'Well I've got two and you've got fifty so we need to get going.'

She sighed. *Her* add the wind closed the door. The wind made the door's lock moan from side to side as if a phantom trying at the handle couldn't escape. When so much in life is geared toward achieving success, Jim stood in the corridor and dreamed what it could be to fail. Yes there's the one who works darn hard at high school. Works hard again at college and university. Becomes his job. What happens to the one that stopped after high school, and who is interested? He may not attain the documents to say he knows success but has he earned more life along the way and is as such more finely tuned to its crescendos and hells? Jim had yet to meet anyone say, 'I'd really like to fail'; he hadn't that is 'til he found himself.

Fail box. Tick the box, fall straight in. What an absolute fail. He failed at high school exams, the gym, snooker halls, women, family relations, money, animals, croquet and very life itself.

The timepiece on the sideboard ticked to itself halfway through the day and Martha found herself in the same corner of the room falling to…

She is remembering a conversation: it is during a date and whilst the guy in front of her is talking, she remembers she can never be with a man that would treat her so well, that would without request provide cups of tea and maybe the odd spot of breakfast in bed.

For Martha, as a dater, he was a one-hit wonder. Martha! She flies she dances she sings she trances to Afrobeats to Kate Bush shrieks to Baudelaire and Keats.

Martha turned over the hourglass, straightened the sconce, lit the green candle with grace. The candlestick had at its centre the initials 'MF.' She mouthed the ancient incantations she had learnt and relearnt so many times before. Abnormal?! What are you talking about I'm perfectly normal thank you, said her head. OK my thoughts scutter. They are droplets of pained ideas at two hundred miles per hour, sometimes, probably, but I'm perfectly normal, aren't I? Someone please tell me I'm normal. I'm normal I'm normal. OK Martha, she now said in the third person to herself, I'm telling you Martha is normal. Normal, normal, thank you very much.

Nobody knew what the incantations were, nobody cared much. Nobody cared about anything much in 2021. Jim biliously averted his eyes from unopened letters as far as six weeks in age and most were tan-stained from all the curries he ate anyhow. To look in Jim's side of the bedroom would be to look at someplace given up. Black of charcoal and death. One could barely walk about as papers and clothes and all sorts of odd bits and pieces bestrewed the floor; to go into finer details would be too odious to talk more of. And the clichés, the clichés! He once had everything and lost it all—that little chestnut. He'd heard about the dropout in films and TV. Books very rarely bothered him.

'Would you do me a favour and close that fucking window? There's an awful chill in here,' said Jim.

Nature mothered Martha's thoughts as she looked up at a smiling gabled skylight replying,

'I like keeping the window open, it keeps me in check with nature. I'm not so bugged by the cars or the people that go by, but that rustling of the trees when the cars have stopped for the night? It's priceless. That rustling of the trees, do you hear? You best get used to it. Soon we won't have any windows.'

'It's the hour of the horn again.' Jim pointed at the manmade scales of time around his wrist, on fawn brownness, of false chic.

'I don't want that now. I thought you wanted to pack anyway?'

'Yeah, but I want to play.'

Martha drove a look into him, a nondescript unforgettable look. Jim was ignored and grew away.

The dropout. Why does nobody aspire to be the dropout? What makes it so bad and where do they drop to? Are they syringed out of the sky, devil's heroin in God's ceremonial dropper, doused onto earth, remnants in its soil? Are things really as bad for you once society plays jury, titling you as such? Or is it a something-system their ancestors manufactured to gauge success, to see who forgot to play the game? Who lies the unwashed success or successor? To this motion, maybe the judges have it right. Maybe dropouts have it hard.

Jim met a girl who helped establish his failure. Failure, to succeed could do with a plan. Enjoying losing also, the lady had not blended with the bad path, even if with tarry ideas, she had experimented to do so. She came from a comfortable family like Jim, had preferred genetically modified men but none had been invented yet. It was Jim that came along with a besom of confidence to sweep up her anxieties. Under his tutelage, she could share impressions of earth. She knew a man called Dave. Everyone knows a Dave. With a little help from peers, Dave had established a New Age hippy commune, or so Jim thought. A commune yes, but an ecovillage too. When things were going right, this place smiled. *She* was Martha.

For a couple of months, Martha had intermittently joined Dave and co. at the commune, where administering drugs, they would brainstorm beliefs such as how in the future, computerised systems will be so advanced that they will be able to read minds.

'We'll get the taxi for quarter past ten. That will give us plenty of time to get our connection. Still sure you want to forget the car?' Jim cheekily asked.

'It wouldn't be right to take it. I want this to be the last car journey I take for a good while.'

Patience isn't a virtue, it's a bloody waste of time. Jim's mind had opened up.

He felt behind everyone. For instance, the people Jim classed as everyone had at least seen *The Lord of the Rings*, and he had long wanted to watch and read it. However, Jim did not like concentrating on anything too long when not bothering seemed so much more attractive. As a frequent occurrence in his life, when he realised it, there was nothing more to do than set about getting stoned or engage in other drug-induced spacing out. He wanted to feel good about his shortcomings, and maybe if he hung around likeminded people, he could join in some harmonic communal utopian failure. Time spoke. Opening the world's wallet in a place of little monetary requirement, it became imperative to spend some life at the commune.

'Get your bin off my fucking property!' Such delights of suburban living echoed last night through the street on which Jim and Martha now stood by grief-leaved flora. Having packed their things, looking back to implant an image, clouds were in a hurry in front of an ailing sun squeezing dying breaths of light on the desolate flat one last time. Of the flat, Jim liked best the overhanging eaves and the welcome skylight. It was too late for second thoughts but that didn't stop Jim from having them. Could he dare to slip in a hesitation? Ambling by Martha, he remained watchful, his confident moment on tenterhooks, his moment amidst a dark promise like wintry early evening. Jim had liked living by the cemetery, it gave him a sense of community.

Whooping cough of an engine, tobacco smoke tattooed on its interior, the beaten down taxi cab—whose driver looked like the kind of person you'd find down the back of a sofa—was due in a few minutes before a future world of few things, and Martha worried three times whether they had everything. Wurlitzers, accordions, finger paints, I should really get that mole looked at, halva, what's Noel Edmonds up to these days? and jaunty self-invented ditties about political soundbites swelled in her brain. Next came: gin, Delacroix, blood sacrifice and what the point of breadsticks was. The brain spat them out in all directions to only where she could see and hear, one after the after; overlap, speed and collision. It was so confusing, terrible and beautiful she could have cried. She then sought to look at the world how it was and not how it was in relation to her. Jim lit a fag.

O anxious Martha. She is like a matador combatting oxygen in an undiscovered continent. She licks the air like a death-defying tree frog, reaching the bough, falls back on her arse.

James Frederick Moyles was alive in 2021, born breech in Queen Mary's Hospital of London in 1985. He was on a delightful pay packet from the government called Jobseeker's Allowance at thirty-six years old. In many countries there would be nothing.

Another day, JSA, you know how it is. Doleful on the dole, you *know* it's bad when you've applied to so many weeks' worth of jobs that you have to ask for a new diary, and even worse when you start using some of that money to gamble on the outcome of the next Pope. On a new system called Universal Credit, all communication had moved online making everything perfect in an instant. Three blooming years Jim hadn't done anything on his 'Things To Do' list—the list that sat in the drawer next to another list called 'girls that never messaged me back.'

'Hello son,' said his father, speaking below a wiry moustache after Jim's first day at school. They said nothing more to Jim the whole evening through, as father carried a hefty chest to the lounge whereupon the catch of his worries could be released, and a lengthy conversation could ensue for the rest of the evening with Jim's mum about the mortgage, adding coins to the worry meter.

Fourteen years later, Jim entered upon his first job: the point in time that you learn freedom is a private function and your membership card just expired. At first, to feel wanted felt terrific, and nineteen is the age where jumps in time feel more poignant and everything seems new, and even the most sapless of environments can be attacked with utmost enthusiasm. As a full-time worker on a crappy wage, and for the most part with affable staff helping out, he did not mind the hours or the photocopier or the printer, staple gun and filing cabinets. Even the awful toilets were only slightly awful. An administrator for a pharmaceutical company, he was happy to be as naïve as possible in expending all his youthful energy in keeping a machine afloat along its expansive journey. Jim did his job, nothing special, a good ordinary. He did not know at the time the extent to which he was a pawn in antidepressant production, not that he had anything against it, in and of itself. However, he would have disfavoured helping multiple future governments have many more multimillion pound glad-handing handshakes with his bosses. He got out, on a quest for higher academia, realising nothing.

Somersaulting to the campus bar, it was rejuvenating to meet new gentlepeople and the not so gentle at university. It was a Welsh one, and Jim soon got more interested in hash than he did people. Broadly speaking it was that good old Welsh soapbar rather than the connoisseur's Afghan or Moroccan that did not have bits of plastic in. As is quietly common in late adolescence, Jim pissed about doing very little of a great many things. Back in the season of his school years he bled success. He always sat with the cool kids at the back of the bus when it was all a front. In scientific subjects and mathematics, Jim was top of the class and curable in others. As a pettable sycophant for the teachers, he read like a bestseller of innocence. Now he wondered: how did I end up here?

Progressing with a jounce here and there, Jim smiled, his now firmly around Martha in the back of the silly taxi.

'I know why we're doing this,' he said. 'I want you to be happy. But if you could narrow it down to one main reason, well, what would it be?'

'The future, Jim. It's for us.'

'Do I even want to be a hippy?' A grin on Jim's face suggested a provocative aim.

'It's not like that, you know it isn't. I can't wait to see Meredith again, it's been too long.'

Martha began reading from a Surrey tourist magazine she had on her lap. 'Anyway we've talked about this all loads, you simple soul. It fits how I'd like to live. Just think, we can get away from the frigging systems of house prices and rent. Another financial strain gone. It's about low-impact self-made housing. The more we build, the more we make councils and hopefully governments stand up and take notice. We can change laws.'

'Do you even know Carringdon that well?'

'Just your copybook south London town. Dave'll tell us everything we need to know. It's not like I've never seen it.'

'Right.'

Martha slouched back into her seat like a puma off duty from a hunt.

'You've saved me from boredom, Jim.'

Jim's words two weeks earlier:

'Well if this is what you want to do, then let's just do it. We'll elope to a field where no-one will ever find us.'

'It's so exciting, I've never done anything like this before,' Martha's return.

Once Jim left uni, there was no going back. With a mind as racing, as multifaceted, as explosive as his, Jim could work the monotonous office job no longer, refusing to be a makeweight for time. At least that's what he told himself. His plan went on hold after moving back and forth to his parents and squalid flats doing jobs he did not want to do for seemingly aeons. It was incontrovertibly now that he had had enough.

There was always feng shui for when nothing else worked. Typical mincy middle-class bastards dabbling with mood-altering room rearrangement, Jim's dated unapologetically unpolitically correct part of his brain informed him. Where did those fifteen years go? Jim often asked this too. He often asked looking at flabbergasted walls and sturdy ceilings. Today, he was off to the land of no ceilings.

The six months on Martha and Jim's rent at their flat had just ended based on a gentleman's agreement. The problem with a gentleman's agreement is there is no guarantee that the male who forms it is a gentleman. It takes more than being a male to make a man, and it takes more than being a man to make a gentleman. Being a gentleman is a refined decision, just ask Jim. Gentlemen use semicolons more often too. When it was signed, Martha could not help but wonder: should there be a common female or gender-neutral alternative to the gentleman's agreement?

Martha rested her head gently on Jim's shoulder as the car continued to chug along, and she thought of life before their flat. She lived isolated. She had so many brilliant thoughts she wanted to share with the world yet only she could hear them.

Taxi ride done and paid for, they got their train alright, arrived at Carringdon Station, strolled through its town afore weaving their way through little country lanes. The sky was overcast, the climate mild and their stomachs full, having picked up some late lunch in their new hometown. A vast wooded area opened before the lovebirds. Off to the right a tall curly-haired woman lulled deep forest, her arms in precise motions, left leg slipping past the right smooth as the light wind, lady tai chi. How striking the vision. What change from car after car on the unforgiving streets. Martha knew who it was, Jim did not. Jim was betwixt and between whether he liked to follow, but Martha led the course for the main gate, after a fashion. Late stages of life strewn around, rolling out the ground like a poster of oranges and browns below the now emboldened yet mute greys above. The pair treaded a new cambering path. Martha remembered the route just about enough to know where she was. Seven minutes later she glanced at the rutted dirt by the entrance whereon stones were superimposed spelling out, 'Welcome To Freedom'; Jim walked past, not noticing. The track gave on to where 'Carringdon Ecovillage' was printed in large lettering at the front gate. A 'section 6' note was displayed below the bulky entrance sign along with a load of other gobbledegook Jim was not arsed to read. Then came the words,

Carringdon Ecovillage is a collection of individuals as one. We are dedicated to low-impact, sustainable living. From disused land we strive to create something beautiful for all

#

The sun of reason is upon us and her subjects are dancing in a clear stretch of air. The commune looking calmingly furnished with oak trees: bulbous fogs of green above gnarly beginnings.

Well, thought Martha, they were probably oaks, or were they ash? No, beech? Maybe lime. Shut up Martha, it's just a tree, she thought.

'Hey Martha, hey Jim, good to meet you, I'm Manny,' a Latino man said coming towards them, sky-high and undernourished with dark features and a good attempt at an English accent. 'So, Martha, you are the artist they keep telling me about. We always want artists here!'

'I try, when I have time. Hopefully I'll have much more time here! There's so much of the natural world to take inspiration from.'

'Yes, sure. There's good camaraderie here, helpfulness, teambuilding, no-one judges you. You can be who you want to be. Make yourselves at home, and if you need any help setting up, or whatever, just let me know.'

'Thank you. Yeah I've been here three times and seen you once or twice but never said hello. Anyway, thanks again,'

'So what made you come here?' Jim asked Manny.

'The thing I say to people is: if you're a landowner, then you have a title deed which says, OK, I own this piece of land. But land is not something humans should own, it is bigger than that, something brought to us by Providence. What gives us the right to say we own it, you see? But then, as with everything, mammon gets in the way. It is too attractive to people. Then you get the ideology of stewardship which means you care for the land, and then sovereignty, but that's by the by.

For thirteen years this land was left unused and derelict. Before this a plastics company was here. We are here to raise awareness of land issues and show people there is another way.'

'And the shower and your hut, they're impressive. I heard on the grapevine you made them yourself?' said Martha.

'The hut yes, the shower I was the main instigator, yes. I learned my trade young. Well, not *my* trade but my sister's. I learned from her. It is amazing what you can find, you just need to look. Construction sites have materials we can use. We use salvaged timber and woven tree branches. Even in the dumpsters you would be surprised what is there. The shower we had before was improvable.'

The former shower, rudimentary in design, had as its main components a siphon, bucket and foot pump.

'Right, I've not seen the shower yet,' said Jim.

'Ah, of course Jim, you've not seen this place before have you, but you know Dave?'

'He's the only one here I know, yeah, from way back when. We hung out a few times, he's a good lad.'

'I tell you what, I need to take care of something, but…' A nearby man caught Manny's attention. 'Hey Kristoff!' he called out. The man came over in a walk that said: I'm guilty for my presence, forgive me for taking up everyone's time. 'Kristoff would you take Jim around on a tour of the ecovillage? Martha knows this place but it is Jim's first time.'

Jim was given the casual tour of the site by some-one that didn't have anything better to do with their time.

Martha started her charm on others, hoping to find a fellow female.

Kristoff asked Jim how he was, in the way that many do, not wanting to know how Jim really was but to use the question as a substitute for hello, in a show of care entwined with polite enquiry. Demure and wholly forgettable, Kristoff's damp deportment only underscored what Jim was about to see. At times he sounded as though he had the craw of a disliked rabbit heading for heaven by the net, having been ousted from his home by a ferret in an SS uniform.

A Muscovite, Kristoff grew in confidence as the tour went on, marshalling the ecovillage the way Zhukov had his men, victorious outside the Kremlin at Red Square. Tall, not lanky; svelte. What was a well-kept thin man doing here? Jim thought.

'What is a well-kept thin man like you doing here?' Jim asked. 'Someone like you, in a place like this?'

'Sorry, how you mean?'

What a wretched picture it all looked. An omni-shambles, the biggest mishmash of crap Jim had ever seen. Shitty little vegetable patches erroneously labelled 'cabbiges' and 'brocoly.' And it wasn't just the brassicas too. There were bottles of bleach labelled 'bleech.' What kind of uneducated James Hunts ran this place? thought Mr Moyles. The shower was an interesting contraption. It measured fifty-five by fifty-three centimetres. Its height, 190 centimetres. Wood, the ancestor's choice, was crudely formed into a staircase of sorts. Its turquoise outside received dreamy psychedelic triangles and rhombi of pink and orange.

'In stove you heat the water and take the water. You go up steps, you put the water in big container,' said Kristoff. The container or barrel sat sorrily for gravity's pleasure, on top of the shower unit. 'The shower, er…it all recycle, everything recycle.' Simple pipework connected to a rusting showerhead. 'Cathy and me, we do the art.'

'I'm sure Martha will like to help out with the art here too,' Jim said.

A blackboard by the kitchen revealed lists of needed items:

> *Blankets, rubble sacks, water buts, containers, hay bales, canvas, tarp, aesthetic plants, edible plants, sand bags, non-treated firewood, DIY appliances*

Situated at the easternmost part of the ecovillage was this kitchen. A handful of overeager midges foxtrotted, their deviltry not unnoticed in distracting Jim from reading the rest of the board:

> *Seedy Saturday Event 2pm*
> *Seed Swap. Bring your seeds along and swap with others!*

Of gustatory sea-salt Jim thought the air and in the kitchen no-one was cooking. Askew shelves, drawers, sin, daydreams, boxes, utensils, cob of mud from a brook, stones, pebbles, cabinets and hopes cluttered around a wood burner in the kitchen.

An ankle unwashed, a poor choice of words, a dusting of healthy humour, a whistling of a song from *Pablo Honey*, dull ache and a moving portrait of sarcasm just passing through. All these and more this day elongated man's decay having this room found their way. Near the kitchen was a tiny building used as a storehouse for stockpiling wood, tools and some foodstuffs. There was a sign by here:

Thou shalt not eat that which is pesticide-ridden
Thou shalt eat fresh from the ground
Big up the plants!

'Have you met Meredith yet?' a northern voice asked Martha.

'Er, well yes, I've been here a few…'

I'll say, she looks like she needs a good square meal. Mind you, that's what they teach 'em at fashion school 'int it. Ooh I don't agree with that, them that's in charge ought to be ashamed. Bad for the soul ya know? Nice girl mind. You'll get on with her, same age an' that. Have ya met Dave? Lovely fella, salt o' the earth.' A woman named Cathy from Derker was talking. Martha was worried if there were going to be many more characters like her. She looked at the garrulous Cathy to see a bit of overdone face, a bit of smoky smoky and a lot of sideward glances. Cathy wore light blue jeans intentionally torn at each knee, one with a better result than the other. Up top she had on a dark T-shirt, label upturned at the nape. Its faded writing spelled out 'The Who.' 'Have you any washing m'love? Ya know you'll need the launderette. We've got a mangle 'ere too what that widow, can't remember 'er name, buddy of Sue donated. They're nice round 'ere some locals, give us lots of stuff, not bric-a-brac mind, I mean useful stuff like.'

'Ah I'd love to try and use that mangle sometime but just want to be quick for now.'

'Yer still of childbearing age aren't ya. Are you an' Jim going to 'ave a baby 'ere? We'd love that, ya know. That'd be so sweet. Havin' a little baby 'ere. Oh we'd love that my lovely.'

Bedbugs neared midges swarming around Cathy and Martha by a recycling receptacle, and a festooned garland of twined twigs and moss hung from a transitory kitchen rail. Outside, abutting the kitchen was the communal area, or communal point, as it was sometimes known. Here, Cathy and Martha were on a bench beside a few logs also used for sitting on. The benches and logs were in a circle around a firepit. 'Ya know, a lot 'ere we get donated,' said Cathy. 'This bench we're on fer starters; from one of the locals this. The communal point we're in is also called *Shard*. It were Peter's idea to jazz things up a bit so 'e likes to call it that. Not many else do. Most stuff is given from the kindness of locals. We get some wood from some o' them tree surgeons an' palettes from some o' them companies.'

Consciences and bodies wobbled and restrengthened like the afternoon winds as the conversation went on apace. Jim was coming back from his tour, shaking his head. Martha went over to hear about his travails.

'God more jargon crap,' he began. '*I* don't know, if I hear words like 'biodiversity,' 'permaculture,' 'low-impact living,' 'eco sustainability' one more time…'

Mind you, it was better than words from Jim's last job like 'outsourcing,' 'profit maximisation' and 'team player.' Jim much preferred words like 'world cup' and 'minge.'

'I can't believe you're that fed up of things already,' Martha said. 'I already think your tiredness is talking. Why don't you have a nap or something?'

An actor against type, Jim's system was shutting down. This wasn't a three-quarter job into logging off mode. No. This was the end with no *on* button in sight. All these sorry hippies were making Jim feel sick. All rubbing up against each other, scabies and lice handed on from one to the next no doubt, thought Jim.

A lantern by Cathy flickered, a wavering swingball in a distilled breeze followed in her mind, a conflation of thought and image. Ingratiation in the making, Jim remembered something.

'There was one thing though that gave me hope,' Jim went on.

'What was that?' With one hand outstretched on an adjacent table, and with the other on her hips as she was peeved, Martha looked like she was imitating a teapot.

'The guy showing me round said it was their Arc de Triomphe, their pièce de résistance. He's not even French. What it is: there's a newly installed charging point and tech area here. Basically, it's a solar panel. I'm not sure how it all works, I got lost in his accent, but it can charge up our laptops etcetera.'

'O that's great. I know they had been talking about that for a while but I didn't realise they had actually put it into practice. Just as well we brought all that electronic junk with us then. Well, you know me, I'm not too bothered but I guess it could help us if we start missing our old life.'

'Too bloody right.'

'What was his name again?'

'Who?'

'The guy that showed you around?'

'O, can't remember.'

#

The ecovillage. Where nothing yet everything happened. The land was twenty acres. They only claimed it because they had to. Their very own love, life, land. Others thought otherwise. This wasn't tree-hugging, flare-wearing, tie-dyed-shirt wearing eco warriors and eco worriers. People, just people, had become land activists. More and more ecovillages were popping up around the country. These gardens of earth.

Martha looked out. Here they were, in this field. Their freedom, what the scientologists call clear, the Buddhists, nibbana; their entire raison d'être lay within a square of grass. How much, if any section, was looking in?

Jim and Martha's unpitched tent was lying on the ground next to a solitary Jim, who marked his territory by doing the dirty: reaching in his pocket for the cigarette packet. All of a sudden, someone walked by, appearing in Jim's vision. It was the tai chi lady he had seen earlier on.

'Hi, I'm Jim.'

'Meredith,' the lady replied, shaking his hand. 'Nice to meet you. Hope you find what you need and make yourselves welcome.' Jim's handshake was rehearsed. He leant in and gave a good squeeze to let her know he was the *man*. It was a long while since Jim had heard an American accent in person. Although carefree, she looked like she could pack a punch. Meredith's eyes circled Jim, finding their way to the cigarette packet in his hand. 'Can I trouble you for a fag?'

O, I know what this is about, you fancy me, thought Jim. In spite of Meredith's impassioned pacifism, she was not so kind to her lungs. What?! What the fuck is happening?! What is the meaning of this illusory game? said her lungs to her brain, as cilia got stamped on. You're not actually a smoker insomuch as you rarely do this, so why do you bamboozle us this way? finished the cilia.

Girlish vagina, you are most female, I shall find thee. Or do indeed you think of me as rotting lowlily? A shoe-shine, knocker-up, pin boy. Yeah, you have one of my cigarettes love. What does it matter? I'm Jimmy Moyles. All this and *then* some, Jim heard his soul say.

Jim had found a smoker and the worst kind of smoker. The antismoking smoker: quick to warn of its dangers and quick to stick it in the gob. She was also good at having the idea to smoke and realising she didn't really want to when it came to it. Billowing, preaching, didactic in her teachings, all the while smoking.

For Jim, her frilly dress was garish, gaunt, bloody awful. Its kenspeckle yellows sharply agleam with ill-conceived floral shapes blobbed on a white background.

What she wore today was as expensive as half Martha's wardrobe. Meredith had dark brown hair and was five foot eleven. Martha had amber-brown hair and was five foot nine. Both were similar in frame, though Meredith had the Wonderbra, girdle and tight trousers to show hers off more. Martha was a liberal snob. She didn't have any money but she could appreciate good wine.

Meredith, notwithstanding her occasional smoking, used a saltpipe for her asthma. It was one aimed at children in the shape of an elephant. She liked the way it made her feel about its apparent restorative properties. She did not trust doctors and the inhalers they gave out. After some small talk exchanging introductory character profiles and origins, Jim got down to business.

'Want to join me later for a spliff?' he asked.

'Sure, why not.'

Meredith didn't think it so bad to smoke the green if she called them naughty cigarettes. It helped her forget she was taking drugs. It was the smell and the funny things she watched stoned people do that she preferred over its effects.

'Well I look forward to that and it's good to finally meet you,' said Jim. 'Martha's told me a lot about you. You were quite a big part in her coming here. By the way, where's the toilet?'

'Kristoff didn't show you the compost toilet?'

'You fucking what? Compost toilet?' Jim said, chortling.

'Come, I'll show you.'

Fleet of foot, she made off scarlet-paced. It looked seriocomic. Her upstairs couldn't keep up with her lioness legs. Everything she had conned in fashion school was slightly off. Shifting through her hips, her arms were dead weights, nailed to her sides against the dog-eared floppiness of her trousers. Her legs were so rapid her brittle torso jerked too far forward with each leg thrust to look comfortable. It was like she was on an imaginary catwalk slightly constipated.

Gangly American, no you don't! We've only just met and haven't established the pace yet, thought Jim. You don't just walk off one hundred miles an hour, silly bitch.

Jim's funny little legs—at least they looked little from Meredith's vantage point—ran a staccato chirpy melody until fastened by mind. Cramp had come on. Finally, he caught her. Aching, Jim never found out why he took the trouble keeping up.

'Here they are,' she said, purely, oblivious to his struggles.

All that to wind up at the shithouse. Jim made it damn sure from this day forward he was only to speak to Meredith on a needs-must basis and never of his own volition. Basta. He could not allow himself to think such thoughts until he had seen the night waltz with camp singalongs under those shining whites like flakes from an erupted moon. 'It was mainly Manny who did this up and Burt helped out a bit too. I'm not sure you've met Burt yet, he rarely shows. You wanna know something? When I first came here, if I caught as much as a thumbnail of dirt, I had to remove it. But then I realised it was all so petty. Now none of that stuff phases me. I'm much more ruralised now I think.'

No place for transparent la-de-das, the compost toilet was essentially a hole in the ground with a well-groomed wooden seat in a small hut Manny had made. Once business was done, sawdust was thrown over despicable acts from the human digestive system with not an air freshener in sight. It wasn't somewhere to read a paper or reflect as flies danced a jig below. Like the makeshift shower, no pursuits of leisure could be sought from such methods of practicality. When Martha first used it, it was like there was an aperture in her coffin. Hitherto, the odour was a little off-putting, so Manny and Burt had put down tarpaulin, which helped. 'Did Kristoff tell you about the recycling or did he forget that too?'

'No he said sod all about that.'

'Hmm, when I was younger, my mom said not to trust people like him. "Don't trust those Russians if you should ever meet them," she said. She never met one herself but I guess now I know what she means.'

Fuck sake, first the compost shitter, and now he had to bother with how he threw stuff away. All this green life. Green this, green that. Piss off Meredith, bearer of green news. Hole in the ground? Jim would much prefer they find a hole in the wall so they could all chip in for a proper toilet with decent plumbing.

At Jim's former places of work, the first ones to know it all were the first ones out the door. Jim learned that the successful man, with the best kind of success, is the one that observes his environment continually. He may have seen the same scene a thousand times but he doesn't take it for granted, doesn't believe the scene for how it was, and never thinks he knows too much.

Sometimes there are better things to do than listen to your own advice.

Jobwise, Martha was lastly a communications-flavoured admin monkey. It wasn't lost on her that the job hadn't completely lost her. She was writing faxes and emails in her mind to directors in the gas industries. It was a time just before she had moved in with Jim, and she was sharing with three other girls. Apostrophes were seldom used improperly and everything was so clean and was everyone was so bitchy. From these girls, Martha felt aloof. Too many conversations about hair extensions, fingernails and whatnot for her liking.

When Jim first met Martha, she talked with ardour about how she had a penchant for travel and a long-felt but never realised desire to go sailing. Jim could never impress her this way: he could not afford a camping trip to Bognor Regis, and he was never going to take her sailing. He had enough problems on the land. The best journey he could hope for was a fast track to her underpants. Pipe-dreaming once there, frankly there was no need to overcomplicate things. Jim could never understand all this talk these days of unlocking the back door when penis and vagina had quite happily been exchanging ideas for generations. And good heavens, what on earth was a butt plug? Jim looked down to his own pants and could not fathom how considerably bushiness had metastasized. No job for cheap razors, more a slash and burn deforestation toolkit.

Later it was time for Jim to reluctantly share that spliff with Meredith, like he had agreed. Though chiefly a liberal environment, Jim was adamant that the two go behind a tree out the way, just in case anyone disapproved. What is more, it provided a safeguard against potential paranoia.

'I'm glad to see Martha back,' said Meredith.

'Good.'

'Presumably she was glad to see me too, right?!'

'Yep.'

Minimalist conversation Jim excelled at. Today was his Oscar-winning performance. Meredith's tolerance was low to cannabis as she had not smoked for a while. Hot rocks on the blouse, scrambling like the smoke from out a smokestack, looking vague and curtain-called, the triumphal misdemeanant ready for a takedown—such was Meredith's look after said joint, surrounded by sunlight and leaves. Her pair of sun-dappled elbows faced the hardy ground.

#

In putting up their tent, stoned, Jim spent much of the time staring at Martha hoping she would do it.

'This will be fine for now,' said Martha, nervously unravelling the peg bag, wapping a few pegs in frustration as they dropped to the floor, then picking them up. 'This tent I mean, fine. Plenty of time to build a little place to call our own.'

Miring mind. Martha set herself still. Wilily she rubbernecked Jim's tobacco pouch. It was a game she played to see how sizzling her choler could get. She felt great now she had more time for such games. A fluty voice trekked through the wind:

'D'you need a help with that, ducky?' A stocky woman with a visor for late spills of summerly sunshine loped toward Martha.

'Ah thank you. What is your name?' Martha asked.

'I'm Sue. I don't live in the ecovillage. I sometimes come down here. Behind yer, I live in them flats over there.'

'O yes, cool. Cathy mentioned you, nice to meet you. This is my worser half, Jim. It's OK, he lets me call him that.' Both ladies laughed. 'First time we've lived anywhere like this.'

Jim's shadow was upon them like an awning the colour of stone. Like a cosy pastel picture from the last vestiges of today's sunlight, lemon drops passing in the sky parented lighter shadow. Jim's attention was elsewhere and his introduction he had not heard. He was looking like an elementary life-form. No, perhaps that was a bit tart; more like a gawping giant trevally. He loved, in workshy fashion, how around calculated activity he could skirt like the oaks the ecovillage. Sue was his new best friend.

#

The evening opened in ebony mist. The people laughed and trifled. Bantering Brits. There were probably close on twelve people living there including the new couple, though Jim never exerted himself working it all out. Ever since those mental arithmetic classes he had to go to once a week after school, he had given a wide berth to counting. Martha always found it startling how hard people looked to find ways to bicker with other members of their own species. Maybe here in this commune, she could find more people with a propensity to recapture a primordial oneness. Fixated on her soup, Martha wanted to get down in her head every sight, sound, smell, texture and taste for her first meal here. She had never tasted newborn vegetables. The potatoes especially, tasted so earthy. The taste of origin. It felt peculiar but it no longer had to.

How different it felt too, sitting by the postprandial campfire. Usually in an evening Jim would be on an iPad, Martha a book, kindle or laptop. There was something else here, a nod to caveperson routes.

As at the ecovillage entrance, Jim reluctantly thought he overheard, amongst the vespertine chatter, that the 'section 6' notice contained the dictates that the dwellers had entered the premises peacefully, causing no damage, and that such an entrance was a civil not criminal matter. Jim, and Martha especially, enjoyed reminiscing with Dave about the old times.

'I'd like to give a toast!' said Manny above the chitchat, standing like a skyscraper, wineglass of his raised. 'I realise I should have raised one at dinner, but never mind.' Most people laughed. 'We raise a glass to our new arrivals, Jim and Martha!' Everyone present gave them an ovation. 'We will treat them as our own. Long live the ecovillage!'

\#

Dave lived in a wheelchair. A quadriplegic, he had a tender by the name of Anjit. There were few problems with wheelchair access as most of daily life was on grass.

Being precise and unsuperfluous in his requests, Anjit did all he was told.

Dave had failed with a year-long appeal. He, along with family members, were not able to receive the necessary benefit money to live together in regular accommodation.

Anjit had a shit immune system. Pain (life's nefarious mother-in-law) helped Anjit help Dave. It could never be said for Anjit that he wasn't a trier. A trier like a cheery old car with minor malfunctions. Responses to stimuli were sometimes delayed, cognitively going fewer frames per second.

'Anjit's in screensaver mode again,' Peter, one of the eco dwellers, would remind everyone. He definitely liked to remind everyone. Was the mode just a proclivity? Perhaps Anjit just enjoyed taking time out. Perhaps.

Everyone has their own reasons for escape. Peter watered his by the lake the dwellers named *Horizon*. Cathy dreamt in black and blue. Martha saw poems as jigsaw pieces of her world. Meredith had a keenness for small moments of lushness she could derive from toasting vegan marshmallows to watching a squirrel get to grips with an acorn. He could not go very far but no-one ever found out how or why Burt got here. Some that visited or lived at the ecovillage were used to states of inanition, from nine 'til five, making money for their bosses, to trying their hands at the simpler life. Jim had a bit more time for them. A bit more. Jim favoured bedewing, then enveloping his world in cynicism.

How it all looked, that first nightfall, to the inexperienced observer: away from neon phone booths and delicatessens, blankets of fields rollicking in a talented changeover of summer to autumn air…dreaming… losing oneself in spirals of the unlit oily dark green.

#

Today Martha thought she'd go crazy and try a spearmint gum and a peppermint one simultaneously; the results were unexciting. It was Martha and Jim's first morning in their new home.

'Take some leave from work, take a break. Your father's married to his work, you don't want to end up like him. Now I'm reading, shut the door on your way out.' Having just awoken, Jim was recalling words spoken to him by his mother several months back.

Just to break, that was all that was intended. Never could his mum endorse or envisage her son ending up in an ecovillage. The bellicose mum and the hidden other. Jim remembered that it was best to follow the example your parents set. The mum always spoke dutifully and without emotion. He chose to speak like her only more serrated.

At first light, Jim saw but with arguable notice: rain-licks on the tips of grass, the moss, the creatures befriending morning dew.

See it come in, daylight broken by dazzling, entangled, fettered, embittered, unbridled fog.

Jim went to the communal water point to utilise toiletries. In a show of masochism, he slapped on some aftershave to remember pain. Jim liked his electric toothbrush, it meant he had less work to do. Martha didn't like them because she didn't like the way her head zzzzzed about the place. Maybe the more it zzzzzed—the same way it did when the bus stopped with the engine running—she would be more likely to get Parkinson's in later life, she worried.

Of mints, of whites, enter toothpaste! The cannon readied, jumping through the morning it went. Too great a squeeze. On to the brush and unexpecting grass it landed. Only when his teeth hurt did Jim see the dentist, and it is an uncanny thing, how toothpaste is the only commodity you realise you need once it runs out.

Hurriedly yet earnestly, Meredith was snipping Anjit's mazy hair at the communal point. Not far away Kristoff was arranging a bug box of wood, slate, stones, bamboo, grass and mulch. In his musty hexi-tent, Peter was warily trying out his dimly understood hammock for the umpteenth time after its having become again unhooked. Jim later took a look at Manny's hut, at first upended by the sound craftsmanship.

'I can build ours like that, no problem,' he said, trying to conceal an unsureness to Martha.

'You don't need to. Just something practical is fine. Stick to the bender, Jim, that's what we should aim for. We'll make the bender in time, but for now the tent we bought is fine.'

Bender tents are shelters made with poles from coppiced hazel-wood or long thin sticks tied at the appropriate points. Most of Carringdon Ecovillage's population lived in their own benders and Manny's self-made hut was one of the exceptions. Martha secretly wished Jim the layman could bind enough brainpower to know how to be able build a hut like his. Jim liked going to his toolbox. It made him feel like a man. He *almost* felt the man when others weren't there to see him with his box.

Dave was feeling particularly mannish today and held his cup aloft anticipatorily as Cathy next to him prepared a Storm Kettle. She felt self-conscious as she was not happy with her tight top, thinking it demanded her fubsy.

Martha's head had just been born; an overdose of freshness: countrified air snorted to the brain, briars singing as lost hair strands from celestial maidens. Parsnips, beetroots and brassicas came to, and on this day, earth orbited a little prompter.

A white-robed figure was walking towards Jim. Dave had wheeled by too.

'Be at one with yourself, your universe, your intrinsic nature,' said the figure clasping his hands. 'Greetings, Saleem Eaglefeather am I. Never one to endorse the ego, dear friends, but people here have called me "The Sage," or "Sage" for short. And what about you? To what do I owe this pleasure? From where have you come?'

'Greenwich,' said Jim.

'Uh-huh. I see you've brought your townie bags,' said a snickering Sage, turning with the ungainliness of a prowling pangolin. 'Hey Cathy look at the townie bags they've brought!'

'Leave 'em alone, you,' said Cathy. 'They're new 'ere, they're not used to it. They're from the city ya know. Pay 'im no nevermind you two.'

'Might I suggest something a little more suitable than valises and holdalls,' said Sage, turning less niftily back to them. 'A giant outdoor rucksack perhaps? And what brings you here?'

'Mainly Martha, my bim's idea innit,' answered Jim. 'But it is nice to be somewhere quiet…'

'I am here to meet likeminded people and I am glad for meeting you. Your minds like our fields, look at where spare time has found me. When I first came here, my mind raced with slanted desires, but now I find them to be more astute. Our politics are left of centre like the heart. As the venerable Lord Buddha once said…well, uh…it was something to the effect of: "do not associate with fools, follow intelligent, wise people, as the moon follows the path of the stars." And what about me, I hear you ask! I say: the best work you can do is on yourself.'

Sage turned and looked towards the lakeside, pointing at a distant figure saying, 'there he is, that's Peter. There's someone that could do with a rocket up his arse. Then he could start working on *himself*. Twenty days of August sun wouldn't lighten that one. Sometimes he sits there, like that, staring his life away to *Horizon*. He becomes indignant about the past. His anger takes a keen eye to notice as he practices contortedly yet never very redly.'

When Jim looked at Peter, it was like looking at a crescendo point in a horror movie only with the sound turned off. 'He's given to brushing his arm against his face when he gets nervous, amongst other quirks. Gets his glasses steamed up, muddied or marked when he doesn't want to be seen. He is used to the rather odd misfortune of happening upon a fly star-floating in his drink. It really *does* happen with inexplicable regularity. It's not uncommon for there to be two or more.'

For extended spans of time, Peter liked to look at people through his glasses on the end of his nose. That's a lot of weight for the end of a nose.

Sage wasn't really sure if he himself was Hindu, Buddhist, Sikh or something else. Verily, he was a synthesization of influences he had picked up along the way. Sometimes, as with today, he wore a turban. He would never admit it but a previous insight into his karmic storage convinced him, that unless he redressed his lifestyle to one of a more spiritual nature, he was sure that in his next life he was going to reincarnate as a turnip. 'You see there's a difference between losing and being a loser,' he went on. 'The loser spends all his time pandering to his ego, spending what little money he has on drink and drugs, and avoids spending money and maybe time on treatment. Now the person that is losing but that has a good intention to change things is very different. Good intentions, after all, are like the flicker of a spark from flint towards glory. In a sense, many of us here at the ecovillage are losing, because we're going against what society wants us to believe is important. We're going against the paradigm that society thinks we need to follow in order to make good. That said, we have ideas to succeed by our own ways of doing things. Maybe not all of us here, but those of us that want to succeed in these ways are far from being losers. If we keep pushing with all our energies, we can experience success in what we understand success to mean, and it will be beautiful and happy and we don't expect any money from it. Would you care for a sugar-free humbug?' Sage asked, searching about his pockets.

'I see. No, thanks,' said Jim. 'Peter is a loser then?'

'In time, I will let you judge that for yourself. The practice of doing tacitly understands there needn't be much thought. Life is but a fleeting miracle, so we need to keep up the positivity! Life is for living and I am no friend of lists. Come. Let us march through the bejewelled field! Planetary change can only eventuate from a consciousness of love and giving, and we are securing the plinths, even if begun on catacumbal debris. Sentiments can change one day to the next from helplessness to hopefulness, but it is all about sticking to the path and never looking back. I'm starting the engine, I'm getting on the happy bus, you coming?'

Jim hesitated. Depends who's on it, I suppose, he thought. He could not stop thinking about all the losers he had met in his life. 'Well anyway, hospitality welcomes you. Have a little think about it and get back to me,' Sage continued before removing his attention.

Sage was a half-person, in the sense that he was unsure of the hallmarks of the colourful half of himself he presented to the ecovillage. The unseen half was a far more timid affair, his kinsfolk knew, Sage knew too. His inner world a time bomb.

'A bit of a character, *isn't* he,' said Jim to Dave, in confidence on faraway grass.

'Yeah.'

'But ultimately a charlatan, a quack. Hurtless mind you. I just find the whole thing with him unappealing, something I want to get away from. That sort of thing's not why I came here, know what I mean?'

'Hmm.'

Zipping blasts entered with darkening clouds. Dave looked at his somewhat overweight slump. There was a morbidity in the look. He took another cigarette, it burned a hole in his heart. He didn't want to smoke and it track-marked his mind to know he couldn't not. Every harsh throat, every morning cough, every inch of malodorousness smote him all at once from a fist tinged with yellow. It was one of those drugs, as with many, that gives off the thought, before usage, of being more exciting than the summation of its effects. Our rose-tinted memories playing tricks with us, resting cosily in subconsciousness. Dave was a daddy longlegs heading for the lights.

He was in two pieces. The second piece, his left leg, had been donated to medical science. Dave remembered that he was an Xbox widower; the machine was the main object of his last girlfriend's desires. No more gamer girls for him.

Martha was checking out Anjit's bender tent and was taking a walk through his knowledge:

'You see how bendy the hazel is?' he asked her. 'That's why we call them benders,' he answered for her in a show of chivalry. 'Sheets and carpet donated from locals are on the outside and these provide insulation. Tarpaulin is set behind these.'

'I've been away too long and forgotten too much,' said Martha.

Some benders were makeshift, others better. Chimneys poked out nervously from each bender.

'You see how the chimneys connect to the wood burners. You can get a good heat out of these things. They're lifesavers in the winter,' said Anjit.

Pruned sticks curved against their naturalness were not killed but tortured like a man drawn and beaten down to face the mud. Malleable coppiced hazel and willow were not from tree species that died easily and meant that wood could be used without having to chop down entire trees. 'For some structures, the ends of posts are burnt black in fire like charcoal. We do this to stop them rotting. The posts we then put into the ground. That layer of charcoal "off the burn" acts a protective barrier against rot getting to the wood. But a word of warning: never use silver birch for structures. It will rot too quickly.' There was a ponderous pause. 'The last thing you want is a damp bender.'

Using timber and recycling from the city helped the dwellers feel more eco-friendly. Think global, act local. Permaculture was the hot word for the Zeitgeist.

#

'Peter seems a nice guy,' Martha said later to her Jim in an unimportant area some way from the firepit. 'I mean I've spoken to him here before but only briefly. It was good to have a proper talk with him earlier. He was telling me how welcoming and loving it is here. He said we could go to him if we need any help with anything.'

Music was soon blaring in and out of mealtime, and afterwards. Both knowing the lyrics, shouting them as they went by as if crazed by some strong stimulant, Martha and Jim were sharing hugging loving in 'Train in Vain,' in the deadening October daylight.

A few days passed. Venomous lava-like shots of sun made the day forget momentarily it was only early morning. Jim felt glum and about as cranky as a problematic crankshaft. He soon negated his indulgency of unconstructive thought when he remembered his granddad had been killed during the 1940s in the Burmese theatre of war. That terrible world war; the first they called 'Great.' Grandad was younger than Jim was now when he died, and for Jim's dad, this indelible fait accompli was immemorial. Jim broke out of his fishbowl mind. Today burgeoned freedom! A sense.

Jim walked over to a small assembled group. A few were breakfasting, the rest looked like they wanted in. Even the overflowing toadflax, ivy-bordered at the side of the storehouse looked pleasant this day.

Caught agaze at the sun overlong, wherever Martha's eyes next averted in the limpid sky, little egg yolks formed, yellow on blue, before invisibly gobbled up. There was a placid edge in the transfer. Swerving her mind in and out of security, she went back to the sun to throw it up for a tennis serve and into her grand abiding.

Headlong into the ecovillage: enter the world of no absolutes. A space is given to aggrandise individualism, away from the plaintive blues Jim sustains. His framed world she can remove herself from, to paint anew for the Martha that you know will be accepted all the while within a community. Here there was no hierarchical domain over nature, here womankind and mankind were at one, in nature simply being.

To feel no frontiers, to feel a person of the world and the person of her world, Martha could not dismiss the similarities; no, not just similar, it was consubstantial: emptiness was freedom. To me, she thought, it is quite clear that we are not free, but for living here we are freer.

Bohemians of the world, unify and propagate! The message. The big fuck you to their bosses. Fucking over economics. Withdrawing from the constraints of so-called normal society. People had come from as far as Sussex to add to the vegetable patch. Work entrance doors were slammed, neckties snatched and shirts ripped free to the last button. Dog Is Dead came on the speakers with a message about being a mess, being a failure; loving it anyway.

The eco villagers came from a world of social meds and social media, people swayed by pixels and frequencies, a generation playing with their smart phones by people not so smart. It could at least in part be true.

Here they were, these eco villagers, doing it on the land and not in offices. This was revolution! A collection of birches veined a hillock, watching twilight's onset, anon a sooty black mess drowning lily pads, bulrushes and dragonflies in *Horizon*. The town of Carringdon was forced to wear the hue of cars. The air felt crisp against the tongue, tree branches appeared as solidified strands of treacle syrup by nighttime's myopic trick; the moon shied behind velvet pillows of cloud, and the sky shut down for the evening.

CHAPTER TWO

Martha was reading a well-thumbed copy of a book called 'The English & Their Sh*tty Rules' by counterculturist author, Kyle James. An important part of the book read,

> *The English, with their aristocratic pomp, purport to be the lord of manners. The way they neatly queue, the way they use knives and forks, the way they uphold rules. What a bunch of twats. I still remember West Ham hooligans chanting racist abuse, homeless men swearing at me because I didn't give them change, upper-class snobs treating my attire with folly. If this is England, I don't want to know.*

Kyle James was English. He had a few problems in his life. Martha liked reading the book because it helped her vicariously get away from it all; away from stress-inspired lachrymation and city slickers summertime-dreaming of Pimm's at the beach. It too helped her scoff at former regulations and became a qualifier in her reasoning for being at the ecovillage. The most happening day in Carringdon was Thursday when it was church bell practice and bin night. Cherryblossom Street was the nearest place that the world decided to happen. Here, buses could be found as could a little market that opened on a Saturday. There were delicately trimmed crescent-shaped hawthorn hedges. Good old topiary, we smash that in England. Under the street's bridge ran a rill, that when cold, spewed tiny streaks of sorrow.

'More than half the world is urbanised. In the UK one percent of the population own seventy percent of the land. Only eight percent of land is settled on. They don't want you to change this. The *more* unused land, the *more* house prices go up. The *more* people become urbanised, the *more* they get away from the natural world and its ecology, and the less they care about it. With what we're doing, even if we can only affect small change and a few people learn and change then we are doing our job.' Manny was speaking to Martha on a sunny day in late October.

'Where did you get that?' Martha asked on looking down from Manny's neck, below the pronounced clavicle. Around the neck were numerous chains. Hanging off some were little parts of animals unknown, and it was guesswork as to whether they were real. In various shades of brown, flowing flashes of dolphin-greys and untrue golds, were tribal and ethnic attachments. Surely too delectable a neck, in Martha's eyes, to ever see a crick, and inviting enough to want to sink her gnashers.

Feel the oozing warmth. His blood, her mouth, awakening gelid, stiff nerves. 'Where did you get that?' Martha asked again, as the first time Manny forgot to listen.

'Which one?'

'This one,' said Martha, lightly diddling the silver object of particular appeal. It had a light-red bedazzlement shaped like lightning, smirking through its centre.

'It's a Thai amulet, or so I was told. I got it from a free shop. Why this one in particular?'

'It's a matter of taste, hang on…go back a bit. A free shop? How do you mean?'

'You will see them if you hang around these parts long enough. We're always linking up with other communities similar to ours. It is an efficient way of getting rid of stuff you don't want, and, most nicely, to share stuff other people might want.'

'Really?! So no money whatsoever, that's crazy. Awesome but crazy.'

'They pop up all the time. A good way to meet new, lovely people too. You've got to feel the love.' Martha emitted some glee. 'Pipe this one here,' he said looking down, with an unforeseen trace of disesteem at a dreamcatcher and arrow design. 'This was inspiring me for my next project. I want to build a longhouse like the Native American style. Cob, daub and wattle are added to the walls made out of sticks and straw. The daub is soil, clay, sand and straw which makes for a thick mixture that dries solidified. A touch of it, one can feel its density. Or, if not, just a yurt I will build.'

'Wow they sound mammoth tasks, both of them. Surely you'll want others to help you?'

'Well. Maybe.'

'There's one thing I've been meaning to ask. Or rather, I've been frightened to ask. Not because I know it to be undoable, but because it may be really difficult.'

'Hmm? Say what's on your mind?'

'I just wanted to know how you guys deal with the winter. The wailing winds and the icy cold. You guys must shiver. I know the wood burner is essential, but I'm not one iota sure how to work that and can it really do enough? I'm worried, I'm only a fair-weather camper.'

'I think you'll be fine. I'm not going to lie, it is not easy here in winter. It was tricky for me at first getting used to it, coming from Mexico. It is not so nice when it is rainy and muddy. The way to install the burner is to put a hole in the material for a small chimney to pass through. Then you use cob around it or something like this to secure it. I'll show you sometime.'

She could hear the salty seas of Cancún in his voice, lapping at her palette, becalming disquiet, intensifying his exotic mystery. No it was Mexico City he was from, that was right, she remembered. 'Tough this is but better than being a celebrity, no?'

'They seem deeply unhappy, celebrities, the vast bulk of them,' said Martha. 'That would be my analysis, not that you asked for my analysis, but I'm giving you one anyway, not *giving you one*, in that way, obviously, I have a boyfriend and everything, not saying you'd even want that or that I would…I mean, what was I talking about again?'

'I forgot.'

It was extraordinary how quickly Martha became interested in her phone lying in the grit and grass. You're welcome, beeped the phone, as Martha cerebrated to rest her straggled tongue. 'Do you ever go on social media?' Martha just realised Manny had restarted a conversation she thought was finished.

'God, I try not to, but like everyone, I fail. I'm still thinking how nice it is with the free shops, to have less so others have more.'

'What is your name again?'

'Martha.'

'Martha, go on the social media and see our Carringdon Ecovillage page and likewise Camden Community and Hackney Garden Ecovillage pages. There you will see when the free shops are happening, along with other events. On that note, if you ever use media, make sure you use it for our purposes not "theirs." You will notice how we and other similar communities like to call ourselves "communities." You will never hear any of us use words like "squatters" and if you do, send them to me, and I will pinch their ear. These are terms the media use to make us sound like the underclass from normal people, you understand? Low-lives…'

'A malign weed in their garden,' said the overhearing Peter. The hum of trees couldn't disguise his voice, the voice like that of a whiny Englishman if you pinched your nose as you spoke. The squashed parrot, the annoying TV, squeaking in the background when you're trying to do something more important. Manny ignored the TV set:

'The other thing: they like to make us out as some kind of anarchists. We really are a lovely people, we are not anarchists. It is too simple for them to call us hippies, but we really do want peace in the world.' Martha hadn't heard much of the more recent parts of what Manny had said; she was too discomfited by the fact he had forgotten her name, adding to her day an unsure burnish.

Manny made others sad about their English. The émigré from Mexico City had learnt English to the point it was a bit too crackerjack to be right. It gave way to oddly interesting, semi-correct expressions, or expressions that strained to be correct. Manny was oftentimes doing his own thing in the ecovillage that no-one ever saw, appearing only from time to time. For the first time ever today, he began songwriting:

All the things that fled her head,
All in silence coloured red

Nah not a song, something more edgy, he decided. A rap maybe…yes. He was writing a rap:

Pointy cornered smile
Swelling at the cheeks

No, change that, he thought, it was all a bit too Louis Theroux. And love? *Fuck* love. Writing about that was so overdone.

Pushing up the sidewalk
Distilling the new talk
Glowing like French toast
Sipping on a dream

That felt righter. And the dream? Ah well, that was easy. That was all about closing the big supermarkets and corporations and everyone living without money to be free on the land, and all that. Manny, ever the dilettante, tried other things today like composing a libretto about time—realised he knew nothing about opera nor a great deal about time, and puffed on a joint the rest of the day.

The elements in equilibrium. The next day was a half-baked, wishy-washy affair where not much really happened, and it was this wishy-washiness by which Manny was de facto leader of the group. With no desire for a leader, Manny was never appointed as such. Peter once tried to gather people around to say something, and only about two showed and Peter made note of this in his mental journal. When Manny spoke, people seemed to listen.

On the half-baked day, Martha drank hot chocolate and when she drank hot chocolate it was compulsory to keep a teaspoon present to stir in two or three vegetarian marshmallows, just at the right moment. Jim had asked for one too but Martha just remembered how she had forgotten to get him one. Jim was unalive to her mistake and it was all too bothersome to get up and fetch him one now.

'You're jittering,' said non-jittering Jim. 'You seem anxious.'

'I'm not anxious, I've just a good imagination,' replied Martha. They both knew she was fooling no-one, though have a good imagination she did. Creation gave boredom an encouraging prognostic. A small dot of dirt on the side of the tent if looked at with intensive focus for long enough could seemingly move slightly as if it were a small insect. As the two settled to watch a film, Martha began delicately swirling the spoon in the mug. Swirling, swirling, swirling, and…whoosh! Out of nowhere, the drink in its very own earthquake sploshed over the pillow that Jim's mum had given him. Jim had not noticed and Martha expeditiously grabbed a sheet to overlap the stain.

She watched with carefulness at her emotions that came in the aftermath of the drink spill, and frightening the world became. What would Jim's mum think? Motion, light and little, to such a stir caused such a stain. Martha knew she had to actualise a plan to divert nervousness. All in good time, she reasoned, all in good time. A system of reprogramming, where in the mindset of the anxious person, action is paramount. The one overconsumed by anxiety thinks about a positive solution for their cure in a situation, then do not act or are not mindful, separating the nervous from the even more nervous. In Martha's case, what helped achieve actualisation was determining the ridiculousness with which, and identifying the reasons for which, she overreacted. There was the realisation, that the practicalities in dealing with the drink spill were easy, allowing for insight into the futility of inceptive reactions. It was one o'clock in the afternoon. A glimpse of her phone's clock told Martha she had spent at least an hour thinking this out.

The two later went outside. When it came to emotions, Martha was like a cheaper model of watch; water-resistant not waterproof. Liquid was visibly swelling in her eyelids. She was usually just in time to swipe any tears away. Today was not one of them. Her chinking thoughts squished inside a single teardrop. The clatterer walked on over to where Jim stood, as lines were digging on Martha's countenance, the flesh fragmenting asunder.

'I'm so sorry,' she said. 'I've messed everything up.'
She shrugged and the subtle upturned corners of her
mouth suggested the tear water was only a little salty.

'Hmm? What's up?' asked Jim, hugging her.

'It's your pillow. I spilt hot chocolate all over it.'

'Oh right.'

A day later, Martha scanned the pillow cover and
the sprawled stain had lightened in colour and lustre,
seeming less real. She took the pillow cover to the
launderette. In no time, it was clean. It was all so
simple.

#

Burt was about as charismatic as a poached egg. Better
now that he had channelled his chagrin through
computer games. The erstwhile coiffeur was older than
his parents. He is the kind of baffled buffoon who by
his loitering continually sets off the automatic outdoor,
making everyone indoors cold. His eyes were kind.
They looked Jim's way as Burt turned. Big Burt was
cleaning his nails with a sim card. Jim took one look at
him and made a valuation: no plastic surgeon, being
paid all the money in the world, could improve that
face; you can't make a chicken salad out of chicken shit.
A gold-rimmed cheque saying five pounds only. Or not
gold. Under sand-blond hair was a face drawn on a
balloon.

Burt always felt a very fat little boy. His mother
made sure he knew it too. Father could not face his
fatness. A big fat little boy. The epitome of the fat fuck.
Bloater boy. He got it all, all that, at school of course.

'I can only presume he came here to get away from it all,' Jim said to Dave later on in the latter's tent. 'He just sort of bobs about from place to place and likes doing things fat people do. That's what you told me anyway, wasn't it?'

'Ermmm…'

'Thought so. Have you noticed how fat people like going out at the same time? Yeah, each morning about eleven o'clock with all the other fatties,' Jim continued, cachinnating. 'They're too lazy to go out earlier, but then they get hungry and go out for food, 'cause they're too lazy to cook.'

Burt's primary class teacher told him that lots of children were big boned, but that some—nodding at Burt—were just a little bit bigger-boned than others. He felt so much better after that.

Burt was in a full-time relationship with his laptop. He called it 'Laptop.' Laptop even made a little sound to tell Burt goodnight. Goodnight Laptop, Burt would say back. Goodnight.

The next morning and Jim got out the tent. It was as if a gigantic vat of morning dew had spilled all around him telling him what part of morning it was. Grass blades had grown longingly. It looked like a thousand-strong swimathon. Strands posing as swimmers pre-dive. Not all played ball, nature only sometimes complies. Rainclouds were having a sedate conversation with each other that only got querulous enough to produce a scanty vapour. A landscape prettily greyed.

Sage was on his search for the new order. In the classroom he looks, pupils glossy. Attendants were listening in the communal area to his guided meditation:

'Peace is underrated. Take a step back from the world. You are in meditation, my friends. How does it feel? Are you anxious? Dispirited? Hungry? Tired? So tired your brain capacity feels like a child's? Nervous amongst the troop of people? Having a hard time concentrating? Find yourself distracted?' Yeah only by you, you cunt, thought Jim. Since Sage never heard Jim's thoughts, he went on. 'It's neither here nor there, if you get distracted. Just bring your mind back to the breath. Don't try to change the breath, just watch it how it is.'

To Jim, everyone else appeared to be fine with the stillness, and lack of activity, lack of ambitious lifestyle, lack of possessions. Burt's crown chakra was blocked because he was wearing a wig.

'What do I do?' Jim whispered to Martha. 'Just sit here like a mong?'

'Why don't you listen to the teacher and he might just tell you,' her peevish retort.

Jim could not concentrate on this beardy unkempt imbecile the other side of reality. He reminded Jim of a truffle egg. Jim fucking hated truffle eggs. Unexciting on the outside and overdeveloped goo on the inside. To try and master some other pie-in-the-sky modality of mind felt utterly pointless. Jim sat there and thought about loads of things: different ways he could fuck Martha, after all how bendy really was she? His next thoughts revolved around cheese, pubs and golf. All assembled sat quietly for sixteen minutes. Discharging Jim's naked angst, Sage rang the meditation bell, and waited awhile for people to rub their eyes open, and shuffle and stretch. Most eventually thanked Sage and left, but for Martha, Jim and Cathy. The subject moved to depression, not exclusively for the threesome, but Kristoff and Peter too, who had walked away from the meditation in a pair.

'I never ask you. What, er, make you come here?' Kristoff asked Peter.

'I suppose seeing as all and sundry seem to know, I might as well tell you too. I lost my mother,' murmured Peter, softly as a kitten's paws.

'I'm sorry to hear.' Kristoff paused. 'Are you OK to talk?'

'Yeah.'

'How did you lose her?'

'It was at a shopping mall.'

'Oh sorry, what unexpected death.'

'No, I mean I actually lost her, in the food court. She wanted to get something healthy, and I went off to KFC. I never saw her again.'

'Oh…right. Sorry man.'

'Well, KFC or Burger King, I forget which, the point is that this too was the time before mobile phones, except for the brickish sorts businessmen and certain types had. I went back home, thinking she might have gone back, only for her never to return. So in answer to your question, when I am by *Lake Horizon*, my troubles seem to fade. I feel still, and at one with nature, like the water. Twenty-odd years ago that was now. Still not returned.'

Jim's tawdry aftershave reflected his powers for vision. His scented neck worked like a robot's, unhappily buttressing a narrow and pointy face on disproportionately broad shoulders. Jim, by nameless accounts, was not particularly attractive. Surly thin eyes. Mousy brown hair the texture of peafowl feathers, sat naturally on his head in a socially polite style. Above a defined philtrum, it looked like he had a plasticised nose that could fall off his face at any moment. Martha shared a like attractiveness to Jim, at least as deemed by societal aesthetic convention, though was probably more attractive. If polled, the bisexual population would agree. In many regards, Martha was an acquired taste. She had a wide face and cloudy lemonade glasses she wore periodically. With the glasses, she was secretarial, yet most marriageable. If polled, most men would agree. Behind the glasses were blue irises, as if starlit, on a whitish visage. She was enamoured of coffee, burst for it too readily, went round sorely tongue-tipped half the time. She appeared hell-bent on laying to waste the only muscle in her body attached at one end. Today she wore an ankh necklace to be cool.

Cathy was forty-six with confidence, and had an awkward fascination with Neil Diamond the older she got. She was not overly fun to look at for Jim. He wasn't overly fun to look at for her either. She looked down to see a body ravaged by drug use, drug misuse and drug abuse. Brow-battered, smoke-shattered puffy old thing. A sureness was written between the lines of her face that told a thousand stories; none of them particularly interesting. Her epidermis like motorways of spider webs. Worn over years, a haemorrhage of animus was evident, having been taken full taken advantage of over the long haul of following every inch of conscience to minimise ethical aberrations and supererogatorily do what felt right. If you're old enough, wan enough, downtrodden enough, wrinkled enough and poor enough to be unable to mask the four formers then it is no longer about looking good but a case of damage limitation. So down on herself at times that she felt if she was a book, she would be in the oversize section, squashed next to her fat friends, far away from all the normal, happy books that people actually wanted to fondle. Flotsam washed up by a seabed. Folds of skin dying that little more now at the waist, Cathy knew more wrinkles would soon come, and more exaggerated, the more she lived the fast life. She fancied herself as so ugly, that every time a man got hard in front of her, it was because he was imagining someone else. Perhaps it was more a case, that she felt there was not anything *wrong* with the way she looked, but she had trouble convincing herself just how much there was right. She rolled and lit a cigarette to forget about heavy shit.

'I faltered sometimes,' she admitted, one afternoon at the communal point. 'But I've always stook to me guns.' Oh crumbs, get the violins out, here comes the sob story, thought Jim, as Cathy's eyes became stuck in memory. On the upside, she had the resting bitch face down to a tee. 'A boy called Jon Roberts asked me to the dance at the end of 'igh school. It were the 'appiest day of me life. I was so touched that 'e asked me to dance with 'im, I thought 'e were the one. Then I caught 'im snogging a real bitch a day after. Like a real bitchy bitch. Fookin' whore like.'

'Ah,' said Sage sympathetically.

Cathy's face plummeted to a near cry, and then a cry.

'I'm not sure I ever recovered. Me mam always did want me to go church more. Maybe if I listened, I would've 'ad more luck by now. Sorry, am getting all emotional now.'

'Weeping is no worse or better than talking. It is merely but a natural human function. The more you meditate, the more you realise,' said Sage.

With her husband a man of the cloth, the mam had followed the necessary formalism to please through the years. She had withstood, by way of gritted teeth, every luncheon, quiz night, holy communion, mass, bringing her nothing but fewer confrontations with her husband. Cathy, busy tapping away her problems, was currently using her ex as a textual soundboard. Not a great fan of men. Big fan of condiments. Her breath felt old and tired. Cathy had had more counsellors than sexual partners and more baggage than Heathrow Airport. On the bright side, she was a superb tile grouter. She longed for a fresh-looking, healthily tanned Italian, with a spirited personality and the patience of her GP.

'I used to have a lot more friends,' said Martha, 'but they just kind of faded away.'

It was easier for people to not know those with lots of problems. Martha, if she allowed herself to think it over, felt that if she ended her life, it would free the burden of all the people that pretended to love her.

'Ah, we'll look after ya here,' said Cathy. 'Ya need friends, they give security and stability.'

'I impugn your latest offering,' said Sage. 'Friends are marvellous but provide a false sense of security. We must all, each one of us, expire, and we will do so individually. As we enter the valley of the shadow of death, there is no-one else to hold our hand. What of friends then? What then of security? We must work on ourselves in this lifetime, as stability in ourselves is our most basic "assurance." When we are happier with ourselves, we are then in a better position to help our friends. Once we have developed such strength, to with efficaciousness, help our friends, we can then help others better, even our enemies.'

'Help our enemies?' asked Jim. Martha inconspicuously elbowed Jim's side, then thought back to her shortage of friends, shortage of money and how outside felt cold and grey.

I am weak before my senses, she thought. I am October through and through. How much does a woman have to suffer for her art? The art that has not taken shape after nearly two weeks at the ecovillage. Can't even get the right prescription for my glasses without fucking up.

'Is the print clearer in one, or two?' asks the optometrist, his hand unquavering through the alterations. I can't tell, she thought. I guess I should guess. It's 15:04 and I'm going down deep. Into the well, afar from turbulence. Pull me up in soaking rebirth for the spring.

She leaves the optician store to leaves on the ground like shrivelled starfish. Her way back to the ecovillage is a pilgrimage to the memory of Leonard Cohen—

ɔn, a voice like rotting leaves in deep
.. Her mind has travelled the course of his life.

In the full bleakness of October sun, amongst the crunch and crackle of an autumn ground, Burt has discovered there is no-one more important in his life than himself. All of Martha's most important decisions are still pending.

#

'O God, really? This food came out a bin?' Jim said later at the communal area.

'What's worse, eating food out o' a skip, or the fact that thirty percent of food waste, and fook knows 'ow much from these supermarkets is comestible? Now get that down yer 'atch and shut it.' Cathy said. She was crabby but a light crabby. Everyone laughed.

'Unlucky, Jim!' said Peter.

Martha sighed.

Cathy was one of those annoying people that tried their hardest to be right at anyone's expense. Jim's mind told him so. Always had to make her little point didn't she. It was another of those loose days, where Jim was left asking himself, how did it get so late so quickly?

'If ya want to live without much money, it's the kinda thing ya need to do,' Cathy continued. 'It's only right we share what would otherwise go t'waste.'

'But, do you not get arrested when you steal it from the supermarket skips?' asked Jim.

'Nah man,' said Anjit. 'We always keep one person on the lookout whilst another one climbs the gate and gets to the skip. They don't really care, as long as you don't take the piss. In fact, it's not unheard of for supermarkets to actually hand out the food they would chuck. I've heard instances like this happen with other communities actually.'

Martha, the only woman ever to make Jim feel it was his birthday every day. If she were luffing a ship, she'd have a sail of rare feathers. The couple went inside their tent with late afternoon sunshine dripping through the tent cracks. Martha had Keltic ornaments, pretty rocks and minerals, gemstones, trinkets, thimbles, charms, plenty of silver, carved wooden bits and bobs, and varied liquids of varying concentrations in differently shaped bottles—for use in libations no doubt, thought Jim. Looking anaemic, Martha's fleece was drying apologetically in the corner.

Jim held a separate ragtag corner of the tent with miscellaneous dreck. One cushion striped black and white, and another with a cretonne cover donated by Sue, seemed to be in joint agreement. Downhearted and rigid they looked as though they would be far better off righted in a nice house somewhere. No matter how much Jim tried to flatten them, they were intent on creasing up. Today on the nightstand in Jim and Martha's tent: a pair of nail scissors, a shoebox and some marble cake. A crane fly had tired of Jim's side of the tent and moved to Martha's.

Every morning, Jim did something that each time left Martha tight at the stomach. It was this: he lit up. Rarely in emotion did he alight, yet in dedicated animation, whether it a roll-up, straight, e-cigarette, spliff or bong, he toked that bastard like no tomorrow. Today, as was his usual method, he smoked rolling tobacco. Martha, calm in her unsteadiness, mumbled something, something indecipherable.

'What?' asked Jim, unpleasantly.

'Are you ever thinking of giving up?'

'What?! Giving up what?'

'Well…er…the smoking. It's just…I'm worried about you.'

She was also worried about all the months of shite going on her lungs from his wont, and wanted to start every kiss without devouring smoke-stench. Jim enjoyed smoking and plainly reminded her he'd give up one day. He just didn't know which day that would be. He realised that after some thinking, like Martha, there was something that did not sit well with him too, only this tight stomach was invoked by something deep within his own constitution. It was dull, agonizing and see-through. In fact, it was invisible, but definitely existed: his conscience. It felt to Jim that there lived in his stomach, an adapted futuristic earthling, originally a scion from the planet Zog. Every time Jim said or did something that he probably shouldn't have, the conscience-monitoring being got out his ray gun called 'the conscience gun,' and zapped Jim's stomach, causing the stomach to tighten each time.

'It's not that I feel bad about smoking,' Jim said. 'It's like my body tells me it's bad, though. Anyway, like I said, don't worry.' Martha felt even worse than before she brought it up. Don't worry, don't panic, stay calm. You would think they would be the phrases an anxious person would want to hear.

#

'He's changed,' Martha said. 'His smile is less than before.'

'Hmm?' said Jim.

'Look at him over there, all by himself, looking down at the ground. When I see Kristoff now, it's a polite "I'll pay lip service for now, but I'd really rather be alone with myself." You know what I mean?'

'We've only been here three weeks, so no.'

The clouds were full of winter news. Bite, bite, bite went the wind to every tooth, every bone, on a new November morning. Second of the month. Icy javelins rained down to the cheeks and ears. 9:30 a.m. and it was fucking cold. The worst part was knowing it was a precursor to how bad it could be for four months more. Martha continued to feel anxious. Hi anxiety, nice of you to show up; have you brought along your on-off friend, depression?

Water was on the horizon. Jim gave an old eye as the cavalry arrived. No sooner had the jumbo water bottles arrived than Jim began to laugh.

'Did you get the new bread too?' he asked.

'Roger,' said Sage, frazzled.

'Good, the old one made good toast, but not bread.'

'How about the toilet roll?'

'No. There were no recycled rolls left.'

'What? Never mind about that, why didn't you get a different brand? I've got to save my arse before I can save the world. By the way, with everything we're meant to stand for, don't you think it's just a bit ironic that, of all places, we're getting water filled up from the local petrol station?'

'Yeah well it's 'ere now, ya want it or not?' Cathy said, panting. 'Why don't ya find something to do instead of complainin' all the time? Heaven forbid a chore to 'elp out. Ya know, we've marched all that way and back again, puttin' ourselves out to 'aul water for the likes o' you. It's piss-poor actually Jim.' Jim had spoken with absolutely no fear for retaliation.

'Well…'

'O, an' why don't ya take yer fookin' library book back?!'

Jim thought a while, stumped about the fookin' library book to which she was referring.

'I've had an idea about the water, actually,' said an overhearing Manny, hooking onto the pack. 'I was saving to tell it once I had developed it more, but now seems a better time than ever. Right, I have devised a water collection and filtration system that I wish to bore. Basic in its design, but it will do the job and give us sustainable water. This is just a feeler idea for now. In time, I hope we can think about irrigation and a hydro turbine.'

'Take it back!' continued Cathy to Jim. 'You'll only get yerself a fine, an' no doubt expect Martha to bail ya out.'

Cathy made Jim think about what a seasoned old cow must look like.

'Why do I bother?' muttered Manny, a breath under cloud.

Jim felt he had got the measure of Cathy: Cathy was not the sharpest crayon in the box. A slight rapping of the knuckles revealed a head as hollow as an Easter egg and the outer shell wasn't exactly Thorntons.

The only evidence that Jim was right: she used to think telesales involved selling tellies. From hard drugs, Jim knew Cathy was clean; as clean as a bubble bath—of a colourless makeup with a frothy head. Howsoever, she specialised in foretelling the past. Before the world of social media platforms she viewed as monstrosities, Cathy would spend hours sifting through photo albums she held as catalogued chequered dreams. Now, she had a hand in the monstrosities. A favourite pastime of hers was to think. A favourite British pastime was to reminisce. Her early teen years remained with her: raggedy, uproarious and unidentified.

Later, with everyone back at camp, and most in the communal area or kitchen, Dave had an idea.

'Anyone fancy a game?' he asked.

He held out a filigree yet rumpled pack of playing cards. There was an extensive dish pileup now looking like a beach littered with scraggy rotting sea wrack.

'Blackjack?' Anjit suggested.

'Brownjack if *you're* playing,' Jim said. There was a cramped pause. 'Did you hear? I said brownjack if *you're* playing.' Anjit looked on in comfy daydream.

'He's gone in screensaver mode again,' said Peter, laughing.

'Fuck off man,' said Anjit, ruefully gazing at Jim and Peter. 'Whitejack if you're playing.'

'Yeah, no need for that guys,' Meredith said.

'Life isn't just black and white, sometimes it's Indian too.'

'There are, er, two blackjacks though, *isn't* it?' remarked Kristoff. 'People call it different names, and people make different rules for the blackjack.'

'Fuck it then we'll play snap, said Dave.'

Everyone knew snap and everyone played and everyone got jaded at the filthy beach. Peter preferred cribbage but daren't mention it.

Martha, feeling uneasy with the kitchen atmosphere and Jim's thoughts, went for a little walk. She thought of her anxiety, how every person has a level of anxiety, how some people, due to their upbringing, their genetics and environmental factors, have more anxiety than what is deemed the norm. She knew that these people were called anxious. With rowdier thoughts, Martha turned back to herself. Now you can insult me from how you perceive cowardice and my overambitious body: my fragile voice, my nausea, my hypersensitiveness, my twitches, my retching, my eye skirting, my quivering, my shrinking from your body language. But you cannot deny the facts. For people superabound with anxiety, there is not always warning. It can stipple the calmest moments.

The moon watched Martha. The dithery folding of a tissue, the seamless turn of worry, the tears that went cold before they could dry, in the early November air. Who knew? A full moon and a crescent Martha. Scrolled towels had been arranged to suppress one or two leaks in the kitchen. With the presentiment that the newer weather would only make conditions worse, Manny and Cathy were working on a more substantive kitchen sunshade. All too easily went day to night. The moon cuddled Martha, in lockdown from the riotous dark.

CHAPTER THREE

C old was here. It sang from the icy ledges and the leafless shrubs. October as a whole was fair to middling. This was November, hitting hard. Siberia had sent her regards and England would feel it five days straight. Some men did some skipping. Nothing to do with bouncing and a rope; this was about supermarket bins.

'I'm sick of it,' Manny lamented. 'Why's it always me, Anjit and Peter that do the collecting from the skips? From now on I'm setting up a rota,' he told everyone at a meeting he had set up at *Shard*.

Rota. That word. It strained every pair of ears that didn't belong to Anjit, Peter or Manny. Thinking he might get windburnt listening to a windbag, Jim was a communication. His pose alone gave all in sight an instruction: leave well alone. It was a reproduction of the pose Jim had used years before in his schooldays when he lied that it wasn't his birthday until the summer so as to bypass the annual birthday beats.

Sinuses felt blocked and Manny thought he was coming down with something. 'Who's going to get the wood for the communal wood burner, or will it be me again?' he asked. Before anyone could say anything,

Manny mumbled under his breath: 'lazy British people.' Meredith and Martha heard, and giggled like bunches-in-their-hair schoolgirls. 'It may be, that you cannot help but laugh, and that is fine. I however can ill afford to. Underneath, remember that we are a team, always. This ecovillage will not prevail without that sense.'

People look to you when you are striven to lead, Jim remembered. Jim never became confident but had learned how to be more willing to show himself up with his limitations.

'Manny has no answers, he's just confident in his mistakes,' said Jim to Dave. 'It's things like this that make you realise no-one in life truly knows where they are going, and why they are going out of their way to keep going in that direction. Everyone just makes it up as they go along.'

'Hmm,' said Dave.

'Watch out for the black ice.'

'Oh yeah, I see.'

'I just said it was icy. Ice tends to be icy you know.'

'No. I said, I *see*.'

#

Another November evening and Jim and Martha were spooning in front of Jim's iPad. *Family Guy* was on. Jim put on his thinking cap: enough with the spooning, let's start the forking. Forks prick after all.

Martha found it tremendously revolting the way Jim spat out time. She could never watch as he watched. Hours and hours of unintelligent television could animate before him without sight to do anything else.

'How else could we spend the evening?' she put down.

'Um,' an unturning Jim muttered.

'I mean, I know it's cold at the moment, and a bit stormy, but maybe we could go…I don't know…to the cinema?' O dear God no, scrap that, she thought. Not another screen. At least it wasn't one of those shows where you watch other people watching TV, she continued in her thinking. If he starts watching those, then there's really no hope. That's when he's given up on life.

Martha paused. She couldn't think but then she could. 'We could see what's on at the Arts Centre? Did you know Carringdon Arts Centre has live comedy now and again?'

'No money.'

'Well, I'll pay this time.'

'You probably need to book in advance for tickets.'

'Well, why don't we just get some fresh air, go over there, and see what shows they've got coming up?'

'Too tired right now.'

Martha sighed. Well that was the end of that.

Two weeks passed where no-one had much to say. The eco villagers were like a conjugal couple of fifty years down a narrow one-way street. With every subject of conversation exhausted and every look reused, to the untrained eye it looked like everybody was just moseying around deciding at times to press on with their own affairs.

Sue's dad and Sue were visiting. The dad, in the Sunday of his years, was named Cuthbert. He had a right-arm tremor and a walking stick made of beechwood.

For the last week or two, Jim had noticed himself gratuitously pick up an irksome modus operandus: if anyone around him looked gleeful, Jim would choose to look as sunken as possible. He found it hard, as a matter of ease, not to feign a frown and look unexcited at anything, even that which bestirred the most magnitudinous delight in him. No light-hearted quibs for Jim please.

'Been quiet recently,' wearily said Dave by the water point. Cathy was there, leadenly listening.

'Aye, it 'as,' she said. 'Strangely quiet.'

'There's that Sue bird here I guess.' Dave was looking at Sue's thin ecru home just three hundred metres away.

'Ah yeah, kind lady she is.' Cathy closed the lid and put down her tall, yellow flask, having filled it with water. 'Brr gettin' colder 'int it.' She started to rub her hands together. 'Need to get me some gloves.'

'I've noticed I've been using the hot water bottle in bed for an extra four and a half minutes lately.'

'Don't blame ya. It's good to see local people an' that interested in what we're doing 'ere. I'm glad Sue is about.'

'She brought us sugar, homemade jam and vitamins. She wanted to make sure we were getting the right vitamins.'

'That's nice of 'er.'

'Yes. Yes it is.'

#

Jim once heard from someone—Sage perchance, but Jim couldn't have anyone know it might've been from him—that contrary to mainstream opinion it actually usually takes fewer muscles to frown than it does smile. It's just that our smile muscles are better trained, so smiling may feel easier. Who was on the money? Whatever. Jim didn't really give a fuck.

Jim noticed a strange big thing just happened. A van was parked at the side of the camp on some long grass by a stand of ash trees. A dog's paw print was on its side and the writing by it said 'Pawfection.' A mobile dog wash van? Enervated, crooked Cuthbert had seen a lot during the war, but he'd never seen *this*. He took a moment to consider what his majoritarian gerontocracy would look like if he ruled the vegetable kingdom at the ecovillage. He had a world-weary look; the look that said he had seen too much to be shocked by anything.

'I am ninety-six now,' he hoarsely confided in Meredith. 'Every time I visit Sue, I wonder if it will be my last.'

'Aww, don't say that.'

'Would you mind telling me what that van's purpose is?'

'Apparently, it's for Burt,' Meredith replied.

'Touch wood I make it through the winter.'

Cuthbert often thought how his skin folds looked like a dense network of tinned spaghetti. He sighed and thought to himself. Spaghetti on toast it is again for tea.

#

Life and half-light emanating from every pore, Meredith's eyes were the same blew green as burning driftwood from the sea. She wasn't really called Meredith. She was called Jane, but Jane was plain so she went with her middle name. She had the aura of a black-and-white era motion picture star, with a Bette Davis hairstyle encroaching her desiderative bone structure. She was funny and intelligent. In Jim's eyes, she was as beautiful a girl as he could wish for and many men would agree. Any man that drew sight knew she could at give any one of them one orgasm to the power of ten. To Meredith, Meredith presented the most agreeable exterior and was of good working parts including an expressive back.

Jim felt like a man that required servicing. He could take the spare parts of Meredith and be insured for life; always read the label. Meredith had even given Jim the odd hint that she liked him. If they were both seventeen, he would have jumped at the chance, domineered by her beauty and his jolty hormones. As it was, none of this really mattered. He hated her laugh and they had nothing in common. For Jim, of his view of Americans, she was so very American. Sealed within were all the necessary irritants. So loud and annoying, he thought, always yapping on about herself. *How* Jim's character had strengthened to turn away such beauty! Besides, he was worried she was the sort to intimidate his penis and the extension of its form. Throw her away with all the other rubbish, thought Jim. Put her in the scrap not the scrapbook.

Meredith came from Madison's Grove in the fairly well-to-do environs of San Francisco, though she spent part of her formative years in Greece. She laughed like a toilet flush. Meredith grew up among delicacies, disinhibition and decency, and a brimful of nonchalance supplied by her parents. Meredith was a modern-day sesquipedalian cruciverbalist and board game nut, with an intention to make them cool. She had all the board games she ever wanted with her safe philosophy of *I do what I want and everyone else pays for it*. If ever a camera flashed her, she would look past it as if too good for its lens. Her father had a face like a pinecone. Her areas for improvement remained playing chess and picking boyfriends.

In Meredith's former life, she is sequins and feathers. She goes to market to sell an unkempt promise. She is in the foetal position, waiting for the drugs to kick in.

#

'I think most women would like to see more spiritual interaction from their partner; a greater sense of connection,' said Martha to Jim, in an evening in late November. Sitting on the mattress, she pulled at the coiled mass of brown and amber on her head, like an immaculate rockery picked and preened. 'When making love, so many guys appear to be interested in getting their end away. But it should be exactly that: making love. Actually caring what's happening for the other person.'

'Here we go,' said Jim.

'It's true! Bloody men. So overcome with their own experience. I think most girls make intimations at the start of the relationship and then end up settling for the same old routine because they know other men will just be exactly the same.' Martha knew it perhaps an untruth; but true enough.

'Why am I listening to this? You know I'm not like that.' Martha's face remained. 'Why don't you speak to Meredith about this? I'm sure she'd love to hear all about it and you guys can live happily ever after in the knowledge that men suck.'

Later that evening, Jim was talking to Kristoff in the kitchen.

'Martha was going on today about how selfish men are. To *me*, of *all* people,' said Jim. 'You know, I felt like saying to her a line that King Edward I says in *Braveheart*, when he says, "Go back to your embroidery." ' Jim said the line in his best attempt at Patrick McGoohan's voice doing King Edward I. Kristoff laughed quite a bit. He prized that one. It was unclear to Jim how much Kristoff actually understood what he was on about, and what proportion of laughter was conciliatory. Perhaps for Kristoff, he could afford to laugh. But deep down, Jim could not stem his worry, that Martha was, by sleight of hand, designating her diatribe closer to home.

#

Of literature, Martha had a predilection for the classics. She loved the way they stirred and stirred and stirred…and then, fortississimo! The horror and the magic is all revealed and they shall remain classics until they are so old they call them ancient classics. The uberclassic.

Somewhere in England the champion in some sport is about to take a penalty in what will be the final kick of the game. While Jim still ponders the evening, abreast in a tête-à-tête Martha and Meredith kipping under a sweet moon beam form a twosome on a hillside making it feel a little warmer.

'How's things been lately?' asked Martha, her jade jumper rucked up in the tickly breeze.

'Meh. OK.'

Martha was thirsty, and her mouth filled wide with talk.

'You don't sound so sure,' she said restively with a sloppy little laugh for afters.

'I've just been thinking about family. We used to be real close. It's a shame they're so far away now, but it's OK.'

'That must be hard. As luck would have it, I don't miss my original family. I haven't told you this: it so happens that by the time I knew who I was, I was being raised in an adoptive family. They took me in as their own. They loved me so, squeezing me tight each night before bed. I was completely doted on. My original parents would have to go some to outshine them!'

'Ah unbelievable, thank you for sharing. What do your adoptive parents think about you being here?'

'I think they think I'm a bit crazy! But heigh-ho, they're understanding. How about your parents?'

'Oh they already know I'm crazy!'

Martha's mother abandoned any sense of the mothership, after Martha—a neat tuft of down on her head, and her body the size of a large watermelon—

left the womb. The father could not cope looking after Martha at any rate, let alone, alone.

'I had no siblings. So I don't say this lightly, but you're like the sister I never had.' Martha knew she said it wrong. She caught her breath while brain cog wheels mechanically ticktocked for a reprieve. 'Forgive me if that's a little premature.'

'Oh honey, that's so sweet. You are great too. I look up to you, even though I look down at you every day.'

Martha sniggered. 'That's funny. You're only a *bit* taller than me!'

There was an untroubled pause.

'It's so still here at night,' said Meredith, after deeply exhaling.

'It is. I like it.'

'So, you still enjoying things then?'

'Yes, it's just so very different to how I used to live. It's nicer in a way. It's difficult though, isn't it?'

'It's the only way for me,' said Meredith, as she turned from Martha one hundred and eighty degrees to rest the back of her head on the grass and watch for sky change. Meredith imagined she wore a gown that went with the wind as she recalled life past, passed as hedonistic arts. She thought of things back home she missed: root beer, firearms, hugs from uncle Jerry, gofers and lonesome pretty highways devoid of gofers. Or at least, to miss them was how she chose to memorize them. 'No going back now. I especially miss Cassandra, my soulmate of a friend in Cali. But like a lot of my old friends, she's got her mummy friends now.

I haven't seen her in eleven years. That's not a friendship, that's just a memory.'

'Really? No going back? Why so sure?' Martha simpered as she asked.

'I love it here. I'm an ecovillage aficionado. It's the only time I've felt truly like I belong someplace. I'm not saying that you should always trust them, but sometimes gut instincts are gut instincts for a reason, honey. You know, I used to really—and I mean *really* be into all that fashion crap. I spent so much time on my hair, nails and clothes. All that silly girly stuff. I still am into it. But I just couldn't live in that mondaine, fast-paced city life any longer, where appearance is everything, or in some way, too important. All that just doesn't matter half as much anymore. I don't even buy dresses now, it's just not practical here. I was looking for answers, as everyone does in their twenties, but I guess I started a bit late. Now that I'm here, like you, in my thirties, I'm still looking for answers. But just for being here, somewhere like this, I think we're on our way to finding them. I think it's really positive, what we've got going on here.'

'Yes, so true. I must admit though, I do sometimes miss being more comfortable.' Shadows hesitated at Martha's leg-side, coming in a little to nap, going back out to saunter. Meredith had seen better legs with a message tied to them in a morgue.

'Yeah, I can understand that, and you are still getting used to things here. What about Jim? Are you happy with him here?'

'If he was as dedicated to me as he is to his smoking, he'd make an epic boyfriend.' Martha laughed.

'Do you love him?'

'Yes, but not quite in the way I think you mean. I mean, I did, but…'

'Honey, why are you doing this to yourself? The guy's a jerk, hasn't he proved it to you enough times? We set a bar in life, and people will treat us how we allow them to. Even Jeremy Kyle says so.' Martha laughed with her friend. She had, at times, developed her love for Jim, as an enviable love. It made it easier. She envied his insouciance and how he could stare blankly with that sociopathic gaze of his at any new human he met, fearless from his own insufficiency to sense danger. Martha dealt with him in splotches of politeness, had learnt to, with no visions for change. Usually an emotional response would kick in long before ratiocination ever could. Love helped pass the time. 'I love him but, I hate him but, I'm not a racist but—meltwater follows the glacier, hun.'

'Hmm?'

'In plain English: if you stay with him, you are fooling yourself.'

'Hmm.'

'Forgive me for saying, but I've already seen far more of that poor excuse for a man than I would have liked.'

Martha had worn multifold masquerade masks before, so to speak, in the course of protean pursuits to impress others and protect mettle. In showcasing the brave face show, she still was not comfortable. There were more masks to wear, yet the wardrobe was thinning. Whose face could she hire for a vital moment? Martha knew she was hiring sense. The end point of a crisis, pen nib Meredith wrote the 'p' in help. 'Look, maybe I've said too much. Maybe I've been a little unfair. I don't want to influence you in your relationship. But life is too short to hang on to the things we don't really want.' Well, thought Martha, she was right about the 'things' at least.

'I think if I can stand up to him, then I'm OK with him. Like today, it was almost like a metamorphosis of character. I could scarcely believe some of the things I was coming out with when I was talking to him.'

'Like what?' Taking out a cigarette to light it, Meredith wanted to get snug for this.

'Like all this stuff I would usually only say to women. About how guys can just think about themselves during intercourse and getting their own satisfaction. I was pretty direct too. I wasn't just thinking about him when I said it, but I think he took it personally because he got a bit upset!'

'Ha*ha,* that's hilarious. High-five.' They clapped hands in a physically yielding settlement of staunch female fellowship. 'Well anyway, it's up to you. Just remember what I said about gut instincts though, with *everything.*'

'Yeah. Thanks Meredith. Gut instincts should undoubtedly be noted. I seem to find myself way too often going to do *this* and going to do *that*, but I never feel like I do anything. It's part of my anxiety, I think. It paralyses me. Fear mocks freedom, and I hate that I preach more than I practice. All the music I want to listen to I've heard ten thousand times before. You get the idea.' She sighed. 'Sometimes, I'd just like to be invisible. That way I won't get hurt.'

'Why not go back home for a bit, and see your folks and friends? It may do you some good. Sometimes it's nice to get a fresh change of scenery.'

'Are you trying to get rid of me already?' Martha asked wryly. 'Yeah, perhaps you're right. It will be nice to have more breathing space. And what about you, with guys at the minute? Are you on the search?'

'No, no. My heart's still busy with someone else.'

'That Jake guy?'

'Yep. Still hung up on him. Any new guy would have to easily be over six feet anyway so I could wear my heels. I'm not sure I'll find anyone else now. It's like when you are looking for an unreachable item you have not long lost. You feel surer to find it the more you uncover the places you think it could possibly be, only to exhaust all possible options. Then the fear sets in.'

'There's that Japanese idea that when ornaments get broken, they piece the parts back together and line the cracks with gold. This is because when things get damaged they become more beautiful. In time your heart will mend.' The friends shared a loving hug, and as they did, please never, thought Martha, remove the holdfast from the safety net. Not ever.

Meredith, to whom Jake was once engaged, now wore the ring on her middle finger to tell all her exes to fuck off.

Martha was trying to think of ways she could be more of an ambivert. When she sat next to Jim, her emotions felt like they were air-locked in a pressure cooker. She liked sitting next to Meredith. When she sat next to her, she felt free. Free and warm like the hill.

Martha went off to bed and Meredith had a smoke in the communal area. The cigarette, once lit, could stand by Meredith for a while until its construction skied away. Cathy historicised while Meredith lived to create history, and one day they would both be bone.

Cathy retraced her steps to the point where she first met Meredith at the ecovillage by the broccoli patch, going out of her way, quite literally, to remember what she was going to say to her now at the communal area.

'Yous are gettin' on well, you and Martha, aren't ya,' said Cathy.

'She has a good heart. I like her energy.'

Meanwhile the shower and its shitty pitter-patter of energy splashed through an imaginary sieve, barely sopping Jim. Biorhythmically disorganised from his experiments with sleep, now in the early hours of the morning, Jim slipped out the shower and walked around in the nip. Didn't even dry himself. Didn't give a fuck. He went to the kitchen, no-one was about. Poured himself beautiful organic coffee from Colombia, imported not far from an avalanche of cocaine in a mogul's warehouse. He buzzed about the kitchen after making it extra strong.

It was at this point that Jim thought he didn't really want to be with Martha anymore. He just wanted to meet new girls to talk, hug, buss, stare the night away with. Mainly the bussing part. Preferably all this would lead to a fucking, but it didn't have to. He thought more. Being in a monogamous long-term relationship? How bromidic. Even the word 'monogamy.' O God, spare me and pull the trigger now, he thought. It was all too normal. But how would it play out if he met someone with whom he wanted carnal embrace? It would be a case of, 'do you want to come back to my ecovillage?' Would she think I swung the other way once she saw my bender?

Jim felt that most girls didn't want all that serious shit and neither did he. Fuck 'em once or twice, then you know who they are. Jim was having a super-duper time with his thoughts. After coffee, he put scolding green tea in wine glasses making it look as if they were ice-cool exotic cocktails. Remembering the struggle he had wrapping up his dinner last night, he thought: in considering all that man has achieved, why in 2021 do we still have to put up with clingfilm?

The following day Martha found Jim with his back to her in the kitchen.

'Jim,' she said. 'I've had some thoughts about Christmas this year. I want it to be special.' Anxiously braced for his response, she fast learned how Jim didn't care a shit for her paralysis. He had heard her muffle a sound—something or other about Christmas—and wasn't even sure it was for him, so he continued looking intently at his phone. Even if it was for him, he thought, why talk about Christmas now? It was only November.

Martha had a thought too: come on girl, you've been mustering up confidence your whole life when you've needed it most; don't let it pass you by now. A minute later, Jim had finished what he was looking at on his phone.

'You what?' he asked, looking round. There was no-one there. Martha, shoulders forward, had returned to the tent to find someone confident within.

Jim started trying to work out how many girls he'd fucked without knowing their surname. He realised a flagrant number were single mums. Well, you've got to give women some jobs, he thought. Give them some individuality. If they were all taken stay-at-home mums, there wouldn't be enough to fuck.

Jim liked the female merry-go-round. He was one of those guys fortunate enough to find another woman to sleep with after he finished with one. They *never* found him. Jim realised that he probably didn't love any of them, and he wasn't sure how he felt about that.

Fucking was great. Not foreplay, not making love, not intellectual stimulation. Fucking. It would have been even better if you didn't have to talk to the subject of your fuck afterwards. That was the part Jim found difficult, unless you were a lightning-quick clothes-dresser, leaving the fuckee like a crime scene. Jim could never be that awful. No. And what made it worse was that Jim always set out to get the woman most attractive to him, and it seemed as though the more they pleased his visual fixations, the worse they were at conversing after said fuck. He looked at the chimera of what it could be, to be the total fuckboy. The walking fuck machine. He opened a can of mackerel and fixed himself a sandwich. He wasn't overly keen on fish, but he heard on the news they were healthy. Such fish were important to keep the merry-go-round well oiled.

#

December saw Cathy get a boyfriend from Camden Community, for about a week. She had to get rid of him.

He was all: could do this, could do that, could do nothing.

The sky was so heavy that everyone uncovered was unintentionally supping rain. It turned dwellers into puddle dodgers.

Just another day in late autumn. Water going hand in hand with life. We see it on the Martian landscape, we see it on patios where the slugs swerve.

And here, there was just too much water, and too many crummy examples of life for Jim. Cloudburst and there's only death, thought he. Dead in manner, dead in spirit, a sodden everyone.

In the watery night was a sweep of eleven o'clock rainfall, that same day. The downpour in bucketfuls had abated. As uninterestingly apparent as a sneck on a door or a rung on a chair, Burt got to his feet as if wearing cold steel armour. Out he popped from his tent with his dog, his footsteps cratering the surface. To see the pair was such a droll and compelling sight. Burt was a great man in stature. Must have been about six foot five and with a belly the breadth of one and a half footballs. By his ogrish feet gamboled a tiny, timid Pomeranian puppy called Fred. Fluff in every direction, he was the only representative of dogdom at the ecovillage. Burt was bedraggled but Fred was dry as anything, making the scene look even more comedic than it already was.

Burt, demurring to do so in the ecovillage, uncouthly bent down at Fred's collar and turned him loose by the entry path. You could not help but stare at them with every comical step, but then Jim had not much else to do in any case.

Burt used to like to do jobs that paid undeclared cash in hand; that way he would get money from work and still claim benefits. He used to have a girlfriend. She blew the whistle on the relationship once she realised he preferred marijuana and 'FootieTeam Manager.' What upset him the most was they had been together five seasons. Now moneyed from a family-run bookmaker's, Burt was enjoying ignoring wealth in a field. *Car Fixations* was showing in half an hour, and Burt did everything terribly slowly. To get back for his favourite TV programme, they left for their walk in plenty of time.

#

'Numbers always drop around this time. This is what separates the men from the boys, the women from the girls. It'll be interesting to see who's really hardcore round here.' Manny was addressing those that bothered to listen one young afternoon, cold as a gravestone in a midnight desert. The group were milling about the kitchen and *Shard* for some event. Martha was whispering to Meredith at the back:

'Spoke to my mum the other week. She's worried how it will look to employers when I explain to them I've been living in an ecovillage for the past couple of months. I'll have to make some excuse for what the hell I've been doing in my "gap in employment." Maybe she's right. It was a fatuous decision, coming here. I should just get a proper job like everyone else. And me and Jim, I'm not even sure we're a couple anymore, and if we are, what kind of couple anyway? It feels like we're just decoration for Christmas.'

'Now then,' said Sage, in bold voice six minutes later, centre stage. He primly revealed banners of red, green and white; the white as white as Walt Whitman's beard. 'Let us consider the Germanic pagan tradition of Yule. Friends, it is the winter solstice!' There were a few supportive yells. 'Some of us at this time may recite pagan prayers and think of the Great Horned Hunter God.'

With exuberance, Sage clutched from his pockets: frankincense, cinnamon and myrrh, plus three bowls into which the ingredients could separately cascade. Red, green and white candles formerly out of sight behind him were now laid out in front of him for all to view, his long arms having agilely reached around his body.

Jim wanted to accost Sage; the cause for his rise in hostility not known completely. Jim's back had almost completely turned against the mummery, and Sage was in his pockets once more to find a match.

'OK, let's get this water away,' said Manny jovially, broom in hand the next forenoon.

Jim gave him a look as spiked as the top of the local parish spire. Owing to recent deluges, Manny used a tatty broom that creaked with every motion to sweep away the water from the kitchen area. That he could attack it in such good humour narked Jim, but the latter just sat there, saying nothing. Jim longed to be told by someone something breathtaking had happened, like opening down the street was a new chav aquarium.

'I don't really want to go home for Christmas this year,' said Jim, turning to Martha in the flooded kitchen.

'Seeing as I'm not a Christian, nor a fan of mass consumerism, I don't really see the point. It's nice for my niece I suppose.'

'Lilly will love it, for sure,' Martha said. 'Remember how excited she was last Christmas?'

'Suppose.'

It was an anathema to Jim how companies try to impel you to care about your loved ones on specific days they choose for you, like Valentine's.

You really should buy something for someone you care about. Now let us make some money.

The companies are quite happy to sell you meagre discounts and offers on carcinogenic perfumes to give to your loved ones.

Jim augured a barmy storm was brewing. That, and that he needed to restock on depilatories, that the kitchen water was getting his dander up, that water too had decided to make a home outside his tent, and for Lilly's sake, he decided he would bide no longer and scram to the family home for this year's festivities. As for Lilly's sake, as to whether he came home or not, Lilly was only three years old. She couldn't give a shit.

#

Inside globed glass lived a fish Jim desired to nurture, so he left it with Martha. Hellbent in the mire to one day crawl out, Jim was back at the hometown he didn't want to see. Real trees, emblazoned and little on Cherryblossom Street beat the adornments here of lightbulbs round the lampposts.

The year was nearly up and Meredith had by her a hand mirror. She served her face for six hours less this month than this same month a few years ago.

A stickler for order, Manny had instigated a more thorough clean-up of water. Roiled water.

How does one measure turbidity?

Everything on the ground was cleansed and tarnished concurrently.

'We'll use weaved hazel as kitchen flooring to keep the mud at bay,' Manny said to the others.

Bits of the hazel were castoff as the make-do flooring was amended with trial and error to fit within the kitchen parameters.

At Christmastime, those that stayed formed a closer bond in a monsoon of revelry. Those peace warmers, those lovers of green. It was Meredith's birthday on the 19th. She felt selfish for having a birthday so near Christmas. Fred was frolicking in the excess water, purling puddles.

'It's like an indoor swimming pool here,' Burt said.

'Step carefully please. I do not want it to break and then have to find more,' said Manny—Burt's tread overbold on the weaved hazel.

The collective listened. The poetry Gods presented a childlike offering:

Dancing in the mud

We're dancing in the mud
Our boots go with a thud

It's wet right here
We've nought to fear

A mess no less
We'll do our best

We're up and down
We'll walk these mounds,
We'll take our mud to town.

They sung it throughout the twelve days of Christmas along with the occasional carol. A small Christmas tree was purchased. Nothing could amputate their spirit. Hammering a nail was not without a spring in the step, or a song or lilt. Cathy did not get a bookmark for Christmas, though she had asked for one. She also wanted a book. She had a cousin called Mark.

'Did you get Cathy the book, Mark?' the cousin thought Cathy's dad had asked him. Mark answered affirmatively.

What her dad actually said was: did you get the *bookmark*? Poor Cathy. She never lived it down.

#

In the spring he came alive with the flowers, as much as Jim *could* come alive; Martha too, as did her creativity. Jim was listening unexceptionally to her in their sorry-looking tent.

'I hate it, Jim. This time of year. I've never put a label on it. Have you heard of SAD? Seasonal Affective Disorder. I don't know much about it.'

'Yeah. I've heard of it but don't know much either. Everyone's feeling a bit off though when the weather's like this.'

'Well, to some extent, I suppose. But there's a difference between that and finding it hard to get out of bed you're so disconsolate. It's possible I'm afflicted with this, that I'm part of a community of seasonally low souls.'

By summertime, Martha would fully bloom and have some sense of cheeriness once again. Autumnal and brumal nights just had her in a low hold. Martha looked to evade her reality and take a hike from the world, when cold and macabre and wet. Despite the fractious nature of her environment, Martha tried her all to uphold a neat and orderly frame. The cold forced Jim to roll a cigarette with ragged edges. It probably would have helped if he used both hands.

Beyond the upper reaches of the North Wind, Boreas and Negafook share a drink. A Hyperborean land lies in wait.

Anxiety, now depression. It was Martha's brain's autopilot mechanism to, at this moment in time, have a song play in the background in mnemonic repetition, to dissuade too great a space for pestilential thoughts and tell her everything was hunky-dory. It didn't matter which song it was, so long as it was fairly upbeat. Impish night playing tricks with mechanics of mind; her mind, a great mind. A mind not simply drained by external outrages and outages but chemically imbalanced.

The wind had ominous fables in its depth. Wheezing, passing up opportunities for sobriety, lashing with unrestful swing, locking onto Martha like an iron grapple.

'I've taken it, Jim.'

'Hmm?' Jim replied. Both were still in the moderate tent.

'Remember I told you how Dr Das gave me a prescription for an antidepressant last month? I was saving it just in case I needed it, and I think now is the right time. I'm a little fearful. I've not had this one before.'

'O right. OK. So will you be happier now?'

With the élan of a leopard on a dinner date, Martha was worried if her mind would return one day. How much of it would get lost or altered once she took the pill? Her mind proffered an undisclosed ransom for the easement of nephritic pain that now bottled her, or at least the bodily tension made her think it was nephritis. Would the amygdala game she cottoned to, be as fun on meds? She would attack the pill-drop like a shivering smolt migrating to the sea.

'I'm going to stay here in the tent, Jim. It's a few hours now since I took it. I feel like my brain has been nuked and some gremlins are tinkering with the results. I'm less sharp and it's like there's something holding me back. You know something's new in your head because you can feel it, but you're not sure what that "it" is. I've all these different emotions and I'm not sure how real any of them are.'

A reductive landscape. So many of Martha's anxieties of thinking heretofore, had gone, but at the cost of creative thinking marginally encumbered. Shorn of access to all the caulked crevices in the gamut of emotion that give on to creation, she could feel the suck on her creative juices, spitting them down a smiling black hole. That is not to say she could not be creative. She could.

But when the blockage is positioned at the instant route to the core, the vibe is with less feeling and of a slower, fragmented value.

Lock went the neurotransmitters, so she thought. Puffiness, dumbing down of emotion, altered perception of risk, unnatural weight-gain and changes in sexual appetite would soon follow, as they had done already for so many millions of others.

For Martha, there were to be too the side effects of the drug that either lessen or pass completely once your body gets more acclimatised to it after a couple of weeks or so.

These were nausea, dry mouth, bruxism and night sweats. Antidepressants created a safety bubble for Martha. A bubble through which she could live a fraction easier. But she felt she could never actually be. The bubble may feel drastically needed in a crisis, but was it necessary when laid low but not buried? She could live her whole life there, inside the bubble. Easier, probably, but perhaps less fulfilling?

Every day is not today. The days went on.

#

Martha had not brushed her hair today. Looked like a burst sofa.

To be noticed during her tussle with life, maybe she wanted a reaction from the world. It was an afternoon in late January. The drugs numbed her, emotions nipped at—pulled predominantly up, and sometimes adown. A general listlessness. A robotic state in full motion. Feelings of extremes nullified. Tips of her fingers and toes sawn off. No orgasmic thought. No totalities of anything. She could not get into the bedrock of lugubriousness, which at this moment felt like a good thing.

Her temperature was unmercurially a little warmer, her appetite a little harder to satisfy. With a first-class thought, she would have been keener to act, but now as thoughts issued forth, they were harder to follow. The best part was that she had no thoughts to commit suicide. A love for escape—from the stuffiness of a car on a hot day—had ceased to be. Sitting in the ranks of freckled past, dark thought felt non-threatening and unactionable. Had her subconscious just convinced her she was safer because she had taken something?

A terrestrial televisual news show on Martha's laptop screen told her earlier that day what was happening in Britain. A government minister was promising Martha and her fellow citizens a huge NHS reform within the next three years. It showed her, with a stretchiness of mind to never underestimate the power of placebo.

'I can't wrap my head as easily around once easy considerations,' said Martha, staring at the vegetable patch. Jim was there, aggravated by the cutting cold. There was his love: beautiful, talented, coiled in inner torment. 'Am I actually still an artist? I've done fuck all. One of the pros of this drug is that as the management of outward symptoms has improved so has my wherewithal to help others.'

'Good. Can we go back to the tent now?'

Less caught in her friendless worries. With all those niggly unnecessary anxious thoughts now easier to shut out, it helped Martha realise how dodgy her previous company must have been to employ someone as inapposite as her. With an extra second or two to take in the world, she felt safer in herself and not so reactive. She could get on with things more and make decisions more easily, but it was harder to see the bigger picture and have days that were as full. The drug felt an important intervention to real struggle.

In the wake of buffered anxieties came dispassion to a day's plan of activities. Days went quicker. She could stare hours away.

Pull down the shutters of the world; I want to be all that sees me, her mind said.

Less racing, her mind, less inventive…distorted like her dreams. Incapable of finishing often simple trains of thought. It felt strange. An unnatural, impure strange. It wasn't just like trying a new perennial herbal tea or fledgling alternative therapy.

Now you are thinking a bit differently, tepid; grain cradle through a clear mind. Your mind is being pushed to a new direction of thinking—one not of your choosing. The redirection starts leading you down the path of confusion though you're not quite confused, but you cannot process thoughts with wholesome liberty. The directors of the orchestras are the drug companies. Their governmental familiars favour the violins. The doctors are told to hand out the sweets. The Gruyère just got processed for your guilt-edged burger. The burger you would have been less keen to go for with the same ease of debauchery had you not been on drugs. Synthetic happiness had just begun.

#

Martha was listening to *The Velvet Underground & Nico*'s 'Heroin,' and at the chorus, everything made pluperfect sense.

There are aspects of creatures, that due to these creatures' very nature, masses of a populace do not zoom in on, like a marmoset's toes or a limpet's poise. In humans, we struggle greatly to see in other humans invisible aspects such as outreach. Fucking up can get in the way. The human condition in the mudslide of human history is such that fucking up is next to mandatory.

You can't put potential down on a page. No-one's interested in potential. Potential doesn't exist. In our fast-food world, people want to know exactly what you're doing right now, yes please, what's your job?— Come on now, and wishy-washy answers won't suffice.

Fuck 'em. Give them the good news with bells on. So many of us have snippety, unstretched memories. There is no point in that things are *going* to be tip-top because that denotes that things are in a process, and that process is called potential. Martha watched for over thirty-four years how people missed her potential.

You can paper the cracks all you like. Mental health anomalies are translucent, and ricochet off people who do not see potential. Many aren't interested in seeing it, others don't make time to see it, and some wouldn't see it if it jumped up in their face and told them POTENTIAL.

How can others believe something they cannot see? Is the world not difficult enough sans the incorporeal?

Meredith later chanced upon Martha's tent.

'If you could somehow translate the mental to the physical: a broken leg for deep depression for example, then everyone bar the blind can see the broken leg,' said Martha. 'They will regale with you whilst you receive well-wishes and cards that say, "get well soon." Now imagine if this was the same for deep depression. What's more, when mentally unwell people get physical problems, the physical problem can be accentuated, attributable to the fact that they are struggling enough with mental difficulties. Do you see? But as it is, the world says: so what if you're on a weight-loss programme, or have intentions that you can lose weight. You are not fit as you stand before me today!

'It's pitiful, this society. Western worlds relentlessly evolve to evermore focus on what we see and not what we could.' The fact that Martha thought this all up meant she had potential for *something*. Martha was an artist and no-one cared.

She could still feel that she had cried yesterday.

'Could everyone gather round please?' said Manny, having banged together a couple of blocks of wood several times at the communal point that afternoon.

So everyone did gather round, like the wood pigeons of London. 'It is a new year and a new start,' he said. 'It is my design that we must have a structural system in place, here at the commune, anarchical and unhierarchical. Everyone 'mucking in' to achieve a collective vision. This vision, devised by myself, is shaped into a mould that would benefit everyone. Having resided in several communes myself, it would be fair to conclude that having one person as overseer, or autocratic ruler, does not work. Leadership breeds resentment, obstinacy and ultimately pell-mell. Is everyone in agreement with me here?'

There weren't any noes or yeses, just weary nods from the couple of people he made eye contact with. Cathy froze to capture her sentiment, with sandy eyes and a work ethic that belonged in a museum. There was so much energy in her facial expressions, and that was all. 'We shall work hard together and lay our heads together from our work. We will eat and drink together. We shall not go to the toilet together,' sprightly proclaimed Manny to Cathy and those others that cared to mentally be there with him. There were a few laughs and a wahey from Anjit. 'Everything we do, we do it as a team, and we try and love one another. We have a sizable enemy in the council so we have to stick together.'

'We'll be as good as Arsenal,' Dave said.

'Ah, we'll be better than them!' Manny retorted. 'We'll be like Man City!'

'Right.'

Snapping his chafed fingers on the word, 'this,' Manny said:

'Some things you can change like this. But to get tuned as a team? That takes time.'

Manny pulled out a mobile whiteboard from behind a hedge with a simple socialist diagram, and a few pointers Peter couldn't see anyway because he hadn't his glasses. Peter may or may not have been missing out. 'I want to see that the socialist model is followed, like by Cuba and Bill Shankly.'

'I thought you said we were going for something more anarchic?' Jim called out.

'Well it is anarchic, but with socialist elements.'

'Who's Bill Shankly?' asked Meredith. Manny sighed.

'It doesn't matter. The point is, if every man decides…

'And every woman,' a laughing Meredith squeaked.

Manny wasn't in the mood. 'If every person,' he continued, again sighing, 'decides that their living place will be cleaner, more aesthetically pleasing, and all-round better than their neighbour's, then everyone, by helping themselves, will be helping each other to build a collective, beautiful, utopian home for us all.

'Environmentally, a reduced carbonic atmosphere will be apparent, maximising the land's productivity, and we will be further engaging positively with our ecosystem. We have been indoctrinated, manipulated— ladies and gentlemen—even in our youth. When we watched TV as little'uns about the joys of vocational triumph, little did we know we were being told how happy we could be once we joined up to the slave force of workers. Financial gain is incessantly sought at the expense of our environment and our people. Well, people, let us be the ones to rise up! Enough is enough. Say it with me people. Enough is enough!'

'Enough is enough,' the crowd hollered. A barrage of half-stoned crowing and chuckling roars followed.

'I cannot change the world tonight. I cannot change it tomorrow. But if I can change just a few people in how they think, and if they then endeavour to do the same, step by step, I tell you, by the collective hand we will change and charge!'

The crowd again showed their support. 'Now that we can all see the lies and manipulation, we can see the truth,' said Manny. 'A new movement in action! From now on, we are the seers!'

A light, apologetically English cheer with some polite clapping followed as though Manny had whacked a single to mid off rather than a six out the park. A higher ratio of men cheered to women, and it was the other way round for the claps. 'People of the ecovillage, let us not forget our past. Let us remember the original Diggers and what they espoused. Gerald Winstanley of the Diggers once said, "Was the earth made to preserve a few covetous, proud men to live at ease, and for them to bag and barn up the treasures of the earth from others, that these may beg or starve in a fruitful land; or was it made to preserve all her children?"

'We must see to it that we carry on the fight. Without the pioneers, from where would we draw our inspiration? They strived for a world where riches are for everyone and not controlled by the few, to create the world they wanted, not what they were told to want. Comrades, that was their future, now it is ours!'

Manny offered up a Q & A session after his speech, and Jim stepped up to the nonliteral mic.

'Alright, fair enough, you've made your points, and I don't disagree with some of them. Call me sceptical, I've only just arrived yeah, but I hear too much bullshit round here. How can we all pull together in a utopian ideal when we can't even help each other in the simplest ways. Like only the other day, Martha leaves clothes drying in the sun on the rocks but that was an unconcern for someone who decided to put their dirty chainsaw on top. Some people here are ultimately selfish. I want, I get, and after I've got, I might just help someone a bit if I'm in a good mood. So, sorry mate, but until people change their ways, you can forget all that hippy bullshit, because we can't just seem to want to change, we have to actually change.'

'Very well. But let us remember the spirit of this place, dear Jim,' said Sage.

'Yeah, I think that's a bit cynical, Jim. The chain-saw incident sounds to me like an honest mistake,' said Meredith.

Jim had a 'walk off' moment. Assuredly. Playing in his head was a wrestler's entrance music.

'Manny's noticed that people listen to him and has taken advantage of it for his own power gains. Sitting in his throne holding court. Pathetic,' Jim said to Martha, a short while later after the speech. 'His speech was demagogic without substance. It may work on overoptimistic Yanks, but we here are British. This is a nation of action.'

Martha, having a job containing her laughter, inadvertently hawked in her throat. 'As the old saying goes, action speaks louder than words,' uttered Jim mutedly to Martha, as if he barely believed his own words. 'And anyway, why's he doing all this? I bet everyone else here is wondering. Some of these people have been here for *time*. So why do they need to hear all this? Why now? I bet he's just doing it to show off to us newer arrivals. Probably trying to impress *you*.'

'What? Why would he be trying to impress me? Don't be so idiotic.'

Manny cribbed parts of speeches from Fidel Castro, Nelson Mandela, Martin Luther King Jnr. and the like—told no-one. He practiced orations in the mirror. A dedicatory reader, snatcher, dreamer, he rejoiced in absorption of information. Manny and many wanted to go down in history, to be named after something the way Victoria sponge was named after Queen Victoria, the way melba toast was named after Dame Nellie Melba. Though Jim wasn't yet sure he wanted to be a dessert.

A week and a half had gone since Martha had started the tablets. She had been treading on the second part of the day with the first going so badly. Crawling with problems: pain in the knees so she loathed to walk, problems with parents, problems with horseradish. Begone pain! Leave me alone for a bit. Go and find another bug to house, clothe, feed. Teeming negativities of thought were at play, but finally she got down to some art. She didn't particularly want to do any. But one she started, the sea change in day was like no other before.

Martha possibly produced her most poignant, heartfelt artwork ever, and well-nigh everything seemed to go heart-stirringly well the rest of the day, such as the way she finished a particular piece a second before the kettle had boiled to pour her favourite peppermint and nettle tea, the way she finished another piece just as the train was nosing to her stop, the way she caught the pizza slice that would usually have fallen flat to the ground, and the way that Jim was nowhere to be seen. Work of art or work of heart? The girl who only playacts for real, who thinks graveyards are underrated. Sound-waves flew to the temples. Word on the street: Martha was the new sound, yet without the soundtrack. Before the drawbridge would close she would hear to read her script.

It came to her, with sensuous intensity, that her art whilst good had a patchiness to it. The antidepressants had dislodged lashings of artistic thought, which she could not recount in exact original detail when it came to putting paint on canvas. A touch frustrated, Martha moved on. The course of events repeated yet she could not curb a smile.

She smelt of stonebaked pizza, ordered some forthwith from her favourite pizzeria, had not showered in the unsatisfying makeshift shower a few days. Last night she had run in the belting rain coursing the finest cheese, chips and gravy this side of town before the shop closed for the witching hour.

She looked to the sky for an impression of Jim, trying her level best to visualise him there in the thick of chants from Benedictine monks. A cloudland of Jim. She loved the contradictions in the sounds. The stillness of pauses between chants, inspected by such powerful voices, and yet there was something in those powerful voices that evoked such calm. She couldn't find the impression she was looking for.

Like Jim in the nip, she could care a fuck no longer. Talking of her favourite four-letter word, she repeated it vehemently that night after having in the shower thought of a simpler time: charades, picnics in wicker baskets in the company of people with names like Mildred and Hubert, gulls gently mewing over the little boy flying a kite by the seafront, beer-soaked tales of mythopoeism from old raconteurs in great glasses on rocking chairs by candlelight.

All this in the unsatisfying makeshift shower. The wandering minstrel and the bard played the sounds of pitter-patter. The thought of the rocking chair reminded Martha of a rocking horse, reminding her of a Tommy Cooper joke. Bemoaning his lack of luck to an audience, he once had a rocking horse but it died.

'Fuck me Jim,' vociferated Martha, straddling the worked boy post-shower. 'Fuck me good and hard!' she demanded, now having acquired the glazed-eye look of a frantic genius. There would be no dismount in a hurry. He tried his best, bless, probably not as good as she would have liked, but God loves a trier.

Stunned into nervelessness, Jim wanted to be a rocket but went off like a sparkler. Diddums. He looked like a knobbed whelk.

Martha had a thought: I have the power to fake an orgasm, you can't even fake a smile you sad git. God was with her, surely, but in her presence, merely a demigod—her mind bleated.

#

'My God, Meredith. Somewhere during that artwork, I felt a new high, and it's like it's continued for the last couple of days,' said Martha. *Lake Horizon* heard her too.

'O really? How so?' asked Meredith, huddled, looking into glassy eyes.

'Like when I went to the chippy, and it was raining, and I just didn't care. I just felt so happy, a crazy happy. So freakishly happy. The corners of my eyes and mouth I couldn't shake off from their feeling a pulling sensation. I've never felt like this on any drug before, nor sober.'

'Please tell me you love me, Jim. I am…I can't think of the words for love nor money, I feel like I'm dying, like a runnel run dry. I'm having very dark thoughts and I don't feel I'm completely in control of them. For want of a better word, I feel scared. Just tell me you love me.' These were the prominent words, the next day, sent to us by Martha in her and Jim's tent, in a spin-rush-bump of the brain.

'I do love you,' said Jim. They embraced, and as they did, he thought: what is this I have as my girlfriend?

'I'm so worried,' said Martha, now mewling. Tears painting annihilation on her cheeks. She had a head like a triangular tumble dryer. 'Can you stay close to me? I just don't want to be left alone with my thoughts tonight.'

Mental, absolutely mental, Jim thought. He was sure other boyfriends didn't have to put up with this, God forbid girlfriends.

Martha felt her way through a pig trough on a ferry to the worst abattoir in history. Overthinking thoughts, the autopilot song was back like the stars you cannot see in the daytime. She did not want to hear her thinking anymore.

Hear me. You're right as rain, you're not going mad, thoughts reminded her.

She felt safe in Jim's arms. For two minutes. She needed to see a doctor. Quick. She called the local surgery, learned she had to call back early the next morning to make an emergency appointment in order to see the doctor that day. A normal appointment, if booked, could only be made for late the following week.

Sunny-side-up-salmonella-egg mind.

She didn't cook the fucking egg properly! she kept telling herself. Maybe on the flip side, only progressiveness could be effectuated from the leaning tower; the voice from the tower shouting 'MADNESS.' What was life without brinks?

Martha was begging her every part to pull in her direction. She was cleaving to spiritualized structures of hope in the form of the Catholic Church that was her upbringing. Thinking back to her time-honoured church as a child, its choral originations and faraway look in the eyes of figures on stained glass.

Liturgy of the Eucharist, are you maddened by my former laughing?! Shrive me! I never meant you mockery.

She gave herself reply in her head from God on up ahead:

Aha! Martha, here you are. Now you're calling out to me, in your hour of need! What of all these years that have gone by since, after you busied yourself at church being a good little girl?! I remember you saying to your friends: since I have no proof of God's existence, nor can I see him, nor do I like beards, why should I believe?

Shut up, she now told her brain in thought, shut up! Don't be so harebrained, brain. This isn't God, it's just you, Martha, from my erroneous brain! My diseased brain.

Martha was shovelling her nails into her arms, smacking her left heel to the ground, but was ungroundable. She was mentally riffling through the pages of her favourite books for sumptuous metaphor to anesthetise short, sharp, injurious thoughts that could, at any time, steamroller her mind. She was calling all sensory receptors at the nerve terminals, thinking she was alexithymic, somatising with the joyful elements of The Beatles' 'All You Need Is Love,' remembering the structures, hoping for the euphoria of Sigur Rós' 'Hoppípolla,' receiving only the complexities of emotion from Bedřich Smetana's 'From my Homeland, Andantino.'

Why, in my time of need, did I fall back upon Christianity, rather than the words of the Buddha, with whose words I these days resonate more strongly? Is the former more sanctifiable from its godly connotations? Was the Omnipotent's presence in conjunction with the magical imagery of Jesus harder to forget than the Buddha, who quested to eradicate the feverish potential of ego, to be an ascetical, humble mendicant?

Martha's mind managed to disengage for a while and she was left with what felt like a mouthful of dusty cherries. Pools of utopian tranquil dreaminess could be found in infestations of issues, and it was with this knowledge that Martha could see out the night…fall into the doctor's arms by the morrow. Martha wasn't so keen on this idea if the doctor turned out to be of the same genital group.

A long-haired, gruff, beardy doppelganger of John Lennon was seen on the way to the surgery the next day, giving her hope. His 'Imagine' brought to mind her Imogen—one of Martha's closest friends outside the community. It didn't matter to Martha how she got through last night, it just mattered that she did.

Light shone, cream-coloured, trampling over demonic possession of thought, tottering at first as it peeked through the venetian blinds of the waiting room. Jim had some tent DIY to do and so he had not gone with her.

'She's overreacting,' he said back at the commune to Dave. 'I think she's trying to get attention. She's just a bit worried, that's all. They used to call it female hysteria. She exaggerates so much man.'

'Perhaps you should question her yourself if you believe her maladies to be fabricated, rather than behind her back,' said Sage on overhearing.

'Whatever. Alright then I will.'

At the surgery, Martha gorged herself on a ploughwoman's lunch and a slice of guilt. After all, she had gotten close to Jim, gaining a knowledge from months and months of his character. She knew, to a small extent, he had been thinking what he was telling Dave. Or was she paranoid? Cremated by anxiety, she was too effete to give it too much deliberation, at least for now. She sat with the same desperation as a 10:55 p.m. dash for cigarettes at the local convenience store before closing time at 11.

Tiptoeing, Martha entered her head, searching for an antidote.

Cue disorder and discomfort. No. She again entered with brazenness. She explored with a prised-open mentality for she knew in the brain could be found the amygdala game. It was something she had heard about online from a man named Neil Slade.

It is widely held that the amygdala is where the brain stores emotion, and the amygdala, if stimulated, will pay dividends to the fondler. Although not manifesting in the same way, an interesting comparison is to look at the way in which cocaine titillates the dopamine receptors.

Where to locate the amygdalae. They are the shape of cashews with the left roughly an inch inside from the left temple of the head, and the right roughly an inch inside from the right temple respectively. Symmetrically apart, each lying behind each eye. The method by which Mr Slade says you can stimulate the amygdala is by imagining a giant feather penetrating the forehead, reaching to tickle the amygdala. You repeatedly imagine this and eventually will experience pleasant sensations.

Martha imagined the feather and it worked, but she preferred to substitute the feather for Manny's hair, wavily curling itself around her brain, feeling up her amygdalae and tickling them for her pleasure.

Tickle tickle tickle went the hair. Tickle tickle tickle. Like an adjunct to meditation but going a more physical route to exultation.

Come on now, focus Martha, she thought to herself. Think about what, and how, and in which order you're going to say what you need to say to the doctor. Got to make it to the next day.

Even with her fears for iatrogenicity and epiphe-nomena, with everything as unpredictable as a soaring Frisbee, her core emotion felt so stormy, so soulful, so potent like Charlemagne's; never had she felt the need to say so much in such restricted a time to one person in all her life.

CHAPTER FOUR

It was done. The tablets were given: a new kind of antidepressant and a benzodiazepine. Martha said all she could in the time allotted, wanted to say more, only realised how much more she had forgotten to say when walking homebound. Cursed herself, so annoyed at herself, how could she disremember such a thing? It was a young blackbird that hovered next to grimy Martha during the walk that kind of said it's OK. There are others alive going through similar. It's OK Martha, everything's going to be OK. Fortitude and forbearance, not shiny luxurious gold but stronger—a bronze-like resilience was going to get her through this with a bit of help maybe from drugs treating drugs, maybe from one or two helpers like Mr Blackbird.

In an appointment, the doctor could only give Martha five minutes and a maximum of two problems when she needed a day. It was explained that the old tablets simply did not agree with her and that she should give the new ones a try once weaned off the current ones. In the short-term, she should take the benzodiazepine as and when she needed when particularly anxious. She didn't want all this sex and violence, just a nice cup of tea and a lemon slice please.

'The new tablets are a security blanket for me if I need them,' she said to Meredith, after explaining to her all that happened on an indistinct area of grass. 'But for now, I'm too terrified to take them. God I hate antidepressants. I've called this "The Anticrisis." I know I haven't been on the last ones long but please help me as now I'm worried about the effects of coming off.'

'Of course hun. You'll be fine. Yeah I think that's a good idea, see how you go without for a while.'

'I've noticed I'm now like I was when I was on these tablets at the start.' Martha was a bit slurred and was talking quite slowly, as she talked out her body-thought. 'I've calmed down but I can't think straight. Remaining are the stock displeasures of coming off. I've had this before with other antidepressants. It's weird. Whilst your body and brain are adjusting to not being on them anymore, you get these, like, electric shock buzzy sensations in your head that seem to more regularly occur if you alter body position like from sitting down to standing up. It happens on the double. With the buzzing, you get what I suppose you would call semi-seconds of depersonalization, and a grogginess.'

'That does sound weird. Just let me know if you need me whilst you're still getting used to things,' said Meredith.

'Thanks. I'm so frustrated, feeling like this. I can't do much. I just want to do my art. There's always something impeding me from just doing my art.'

She had lost a bit of Martha, like a muffler on a piano. The only artistic thing going on in there was a hodgepodge of inanity. The pilot deplaned and parachuted. The artisan had become a human drone.

The queen bee flies high and fast. The drone briskest off the mark to fly highest catches up with the queen bee. The queen, thankful for his efforts copulates with him and afterwards bites his head off. She rips out his dead genitalia so that she can repeat the process with the next highest and briskest bee. Life's a drag, just ask a drone.

O, this bee's only got one wing, don't worry, the chairbee at The Board of Bees says that bee can be a drone too.

Between 1930 and 1980, eighty percent of wild-flower meadow was sold off to private developers and destroyed, helping the bee population to die out faster. The bee does not realise how lucky it is to be able to fly nor how unlucky it is not to have a brain smart enough to know any of this. Bees have a song:

'I'm a beeyeeeee. Bee bee bee.'

#

Create your future, add to the economy, keep the machine going. Martha was remembering a foray three years ago into antidepressant land. At antidepressant club she had been complaining of anhedonia and couldn't-give-a-fuckery, so they selected a tablet for her they thought would be just the ticket. They fed her a low dose, didn't do the trick, so they upped it, stuck her on a supermarket till. That shut her the fuck up.

Nametag on the laniard: Prisoner
Number: Infinity

Martha once ID'd a man for buying bread.

Hello Martha, we need you to get back to the standardization in modalities of correct behaviour. Here, take this pill. All will ameliorate.

It was either that or wait for endless months for your six fifty minute sessions of CBT.

Stand to attention! Sea shanties directed from the capstan of the DWP schooner careening as its pace narrows in. At the foghorn it went:

Most countries don't have it
So
You better be grateful we pay you so,
If you're on JSA, get cracking on your search!
We'll leave you, cackling, in the lurch.
If you don't comply…
Loading…Our admin system is experiencing a fault.
Quick, put on some Vivaldi. We no longer make sense, we have no steersman. We never knew patience and we've forgotten how to rhyme.
Our rhythm section was never our strong point anyway,
We're the DWP so we don't even need to finish this…

The boat's wash along the waterline had a foul colouration. It was just a boat and we need boats to get away.

#

'That's like well good what you've done there 'int it,' said Cathy.

'Is it? Thank you,' replied Martha.

Amongst the verdure there were explosions of amber. It was a sunless day outside Martha's tent. Not too chilly.

Around forty minutes ago, Martha sat and stared at a blank canvas amidst wispy smiles of air scampering to encircle her like wingtip vortices. Wishing a cessation in stasis for about twenty minutes, she did eventually paint. Back and forth lifelessly over marks she had made, back and forth, back and forth. Martha could not fully get into anything and spilled the coffee that had already burned her lips. She was mindful on a question: how was it to be a creative and be stymied? Her mindfulness lasted up until Cathy came by.

'What's like the meanin' of this paintin' then?'

'This is memories and visions of harmonious futures, and utopian green worlds. Have you ever heard the Brian Eno track, 'Another Green World?'

''Oo's that?'

'A musician. A very good musician. I was thinking about this track as I painted.'

''Ave ya thought about putting ya stuff up on Etsy or sommat?'

'I'm doubtful I'm good enough for that, Cathy, but thank you.'

'Yer being daft, you. Give it a whirl like.'

'Yeah…maybe.'

Her art is peerless. But who said? Her art was life itself, at least before the worry, all that was. No-one else quite understood; it helped to see her inscape but you didn't have to. How could she tell the others of the motifs swishing her mind from the painter's brush?! As an initiation for an outsider's mind: a protean extravaganza condensed to the singular of pot-roastable skewered humans in only loincloths tasked by underworld guards to make sure of their smooth about-turns, ripping masses of flesh in the process. To resist would mean another skewer on its way over to them, by the hand of another guard in a choice of nightmares similar to what the Jains call Mahatamaha Prabha and the Buddhists, Avīci. It was only Martha that had to go to bed with such visions, Martha that lived in its juices by the appeasement of day. Martha that now laughed with the brush in her hand!

What lies beneath hells? She is tomorrow of a next-day dream. She never wanted top shelf.

Martha carried an unremitting expression of blankness for the day. There was something there, an exciting je ne sais quoi, but it could not be accessed easily for it brimmed behind skin.

#

'I now know what Cathy meant when she said she felt like "used goods" the other day,' Martha said a bit later to Meredith, who was the next solo arrival to look at the painting. 'This piece of art is just…abominable.'

'No, you're so hard on yourself,' said Meredith. 'It is an expression of how you are at the moment. And well done for getting to do something. I think you'll look back at this once you feel better and be thankful for this work.'

'I guess so.' She didn't so.

Martha didn't believe her advisor one bit; a world first. Martha mused over how she should feel; cerebral vs visceral. She wasn't sure whether to laugh or cry but she couldn't do either very well. Internally conflicted as usual, feeling a diversity of sensations all at once, sometimes overwhelmingly so. A struggle with complications beneath the surface to the even greater struggle once these whirr and meld with the external world. It was as frustrating as being plumb innocent of a crime yet cemented by a set of events so incredibly implausible that no judge in the land would believe. A triplet of unlinked Martha thoughts, one after another, came rolling by: a cigarillo, a ship nearing in, something heard in a film. Jim came along just as she got very still. Wispy smiles were back, but this time in the form of smoke from Jim's cigarette. Martha came at Jim with a face transfigured as if a truck had just pulled out in front of her. He wanted to know why her pinkish lips were trembling, so he spoke to them.

'Disturbing you?' Martha was half open at the eyes. She closed them to.

'No,' she replied. Suddenly things weren't looking quite as green.

'Good good. Oh, alright Meredith? Didn't see you there. Hey, that picture's alright,' Jim said, looking at Martha's latest shadings of orange, raw sienna, coral and onyx. Some might say none of the colours seemed to have any discernible relation to each other, or purpose, nor any delineations of trees or other features of landscape one might expect in a utopian green world. There were lots of globs and long rectangles, inclusive of the greens.

'Cathy liked it too. Do you really think the picture's alright?'

'Yeah. Maybe a little dark.'

'OK, I'm going to go and lie down for a bit.'

Therewith, tentward, Martha had gone.

A Jimless tent of peaceable stares.

Once I am fully off these pills…Martha started to think, and as she did, no more thoughts came forward to make themselves known, other than an image of a shadowy brook.

Jim thought of his own creative pursuits while chomping down a sausage. All he knew was he liked to write. Never judge a book by its cover? Fuck that. The cover to his book would be freaking amazing. Then they would judge it. Then in about fifty years he'd be dead anyway and we can all go home. To not judge covers does artists a disservice and initial covert-to-conscious suspicions remind us that we have anxiety in our body for a reason. A judge didn't seem necessary for book covers. Not to Jim.

It was not fashionable to be a writer anymore and Jim had poor penmanship anyway. Jim thought no-one cared what you wrote about unless it involved *them*, so he never had a stab at it, even if he felt he could do an awesome job. For the never-ventured book, he even had his opening line:

I am a cunt and you are fucking me by reading this

For Jim, it was the profession for the lucubrator, the affected solipsist. Iambic pentameter really pissed him off. He knew that we have so many words that we don't use and that some of the best lines are when we're not trying, or are keeping it simple. That feeling from a breakthrough idea or a favourable choice of words is spine-tingling, and you're the only one that can feel it. It may be years before you can share these isolated cases with others, and for you in that moment, it can lighten a dreary afternoon.

Sure I could start a book, Jim pondered, but I am not fooled by the fleeting, fickle entertainment world! Bespectacled introverts trying to improve their knowledge of idioms and showing off their silly words on paper from the trees that we're exterminating. And why is grammar there to simplify yet so complicated in its design? Even 'em-dash' has a hyphen in it.

The modern writer, Jim thought, with their Americanisms and intent on expanding their vocabulary at the expense of rhythm and clarity? None of that for me thank you. And I don't have a cool name like Mazzy Martin.

The hardest part for any writer is to look your work cold and hard in the eye; foregoing your attachment, you ask yourself is this really any good?

Jim wanted no part in that brutality. Not least, he realised that in ten years' time, there would be someone younger, hotter-footed, better read, better educated, with more contacts, more influences and more influence. So why bother?

#

Martha was the first drop of February sleet to fall on your forehead, too interesting for rain, trying to be snow, feeling like a shy kiss. She looked as though she had been recently crumpled under a sumo wrestler. Breathless yet serpentine, motes of midnight in her hair, a glass ceiling below her aureole. Doing naught for her comfort, in her tent but not *in* her tent, somewhere in her head the bully voice of Martha was back. She was forecasting future events in future tents while Dave wasn't thinking particularly about anything much, although he did for a steep time wonder whether his latest grunts of acknowledgment came with the desired inflection.

A little earlier, crepuscule commingled with clouds of light grey on Peter's glasses; dozy sunshine having varnished late afternoon. What a nice finish. As anti-depressants relax muscles unnaturally, once you're off them, the muscles have to relearn old tricks.

The process in motion, Martha mustered a laminate smile. Positivity with drains.

Yet in a few days, her brilliant mind was coming back, at least in shavings.

'You can do more when you're nearer the destina-tion,' said Martha to Meredith, in Meredith's bender. 'The fact that I've been there hopefully means it's not too far to get back. I will calibrate the increments. Wing parts need to repair. The Anticrisis is over!'

She was to go to the shadowy brook, where no-one would disturb. It was a place she could paint time away and think for the fairytale images that settled in her midst. Her art had an idea to pearl the outline of a humanoid. 'When it comes to antidepressants, and not just this last one, I'm realising that you cannot underestimate how much you can change, nor how much of that change you maybe cannot see whilst you are on them.'

Maybe equals maybe not, or is that a glass-half-empty way of seeing things? thought Martha. The depressive's choice!

'It's good you're off them. You seem more perky,' Meredith said.

'Unquestionably, and I've already theorised with myself for myself that I do not want to take antidepressants anymore, even if it means crying for long periods of each day, because I want to experience life as it truly is. To resort to pharmaceuticals means a masking of reality. They're anodynic, yes, but henceforward, only a last resort.'

'You're already using more words than before. "Anodynic?" I can't say I know what that means.'

Spiritless from months spent being someone else, with only tints of Martha about her.

Let someone else be me for a bit, she sighed to herself in thought. I want to shirk the necessities of being a human being right now for an indeterminate period.

Martha wanted to be heroic like Blaise Cendrars, the famed painter and hardened veteran of World War One she had read about, who near the time of his perishing, had tears streaming down his face the pain was so great. Not his mind telling him to bawl, but his body speaking for him. He was determined to find out what death felt like.

Martha noticed her behaviour a little straightened now as before medication. The raiment now bought had tempered in chromatic loudness and her mind no longer careered down its more tumble-down tarmacked avenues. She thought that analysis can be helpful, overanalysis usually unhelpful, and that to think any more on her theory would be to overanalyse. All of her muscles were awoken and jumpy, on guard for flight. She was wishing over false hopes, skipping on a dive. Uh-oh, said the right corners of her and Meredith's eyes. The sewer rat, the swift romancer, the black pudding was coming closer.

'So…' Jim said. He went to touch Martha, but it was too late. She had netted hypnotic, oneiric captures of thought. Martha searched Jim's doorway to his brain—have them us all: the eyes. She found numb mindlessness among the dispelled brickwork. The Buddhists have it that the mind is actually in the heart. She searched there just in case they were right. There were no stores of patience and humility. Amongst the junctures, besides arterial waves she found unmoving vessels for change. The poets and the clergymen inform us of a soul. Whether it held good or not, in Jim's case, there was but inviolate invisibility. Sometimes only, logic works.

'Sorry I have to go soon,' said the artist. 'I'm still getting used to coming off the drugs. That is to say I just want to head off and be on my own tonight. Sorry.'

Jim's extremities imploded. He searched for blots on Martha's mug to make him feel better about his person. Twin anger marks, their bases starting either side the top of his nose, told Martha all she needed to know.

'She's been a bit funny recently hasn't she?' Jim said to Meredith a minute later, with Martha having followed through with her intentions sooner than soon.

'Just give her time, she's still feeling her way.'

117

Martha's disgruntlement was her launch pad. She tore free her topknot with pugnacious whim.

Where's the easel? Where's the fucking easel?! she asked herself in thought. She found it, underneath Jim's miscellaneous dreck that had worked its way over to Martha's side of the tent, making her even more disgruntled.

Gathered her watercolours, mop brush, round brush, any bleeding brush—just grab it. Palette, tape, liquid frisket, jars, paper and a dark red cardigan for when it got cold later. Off to the brook where she produced twenty-four-carat art.

Enough of the bent bollocks, there was a new home rule down by the brook, and Martha was both chieftain and sole functionary. The throat of the brackish brook gasped for breath in the winter winds. Containing peat, there was an acidity for the runoff of ideas at Martha's factory of creation. Her images were peppy, watered-down angers. Malice altering every brush stroke painting the landscape. Far-off trees merged in a cluster: little brown sticks with green hair.

Budding by the brook, Martha's inner problematic thoughts that amount to labels given them, were her captors. It was her captors that coated her beautiful art. Not that they always had, or even ever had to, but to play down their role would be to disregard process. They clung less during chemical strangulation.

Martha's dress gave a soft blue to the sunset. It was one of only two she kept in her tent. A quiescence of mind, a full taste of water, a splash to the eyes.

Starting off unnoteworthy in fringing reeds and grasses before unlocking a deep blue crack through a stony declivity, sometimes sputtering, sometimes trickling, the brook offered a lovely Aussichtspunkt. Up on the brook, in panorama the ecovillage tents and benders looked like little pointed hats for Lilliputians by a thin wire of smoke, *Horizon* a miniature puddle meticulously made. The female maestro and mother nature in full accord.

Meredith used to edit a magazine called *People who Pout*, which was far more a success than the prequel, *Quantum Cappuccino*. With a crossword on her lap, she was reading *Grazia* magazine by the vegetable patch. She liked tall men, she liked men with beards. Growing beards takes patience, the kind it would take to put up with her. It wouldn't matter if the tallest, handsomest, beardiest man walked past, nothing was to remove that violent gaze from such a fine weekly issue.

#

The 17th of February and it was Jim's birthday. Thirty-seven solar orbits the world had to put up with this shit. His girlfriend was buoyed by her new art and new mind, and for the last few days this was so. Martha seemed pressured to find the right mask for the conditions she felt today demanded. She had bought Jim a book about gardening, a torch and some silken male underwear for her amusement. Her balmy naked flesh with breasts ripening for spring, ever so gently brushed against the corner-cover of the mattress before she climbed it. She reminded Jim of conditioner used to soften clothes. Her bare back artistically shadowed in dim lamp lighting, consuming blacks and golds.

Shoulder blades rushed to the front of the scene; amalgamation of form: her ascendants had shouldered upmost care for symmetry.

One is not dancing if still, yet under the underhand light source and its intermittent flicker, the delicate back illusively slipped and slid. A careful lowering of the back communicated that she was not yet one hundred percent comfortable to be braless in the company of a man. But the fact it lowered, and to the mattress, lowered all the way, said to Jim, from Martha's back, on behalf of Martha, that she was ready.

Now that you've seen my bits, what are you going to do with them? she thought. The point at which you know something between two people has clicked: when silences become snug as a bug in a rug.

Night had gently fallen, her head against his. They kissed and hugged and shared in love. Halt the time machine, in this moment she wanted to stay, tugging back the heels of aurora a few lingerings more. Her black-as-death pupils dilated with Jim's as they stared, stared and stared, totally at ease with each other, themselves and every part of the multiverse.

Jim was awoken the next morning by sincere shrieking.

'Spider! Spider!' were the first words Martha decided Jim would hear as a thirty-seven-year-old. There it was, scurrying just above her, weaving with great purpose. 'Try not to squash it, just catch it,' she said.

'Martha, it's 6 a.m. so right now I'm not too worried about the spider's emotional needs,' said Jim, and he dealt with the arachnid in his own special little way.

In short order, the partnership of humans gently watched their chemistry smoulder after fizzing.

Jim found himself in and out of frosty hypnopompic thought. He had tried to get back to the land of Nod but only managed non-rapid eye movement sleep, stage 2. When he came to his senses, Martha was cleaning. Her loveliness wafting in his eyes, she made things better like blossoms shedding to the floor during a funeral dirge.

'If you were a film, you would be exempt from classification,' he informed Martha.

'Thanks,' she replied with a titter, tidying up his crap.

'When you dust, it's like a little faerie would. Your magic wand at work making everything nice and sparkly and pink again.' It reminded Jim of something else—a dredging barge he had seen in Porto, excavating in proximate waters for navigable approach. He didn't mention that.

In what the psychologists call transference, she reminded Jim of the only girl he had fallen in love with, by her gum line and shape of her forehead. Oh that previous girl! Of his being, she took over completely. Shouldering a double-barrelled shotgun, she his prey, girl in the crosshairs, Jim dropped the gun.

You meet the perfect gentlewoman and decision-engineering falls to pieces; how it went. His feelings for her meant his feelings for Martha. And, much to his sense of antagonism, it was because he was deeply in love with Martha that he was deeply in love with the ecovillage, deeply in love with Cherryblossom Street, deeply in love with Carringdon, and most stomach-gnawingly, deeply in love with London.

Skin-tight jeans were not Martha's best idea for cleaning in. 'I like your dimpled smile,' said Jim. 'Behind it is where the palatial faerie lives.'

Women are very strange people, thought Jim; him there with the caught-out eyes. Jim was thinking over Martha, overthinking Martha. With currents of memory gently circulating, her shapeliness soon again came into view as she sponged off some guck on the inside of the tent. 'Thanks a lot for all you did for my birthday,' said Jim, as he saw that Martha had finished organising the last of his pile. 'Look at you,' he continued. 'You're too gorgeous to ever have chickenpox. It would have to be something that sounds more sophisticated. Something like quailpox.'

'That's OK. That's nice. What time does *Diagnosis Murder* start?'

Watch him lowing above, her the udder of his world adding him days. The midwife at the birthing of his new year. She sang in coils, twirling twisty lovely Martha! Better twisted than bitter, Jim knew oh-so well of her courtly altruism, enkindled not by religious beginnings but from an unblemished heart. She could rearrange the sky with a smile.

Martha infatuated with Sisyphean tasks, once affected, remained so the remainder of the day. It was only just that Jim should help out.

'Here, I'll get that for you,' he said, lifting up a kitchen chair as Martha swept underneath.

#

On to a morning dripped with affectionate rain. Gale winds chuckled for winter. They were British, they would endure. There was however just a month to go when March would offer the promise of spring. A jungle of voices zigzagged in the bluster. Amongst them, those of Jim and Martha. One voice hung for a bit, consorting the other. An interlocking or confluent return?

'It's fucking 'orrible,' said Jim to his girl.

'I know.'

It was the 19th, 20th or 21st of February. It didn't matter which seeing as human dates were related to the Gregorian calendar imbued with Christian history, and Christianity, most at the commune did not relate to. That there was no God was a given among most there too. A February everyone knew, at this time of year for the depressive, a galling fact is knowing how temporary winter sunlight is. The problem for the thinker is there is not long enough in the day to do all the things you want to do. Martha was a thoughtful depressive, and didn't the world know it. How then of the upcoming meditation, this polishing of the mind!

Sage decided to postpone the upcoming meditation until early March as it clashed with his pedicure appointment. Time pressed the fast-forward button.

'You get those moments in life where you feel so relieved after a nightmarish incident clears. Like if a car nearly nicks you, you think golly, how lucky am I?' Sage was once again giving a talk in line with the meditation. Wrapped in winter wear at the communal hub, fewer people were present this time around. 'If I'd have been an inch slower getting out the way of that car, I'd be in the hospital or dead. But then as life elapses, you have a week, two weeks, a month without any such incident. You get too comfortable and your level of generalised comfort reaches a plateau. You forget how lucky you were a month ago when that car nearly hit you, and even if you again remember the incident, it feels an age ago so it can't hurt you. It's the edge that keeps us on our toes; that little item of captivation that enables us to strengthen and push towards our dreams because in that moment we realise how lucky we are to be alive. Without it, we're indestructible, all until the next lucky or unlucky event. Maybe next time you won't get so lucky.'

'Fuck I agree with you,' Jim said, and all present laughed. 'That's probably the first time though.'

'Thank you. Life is not absolute if not on the edge, hey Jim. I am surprised you are here when others are not. God bless.'

Jim started to question his choice of saying anything. Such self-question represented an atypical trail of thought. 'If a man is stabbed he is forced into presence. He is forced into his body, feeling it, aware that the blow could well be serious. He knows his time might be limited and must perforce think of his loved ones and what he has achieved in his life. He is aware of the pain.

'When we get too comfortable, we need to figuratively stab ourselves to keep in check, be in our bodies, and realise the most important aspects of our lives.

'A duality rings true. Investigating the absence of things, is too, an advanced meditative technique; for noticing is also noticing what you don't notice. If one is not curious about the world, does one deserve its riches?

'A four-year-old is probably more mindful than any of us insofar as they are so curious about the present moment. Mindfulness is just what we forgot along the way. Believe everything and nothing of what I have said. In other words, it's probably best to take that which most strikes a chord. Leave the other bits behind. Question it all, test out the bits you are unsure of, if so inclined.'

What was he blathering on about now? Jim sort of knew but it was cooler to remain in disdain. Sage instructed the meditators to now close their eyes, sit upright and be calm yet alert. 'Just be present of what is here,' Sage said quietly. 'It doesn't matter about the past or future. Just be here, and don't judge.'

Jim used to have an idea of what presence was, but it was now he was truly now. For fifty seconds.

Jim *is* present. Injuries to cognizance were oceanic and never-ending. Trepidation about the destination of the meditative altered state was of marked trickiness. How safe really was it to let go? Sage was alright with letting go but Jim had no intention of being like him nor did anyone else, probably. Almost everyone was more sleet than snow. Jim the hailstone was untidily curious. For him, there was nothing a shag and a cigarette couldn't solve.

After the meditation bell to end rang out, Sage said: 'I don't like to call it letting go. No, I prefer *letting be*, a bit like what The Beatles were talking about.' He gave a long laugh and croak. Jim was not amused. 'I don't know much about depression, but I read about it in a book once. Snubbing depressing thoughts allows one to live pro tempore. Suffering them into your nonjudgmental sphere of consciousness is evolved thinking. Counselling helps peoples' tangled thoughts through the medium of someone else. It's great to talk.

'Meditation allows you to work through these thoughts yourself, giving a spacious place for all these thoughts to go, where they are not attempted to be "corrected."

'In meditation, thoughts are watched without judgement. This allows them to naturally process without being poked, and it allows your backbone to step away from being tangled itself, within the thoughts. In substance, it is all about seeing how life really is and not seeing it'—he glanced at Peter—'as how other humans have moulded it for self-interest. Forget unrealised potentialities. If you do not have this moment, then what do you have? Mindfulness doesn't give you the destination but it affords you the map.

'Friends, I will leave you with this: It is the eighth of March. As some of you may know, it is International Women's Day today, and that is nice. What I think would be commendable is if everyone celebrated an "International Equality Day," every day, but without the label. That way, there wouldn't need to be any day to honour women, gay people, and ethnic minorities to name but a few. Everyone would get on with their lives a lot easier and the world would be a better place. Thank you.'

People rose and slowly walked around. Jim had an expression as if he was febrile. Martha, feeling meaningful, ferociously grinned at Jim and said nothing; for what can you say to the man who has realised he has spent half his life disgusted by the world and everyone in it?

It seemed like anyone Jim had ever encountered who 'made it' did it by one, two or all three parts of the magic three: trickery, selfishness and greed. This anomie and the morally fibrous exteriors within for a socially dissolute miasma could surely only adulterate us. Or was Jim just thinking his way to being a grump, whom one day the grandkids would call Grumpfather Jim.

One thing after the meditation Jim *did* notice was how much we *don't* notice so much of the less appreciable components of our biosphere. Cherryblossom Street in mundane, restless flow sprung up answers: the potholes, manholes, lampposts, sights of workers, drains, the little bobbly bits where blind people go to cross roads Jim labelled 'braille for feet,' all became as wakeful as the other elements. Growing up in street life had conditioned Jim to see the world a particular way. Perhaps it had nix to do with the meditation and all the time in the commune was rubbing off on him, but now he was starting to see, with microscopic goggles, the way things actually were. Jim had a mindful smoke.

'So many of my anxieties are in the future. When he said, "If you cultivate presence, you can shape a better future," I was reminded in this moment how important presence is,' Martha said to an undecided Meredith.

'Darling, you walk awful slow,' the American replied, as they walked and talked near Peter's hexi-tent.

'I know! Sage helped me realise that humans are the worst storytellers.' Martha went on to explain how our multi-layered presuppositions rarely play out the way we think they will. Even if they do go in much the same way to how we think, there is usually some dip or twist or leap. 'Such misgiven thoughts just ensnare us. You can't be happy.' Martha was content that it seemed possible to refind a potential deity within herself.

Jim meanwhile on his lonesome outside the compost toilet had a mist in the brain. He realised that to an extent more widely than originally first thought that neurological activity and his subconscious, at the time of meditation, had been in cahoots, as Jim fell upon remembering some of the key points. What was it like to embody stillness? Jim was now apparent for, and nonjudgmental of the susurrus of distant voices, the waviness of the briars, and old-lady-hair ferns as they acquiesced in musical arrangement a modulation from E flat to D with nimble swirls of wind. He was apparent for the shadows of soughing trees winningly correlating with the look of the gentle rill in shadow, or so it somehow felt and seemed. He then thought fuck all this and opened a beer.

Meredith went to bathe, Martha read her book. Liking the look of the book, something new happened: standing weightily on the tippytoes of pleasure, Martha became desirous of it. A coffee just made, a tongue just burned as on her lap she opened the book to be engulfed.

Refuel energies, block adenosine, dress nude attention.

That was Martha. Not the sort to skim-read book after book, accumulating a creditable collection, getting only a gist of what they all meant. She would just as soon read only five books in her lifetime in every way she knew how. Commemorating them, cherishing them.

Martha was about a third of the way through her current book. She turned the page and Kyle James was flying:

> *I was fucking delighted when they authorised my new passport. Now I'm in Argentina with my gun and pool table, and guess what? The weather's not too bloody bad either. Go and stand in your petty queue you fucking English twat! So glad I'm not back with those misery gut poms. They look like fish guts, all their faces rot and mumble a seabed of lies…*

So it went. Martha stopped. She wondered if reading the uptight infrastructure of the book would sully her. Time spent drugged up had felt like time wasted, and as her memory kissed eventide it grew tiresome and horrorful.

*

\#

Kristoff, standing shyly let his eyes fall on Martha in a way no-one else's did: a rose-water orb of sun illumined the lankiness of her frame; the ribbonfish that swam in gentle majesty through *Lake Horizon*. She was absolutely beautiful, dainty, quirky, female. Every new sky awash with lime-green gallons of snow, felled from tears of Goddesses too unearthly to unfreeze. Tears enough to overload pails, making others jealous by their drought. She had stories in her hair. Amongst the tassels of gold could be seen chasms, seas, questions of metaphysics, bedposts, carousels, symphonies, guillotines, indigo deserts, Monet, al dente pasta, enlivened aspirations and sour sweets.

No-one in the twenty acres of land was more feminine in the historically formed social fortifications humans had framed for the patent of womanhood.

Everyone at the commune was daring and fickle and tense at least for small journeys of time. A March day. Much of Cherryblossom Street looked uninvitingly at the shoddily clad rabble from the ecovillage whenever they turned up on *their* street—why how unsavoury a sight! When it was inclement at the ecovillage, there was at least a welcome natural backdrop.

Jim remembered how much he hated London. Overcast or a sky in ninety-five percent cloud cover in the city, was different; the greyness in London just went with the buildings, Jim felt. Deep, dreary drudgery. With Carringdon Ecovillage's position reasonably near to billboards and vehicular playgrounds, traffic could sometimes be heard giving cheerless reminders.

In some posh places of London, people seem happy with their world but not so happy with *the* world, thought Jim. Walking round town they are looking at their phones or past you. The only time this seems subject to change is if they are directly addressed, or money is shoved in their faces.

So sorry for being a human being and not the latest phone. Yes it is me, the amorphous rubble. O I see you've decided to stop by and chat on this occasion. Probably best if you hadn't, but I know you have to be seen to be busy. You usually pretend you haven't noticed me and pick up the pace, or shun me the other side of the road. If you did stop and chat, it might be along the lines of:

'We've just come back from Tarquin's graduation at Oxford. We're so very proud of our darling boy. Oh you should have seen him, he simply looked to die for in his graduation cap! Such a delightful ceremony, and his sister, Tabitha, is travelling with her fiancé around Australia before they get back to their lovely flat in Notting Hill. Oh, and how about you? Has the croquet picked up? Tarquin said you weren't very good.'

And in these parts, there had been for years an eroding of effort given towards manners requiring more time. In these parts, the underdone 'hand up' signal to identify to a fellow driver of your thankfulness in voluntarily giving way, can easily be mistaken.

Why's he waving at me? Do I even know him?

Jim heard his thoughts end and bottom out.

Could Jim have had a point, if only that politeness could give us all a hand? Do such activities play out in undersea life? The clam and sponge on the seabed acknowledging a shoal? A multiform of drivers in certain areas would look at the hand and…who cares.

There goes the middle-class townsperson, their life is an ice rink. They idly speed, it is haiku, it is flood, it is high theatre, it is the mad conductor with the Einstein haircut. They have turned full circle, their life is an ice rink.

Jim's mind wasn't done yet, but en route to town a certain girlfriend in his company was revving her mind for an internal rant of her own:

It's funny how the world of distending media that was meant to set us free can freely do us such disservice. The process of exchange. We have gotten so used to exchange being engrained in our culture, we seldom seek to question or look askance at the process. I'll only do this for you if you do this for me. Even if you've scrubbed up in your best garb, you can walk around town pretty much invisible. Jim wouldn't agree with me but it's not just a London thing. Other UK cities and to a certain extent other UK towns have this too though with the insanity of London you have a front row ticket. What about my car? My earnings? My kids? My husband? My wife? My vajazzle?

She went on: other people aren't as important, but friends and their attachments are a bit more important. Too many people placing too much interest in money and showing off dear clothes, too caught up in themselves, not looking up enough at the world and its people. What happened to the young minds of creation?! To the Dadaists, the Romantics, the civil rights movement? The only movements *we* have are peoples' fingers moving over the mouse to put up the next social media post. The problem is not people inherently, it is the way they have decided to adapt to their environment, and then how they have followed like sheep to the herd.

Jim was still thinking about London: Too much stress around London and people could be unmannerly at any moment, even fairly decent people. Jim wasn't sure where 'unmannerly' came from. He continued: I don't blame these London people necessarily. They are, to a certain extent, a victim of their environment. They travel on the jam-packed tube to work where there are a number of worried and woebegone looking faces. They get aggro from their boss, come out of work to where it's raining tabbies and Alsatians, only to go back again on the jam-packed tube homeward and make the conscious decision to do it all again tomorrow. Then, sooner or later, something can give. Some people love living in London…they get hooked on its adventure. But others that get stuck, and after a while exist to forget what it is to be happy. You can get so wrapped up in a city like London, so wrapped up in a system of living that you can forget to think you can live and think anywhere different. Jim could hear his thoughts end once again: woebegone? Homeward? I have been too much time with Sage.

Jim felt it better to be bored and happy than stressed with everything at your feet. Could Jim admit to himself he was grouchy and depressed? And how much of it, if so, was borne out of general London or the London he grew up with and latterly lived in? How much was about his London now? With the police station at the top of Cherryblossom Street and the church at the top of the neighbouring Birch Street, Carringdon was well looked after.

Around town people don't walk naturally. They've learnt ways to walk. And at roadsides, they don't all look for cars but use human shields as they cross. Man created roads which in turn led to laws against other creations such as jaywalking.

Jim was jaywalking, Martha and Peter were to his side on the pavement. There was a stubby plump sixty-something sir with 80s glasses and advanced hair loss. Distinguished yet drooping, he was holding a wad of Christmas cards, and was, with the same delicacy with which you would have thought he wrote them, individually slotting them into a pillar box, three months too late for Christmas.

Across the way was a man on a sunny bench next to a cider, gazing at the end of his shoe. A fire engine haughtily sounded with the slogan on its side: 'never leave cooking unattended.' Five fifty-plus ladies were sharing differences about their Sunday roasts. One had started to look like a catfish after growing dangly bits of hair from her chin. And there were those independent shops coyly trying to save face, poking out resignedly from the multinational chain stores. How they coveted to be many years younger when they did not need so much marketing makeup. Many of the multinational stores sat like beautifully raw acoustic pieces of music doctored by synthopop autotuning to fashion something as colourful yet tasteless as turmeric. Near a pub of choice for the eco dwellers was a small war memorial with a single wreath of poppies resting in its misery. It had been pissed on the day before by a night-going drunkard.

Today Martha convinced Jim to look at peoples' reactions to Hare Krishnas singing up the street. Some of these read: well I really could have done without that. Nosing our streets, what a racket!

Despite his bad start at the ecovillage, Jim did not want to be concomitant with such people anymore. He could only think that the Hare Krishnas seemed a lot more fun. So did the Buddhists, the poets, the greens and the underground scene.

The door swings open of 'The Green Lion.' A sea of pub goers stare at the eco bunch as if to say, who the bloody fuck are you? Jim's pair of eyes find themselves caught with another. The look of a dusty patron with a watercress-green jumper says: don't look at me like that, you turned-up trouser twat. Feeling a part of the personae non gratae, Jim is reminded of a song about gentlefolk of the North Country a school friend had told him about. 'Yorkshire Bastard' bolts through Jim's head on the way to the démodé bar.

'What you drinking?' asked Jim to a following Martha. Martha started to speak and as she did, she realised that she didn't have the self-esteem nor energy to fully communicate as she would have liked. There were too many people, for her. The music was quite loud and she had no bother to raise her voice over it, gabbling:

'G & T.'

Whatever, she thought. Defibrillate woman! said an inner noise, but she had no reason to act on it.

The barman, slick-back style, looking about on a quarter-turn pressed imperturbably his palm against the pump. Jim ordered a pale ale. Good old England was holding its breath.

'See him at the back, in the corner there. Looking stern, mumbling to himself? That's Benny,' Peter said to Jim. 'Now Benny doesn't roll, he just likes the smoke, you know what I mean? He always wears a duffel jacket and an eye patch—idiosyncrasies he likes the best.'

'Eight forty mate,' said the barman.

'Is it?' asked Jim. 'That's late.'

'No. Eight pounds forty, sir.'

'Oh.'

'Rum and coke on the rocks, half a cube of ice cheers,' said Peter, leaning across before Jim could even reach a shallow pocket. The barman gave Peter a perverted look.

'Well, you mean on the half rock,' Jim said to Peter. 'You're in a different mood today: "You know what I mean?" "On the rocks?" Have you been watching those American gangster films again?'

'I have, but you've got to ham it up a bit. It's not every day you see a guy like Benny.'

'Yeah, why does he dress like that?'

'I've never asked him.'

'Right…Sage not coming then?'

'Uh-uh, he abstains from alcohol and he wouldn't be seen dead in a drinking establishment.'

'Thank fuck for that.'

'Touché!'

'We should come here more often.'

After Jim's brief moment of elation, his expression turned to the usual.

'Cheer up, it could be worse,' a woman at the bar said to Jim, divorced from the hordes amassed, rifling Jim's brain, wearing a technicolour raincoat. Jim pretended he had not heard the woman he decided was a kook.

'Who was that?' asked Peter.

'I have no idea'—Jim's reply.

'Oh right, I thought you knew her.'

'God no. After she spoke, I just thought: oh you're one of *those* people.'

The pub was by the town leisure centre whose crowd puller was a swimming pool. 'I hate swimming in those public swimming pools,' Jim trumpeted to Peter. 'It's not particularly good for you to be in one of those pools with their high concentration of chlorine, especially when you swallow the odd mouthful. And the other thing I hate about being underwater is when you accidentally breathe some water through your nose— you are just left with an unhappy windpipe. When the pool is so busy, you can't even get a few strokes together because you're too worried about your arm hitting the person to your side. Martha likes to swim, don't you Martha,' he said looking round at her.

Martha stared blankly, pretending she was not listening. Jim turned back to Peter. 'The best part I like is just lying on my back, getting out of this world, pretending I'm a starfish.' Peter laughed. 'And you've got to swim knowing that some kid's probably slashed there not long ago. After all of that trauma in the stupid pool, you've got to go and get changed where there's always one or two elderly gents who think it's perfectly acceptable to just walk around, no care in the world, completely bollock naked. And you're cold, shivering like an idiot, too cold to bother drying yourself, waiting for the water drops to drip dry. Once you get to your locker, here's hoping the wristband with its key hasn't already fallen off into the pool. Public swimming pools, no thanks mate.'

Martha tried to make eye contact with the colourful-coat lady at the bar to strike up some conversation. She'd heard Jim's pool rant so many bloody times before.

#

'It's just food isn't it. I've never killed an animal *just* for fun,' said Burt assuredly to Jim, several days later. The former had somehow managed to have in his possession an adapted, loaded gun with no-one else knowing how or when Burt and Jim formed some kind of alliance. Their shirts stained with activity, they were quite a way away from the ecovillage in an area of woodland their eyes had not laid on before. Rabbits especially seemed pretty fool creatures and Jim could not envisage them having had much of a life anyhow. After a first rabbit was felled it felt easier and easier, almost mechanical. 'They're pests, the foxes. All those city boys and girls that don't live amongst them stand up there with their anti-hunt placards because they don't understand what it's like to have to live with them. They don't know the damage these foxes do to farmers' livestock.'

'I wouldn't even know about all that, though it's quite engrossing, this shit, once you get the hang of it,' Jim responded.

'Too right mate. Let's see how much of it we can sort out before dusk.'

'Sounds good. Oh, and not a word to Martha about this. You know what she's like.'

Burt hadn't had this much fun since Crufts. Jim was so into it, he could forget about time and circumstance in a commune. Everyone could fuck right off!

Jim's noggin sang him a song: The women can wait, the men have work to do.

These days Jim would rather go seal-clubbing than nightclubbing. He felt so independent, so at ease and in control. He hadn't felt so good since his birthday in

Martha's arms. The only frustrating part of it for Burt was that there were no riled dogs, no horses, no uniforms and no hunting horn for the mort.

CHAPTER FIVE

Burt was pissing up a very English deciduous tree. In a welcome rest from the bloodshed, something happened that always happened when he pissed, and that was that due to his corpulent tummy, he could not see his genital collective. With an awry gaze a discovery was made: by the side of a neighbouring tree was a miniscule, carved animation, painted and all. It seemed a take on the *Little Red Riding Hood* story, only the little girl was blue and had a wolf deep in her mouth with only his tail and hind legs hanging out. Riding Hood looked wrathful. There was a groove in the gullet of Little Blue Riding Hood where the wolf's jaws were. Here, a little speech bubble cropped up, exclaiming, 'Up the Chels!'

An accursed wolf, a deranged Blue Riding Hood, and a reference to Chelsea Football Club. What a surreal five minutes, thought Burt.

'Just a minute, just a minute Ol' Jim boy,' said Burt.

'What's that?' replied Jim, making his way over to the tree.

On closer inspection, a hole beyond the groove went deep and opened out wider the further in it went. Burt could reach in with two fingers and a thumb.

He dragged out a bitty box, and with the other hand, did up his fly.

'Heavens above!' mellifluously said Burt, regardful of the box in his palm from which his eyes would not unbind their interrogation.

'What do you think it is?' said Jim, beside him now.

'There's only one way to find out, Ol' Jim boy. There's only one way.'

Overseeing charily that the catch was released on the wooden itty-bitty brown box, slowly, slowly went the lid. Slanting, grinding, creaking…the results betrayed the pair's second-guesses. Voilà! Inside was a titchy scroll.

'Bloody hell. What's going on here?!' said Jim.

'I don't rightly know, cor blimey, I don't rightly know.' After Burt had spoken, he emptied the box into his unsmooth hands, unrolling the scroll a great many times its size. Its words from a story long ago:

In a valley of surprise perched two golden sons. Drunk on their champagne-standard God, a single blossom looked thousands on a tree more magnificent than Earth could accommodate. These are my sons, this my tale:

1231 Theory

The above number is the only time I can ever write or say it, and I write it here expressly for the reader's educational purposes. The number is not said as it would be in this world i.e. (one thousand, two hundred and thirty-one.) In lieu it is said as a combination of numbers, singularly said of their own. To illustrate, as in the combination of numbers for a money safe, they are said, 'one-two-three-one.' The number talked about is the creator and divine being. Ergo, in a similar way to the creator being pronounced 'Adonai' in Hebrew, defying the way it is spelt, the number I mentioned has a subordinate proxy combination number that's used to refer to it in an expedient manner, in speech and in writing. The combination number we use is 1237. The number that this proxies, if said or written, is adjudged blasphemous to the way of life of the divine creator via the expressed form of a combination number. As far as this 'ties in' with me - I am controlled by a man called 'Captain Fuck.' Fuck lives and works in the spaceship that is my brain. He has subordinate colleagues but they are of little importance. He has many buttons that he controls - buttons that control fork-in-the-road decisions in my head. He is enjoined to press the buttons I decide to select, and his job is done infallibly. I will speak more of the buttons at another juncture. Please, we must not get bogged down with the right honourable Lord Fuck, who is merely a praiseworthy figure in a much larger and significant dogma.

Captain Fuck = Engine Force of Structural System

Structural System = (The Theory; i.e. 1237)

Singular Numbers

Singular numbers are numbers in their own right, singularly e.g. 17 and 1, and what have you. It is only within combination numbers that these numbers take a different form and are part of a different number power.

When talking of single numbers, the number '3' is the best singular number possible out of all singular numbers beknown to man of this world. Don't ask, just accept it. Naturally so: Best number = Most powerful number.

'1' is the second best singular number.

1237 - (the way of life) was not thought of or devised with a view to be portrayed in written form as a thoroughly polished theory using numbers. There are therefore numbers that carry no particular value.

Scale of Singular & Combination Numbers

Rank	Singular Numbers	Combination Numbers
1	3	123(7) x 4 (4 is not considered a cool number and so it is said that it is multiplied '1237 times')
2	1	123(7) x 3
3	6	123(7) x 1

It should here be noted that the number 7 is also a very good number.

A Note (On This Way of Life)

Without an explanation of this theory overmuch, through nuanced readings and examinations it would appear that I will obey this order, and no more shall I suffer embarrassment - something I repeatedly experience. There is a notion that countless, and sometimes overwhelming intrusive thoughts that enter one's mind are 'cancelled out,' so to speak, if the thoughts are negative, and more so by means of specific actions. This is seen within 1237 theory whereby a systematic and sometimes negative way of thinking is tackled by 'attacking' such thoughts with actions, among which are blinking a certain number of times, (in the number form of 1237) in a right-to-left direction. To endorse positive thoughts, blinking is done from left-to right (usually initiating from the top left of the object for extra strength.) Of course the theory is a numeric system of order - an order I knew whilst growing as a youth, and that I saw develop during my adolescence. It still remains.

The numeric system could be analysed by some as a contrived spiritual order of things, or by others as ultimately meaningless. One day when not so clear you may see what really lives out there, in the hushed night. I had no power over this theory - it came to me like a scald; whilst aspects of it prove vexing, it should here be mentioned that I look back at the minutiae of this theory with no degree of jocularity, and once accustomed to its power, neither will you.

1237 Active In A Situation

Example A: In a situation where negativity is present and presents itself in an active role, the aforementioned blinking system can be employed so as to deal with this. It does this in two ways. Firstly, it filters out the negative vibes; secondarily, it will, working now with the body of neutral contentment, integrate positive thoughts to the mind.

Neutralise negativity, incorporate positivism. This blinking system is probably the most favoured and used manner in which to deal with negativity out of several variegated systems. It will be so, that another system will now be discussed:

When The Roles Are Reversed

Although the right side of the body lends itself to effect a positive vibe as illustrated by the common equation, right = the right side for positivism, there can on occasion be methods of positivism by way of the left side of the body. This can be the left arm or the left foot. If on a desk, the left elbow is positioned erect on the horizontal surface whilst the right palm is pressed against the thin area of wood between the top surface and the underside.

Please note that we must use such positive forces in warring against our own antichrist, Minus 1237 (written '-1237') also known as the religion of the snail. They believe in a satanic doctrine of thought that threatens to blight and attenuate our way of life. They have the erroneous belief that our way of life is nonsensical, belittlingly believing that 1237 is simply, 'what people do.'

The text and imagery that followed was faded to the point of being unreadable owing to its age and scraps with earthly material. This remained true, up until a subjoined short passage of fresher ink:

For a relatively young man I think about death more than is probably healthful. I go to a friend's wedding. The master of ceremonies is playing pop music with highly sexualised content. It is all about getting down and dirty. Two girls, just shy of twelve I would guess, are jigging about the dancefloor and know all the lyrics. They do not even know what they're singing about. It looks so wrong, I cannot watch. I realise I must be sounding like an old man but at least I am not a dirty one. It does not taste the same from the plastic bottles. I take a swig from a can of cola. I love the feel of metal against my lips.

'What bollocks,' said Burt. 'I can't believe this, I just can't. I don't understand what's going on. Have we dreamt this?'

'I don't know how the second bit is linked but the 1237 stuff I think is maybe an in-joke between some bloke and his mates, but I'm not so sure.'

Was it a joke at all? Something aside the conjectures? An in-joke inside oneself? The two shared the images they held off from anyone else until the unwinding of a new morning.

#

Martha had snoozed off. Having taken a break to see her adoptive parents in Holloway for a few days, Martha was travelling on the afternoon train back to Carringdon. She awoke to find the light sharing with her that it was five-ish. Can't be too long now, she thought. Martha awoke with a problem. It found itself at the back of her head: An erstwhile chatterbox was sitting therein, reeling off thoughts like a flicker book through other parts of time. Her phone was buzzing and shrieking. It was Jim.

'Hi,' Martha answered. Jim could hear her smile the other end.

'Hi babe,' he said in an oleaginous manner. She pulled a face like she was foaming at the mouth. Familial varieties like 'hun' resulted in similar evocations and she was sure she had told Jim about this at least once. 'How's the journey?'

'Yeah OK, been slumbering most of it. What time is it?'

'Twenty-five to six.'

'Argh, I had no idea!' Her train was due for arrival in five minutes.

'Listen, I'm going to be a bit late meeting you, sorry.'

'What time will you…'

'About fifteen minutes late.' Martha lolled.

'OK.'

'Did you have a good look through my old stuff at your parents' house?'

'Yes.'

'Did you remember my digital pet?'

'Yes, even though you haven't played with Marmaduke since 2003.'

'He's sentimental. How about my old laptop?'

'Yes.'

'What about the laptop charger?'

Waylaid and stinging, Martha was in the dungeon of anxiety.

Thought of Martha jabbed mind of Martha for an answer. Her body rigidified.

'O my…I forgot about that. I looked all over for it. You know I've a horrid feeling it got mixed up when I was doing a sort-out and'—her voice went an octave higher—'landed up in the tip.'

'Och, fucking hell Martha. What the bloody fuck's wrong with you?! I ask you to do two things!' She felt his face reddening down the telephone and put the in-call volume down a couple of notches. Martha did not feel he was in a mood to be told he had undercounted the actual number of things he had asked her to do. 'Fifty-five pounds that cost me! I can't exactly have it posted here. So I've got to wait to have it posted to my parents in Greenwich to go and collect it there, or else go all the way to Holloway to collect it from *your* parents, and then come back here before I can use the laptop. Can't I just use my laptop?! I just want to go on my fucking laptop, why's everything so difficult with you?!' He sighed. 'See you in a bit.'

The train's drone swallowed Carringdon pretty well on time. Whilst others stood and sat and riveted their eyes on newspapers and mobile phones, Martha walked the platform to give room for her thoughts: last thing I need is to go back to the community stressed. I hope he's not too mad with me.

Sage and his thoughts had made a new plan: I think of something I'm really passionate about and pretend I don't care.

A few hours before, he used this technique while talking to Cathy about spirituality. She was smilingly taking a gander at him, beaming like never before. His thoughts were:

This is brilliant. She blatantly likes me. I could try myself at writing one of those self-help books about how to understand women, only this one wouldn't be made up, it would actually be real; my real experience of understanding women! I can tell everyone in this book that wants to know how to pick up girls and then I'd make millions!

Sage had barely finished these thoughts before his phone vibrated with a text that read:

'Cld u get sum profiterolls when u go shop later, this guy is visiting and I want 2 impress him, thanks,

- Cathy xx.'

Sage suddenly looked every part his age.

He was talking a little later on, profiteroles in hand, with Cathy the executioner. Sue was visiting for the evening.

'Nice o' that Sue to come 'ere an' help out again 'int it,' said Cathy.

'She is quite the delight,' said Sage. 'It saddens me so, however, that she has much to do on her own. Most girls want to be loved implicitly and for the entirety of their lives by their man. Single-parent mums were girls with dreams too that just didn't work out.'

'Aye, true say. Cheers fer the profiteroles.'

Sue's children did not have to think because she did that for them. Five kids she had. Must have had a minge like a fire escape, Jim thought. Jim liked that she probably did. There was more to delve into and explore. He was back at the ecovillage with Martha now. He had planned on getting Martha a vegetarian dessert, but that wasn't going to happen now, not after Chargergate.

Tonight Martha wore a torsolette for him.

I hope he notices, she thought before bed.

Martha enchanted their tent with soft candle-light—pear and orange, her favourite. It was a little after eleven. She excited like a cloudless daybreak. A springboard of inspiriment.

'You'll never guess what Dave was telling me today,' said Jim, striding into the tent, a fork and microwaved macaroni cheese flawlessly browned in his trailing left arm. 'Have I told you about his mate, Cockney Alvin? He's only started selling vaporizers and all sorts of paraphernalia for half the price of what they do in shops. He's in town tomorrow morning, I best be up in time.' Jim hopped onto the mattress and pulled the covers over him, plunking down the meal and forgetting it on the nightstand. He was sawing wood quick as a wink.

Martha's foremost thought: right, that's it.

She stared up at the tent's roof, straight-backed, feeling constricted as if wearing a corset.

That's the last time I try with him. I don't know why I bother. Running out of fucks to give. God I'm even starting to sound like him—what a loser. I'm just going to do my own thing from now on, and if he wants me, he'll have to come and find me. Whether I'm in the mood or not, he'll just have to find out.

Martha's hair had been growing like a pain. She was like Rapunzel only without the patience.

Adieu, she proclaimed furtively from her tower's oriel. In thermoweave vestments, she would rather dive-bomb out its glass as an hors d'oeuvre for the agony below than wait for her tosser in tin foil.

#

Next morning and Meredith gave a searching look in the undergrowth by *Horizon*.

'What's up?' she asked Martha.

'Oh nothing, It's Jim. Can't be bothered to talk about him to be honest.'

'Ah honey, I'm sorry.'

'Just Jim being Jim.'

It was a day that was to be a busy busy affair. Without delay, Martha had hightailed for the trees, and almost seemingly without as much as a sound of a human breath or footstep, Peter had somehow snuck into the position her body had come away from.

Peter knew that Meredith knew he was there, yet without notice. He knew he liked her because he adhered to the sum total of her words and watched her every moment. He looked at her in daydream and awe. As she stared off, he searched *her* daydream. Peter always liked the foreign ones—probably for the best as it meant they were less likely to understand all the crap he came out with.

Peter felt he could have been any of the many freshwater leeches that wanted to suckle Meredith. He gave her a misfiring wink, for he occasionally forgot that a wink involved just one eye and both would go at the same time resulting in more of an effeminate eye-flutter. He really was a winker.

Peter and his thoughts:

Overlook your error at the landing fields, Peter. Meredith's scent is stuck in my throat; I must retreat in my operation for conquest. Abort Peter! Back to Tent HQ to regroup and rethink strategy. Maybe I should go direct with Meredith, something like: will you be my twat? No Peter, no; you're not a gangster rapper.

A coquette of the highest order, this diplomatic tease from the west coast of that dizzying, seductive land of America showered Peter with untreated saccharine. There were inexhaustible uncounted rains of tumult from those relucent eyes of hers in all directions, microwaving blood, discombobulating brainwaves, crashing Peter's shockwave flash. She could even get Martha to twist her eyes to meet hers, make her yearn; a gun carriage, a Chinese lantern, a chalice full of thorns—bonny and dangerous in unequal measure. Such a sultry entrapper, in her company nothing safe. She had the most splendorous eyelashes she would sparkle her prey with. It does not afford me any pleasure to insist that you, too, are in Meredith's snare.

World filterer and dallier, she flirted with wild-flowers, she could sharpen a pencil with a glance.

She waved at Jim walking by. Her hand was made up of black silk, skilful to the touch, deathlike. Once upon a time she was worse and would give as much of a fuck as the female praying mantis. In those days she was a social chameleon, one minute playing in the touch-rugby team and the next in fancy bars sipping martinis. She could make her voice as spongy as her calves to cajole men, whipping them up in tornadoes of lust, moving on to her next victim at the drop of a hat. Not manipulative just thoughtful, she would have it.

Many moons ago, Jim felt that he was spending too much time letting women penetrate his mind, and not enough time penetrating *them*. There was Andrea, the high school stunner. Every zitty-nosed kid was after her. Jim had been close to going out with other girls, like Annabelle. She was far too close to her parents for Jim's liking. Then there was Sophie, her energy was too tame. There was Sam. She was alright but too many pardon me's and no thank you's for his liking. He liked her for what she wore and how she wore them. When Jim's best friend asked if he fancied Sam, he replied in the affirmative. When another girl Jim was thinking about going out with asked him whether he fancied Sam, he replied that that would be going too far, but he had seen some potential. He wanted to verbalise to her that he fancied both her and Sam a bit. The truth was somewhere in-between what he had told his best friend and what he had told the girl, but he could not find the words so he learned to start changing his response depending on who was asking. There was also Michelle who was a practicing Anglican. Jim had a problem in sharing a woman with a guy with two thousand years of experience:

If I saw you in the week, would Jesus come round at the weekend and babysit your sister? Do you have to wear that cross so often to remind me of our bilateral relationship?

Jim always detested pretension so he never took to poetry, nor did he ever understand women. He was sure they had a secret language men did not know about.

People say they do not know how they would cope bereft of their pard. Jim felt this way about two or three girls yet he was not with any of them. How did he manage? For three months, in an unhappy job with no sense of stability, he managed. Then he met Martha. He was dubious about her but she was a woman. Whenever Jim was unsure of Martha, he could not look, even detachedly into either eye of hers. Whenever he felt love for Martha, she would slacken the tension at his heart centre with only his crotch left taut. Martha, the splendid enigma.

She is Kasparov, Grieg, Jackson Pollack, Joan of Arc, Des Lynam, a Mesopotamian tablet of cuneiform yet to be found.

From a provenance unaccounted for, as though a nimbus around her, somewhere deep-seated, Martha found how to think Jim a poem in his voice to make him king of the page:

> *I love you like the moon loves the sea,*
> *the stars allure the sky.*
> *Old and grey I will end,*
> *I've nothing on*
> *maverick young stars.*

Professedly as the crux of what mattered, somehow Martha understood Jim to some end.

Like Jim, Sage also tried to understand women but found better things to do. He knew it unsolvable. He knew men of great penitence, of husband material never to reach the Holy Grail. Burning calories by thinking, Sage's pate told him he was a hard man to please:

I have found myself a number of times in my life where there is a lady I have not before seen in front of me, and she has her back to me. Paradisal was the plurality of these sights, and in a staggering number of such cases I preferred this view before they turned round.

Sage wanted a sophisticated woman. He quite liked Cathy but couldn't stop thinking how her chin seemed almost the size of his forehead. He preferred her farther away than closer up. The turban, nightcaps, shower caps and caps may have made him forget how big his forehead actually was. Sage liked to use breath spray before he jabbered with the ladies. Cathy need not know about the halitosis.

#

'Life I find very difficult,' Peter confided in Martha whilst sharing falafel out near his hexi-tent. It was around lunchtime on the busy busy day. 'I don't expect anyone else to understand.'

'Thanks for telling me, I know what you mean. I've undergone a bit of a rough patch lately too.'

'I still think about my losses, what could be better, the real and the not-so-real thoughts my mind thinks for me.'

'O I know what you mean there. I'm such a negative over-thinker.' Martha counted the coppers she had left for chocolate.

'Why are you over here? I am not the most personable of fellows.'

'I see that in you Peter. You were so welcoming to me when Jim and I first arrived. I mean, I don't know you that well but I can tell you are nice inside, but have trouble showing others perhaps?'

'You are only half misinformed.' Peter sold a little smile, just for Martha.

Bloated with unrequited love, it swells in the stomach as it comes alive.

Unrequited love? Peter was an A plus student in that. There was Daisy, Megan, Jen and Tabitha. Peter did not fall in love very often so when he did, he went for broke. One-sided loves obsessed him and made it burdensome to love again. Not in the right place for women, walking through his mind revolted him. Whenever caught in a love triangle, Peter was always the part that no-one wanted, and with Meredith never had he been in such a poor state to meet his one girl. As pointless as a tiered stand of canapés on a starched tablecloth, would Peter dare to make Meredith his last try? Oh well he thought, it's all good material for the psychotherapist.

#

'Come on, let's have a piggyback race,' Peter vocalised. 'Finish line is that tree.' He pointed at a heavyset oak yonder the vegetable patch. 'Last one has to cook dinner.'

It was late in the afternoon that busy busy day. Meredith was right next to Peter and he knew she was. He looked at her and she clambered aboard. Peter was delighted she had chosen him to be her very own piggyback man. Meredith, alarmed, thought he might have taken it wrong. She remembered that if you give a man just a hint of a flirtation, misplaced or mistimed innuendo that they could start thinking with their todger they just replaced for a brain. Peter was a distant car alarm she wished to turn off. He looked squashed-faced by her; rind against brie. Kristoff heard about the event but said vying was not for him. Sage seemed pretty chipper about having Cathy on his back as well. It was Cathy and Sage vs Manny and Martha vs Peter and Meredith. Jim was watching one of those TV shows where you watch other people watching TV. You heard it here first.

Manny ran stumblingly yet well, transmuting breath to a smile. Sage ran with a gallant fight.

'I don't eat all that wheat for nothing you know,' he said, chuffing. Others laughed. It was the first occasion Martha had been higher than Manny, and looking down at him, in an unassailable lead, spellbound by the hyacinth, she had thoughts with feeling:

If just for one minute of your time, I could share in your happiness, that would be perfect, thank you. Why not take me on a seven-day trial? You could date me out of pity, that could be fun.

Manny and Martha more adroitly than the others slalomed their way past bits of stone and unevenness to the finishing post.

'Drat,' said Peter. 'Last again. I just could not get going today. I think I overdid my walk earlier on.'

Piggyback politics was done for the day.

By the evening, Jim was bored and wanted sex. Hopefully she'd put out as she hadn't last night, he thought. His libidinous visions pulled him by the ear to the tent to see if Martha was there. She was, but so was someone else. It was Manny. They had not noticed Jim and he listened pressed up against the bark of a close-at-hand tree.

'I'm loath to do the next speech though, I'll get all nervy. But I'll definitely help out with the design and marketing side of things,' said Martha.

'Good. It's a real help to me, you realise. You're the main one here that wants to help. OK then, I'm off, but come by if you need me for anything.'

'I will. Thanks.'

Manny did not notice Jim behind the lank oak as he strutted out the unremarkable tent, happy-go-lucky. Jim went to the unremarkable tent a few minutes later. Urges relocated.

'How are you?' he asked Martha.

'Ah I'm knackered. I sometimes feel like that after cooking.'

'Cooking?'

'Yes, I cooked a meal earlier if you remember.' Martha had a taste of leftover sardonicism in her mouth. 'You had some, and Manny had some too.'

'So he did, righto.'

'Yes he did. He thanked me too. Right, as I said, I'm tired. See you in the morning.'

'Just a moment, before you go to bed, what did you do this afternoon?'

'Oh not much. There was the piggyback race though, that was funny.'

'There was?'

'Yes. I didn't know where you were.'

'I was keeping warm in the tent, I wasn't feeling myself. Had a headache.'

'Are you any better now?'

'Yeah.'

'Great news. Goodnight Jim.'

Martha in repose for bedtime with her Kyle James book did not read a word from Mr James tonight. There were no thoughts too about the guy next to her, as de facto leader guy tyrannised her state of mind. She hoped in the several times their eyes met as they did that day, that those looks had not now withered, that ascribed to them was a great drift and depth. She lay ensconced, nursing her favourite childhood memories, pristinely devoid of worry as though embalmed by a naked sun. Thoughts in pyjamas. She felt cosily high up on Mount Manny, safe as the interior of a Popemobile, light as the peignoir she never wore.

#

There they were. The next day. All the vegetarians, vegans, hippies and green people; a big grey cloud of douches, Jim thought. He in particular found some new ill will toward hippies:

They have this pleasant veneer but scratch under the surface and you realise they are just the same as everyone else. O God is this my future? A bunch of grubby lefties in a field that all look like they need a good spin in the wash. Of course there is a small collection that babbled about the fiendishness of globalisation and capitalism, and at any slight opportunity would vent their grievances. Not that anybody could hear what they were saying as their mouths were often overflowing with vegetables. Green-fingered, lily-livered bastards. So vapid, of a similar calibre, all their egos in splintered homogeneity.

Jim's thoughts took a rest on this day following two without sexual relations. Was it just Jim or was everyone else becoming more misanthropic the more time went on? Most of the eco dwellers were either smoking, drinking, on prescription drugs, illegal drugs or were drinking cups of tea. Because the world as it was was not enough on its own. Death + silence = deathly silence, throwing down eeriness like never before. Martha was the sobering force of the day, eighty percent unsure of everything. Jim suggested she go back to the tent with him, so she did.

'The sense I had of quietude is now gone, Martha.'

'I beg your pardon?'

'It has been replaced with hatred. I cannot relax in somewhere for which I feel so much animosity.'

' "For which?" "Quietude?" What the…? What have you been reading lately? I think you need to remind yourself of why you came here in the first place.' Jim felt she had a sound point, yet he was too het up for it to sound right.

'Forget that, I'm just not happy with how things are, alright?'

'Fine then, leave. Go back to the perfunctory job and live in your little hovel in mechanised Greenwich. Me and Manny will be a person short but we're devoted to running this place.'

'Running this place? Oh please.'

Following Martha's suggestion, Jim thought of immunogenic, genotoxic compounds—how his body would deal with all those molecules—the genotoxic agents damaging DNA bio-accumulations that his body could not jettison unless he breast-fed.

Peter, rubbing his eyes from a distance observed the bellowing, overtired ill exchange without his glasses on. Martha was wearing a grey onesie. To Peter, she looked like a giant brillo pad. 'Last night, you and Manny, what the fuck was all that about?'

'What?'

'Don't you give me that, I heard him in our tent.'

'So what? We were merely alluding to things that need doing, i.e. things that other people should be doing but in the end it falls to the people that actually care and want to make a difference round here.'

'It's always you and *fucking* Manny isn't it? Peter was telling me you had a piggyback on him yesterday. Why him? Hmm? Martha and Manny saving the world…why don't you just screw him?!'

She looked normal. She felt like pins and needles in a jar. Martha scuttled away like a loud bang. Jim thought about Manny:

He just has such a nice accent. He seems manful and she's so right; so proficient at what he does. Even I'm starting to devote a man crush on him. No, forget that, he thought, I don't know what a real man is anymore. All the real men are dead.

Jim's mind, whilst it was thrown these inconvenient thoughts was far too busy and far too rageful to back down. He reached for an orgiastic chocolate bar hived in his trousers; the chocolate whose eaten effects were like his paroxysm: a short burst of energy then flat on your face. Throughout the day Martha carried his words. His words were biting. Surely while he slept, she would throb at the vein, vent with emotion. Her pallid eyes would be full of night, and his spine would dance with anguish from her acts.

Shapeshifting werewolf you will slay me, he shall say, but too late I am gone and the pain I deserved.

While the others ate, Martha filled up on nausea for the evening. Not much was said in the sexless tent. Jim found it hard to get to sleep that night. Martha was next to him but kept her body pencil-shaped and as close to the edge of the mattress as possible. The couple of times Jim tested the water with a hand on her, Martha held still. The triangular tumble dryer resurfaced.

Was she simply affected by Jim, or was it how she related to him, or how it all affected her anxiety? How much of any of it was true? She was off to dream about Barry Supperquiz. BS was an aging Scottish singer who wore sunglasses indoors and was a big hit in Azerbaijan.

Martha's tossing and turning mind finally slept, and entering dreamscape, the tumble dryer hit the turbo setting:

Picture this. Barry Supperquiz flies down from empyrean. Khachaturian's *Adagio of Spartacus and Phrygia* plays whilst a kazoo rests on Barry's right shoulder. He has magical powers to detour softball-sized snows as they waft by all sides of him. He is wearing little. He is wearing a violet fluffy dress just for me. A decadent crown takes a seat on his head, for he is either my tooth fairy or fairy godmother.

Kraken armed with a failsafe Panzerfaust, listening to Dennis Brown, sidesteps across the scene for two seconds.

Barry, flying to my room where we meet, sings as though his tongue is made of down. His warm Glaswegian tones give a little tingle to my ears.

Touch me Barry, make me feel alive again! He wraps his arms around me. His large hands make me feel so safe. He lends me his sunglasses to shield the paparazzi whose attention we now draw. As my recourse, he can at once liberate me and the world tonight. I am there, safe. Safe I think, but no! He turns into a hybrid of a lobster and a scorpion, hulking and looming over me. With a moue he looks into my eyes before salivating and revealing ginormous pointy fangs! His voice becomes deep. His voice could use a cough sweet. He is absolute in his praise for me though I am incredulous. Pitchforking piled bodies into place for his human sandwich, he knows I am in his snare. He is to fatally strike! A mistrust of azure circumnavigates me. I edge out of phantasmagoria to south London.

I realise the guy next to me is no Barry Supperquiz. Jim is snoring like the kazoo that never sounded in the dream.

Frustrated by her consciousness, Martha closed her eyes, watertight. She had to see if she could meet her Barry again.

Listen you fucker, you fucker, you fucker, I'm going to tell you how you make me feel, listen you dour ponce. These were the first thoughts of Martha on waking, with no recollection of further dreaming, meaning no revisit from her new favourite gent. Jim was in *her* mind just an offshoot of the Jim she once knew. The incarnation was dressing himself.

'I'm making a tea, want one?' he said. Nothing says I love you like a cup of tea.

'OK,' said Martha, in deferential fashion. Shrill banshees ululated echoes down the neural pathways informing her of their dissatisfaction as to her conduct:

'We thought you were part of the sisterhood, Martha!'

Martha was remembering the *Button Moon* episode where they ended up on Planet Donut and she was wondering how they got there. There was new ideation. Martha thought herself a scenario: what if someone held a gun to my head and said that I had to choose someone to be shot between either Jim and Meredith or else the gun would go off on me, making my brain do what it feels like doing half the time.

Martha hemmed and hawed a little then felt herself swaying towards having Jim shot, but then she thought: who is this person propositioning me and why do they have a gun to my head? Do I have to decide right at this moment? Can't we all just get along and play hopscotch together?

As rare a spectacle as English ducks sunning by a frozen lakeside, that night's conversation was largely dominated by Burt's communal presence.

'I used to live in a big house,' he told them. 'With valuable items in it too.'

Martha still had an abundance of unanswered questions flying around her mind.

Burt was in one of those vexatious positions many middle-class fairly well-to-do former businessmen found themselves in: 'My predicament is that I'm at that stage where I have more than enough money not to worry about living, yet not enough to have to worry about nearly everything else,' he said.

'I feel for you,' said Jim. Not for one minute did Burt detect any sarcasm and felt thankful to his ally.

'At the current rate, I'll still be paying off the mortgage on my house up until my late 60s. I've protected the house by getting a security firm to install a burglar alarm.'

So that the burglars knew, it was becoming to give them fair warning by siting plastic eyesores at the front and rear of the house with the writing, 'Surefire Security Systems.' Burt suddenly looked contented. 'I still remember their telephone number. The alarm makes a particularly piercing noise and just to make extra sure of my security, I lock the kitchen, downstairs, bathroom and hallway double doors if I go to sleep there at night. If a burglar manages to get inside the house, the sound of trying to get through one of the doors might wake me up and alert me to the danger.'

Burt also talked about other aspects of his previous life like how absurd he found it when a former leman he had living there made it so that a certain cushion could not be displanted from a side room. To reposition it to the sitting room would mar the sitting room's 'aesthetic arrangement of items,' but this was by the by. 'Now I never have to worry,' he said. 'Happy as Larry I am now that money means so much less.'

'But you still have the house?' asked Anjit.

'Yes.'

'But why?'

'For backup.'

'Hmm?'

'Ecovillages are not secure.'

Everyone looked bored as fuck.

'Funny about that bird though,' remarked Anjit.

#

Spring had just arrived. Martha had pissed Jim off by nothing special. Near their tent, Jim went to Martha in a high-octane flurry of what he thought were seminal ideas about Martha's place in their relationship. Pulsed furies swelled in his head and burst from his mouth: a spicy platter of words. They consisted of nothing you or Martha or Jim would not expect Jim to say. With a crying flounce, Martha faced about to storm their tent where she could look him in the aorta. With Jim words inseminating her wrath, before she got to the tent he received a donation:

'You can fucking sleep somewhere else tonight!!!'

He'd really pissed the bed this time. Guess it left him something to work with. Better than a teary walk off, he thought.

Gobby love. The lights turned off in the tent and Jim was left to figure out where he would sleep that night. Still, he had a really good wank by a hornbeam. Perhaps it was best to go solo. Martha was never that keen on sex, or at least the word. The 's' and the 'e:' well and good. But the 'x' sound at the end gave it a trumpery edge somehow. Jim just thought: stick it in, hope for the best.

How can I hang onto this one? Thought Jim. A bird in the hand is better than two with each a bush.

Meanwhile Martha felt preternaturally lofty. The language she had used—one would never suspect she had once been the focus of baptized lustration. Martha could not believe she found the confidence to talk at Jim like that and she was much the merrier for it. All she could hear was the wood burner.

A fog of love descends from the mountain top to the house of my spine
and filters the air we share

there is nothing there is only us

but

I was too busy chasing the dollar, my unplanned American dream
treading water downstream to
lonely counsel.

As a change from Mr James, whilst listening to Frédéric Chopin's 'Nocturne in B-flat minor, Op. 9, No. 1' as interpreted by Idil Biret, before Nobuyuki Tsujii's 'Elegy for the Victims of the Tsunami of March 11, 2011 in Japan,' Martha was reading from her favourite eco poet and singer-songwriter, Jilly Wright. Wright was born in Northern Ireland but had been resourcing painted prints of camel shrimps, the red with her blood. Reflected in the water from above, an astral forefront on a navy-blue afternoon.

Martha remembered that the wood burner that now comforted her had been fitted with the assistance of Manny. Although ideal for benders, wood burners could not just be fitted in any old tent but Martha and

Jim's tent was canvas so it could be done. She felt a tear for yesteryear. The secretarial lemonade glasses Martha held in her hands made her feel anachronistic. How easy it was to let things slide in a world with prospects none too good, generating just cause for retiring to bed.

#

Sunrise gilded the haggard, rickety landscape, prodding it with a collage of colour. Left behind were inclines of hills the hues of branded Welsh rarebit. Jim was astir. He had no set routine for bed. His order was that there was no order.

Following the argument, Dave who had agreed to put him up for the night, had wheeled out of his tent for the morning a while ago.

Jim picked his teeth for breakfast remnants then got to work on rolling a J. The smoke blew up and he looked at all the green. On the grass outside Dave's tent beside him was his go-to liquor, an Old Fashioned. As energetic as a sloth muscling in water, he felt good, he felt stoned, but unlike the extricated food remnants his unquiet remained. Anything and everything fluctuated in his thinking in rebellious tohubohu. Deep deep down from parts unknown in his psyche, and unadmitted to his consciousness, he wanted to be like everyone else. He wanted a job, he wanted a partner, he wanted a house and he wanted to be liked.

Every man has a mother inside. Every man some-where has levity, a softness, a thought to do right, even if outwardly it is not shone. Some close it off, helping their place in society. Others embrace it, crying at every opportunity. Most are part of the struggle somewhere in-between. This was where Jim swam about too but he would sooner ward off his adversary—emotion—who lived in the deep end of life's swimming pool.

Jim started to think of Martha and how it would be if she was here. A suckling on the teats of a time before. He loved her so much that after death he wanted to transmigrate to the body of her next cat. His chest was weighty as if a boxing glove there had landed, laced in vinegar. Freshets of love throbbed at the heart, wanting to pour from his to hers. Suddenly he felt nothing. Sensory deprivation from dune after dune in the desert sunset…heavy eyes rolled upward and there she stood, looting his dreams through a stare.

One set of eyes bloodshot, the other bloodless. Cacoethes iced.

Jim had the posture of unused hairbrush bristles.

The eyes have it. It was that little glance there, the boxer's jab too quick for the camera, her perfume eyes glossy in a melting sorbet of sun. Jim got caught, stilled by her gaze. Medusa had appeared yet this version was heavenly.

Today Martha felt deathful. A conceit about Jim looked to her: Jim is now a thing.

It was the only way she could think of him. Like a bad cough, the more she thought of it, the worse it got. No longer did he meet the criteria she looked for in a man, let alone a suitor. She preferred Ed Balls. Mr Balls, put your picture on my wall. Or in this case, the side of my tent.

Martha. She is wearing rage. The armourer is out of stock. Jim. Complaining complaining, the head within the him, the him within like a funerary dawn.

Jim looked at her, she took a glance at it. It reminded her of dirty wells, dust that forms in crevices and the solitude of a black sky.

'So…' said Jim, hoping she would complete his sentence to show him she still cared. It came to pass that this was an odd time indeed to be Jim as Martha failed to answer to his expectations. He asked how she was. He didn't care a fat lot for her answer but wanted her to say something so that she could ask how he was.

'Hmph,' was the mildest possible acknowledgment of his presence she could muster.

'Is this how we're talking now? Are you just going to talk to me in grunts all day?'

Martha always wanted a positive, get up and go type. Instead she got sit down and shut up. She did not respond to her beau. He became a fletcher making arrows, piercing her temples, reaching her inner eye to find a convolution of mismatched cogs. Her mind like a grandfather clock windable no longer. The arrows were blunted and lapped in cotton to mollify hurt. Sanguine cartooned mice danced around and bounced on trapezes making Barry-Supperquiz-like noises.

Jim snapped out of his time in Martha's head and focused back on her. She was thinking about the history of Zoroastrianism and ranking chocolate bars. All Jim had for company was a disapproving cloud and a silent woman.

Martha writes lists, Jim does not own a pen. Extraneous activity in his head equalled a maelstrom of ideas etched on his thinking face. He tired his own mind into stagnance. Suddenly a rumination turned out:

'What are you up to today?' he asked.

'Not sure yet,' and during her reply, the ground looked more interesting to her than it ever had.

'Where do we stand?'

What did he just say? she thought. Where do we stand?! What is this, *Home and Away*?

Martha mumbled a neutral response. He lit a cigarette and finished the Old Fashioned. She ran along hoping she wouldn't see him the rest of the day. Everything was solved at least for now.

CHAPTER SIX

'I'm so happy!' said Martha, on an unmemorable expanse of green.

'Why's that?' asked Meredith.

'Little Delora's coming to stay.'

'Who's she?'

'You know, my godchild. She's only three. She's so sweet.'

'Aw, I'm super psyched for you,' said Meredith.

'On another note, Jim, are ever going to build our own place to live, or, I don't know, just show some initiative to get the bender rolling?'

'Tent's alright for now isn't it?' he answered. Jim made a break for it to talk to Dave and Anjit seen within eyeshot.

'What's happening with you guys now?' Meredith asked Martha, making quite sure Jim had gone.

'Tensions between us have been refrigerating the last few days and we're talking again now. Well, in some sort of way.'

Martha thought of Delora's elfish charm, of how Delora's nose when cold reminded her of roses pink. 'It will be good to see Sara too, Delora's mum. You've not met her. We go back quite a way from college but recently we haven't been in touch much.'

'That so easily happens.'

'She's driving over tomorrow night. I can't wait!' And with that, Martha turned on the spot and clasped her hands. 'Sara always says that with Delora she's lost her freedom, that she feels guilty when out partying and so on. But it's no use her complaining, she made the conscious decision to have a child.'

Or in Sara's case quasi-conscious because she was pissed.

#

'I like girls with a hamster look. Goofy teeth, skin as pallid as ivory, quite tall, 5'6 to 5'9 at a reckoning, slender frame, eyes you can get lost in, hair red or the colour of the hamster. Yes, this is the girl. She infiltrates my poise. She does not care for earth's magnetic field! She charges me like the sun its particles, taking me to the firmament of my being!!

'What do you love so much about the subject of your suffocation anyway? She's one of those all the rage, hashtag girls.

'Don't worry Peter, that others have desires for others. These desires will fade and bury themselves. Such is the transience of life.' These were the first words of The Sage after Peter had given a long list of the facets he loved about Meredith he could not stop from coughing up by *Horizon*. 'At least you don't want to be like Jim. The world of love is one that confuses him. He speaks of it often yet he does not know its meaning.

He goes along in life like it's always 5 a.m. No wonder his world feels uphill when his eyelids weaken. He is a walking encyclopaedia so why should he seek help? If there ever has been a man that is content and has never asked for help, find him me, and his contact details I shall take.'

'Yep OK,' Peter said in reply, leaning to the side of his farthest from Sage representing thoughts to make tracks and evacuate unsought guidance. Peter regretted he had said so much. He liked to shake his head when he heard stories of Weltschmerz in the news.

It shook distinctly today. Peter read from a tabloid newspaper. Shake, shake, shake went his loft and out steamed a wistful tone.

'Terrible, just terrible. If it's not a mugging, it's something worse,' he soliloquised at *Shard*. 'Straight-out assault is bad enough. What is wrong with the world?! I'm astonished how sombre this all makes me.'

The world had gone bad. Really bad. Fungus-ridden dishes festering for months couldn't keep up with this lot. Whenever his despondency developed to a rodomontade style, Peter always felt a shred better about himself. The problem he had was no-one was listening, except Jim, and he had not even noticed that Jim had been.

'I spent another night in,' Peter said earlier on, to Sage. 'I realised it was going to be another night alone. Something I learned, at least about myself, is that we as humans can be at our weakest moments when we are going to go to bed with nobody there to snuggle with.'

'That's an ipse dixit. The repeated realisation can be difficult, but really when you have been through the things I have in life you realise that things like that are not all that bad. Trust me old fellow,' said Sage.

'So you don't think I've had more difficult things to deal with?'

'I'm just saying that your life is probably easier than you think it is, if that is one of your "weakest moments." That's quite a strong assertion.'

Away went Peter. It rankled him the way that Meredith could look away from a strawberry in the vegetable patch just as easily as she could from him, and then look towards the stars as if searching for another. I'll show her, he thought. I'm going to get buff.

Later that day, back at the vegetable patch Peter exercised thinking he was Colin Jackson. Everyone else thought he looked like a beetroot with emphysema. Peter, of a fair complexion, a fairness like faint signs of morning, had premeditated the use of sunset to remind Meredith how golden his forelock could sheen. For the three seconds she saw eager Peter, the only colour she noticed was beetroot.

#

Late March and Sara and Delora had arrived. Things were going swimmingly.

'What you guys are doing, it's so amazing. You're ace!' said Sara, talking to several gathered on the grass near Sage and his bender. 'Martha showed me round earlier. I just get so inspired here,' said the woman with the clement mien.

'Indeed young damsel,' said Sage about to use a hammer. 'At times we are a collective voice in full song.

I stress the phrase, "at times." ' Sage was doing some light repair work on his bender.

'He's funny,' said Delora on Sage.

'I'm funny am I? Aw, how lovely. When I see Delora…when we see children, it brings us happiness in a very positive way.' Yeah I bet it does you randy old git, thought Jim. 'We see the simplicity of their world and without us consciously realising it we can see that such happiness, as they have in their eyes, can be achieved by living so simply. It reminds us of what is important in life. We become a little less frustrated when the next lightbulb fails on us. Moments that seem so poignant for us when we are children and young grown-ups transform into little weightless memories as we look back.'

Like Meredith, Sara was conventionally comely. Day was dingily at death's door. Jim seesawed over what to think with Martha in the middle of the prementioned two women, but he was reminded by something the beardy one, for whom he still carried unresolved opinions, once told him:

'Jim, you must know that it is a syncretic pastiche of thought and emotion when you should find yourself among ranging glorious girls; the ambiguous twilight from a perfect sunset is sometimes more perfect than its source.'

Jim had no reason to take pains decoding Sage's codswallop but he did feel smug about having a meritable memory. For many reasons, Sage wasn't sure about 'syncretic pastiche' either. Still, sounded good.

One day later, Delora drew a picture.

'That's nice,' Meredith said, but did not really mean. In the picture were versions of foxes Delora had seen the night before. They were really crap drawings you would expect of a three-year-old. They looked like large squirrels at a psychiatric unit for animals. If spelt correctly, the next picture would have been titled, *Daddy's Short Fuse*. Delora limned her dad with a very red physiognomy wearing a shirt with its buttons near bursting. Daddy was about to blow his top.

Very much in the throes of wonder, steeply in the vaults of toddlerhood her innocence could effortlessly unfold, but how soon and by whom would she be told of a lifelong learning in what to fear and what not to?

Later on, Meredith and Martha helped the little lady deck the sycamore trees with powdered paint. Pink and mellow gold spirals and multicolour pentagrams were painted. Delora stepped back to admire her work though she didn't much care for the other two's efforts.

Meanwhile Peter in his hexi-tent had cooked up a confidential moment with Jim, speaking with a view to a reveal:

'Let me tell you something about Sage. His name's not Sage at all. Nor is it Saleem Eaglefeather. Nor is he a sage. His name's Bruce Clarke. He used to be a stock replenisher at Bargain Borstal Foods. And he only got *that* job because he got suspended for chatting up the mums working in Santa's Grotto. You know he was such a bad worker. Lazy worker, always late. He's the kind of guy that never shows up for'—Peter stopped to hand-signal quotation marks—' "personal reasons." In the end, Bargain Borstal ditched him. He never got over that—the fact that he couldn't even do a menial job.

That's why he is who he became, it's his own little fantasy world.

'Never has he been worthy of his epithet…oh yeah, and that story of how he became celibate? Go on ask him, I dare you. I caught him the other day looking up the word "thesaurus" in a thesaurus. But that wasn't enough for him, oh no. Then he went to look up the word "dictionary" in the dictionary. Because he's a dickhead.'

Jim knew he was partial to this news but he was left in an unfamiliar state of not knowing how to react.

Most gathered in the late hours to settle around a campfire.

'What is it about the white man that we serve to make less white?' asked Sage. 'Is it his history, his shameful undertakings in slavery? As John Agard helped it be so, we can no longer use the word half-caste. Fine, then let us say the politically correct term, "mixed race," a spade a spade. Barack Obama is no more black than he is white. Of course it also holds true that he is no more white than he is black. A mulatto, a mixed race man. We do the same when we talk of Native Americans that have a moiety of white. We often call them Native American, but why, when they are mixed race? I can only imagine that the white man's history has cast a shame on him especially when considering his role in his mistreatment of these two sets of ethnic groups. To this end, if some of someone is part of somewhere else, many will jump at the chance to call him from that somewhere else. Maybe the commentariat has a role to play in all this too, telling us how we should categorise people rather than just saying what they are.'

'Yeah I have a good idea what you are,' Jim said.

'Very funny, but I was actually, you know, trying to have a serious discussion about something. Something I don't see you doing very often.'

'Alright then, what are you?'

'How do you mean?'

'You have a turban on your head even though you're not a Sikh. You look white but most of the time you're dressed like an Indian sadhu. The only white I see are your white robes. Doesn't sound very white to me.'

'Whiteness is not defined by dress sense.'

'Others might disagree, but carry on.'

'The problem we have is that terms like "mixed race" fail to satisfactorily describe someone. If we have never met someone and they are described as mixed race, then we don't know of what mixes they are. There are innumerous mixes they could be. That is the problem with political correctness. At the risk of tiptoeing not to upset a few, it creates obfuscation for everyone else.' Martha weighed in,

'Probably in a few hundred years from now, such is the rates at which whites are being outbred, this conversation will be irrelevant as we will pretty much all be mixed! In the long run, we need to interbreed if we are to keep the human population going. But we must be able to talk about controversial topics. Free speech, or at least the concept of it, is a realm of the past in the UK, or maybe it never really existed. It was just a nice concept. But even more so now than ever before is this witch-hunting culture. Everyone records stuff on their phones these days and someone can say something in what they think is a private conversation but it is secretly recorded. It is rehashed in one hundred different media, perhaps misconstrued and taken out of context. The person is hounded to apologise so that they can recontinue their career. The public loves a scapegoat and we've become baying vultures. People seem to find a lot of time for being offended. We're bored of your outrage, of the thought police telling us things we should and shouldn't say, or when it is OK to do this or that. I'm offended by your offence, and people should be forced to apologise for forcing other people to apologise.

'I know it's been said before but I am of the opinion that it's bizarre how often "black" is considered bad in language, like in the phrase, "being the black sheep of the family" for example, or "black hat." Yet white can be used as a symbol of purity.

'Black people are actually dark brown and white people are actually a peachy colour. So are black and white terms for people because it is a system of control implemented to divide us and make us feel we as human beings are further apart than we really are to each other? I see this system too with God as a 'he,' as an all-powerful being we should obey perhaps to make females feel inferior, and to that end, develop a patriarchal system of control for our society.' Particularly in relation to talking a group, Martha suddenly realised how much she had said and could not believe she was confident enough to say any of it.

'Without question we affix a badness to black,' said Sage. 'White is pure goodness. Yet, as you say petal, have you ever met a white white man? Even the whitest of men have a little peach in them. If you're straight talking, then that's a very likeable quality. People like candour. But why always a *straight* talker? Flexible chats are more fun.'

A character brooded over a far light. Coming toward them, haphazardly trundling, a back arched backwards and wide gapping between the feet as if caught in a zesty haboob. He continued as if his pelvis was unstable in a myopathic gait. He paused a while to glare at a glare. Of those there, the group had in their entirety noticed him, as they nestled closer together by the firepit. His greengage-coloured hat was more eye-catching than anything else. Over his shoulder was a chrome-buckled, scarred brown satchel. Wending even more cautiously in their direction, Manny would have hoisted his hand and called out had Peter not pinned down its uprising. The latter wanted to watch the shaky apparition make its own magic. The character's left hand, lightly inked, had a topless Belgian beer three-quarters full in its grasp. His gaze improved by drink, the snaggletoothed man's teeth that remained were jaundice-yellow and caramel brown. Many tales of outdoor life had caught in his beard. Jim decided the guy was quite clearly pissed, quite clearly a bum and quite clearly looking for a friend or two.

It is wise to have at least two friends in case one becomes fly-by-night.

The dodderer now within a stone's throw, his profile in fireglow and Cathy's torchlight. He caught sight of Meredith. His sclerae: red intrusions on carpets of white. He looked over Meredith and it was most definitely *all* over her like the leering headmaster, the sweaty palmed professor in lechery.

'What's all this about?!' the gruff character demanded to know.

'Hi,' said Meredith.

'Alright treacle. What's it all about though?'

'This here?' asked Meredith, pointing downwards.

'Affirmative.'

'This is an ecovillage, honey.'

'Yeah but…'—he pointed at Jim—'You know what I'm saying though don't you. What are we going to do? I mean what's it all about? You know what it's about, I know what it's about, every-blasted-body knows what it's about. Or do I? Or do they? You do know right?' The character then looked at the others, pointing at Jim. 'He knows what I'm saying.'

Martha was a painter and no-one cared. That was all she could think as the ranting man carried on and the group got lost in the maze of his words. Maybe if I drew this drunk he could care, Martha thought. Not still life nor its crony, hyperrealism. She wanted madness on the canvas. She had no need for loud people in her life, her head was loud enough already. The boozer's beard was thick and ginger with hoary strays of white. He frothed as he spoke, made those that listened laugh, and raised his arms at intervals like a gymnast's. He gibbered on for half an hour, haggling with inhibitions.

Flies were only too fond for a friend in the man. He was one of the few humans that did not move a muscle in their presence, and they tolerated better than humans his trite conversation. He spent much of his silent moments, mouth open.

People think if you ofttimes have your mouth open you might be dense. But you could just be one of those to never get braces or have a particular fondness for flies.

As the hours lapsed, the oddball's obtuse energy decelerated, but the group he still tipsily commanded.

'So what's an ecovillage then and why are you here?' he asked them, his left hand resting on a left thigh that lived under moth-eaten dirt-yellow trousers. 'I haven't even told you my name yet. I am Paul. I know about some things around here, believe you me.'

Meredith explained the ecovillage concept, and heedfully the community continued to keep tabs on Paul.

'So tell us,' Meredith continued afterwards. 'What things do you know about around here then?'

This time, Paul's expression became severer, his voice deeper, his language knottier, and his eyes a tribute to the owl.

'You really want to know? You must keep it so that I never told any of you any of this.'

Sheets of wind intoned with a high-pitched warble clobbered trees and speech. 'Since you asked so nice and have welcomed me here with open arms, I will tell. There is a mysterious fog in these parts that enters when the children sleep, that beckons the one they call "The Gren" from its lair. The Gren has the face of a hag and the body of a jackal. It does not use its "feet" but glides along its side on the ground. How it does this has been discovered by no-one.

'Urban legend has it that within The Gren is the trapped soul of a young woman, who lived two hundred years ago. She is said to have committed adultery with a whole slew of men, most notably the nobleman, Horace of Little Horwood, for his sapphires and pearls. Townsfolk labelled the pert filly's chamber, "The Haven of Friskiness." Although she has the body of a jackal, she cannot fornicate by virtue of the strange way she moves on her side. She is deformed by the most grotesque proportions. It is said the fog is her nectar, giving her a spiritual power the ancients called mana.

'Just do me the service of remembering it was not me that said anything. Frankly the whole thing boils my bones. I can only think of what forces may be at work behind these dark arts.'

'You know what, you can stick around here, I have decided. You're good entertainment value,' said Manny's voice out of wedlock for the hand of Paul to be taken in marriage to the ecovillage. Only Peter had known Manny was even there.

#

The next day, Sage pulled out from his tent a chipped mandolin, twenty years old. Strings unchanged for eight years gave its voice yearning for renewal; it was spring after all. He played some Americana classics around the communal campfire, and Paul and Anjit joined in with the words. Paul had a stick and empty tea tin he used for a drum. He actually had a rawhide drum in his tent;

no need to tell the others that he couldn't be bothered to get up.

Paul's smoky voice dipped in ethanol brushed against overgrown moustache hairs as it exited like that of a folk singer's you'd find at an ale festival. The old strings hummed and brightly screeched as though its body was anoxic.

Delora was not sure how to digest all the irregular activity as Sara dandled her from time to time. Peter looked perplexed by all the merrymaking but tried to give an English gaze. Kristoff got a charge out of it but did not want to show anyone. He muttered a few words of song now and again, and his mind pulled at the lines on his brow where could be found a softer shade of yesterday. Jim copied his look. Meredith and Manny showed every sign of looking normal. Dave looked incurious.

A coarse gust of wind fretted the fire wreathed by all humans of the ecovillage, except for Burt. Cathy made a start on rolling a joint. Jim preferred to smoke his own in his and Martha's tent, as to share too often would mean there was not enough for him. Martha looked down at her clacking phone with thanks as it gave her excuse to get away from the scary throng of people. She hied to a sweet-tempered shade of trees. Incoming was a call from Imogen.

'Martha! How now brown cow?' said a mildly posh voice.

'Imogen! So good to hear from you. I'm alright thanks, I've missed you. How are you bearing up?'

'I'm stellar darling, ya ya, so like, what the flip, you're actually still at that ecovillage?! Wowzers, that's totes amaze. Must be so interesting.'

'Yeah I can't believe it's been round about half a year now. Still getting used to things. It can be challenging but generally it's a lot of fun. With winter now gone I think it will be easier. Sorry I haven't been in touch too much, phone signal here isn't always top-notch. That American called Meredith I was telling you about—she's really nice. She's helped me settle in a lot.'

'Ah ya that's fab but don't forget about your non-eco friends! So do you think you'll stick it out there?'

'Yeah it's early days but I had the rationale before I came that I'd try and stay as long as possible, so I want to try and stick to that.'

'Ah lush, me and Beth will have to pop over at some point. Will be bonzer. YOLO hunni YOLO.'

'By all means. That would be lovely. What have you been up to?'

'Still helping my aunt at the pharmacy but obvs hoping to start that PGCE course soon I keep saying I will get round to when I'm not povo. Can't wait to try your yumtastic veggie stews at the village, sweetheart. Anyway speaking of food the dinner's on and I've got to run.'

In truth she had run out of mirth.

'OK, sure, bye. Speak again soon,' said Martha. Her reply was a phone put down.

Martha had on mini-holed tights and a frayed homespun jumper in front of a singlet. Formerly appealable garments, their advanced age made for a rugged beauteousness.

Martha looked back at the bunch. They looked like a gang of wasps. How pusillanimous, she thought. She didn't want to face so many but felt compelled to rejoin them. Martha felt she was the crumbs of life, everyone else the bread. Jim was sourdough, Meredith was a Tesco finest tiger bloomer.

'Are you alright?' asked a voice that interrupted Martha's thoughts.

'Yes thanks Meredith. Well, no actually. Just a bit anxious in the group.'

'Just talk to me when we go back to them, you don't have to talk to the others or feel put on the spot.'

'Thanks.'

The gift of time-lag: roomy mind before the event, so allowing joy of mind and plague of mind to miscolour thoughts. Martha's tight stomach made her feel she was in a composite afterworld that had a lift. The lift only went up and down different levels of hell.

I can't do anything right so I don't know why I bother, was Martha's next thought. Not to Meredith but to any of the others, Martha felt she was of phytoplanktonic significance, gluing to her yawper boyfriend. Yet, such was the anatomy of the ecovillage, she was necessary to the functionality of an inclusive ecosystem. How was she to become the successful curry-favourer?!

'Sara was telling me it's her last day here tomorrow,' said Meredith. 'She says she wants to join us at the festival before she heads home.'

'Really?' Martha sighed. 'Typical Sara that is. What about Delora? She's not coming too is she?'

'I don't know. She didn't say.'

'I hope not, the festival is not the sort for kids.'

Martha's slight irritation made her confident enough to hope that it did not all that much matter about naysayers in general because no-one was harsher on her than herself. By the same token, she knew that the same brain was furnished with the service of chief motivator.

It is not so easy for the unconfident, fucked around by the more confident because they're not confident, to be confident.

Martha slipped meekly back into the group at close quarters to her main ally.

'Who was on the dog and bone earlier sweetie?' asked Meredith.

Martha laughed. 'Dog and bone? Huzzah! You really *have* become one of us. Oh, and it was just my friend Imogen.'

Everyone around Martha looked like hyperrealist paintings, wired in the bonce, quick on the draw. Martha was hyperaware but only in the sense that she worried her words would be analysed at every angle; that the important parts would be plucked from the sky where they would meet the salubrious air and be used to best her.

No you simpleton, she thought to herself, remember the advice Meredith just gave you. 'Imogen's a lovely girl. Lovely, but off her hinges. She did this thing at uni called the spatula blues. What she would do is she would thwack her head repeatedly with a spatula whilst singing the blues.'

'Right…erm, that's interesting let's say. That's nice for her.'

'Whilst drunk obviously!'

Paul spoke with an Estuary English not because he was brought up in it but because it was fashionable to adopt. As bald as Humpty Dumpty, he seemed like a good egg. Such a good egg in fact that he was most certainly organic and free-range, just like Humpty Dumpty before he fell. This was what Jim felt at least, humoured by the antics of last night. The musicians had come to a standstill.

'The multinational chain store workers, the termites of my generation…I was a termite too! Termite power!' Paul said, and he laughed rambunctiously. 'In fact I was even worse, working for low-down shitty private companies that fucked people over. So I started my own cheeky little business ventures. "Schlockmeister General" they called me. Firstly, I'd go to doctors' surgeries when it was raining and there would sometimes be a box full of umbrellas in the porches before you got to reception. There would be the check; if there were no security cameras, I was in. I snatched the more expensive-looking umbrellas, dried them off and sold them online. I made more money by coming up with the plan of acquiring prescription drugs for free in Wales at the border, then going across to England to sell them for a fee. I was taking advantage of laws passed by the Welsh Government in 2007. It was great being an Englishman living in Wales. It felt like constantly being on a budget holiday. I couldn't afford a decent waterproof jacket, unfortunately, so the rain soon got to me.'

The rain is of a different quality in Wales. In England, rain is of pockets of hard and fast, and then it's over. In Wales it dribbles on for years…

Paul had sobered up. Aside from alcohol there were used needles about his person. But what can be said of a junky that hasn't already been said? Blotchy and eyes red raw. And freedom saw no headway in his soul.

A life of surrounding himself with errant kids and yes men. Skint. What then of this commune he'd come to? What better place to dream!

#

'Are you sure Sara, about going to the festival tomorrow?' Martha later asked in the storehouse, fetching a tin of lentils, reshuffling provisions to make things less unsystematic in there. 'Don't you think it might be a bit loud for Delora? There'll be drugs and lots of swearing.'

'She'll be fine. It will be a good experience for her.'

In the evening Martha found some alone-time with Delora on the brow of a quiet hill. It was a bit like the one Martha and Meredith had talked on at length before but not quite as hilly. It was a little past Delora's bedtime but Sara had let her stay up extra late as it was their last night in Carringdon.

'So have you had a nice time?' Martha asked, holding her goddaughter's hand.

'Nice time, yep.'

'Soon, you'll be a big girl going to school. How does that sound?'

Delora replied something unhearable in the temperate night. Martha went into advice-mode. 'The thing about what you learn at school—nobody teaches you how to dream.'

The sky wonderfully jewelled with inestimable value, as though God had tidily arranged them a private viewing of the stars. 'See that star over there. He's waiting on a friend. Very, very rarely you get a star on the run. They're called shooting stars.'

'Shooting star.'

'That's what you are, Delora, my star on the run. My little shooting star. They make the other stars jealous because they're so rare and pretty when they fly across the sky. *Why*, you could even be an exploding star, ten billion times brighter than the regular: the supernova. You are stardust. Every atom in your body comes from an exploding star. Your DNA makes you unique in that no-one else in the universe has the same…I'm getting ahead of myself. One day you'll comprehend…or understand, I should say. But just imagine all those other stars are the normal people. If you dream hard enough you can be that supernova and star on the run both at once! Too quick, too bright for everyone else.'

Delora felt so little and so powerful.

A day after this day, hot drinks were being passed around *Shard* just as morning kicked the bucket. Paul was inflicting his charisma on the others once more:

'I wasn't just in the underground scene, I *was* the underground scene.'

Paul remembered those days, the good days anyway. In some, he was booming like a high ant, pre-eminent to mushroom-head explosiveness. 'It wasn't that easy to find it all either. It was a long town where nothing really happened. I was lucky enough to find the right connections.'

'What kind of shit were you doing?' asked Kristoff.

'All sorts, man. Pretty much everything that didn't involve a needle. It felt fun and exciting doing coke in the khazies during the so-called cigarette break at work. I would put anything up my nose. One time the coke ran out I was snorting cold-remedy powder. I don't do any of that shit anymore, man. I just drink now. But after a while, at the same time it felt'—Paul sighed—'you know…a bit tragic. Sad.'

'Yeah, I know all about that.'

'Long gone are the days of crystal meth and opiates. These days I get a buzz if I find my food-shop coupon is still valid.'

All present laughed. 'The fact was I was an innovator,' said Paul. 'Still am. I was the best roadie you could find. And you'd do well to find me five decent musical bands or artists in their own right, that didn't at one point dabble in drugs. And I'm talking decent, not 80s disco.'

'So that was your dream then, to be a rock star?' asked Kristoff.

'Nah, sounds like too much hard work,' Paul said, followed by his characteristic noisy chuckle.

'Like my taste in books, my music taste is eclectically selective,' said Martha. 'Hence, I am widely influenced yet at the same time realise there is only so much time I can feasibly factor in for listening to music in my life.'

'Bless you my dear.'

'It sounds like you had a lot of fun, man,' said Kristoff. 'I wish I would have been in underground scene. There wasn't much happening like that in my part of Russia when I was youngster.'

'Then I was on ESA for depression from my alcoholism,' said Paul. 'It wasn't all bad though, one of my mates thought I worked for the European Space Agency. Yeah, "Blighty Bill" we called him. My body loves drink and I've got a handle on it.' Paul motioned to show everyone he was holding an imaginary handle, then laughed roaringly. 'I'm not depressed anymore. I don't get too-bad hangovers. People say, "Paul, you look so well. All the colour's come to your face." Well that's 'cause I'm drinking all the time.' He laughed again, as did one or two others to be good-natured. 'Strangest thing happened the other day. So this guy comes up to me; the look is relaxed. He's like, "Psst, you know I can offer our spiritual wellbeing course for half the price of these guys." He's offering me a crafty discount right there at the back of the meditation hall.'

Meredith laughed and so did a few of the others. 'No way!' she said.

'I'm like, man, not here. I thought we're all meant to be on the same wavelength, all trying to get enlightened together, looking out for each other. Man, playing business off against each other, that's just out of order.'

Paul dreamt of a world where drag queens came out like leaping salmons. Where gay marriage shared equal status to heterosexual marriage globally, on paper, in attitude. Where when feeling for the light switch to find the new you, a sex change could be made that bit easier. 'It's the paracetamol diet for me. Nothing else for it. This bit of old jip won't leave me alone.' Paul pointed to his knee. 'All this talk of money and shit; I just want to be free by the water, and fish.' Martha could see Paul's sentiments but all this probably was not very fair on the fishes in question. With such sentiments at his side, Paul could not wait for upcoming sweet carnivalesque release.

'Right guys, are we all good to go?' asked Meredith.

'Yeah,'—the response, by and large.

'Whereabouts is this place again?' asked Anjit, his hands at the ready to push Dave.

'Hackney Garden Ecovillage. First the Tube then we bus it,' said Meredith. 'They haven't done a festival like this before so it's exciting. There's no way of knowing what to expect.'

On winding paths, behind her iron demeanour Meredith hankered for a conscience of salt-white sublimableness she could impress upon Delora. Fortified with a placard hoisted loftily in one hand, and Meredith's firm hand around the other, having traipsed along a detritus-smothered pathway, Delora maladroitly baulked at chilblained feet—sojourning in Jim's shoes. Delora had happy soles because she wore UGGs. 'Hold your arm lower down,' said Meredith. 'It will be easier for you.' Delora took her advice.

The placard said: 'Carringdon Ecovillage Comes In Peace.' Carringdon Tube Station was just around the corner from its sister national railway station.

Within seconds of arriving, the festival imagery pounced on the Carringdon lot, in iridescent beauty. People of every ilk, of distances little and long. Mock smoke from smoke machines, real smoke from cigarettes, e-cigarettes, incense, marijuana and shisha coals whipping the gentle breeze. Blue and green mohawks, women painted head to toe in rose gold, enough tattoos and piercings for Camden Town to be impressed with, and naked adults and children running around reminding humankind of its primitivism.

Jim walked down a path called 'Peter Pan Pathway.' A woman and her child walked past him.

'You have to stay closer to me,' the mother said. 'People are very nice here, but it only takes one.'

From the path, Jim was witnessing Martha's reality from afar as she partook in a walking meditation with strangers. Before and after the walking meditation, Carmel Yap, an erudite Buddhist teacher from the Philippines was giving a guided metta bhavana meditation. Inspired by ancient Buddhist literature and At the Drive-In, she liked to express herself in a far-out way, splintering sentences with phrases that at first didn't quite sit in sense to the human eye, like 'selling inhibitions of grandeur,' 'skidding on the foolstep of intellectual chins.' The meditators looked at each other a bit more than they usually would and went away with hearts warmer than the sun. Martha remembered her favourite line from Yap:

'You know you are somewhere with meditating when you no longer need language to get in the right state. When it just becomes. When *you* just become.'

Sage didn't think much of Yap and picked up a mallet at the high striker. Amongst other things, Cathy carved a small bowl at a woodworking event, Sara supervised Delora as she splashed about the children's fountains, Meredith went in for seven helpings of vegan popcorn, Dave and Anjit tried to win a goldfish at the shooting range, Paul set foot in the ecstatic dance hut, and Jim watched a folk band called Huley & The Hulagrams. The others didn't go.

Martha was glad to be in a new mindful world. The suchness of the moment, the inherence of the moment. How she all was of herself, and the other, at each passing minute. Now and here, each moment individualised in the patchwork of time. *They* seemed far away.

Sara and Delora went back to their home after the festival and said their goodbyes. Soon enough the ecovillage community were reunited back at Carringdon.

'You know I was having a lovely little conversation with Delora last night,' said Martha at the communal point; her confidence upgraded by the meditation. 'I was saying that even in 2022, they still don't tell you how to dream, nor tell you how to *be* here. We are taught by the media and our parents and schools how important our "selves" are, and how we have to make it out there in the big bad world for our own sakes. All this is yet another intellection to be broken down.'

'I second that, and some Buddhist monks live as collective units, especially when they clean and eat for example,' said Sage. 'Self-importance is a creation, then a conditioning of mind, then an insistence, then a habit. They teach of the relearning and improving of self-importance in schools, but to what end? The words "self" and "importance" aren't as powerful without a hyphen between them. The children are helped to be ignorant of inner growth, helped to be ignorant of increasing grey matter in the brain, and helped to be ignorant of how meditation can lead to mental wonders.

The last thing capitalism wants is people who can fix things for themselves. In the 70s, it was common for a man to be able to fix his automobile. But it's best to keep people ignorant—that way people will get useless jobs, like sewing up hems for dimwits' clothes. Depreciation always objects to being left out. They want to keep you at a level, hardwired as the perpetual consumer to invigorate their capitalist model with new life. Maybe we are all in some way *they*.'

'Oh Sage, there is truth in what you say. I can't stop thinking about Delora. It was great that Delora was here, don't you think Jim? She'll be at school very soon. I forget Jim, whereabouts did you go to first school again?'

'London.'

'Yeah I gathered that much. I mean which school?'

'Why?'

'Never mind.'

A bit of time passed. It usually took Jim a month to catch on to the clock change of British summertime that now presented itself. He refused to lose an hour's sleep just because British summertime told him to.

Martha had a thought, etched in time. She bethought herself of the multitudinous losses and few gains in her life. One step forward two steps back, one step forward two steps back, she kept saying to himself. The end.

Howbeit, after prosaic diurnal activities added some more time, like a cat in the rain waiting by a hedgerow for an animalistic ruffling, Martha listened to a snip of new thought she had dug up. It was telling her to alter the phrasing a little, so she did as thus: one's step forward two steps back, one steps forward two steps back. Suddenly she was the one. It was only *her* that was saying to *herself*, one step forward two steps back. She was now one step forward, the two steps back didn't have to be hers. She could even go one step back two steps forward if she really wanted to; how fleeting our matters of perception.

When Jim next found Martha, it was all:

'Delora's so talkative at the minute, Jim. Don't you think she was so talkative? Don't you think she's so cute?'

How could there be an answer.

#

It is a new day in the new month of April. The light from the day will shortly be fading and Martha will like it, for everyone will start to look less ugly.

'Nice day today. Peter around?' a woman asked.

The woman Martha not seen before surprised Martha and Cathy from behind. They were at the communal point and everyone else was either in town or their eco homes.

'Tracy Beers,' said Cathy.

'Yes, it is I, but you can call me Mrs Beswick, if you don't mind.' Beers ended her words with something between a grimace and a smile.

Born Tracy Beers, she often used the pseudonym, Mary Beswick as to have only the one name just wouldn't do, and the last name mentioned sounded more befitting of her person to boot. Beers, a person of some standing in certain circles was from the more spiffy parts of London. One could tell from the blazer, brooch and botulinum; forgetting not the highlighted hairs and chiffon scarf. Her cheeks luxuriated in redness from all the cow she ate. She smelled of a mix between ultra-chemical cologne and wet dog hair.

'Peter? I've not seen 'im,' said Cathy.

'*I* see. And how's hairy back?'

''Airy back? Oo's that?'

'You mean to say you don't know?' Beers laughed. 'I'm talking about Burt of course. Haven't you seen his back before? You're in for a real treat!' Beers laughed as though she were on the beers. 'That little squire's got hair in all the wrong places. Trust me, I know. He used to go out with a friend of a friend. Don't worry though, have you seen those people that live up the old Commonsworth Hill? You're not as grubby as them, I keep them at arm's length. "Tentacles of the earth" I call them.'

Martha felt uneasy about having negative thoughts about someone she just met, but on this occasion she couldn't hold back: Tracy Beers is the shape of a Christmas bauble. Her square-cut hair makes her look like a plump lamp. Lamps don't talk much, and if they do, it is only to alight. On this one the fuse has blown.

'They call 'er "the needlewoman" 'cause it looks as though 'er 'ead 'as been sewn together,' Cathy whispered to Martha. 'Also, Burt said that she likes to use a feather duster down 'er unmentionables.' Cathy liked to whisper as it gave her the edge of a gossiping washerwoman, but there was no need as Beers had long gone to run a bath and put on some soft rock.

'I see what you mean about her head,' said Martha. 'She reminds me of a toppling sandcastle.' Both women giggled together. Every body part and item of clothing looked pieced combinedly like some character made out of modelling clay. Any piece could be lost as easily as Jim's nose.

Mary Beswick was Chairman of Brighton's Conservative Luncheon Club. Her favourite television programme was 'Paul Hollywood's Pies & Puds.' For reasons unknown, Tuesday was the only day she was willing to make an entrance her husband could pop into. At least she was consistent. At the pastoral playground, whispers grew louder, rumour had it she now lived in Balham with two kids and a merkin.

#

Jim's ears met with a brand-new voice the next morning:

'Have you run the BIOS?' said a rich Indian accent down the phone.

'Have I what?' Jim said, punching his fist onto the ground next to his laptop, microorganisms perishing as he did. Yet not a squeal was heard and not a mouth spoke for an inelegant several seconds.

'Sorry, the line is very bad. Just to check, is that Mistaaa…Moy…lez I am speaking with? Mr Moy-lez?'

'Yeah, Mr Moyles actually, but never mind.'

'Sorry?'

'Yes, Mr Moy-lez here,' said Jim, sighing in his tent.

'Good afternoon Mr Moy-lez, thank you so much. I was just asking about the BIOS check, sir. It might help us see what is the problem with your computer. It sees which parts of your system could be faulty.'

'How do I do it?'

The conversation continued in much the way it started. The problem soon fixed, Jim was brazen. He turned to Martha and began to rap 'Gangsta's Paradise.' She laughed, he didn't. The world was a happy place once more.

At moments like this, Martha could circumstantiate a little more why it was she was with him. It was a Thursday and heard and felt was an atavic companion of a rural setting in the shape of parish bells. At bell practice the church sang many colours. A plethora of chirpy melodies. For Jim, it was that single stroke of the bell—the death knell that did it every time. Martha loved how the death knell was Jim's favourite. She stilted herself with her toes and lipped him on the cheek. Thanks to the serenity about and her poise therein, it felt like twelve at once. All Martha wanted was someone to be kind with. And by God she loved him! He was someone for now. She really needed a someone.

To Jim, Martha was no ordinary biped. The female was back by popular demand. She was a girlfriend, Jim's girlfriend. Now and then he wondered if he was her boyfriend. He wondered how happy each of them actually were in the situation, but for now he thought it better to be with someone than not. He looked at her in the manner of a man in love yet unsure how true the look. She gave his erections new meaning.

That night Jim wanted to slam her. He received oral only. She came at him like a burrowing sandfish; it was lonely down there for Martha. Still, blow job's better than no job and the lack of job was grating a little for Jim. After the dyad finalised intimate proceedings, Martha gazed up at her romantic companion and here Jim witnessed the eyes that said: you best have fucking meant that. Was there love or lust? Alas! Martha found the latter: love overmastered by lust's hangover.

Is love but a tamer side of lust?

Jim sagged. Perusing his wallet, fingering its insides the penny dropped. His mind at varying orders and angles, through fumbling and force, cards with mortified histories had found their way to the backs of slits. Aged and dilapidated with yawning zip, the wallet carried three pounds, seven pence. In Jim's bank account lived the only other finances to his name. £167 and dwindling.

He'll be heading to the sperm bank at this rate. He had a boy's toys dream in some pithy moment of freedom. Rapt in thoughts of what the newest phones were really like, what the newest laptops were really like and whether his niece, Lilly still called them 'lappops.'

Those boys in factories busting their guts to make us all these technological lovelies. The 'net' and 'web' are names of places one can get caught. But the internet is also where one can surf. The internet was almost adequate at the ecovillage but it cut out now and then, so Jim had an itch for a different provider.

He came out of the sleepwalking haze taking umbrage in the fact that he no longer had the means to afford such items and that there was hardly any phone signal nor passable mobile internet coverage in the general area for a nice new phone. What the bloody hell was he doing here? This was nonsense.

Fully with the programme, Manny was someone absolved from fear of state retribution from the secret police, and police. The outside world that could dragoon him to get a job was not on his mind.

Jim could not refrain from having his attention averted now and again to how much money he was missing out on not full-time employed. Despite the job gaps, his CV still read to employers: possibly of use to someone. Was a 'normal' life as bad as he remembered? He missed the welcome skylight that looked on to the summit of a kindly neighbour's apple tree. The street in his blood, Jim's mind could toss just as easily to think of the good things about his previous jobs. He refreshed his memory of the contrasting opinions about his most recent boss: some said this nouveau riche man with a sports car and pug was a manly man, a successful man, a man with a plan. Send home the postcard to ma, tell her the boy's done good. An alternative view of this individual from the lower down colleagues was: overeater, overheater, overrated, overpaid, over-moisturised.

Get enraged, worried and stressed enough whilst marching to success to form lines in the forehead, then smooth them out from all the money you've made. In your 30s you want to do your teens and 20s again, though this time slick as a whistle thanks to the highchair of wisdom. You could wolf down the confectionery and coagulated dish before, but now when you try, your body says you probably shouldn't be doing that. Go to the hippodrome instead, or there's always the ice rink.

Jim also thought about what was formerly his closest friend on the planet and the only one that could ignite his debauchery. Jim remembered him as liking clubbing, winning fake-money board games, and running off at the mouth. Other hobbies included sitting down, freeloading off peoples' kindness, the art of equivocation, and holding ladies' hands with his eyes closed. Four girlfriends and only three restraining orders, he liked women, big women, the type that could squash weedy little shits like him. Bossy women in yoga pants was another household favourite.

Last Father's Day he had so many cards; he just wished he knew who they were all from. There was even one from Bucharest. A cross between an assorted pick 'n' mix bag and Beelzebub, this recherché young lion was prurient, cretinous and conceited.

Nowadays he lives in the cupboard of his mistress. When he's allowed out, there are floggings, tie-downs and back-to-school nights. They explore furry conventions, sex magical practice and have-you-met-my-wife nights.

She is one sick bitch. It is not enough to handcuff the subby hubby. If she had it her way, she would kill her cousin leaving only his husks and use his entrails to tie the gimp—who suffers his bonds 'til she fucking feels like it. The cousin was only her second worst foe.

It was over the microwave meals in Bargain Borstal that the couple's eyes first met, and he recently proposed to her down a well. They have just come back from a UK tour of shagging in department store toilets.

Despite recently overdosing on pistachios he is health-conscious to the point of nosophobia, and tonight when Prince Albert shall meet her Vajesty, she shall administer lavender upon his person. He's an antimicrobial gimp and that's just the way she likes it.

She's a creative too don't you know. Yessterday shee woz riting a hiku how werds sownd. Currently she is writing a cross between a poem and a song she called a pong:

Peyote Crayon

Gazing through the desert heat
Peering down at stone-cold feet,
I can see a boy
Who used to be my toy
Climbing frames of
All the dreams he keeps.

Words will not right me now
Lizard eaters coming to town…

The next line involved peyote and an arse. It was horrible.

Jim had to learn. Intensity, if used all at once burns and the skin peels from the self. He knew he had to more readily acknowledge it so as to hone it and extend it over a longer period. Jim felt the need for a quiet confidence aligned in control. If only he realised this at twenty instead of thirty-seven, he could have saved himself many a problem. He remembered the orgiastic chocolate bar and how a prolongation of short-term pleasures leads to breakdown. Forget the very serious plan and do a deal with the calm, simple plan. Yes. Now *that* sounded more like it, in what was to be, in nothing flat, his new plan of action. And what was the plan again?

CHAPTER SEVEN

'I'm heading back home for a bit,' Jim announced, sitting next to a reclining Martha in the tent of mediocrity.

'OK.' The pregnant interjection unfurled from a tired tongue in response, quite happy on its tod.

'It's good to get away for a while. It will be nice to be in a proper house again. It's only a weekend, I think it's for the best.'

'Yeah, I should think about following suit. A change of scenery, not to North London again, it's too out the way. Just to Greenwich to see friends I haven't seen for donkey's years.'

'Right. I'll pack my bag.'

'You're going this instant?' Martha queried, removing herself from inertia to come to grips with an urgency she felt the situation asked of her.

'Pretty well, yeah.'

'Wow, that *is* sudden.'

'I've been thinking about it for a while,' said Jim, zipping open the front of the tent. 'What are you going to do without me?' he asked.

'Ha, I'll think of something.'

They kissed. Martha saw Manny in the distance, locked by purpose, making a fire to draw a smile. Jim grabbed his house keys like he would a pair of bollocks. He packed and went without saying a pat word.

#

'Hi Manny.'

'Ah, hi there Martha.'

'How's things?'

'Not so bad, things could always be worse. Just trying to get this fire going.'

'I've had some more ideas by the way. I've come up with some better design ideas for our website I will show you. There is more purple and it is generally more user-friendly for a start. Furthermore, I noticed when I went to Hackney Garden Ecovillage that they are equipped with their own t-shirts that they sell in association with a few other souvenirs for when outsiders come to visit. Plus they have lots going on there now, more open days and festivals to come that will help give them more publicity. I was thinking we could do some similar things to this.'

'I like your thinking, nice going. I will think about a pertinent meeting again sometime we can have.'

'Got it.'

'What are you and Jim up to tonight?'

'Actually, he's just gone off.'

'Gone off? He's always been off, hasn't he?' The duo cracked up.

'Not like that! He's gone away to his parents' for the weekend,' said Martha, her voice unanticipatingly breaking. She noticed and tried to cover a tea stain with her left arm on her salmon-dyed muslin top.

'I daresay he'll be back before then.'

'Really? Why's that?'

'He'll miss you too much.'

'Pah, I doubt that. He's only two days away.' Martha was girning, twiddling her myriad curls and going the colour of her jumper.

'You look blushful. Why so?'

She reticently declined her head. There were strategic doubts. She moved her lips and her mother's cautiousness filtered her words.

'I don't know,' she said. It was true, her dear mother lived in her, improved by age, a still, loving cantankerousness—the one whom she called mother, not the one on the substitute bench.

Are spectres in existence, and, if so, do they breathe? The flesh of the body painted on the earth, the reserved Martha; moon on the horizon looking like an astronomical chocolate orange. Hear there, O moon! Does a spectre's breath coolingly haunt her sky this night?!

Martha couldn't find the right thoughts for herself. Stop being so nervous was one of them. She decided to channel her thoughts through the brain of Sage as if she were him herself: In a hundred years from now, we'll be dead. In two hundred years, no-one will remember us and we'll just be a name on a family tree chart at most. So why, in this lifetime, do you care so much what others think?

'But you don't think he'll miss you?' asked Manny, unseemly interrupting Martha's thoughts.

'Who knows what goes through that boy's head sometimes,' she said giggling through her teeth. Her tongue overruled thought. 'You reckon he would then? Miss me, that is.'

'Why wouldn't he?' said Manny, his mouth more upwardly curved than ever she'd seen. Martha went all skittish. With his energy, Martha felt unnerved for Manny's capacity for violence. She breathed and composed herself, recollecting words from Sage, Yap and Thich Nhat Hanh.

'When we first got here, we were so into each other. So into this place too,' said Martha. 'Well I was anyway. I can't tell you how nervous I was coming here, even just thinking about the prospect of coming here. With all my anxieties, I wasn't sure I could do it. But then love conquers all, right? Or so they say. I was so excited and that masked almost everything, and it's not always easy to tell Jim deep stuff anyway. I think he was just humouring me a little at the start by coming here in the first place but I think he got off on the grounds that I was enjoying it. Like I say, who knows with him. But we were strong. Now I don't know. I just don't know anymore.' Manny had a small stash of Latin-American beers by his side.

'Here,' he said handing her one. 'Forget all about it. Think of tonight as being the start of the present and future rolled into one. The past is the past eh.'

They fucked for an hour and a day. So it felt. Certainly to Manny, that's how it felt. Nobody ever could keep up with the quiet ones.

Quite the erotic multitasker, as it happens, sharing Manny's post-coital cigars in bed, Martha forgot for a minute she was not a socialite in a New York apartment.

'I'm out of weed. Do you ever do that shit?' he asked.

'Nope. I mean I've tried it a couple of times. I've never tried cigars before though.' She rolled up to his forearm and looked in more detail at the inside of Manny's self-made hut, which was just as impressive as its outside.

'Do not inhale. Just collect the smoke in your mouth then let the room smell the smoke. When is he back?'

Martha learned of Jim's eyes, their stare, their hold, their true nature and formlessness, not by their nearness, but by remembering how they were before he left and came.

'I don't know exactly, he just said he was away for the weekend.' Martha cracked up again, but this time it was just her voice and not her. 'He didn't even say goodbye…I should go.'

'Wait, wait, what's the rush?'

'I should j-just go, OK.'

'Martha!' Manny called out, but to the dead of night, for pfft! She was gone.

She left her dainty nightgown under Manny's duvet in the hope that by the time he would see it and return it to her, it would have picked up an infinitesimal of his scent.

#

'Are you going to "ye old craft fayre?" ' Jim texted Meredith the following night, with Meredith knowing the most about the upcoming event.

'No doubt! I'm going with my BFF,' she texted back.

'Your what?'

'My BFF.'

'Are you talking to me in abbreviations now? What does that even stand for, best fucking friend, or something?'

'No silly, best friend forever.'

'Really? You and Martha are that close now you'd regard her as your best friend forever? Forever is quite a long time.' The world according to Jim had got so fast-paced now that people couldn't even stop for full words.

'When are u back?' continued Meredith in the text conversation.

'Tomorrow. God I fucking hate London.'

'Haha OK, though through aggression can come reverse psychology :P. I'll let Martha know ur back tmrw.'

The next strangling of Jim's pocket by his phone was in the mould of an incoming text from Greenwich mate, Schemey Sven:

'Seen, i overstand blad, just cotching browns an ting u get me. me an ma bredren will link u ur village some time fam safe yeah.'

Meanwhile, Peter felt as unattractive as the word 'slurry.' A rack of ribs in his belly, seared to a crisp. By his side was Anjit and a squat book about Mao. They were in the kitchen, only them. On the kitchen side was a pan half-filled with glop alongside other graves of supper. Arms out in front, palms pressed against the unsightly side, Peter had his back to Anjit, who was bearishly munching on nachos while seated, and who used the apex of his tongue like floss for his molars.

'I know it's only been a day but it feels like Jim's been gone a while,' said Anjit, and as he spoke, a look of sham concern stretched out his forehead.

'Sees vaginas as toys, that boy. He doesn't love Martha,' Peter said, stance unaltered. Forcibly, he turned on a sixpence, his face within a hair's breadth of Anjit's, his face most sour. 'He doesn't know what love is.' The face looked as though it couldn't keep up with the strength of his emotion as he spoke. Candid concern sewed up Anjit's forehead—now he knew how Mrs Beswick felt.

#

Next evening's clouds sniffle a few drops for a return. A thirty-seven-year-old man is bolstered from the charm and repartee of old London. His acquaintances there and the edificial world where quick results are makeable sealed the deal.

Jim was reminded of the jaunt he had taken from the ecovillage back to Greenwich on the Tube first of all: High in the Underground crowds were banked the sighs for escape. Then Jim hopped on the bus not before tripping over a bottle of vodka. 'Alright,' he said to the driver, who just looked at him as if he was mental. Aah, it sure felt good to be back.

The bus driver careers round the corner,

Passengers are hanging on for dear life,

lots of empty seats,

you might have to sit next to someone else. Perish the thought.

But no,

got to be a man,

got to appear manly,

got to be strong,

stand up and hang on for the rest of the journey, Jim.

Back now at the ecovillage and he thought he was hard because he donned his new shell suit as though it were his shell, 'round *him*, the tortoise. Wading through the ecovillage, Jim recoiled as he came across a sight unseen until now. Battery-powered flashing lights reminiscent of a tacky 80s casino spelled out 'happy' over a tent. Dangling down were fairy lights in the shape of a rose. A small alabaster Buddha statue guarded the entrance. With his thin eyes fixed on the colourful abode, Jim saw Anjit walking close by and said,

'What the…?'

'O yeah. Paul's pimped up his tent,' Anjit replied. 'He was working on it all last night. How was your time away anyway?'

Before Jim has an answer, it would be unfair not to have the reader learn of the lividity going down only a few tents away…

'Two nights ago. It's all about two nights ago,' said Peter to Sage, from Peter's upswollen head, over a burrito in his hex-Mex tent.

'What is?'

'I heard noises. People always forget how close I live to Manny. I know that he is not in his hut right now. Manny always sleeps on the left side of his bed. That's why he is the way he is you see. The left side of his brain is always rested on waking and it explains his general dearth in abilities associated with how the right brain functions. Yesterday morning I too saw ripples in the bedsheets on the right-hand side of the bed that were more, er, you know…more ripply than usual. Martha was alert enough to ensure no-one saw her in the night. However, there was one thing she was not so clever with. Like today, if the mud is too dry, it is harder to mark. Too wet, and any pressure against it becomes too indistinguishable against the rest of the soddenness. Not too soft, not too hard, it was perfect for footprints two nights previous. Earlier on, I went to Martha's when she was not there, and I saw that the pattern inscribed on the footprints leading to Manny's tent match exactly the pattern on the sole of her shoe.'

'Those noises…that you heard…you don't mean…'

'Yes. I am afraid so, Sage. It is what you think.'

'She's always sought the kind of comfort Manny has in his hut, so with Jim being away it gave her the confidence to ask Manny to swap beds?'

'No, you imbecile! She was in the bed with him…they…you know…'

'*Why* I never. Where do people find the time for polyamory?'

'Now not a jiffy. I know you're no more an enthusiast of Jim than I. I'd have his guts for garters if I could. Regardless, Martha needs protecting.'

Jim was polyamorous too as he was already in a relationship with himself. And things had only been hotting up since the shell suit.

'I think you meant to say "not a word," not "not a jiffy." You don't need to worry, I'll keep this under my turban. Manny is a fool and he will never change a whit. He has left things here like putrid roadkill.'

Peter poured out some Sailor Jerry, looking cocksure.

'Never forget your rank and file, Manny,' said Peter, firmly holding the glass to his lips. 'Never!'

His friend, Jerry, was thrown to the back of his throat.

#

Martha noticed that if she read enough, it made her felt thirsty having said in her mind all the unsaid words under her. She reached down for an Old Fashioned, fixed antecedently. It was either that or the dregs of the Prosecco bottle from the night before. I'll go for the Prosecco, she thought. Old Fashioneds just remind me of Jim. Bottle in one hand, book in the other, Martha was back to reading about the English and their rules:

I fucking hate the autumn in England. As soon as it…did I forget to mention that you're all imperialist bastards? Did I?! Did I fucking forget to mention that? Well I have now.

…Where was I? Ah yeah, autumn…as soon as it hits there's just so much to look forward to. Half a year of crap weather to come before you can start to get excited about your 5 days of summer.

An Argentine asked me the other day, 'are you ever homesick?'
Am I fuck.

James sounds like how I feel, Martha thought: This spit in the face, an homage to Manny reserved for Jim only. I love Buddha, he's way better than Jim. Maybe, in after years I will go to the worst Buddhist hell of Avīci where Manny and I will be grappling to thorn bushes with vicious dogs and spears poking us should we fall. Ah well, I've heard the music's not so bad down in hell. At least we'll still be together, side by side. Ballsac I don't care anymore. It is hard being sensitive because you forget that most people around you are not as sensitive. Bollocks to that. I'm fed up with being the good girl. That little prudent parti-coloured good-for-nothing goody two shoes that everyone pretends to love. Fuck you all for not realising my potential for bad behaviour.

Martha's thoughts came to a close.

They call it the parasites, the demons in a person; any which way you want to depict them, every un-enlightened person has them, perhaps the enlightened too. Where do such influences hail from and what are their ulterior functions?

Martha's lemon slice was looking at her, it told her 'open here' at the bottom corner. I'll open it where I fucking want

—that, her last thought, before she heard a distinctive voice.

'Hello, it's me, Peter. Can I come in?'

'Sure, hang on.' Martha drew back the covers.

'Aah, it's nice and toasty in here. You've got that wood burner going nicely.'

'Yeah, it really is first-rate, that burner. I'd be lost without it. Manny helped me set it up.'

'He *is* good with his hands, isn't he.'

She looked up at Peter and she somehow sensed, by the expression on his face, that it was possible he understood her better now than ever before.

'So. Is everything alright?'

'Just shipshape, flower. I'd like us to go somewhere private, where we won't be disturbed.'

Martha and Peter adjourned to his hexi-tent. The hammock Peter still could not make head nor tail of, was lying on the ground.

'Jim was talking to Anjit, but is now over in Dave's tent,' said Peter. 'He was saying to Anjit what a funny man Paul is for pimping his tent. Have you talked to him since he's come back?'

'Well, briefly yes. Just to say hello really. Why?'

'Did you have a nice time while he was away?'

'Well, um…he didn't go very long. I've just been chilling out really.'

'Chilling out. *I* see.'

Peter sounded curious. He poured out some more rum, topping up his glass. He pointed at a lightweight version of his glass empty near Martha, whilst making eye contact.

'Oh, no, I've just had some Prosecco. Thanks.'

'I have not done much this weekend. I have been studious. Watching history documentaries and reading up on the Crimean War. Though, with exterior noise from wildlife, and suchlike, I am easily distracted. Do you know much about the Crimean War, Martha?'

'I don't.'

'Albion against Russia. We had a few others helping us too. We sure had to work hard together in order to succeed our objectives. But then we Britons have always been good on that front. On the occasions that we're not, that's when it all goes haywire.'

'OK, can I ask about the private thing you wanted to talk about?'

'Ah yes, that little matter. Martha, I need you to listen very carefully…I know.' Martha, about to vomit, like a sinkhole was opening beneath her composed herself to continue looking at him roundly, as if she had no idea what he was touching upon.

'What? What do you know? What do you mean?'

'Brits working together, the noises distracting me, having a nice time. Have you joined up the dots yet?'

'Oh my God, you really *do* know. How do you fucking know? Fuck. What's going on? How do you…don't tell Jim. Just don't. Please!'

'I am distracted by wildlife and wild life, but fret not. Your secret's safe with me. It must be a surprise, not just to me Martha, not just to me. It wasn't very chill. I don't mind his sake, but I do yours. Jim looks as ugly as his personality. I'll tell you something else for free: if Manny knows what's good for him, tell him to do away with his shoes or else cover their marks, as they have shown on the mud where he neared your tent. Mum's the word, I've got your back. Just remember this.'

#

Only a new morning could make Martha feel less anxious. It found her alone in the familiar setting of her tent. Jim was in the ungroomed kitchen getting some breakfast together.

Broadly, these had been the contents of the first conversation that had taken place between Jim and Martha on the former's return:

'How did it go in Greenwich?' asked Martha.

'It was alright cheers. Met up with the old boys, had a few drinks, you know how it is. Have you missed me?'

'Maybe,' she said with a half-smile and full hesitation. 'It was pretty quiet really. It was quiet in *our* tent. Principally I was hanging out with Meredith.'

'Are you looking forward to the craft fair Meredith was talking about?'

'I don't really know much about it. I'm at a crossroads if I'll go now. I'm feeling quite apathetic. What's with the shell suit?'

'I know, it is pretty naff. Got it for a bargain though off Schemey Sven.'

Martha stopped thinking about that conversation with Jim and disrobed from her cerulean womanly outfit.

How was she? the natural flesh asked the looking glass. Misshapen, I once thought, my body is not too bad. My body is slight. Why do I give it to him? thought Martha.

Martha remembered something that Sage had said: if you believe that beauty is measured by looks then you do not know beauty my friends.

Hereditary peers, Martha reasoned in her mind, should not have been banished from the House of Lords in 1999, if you yourself judge others in large on their looks. Nice looking, I like your genes, where'd you get them from?

Jim was greatly intelligent, yet its construction he never commissioned, rendering him eternally absent above the shoulders.

Why then—Martha wondered—does he try to be quite so dreadful?

But this wasn't his most exigent concern according to Martha, no. Jim's real problem was how he could remain humble when he was so brilliant.

Martha put on some slacks and a hoodie to make her feel comfortably less attractive. As she came out of the middle-of-the-road tent at a bent angle, there came the realisation that the sky had decided to swallow all cloud leaving Martha an overkill of blue. With her mind still in a jumble over Jim, she could see Mr de facto leader watering the stalk of her attention. He was sawing outside his hut; the clamminess of his hands too far away to be evident. Martha had gained an incautious attitude to prying. She loved to watch Manny wood-working, baring his back. *How*, from industriousness, his living quarters were made with such refinement, as opposed to Jim's base efforts. *How* she looked up to his mountainous range. *How* he made her feel she was growing young!

Egregious!! Hammer a nail into your arm with dexterity and let me lather in your blood! Where did that come from? Did I really just think that? she asked herself. But Martha's fluctuant, licentious inner voice wouldn't go away that easily!!!:

I am fucking Manny with my mind! A consigliere, my liege! A Romeo higher than Juliet's. Lob me onto hot coals, exact my information, salt me in your kench. Manny my tonic, my Eleusis, my elixir of life! Amidst steamy conjuration, investigate my shew stone, corrupt my future! Provide palmistry for this soubrette mad as a March hare! Could you father my thoughts? Soothsayer, necromancer, turn away from this ugly Witch of Endor! Manipulate me with jiggery-pokery; you can poke me any time. Bekiss my neck, lacquer my pneuma, make me feel new morning. Gargle me, toss me round the room, let me feel all man! Inguinal pulsations!!

Fuck me! Take it! Take it bitch! said Manny back to her, in her head, and it was her turn again:

Fuck up, brain my poor excuse for a boyfriend! Collapsible, emetic, syphilitic companion! Send him to the gallows of doom! Hang him dead slowly on viscous meat hooks!! Ooh yeah wear your priest outfit for me! Exorcise an inner existential continuum that so frightens me! The beast sees you jaculating your spear; look at me! Bogwash insecurities Look!! It's me…Martha…your fucking bitch!!!

Shh shh, now she begged of thought. She didn't like how it made her feel. The world was losing its innocence as Martha went away from the shameful crime scene. As she did, she remembered that what could be said in meditational instructions could be said of life: that there was nothing in her experience that didn't need to happen. Whether these were the right instructions, well, she was willing to go with it for now.

Her ability to concentrate on the flavourless was hampered by the fact that she wanted to starkly drink in every dulcet note the world could sing to her. Nonetheless, she felt her head more expansive when she allowed room for every sight, sound, smell or thought that passed the present moment, without passing judgement, without being for or against any one of them—the process the sages name equanimity. Saleem Eaglefeather was one of its proponents.

Oil my pipes!!

—the voice rattled forth once more.

#

At the Easter weekend, Martha was having a great time facing the fact that she was not coping with life as well as she pretended she had been. She had trialling a new antidepressant, not the NaSSA she had tried before, but the more common SSRI. It was the second drug Martha had received from Dr Das that she had kept as a backup. It made her feel numb and even Jim's moaning could not muzzle her any. Sure enough, the other relatable experiences of feeling lethargic and drug-slow thought took the limelight of her days. Martha opined that there had seemed a scintilla of freedom, but was reminded how no drug on top of, under or in the world can make you feel high all the time.

It was back to see what no drugs felt like. All in all, she just hoped spring would pass without the prospect of a black summer.

In mid-April lightlessness, in a pitch-dark coat to camouflage, Martha attended a discussion from afar in her mind. Dressed to the nines for Manny, the wind holding converse with her hair, locks looping like tendrils.

'Tousle! I'm gonna mess you up,' the wind said. 'I'm going to ruin all your hard work, ravel your confidence, blow over guilt.'

Martha put on that her ears were attending Meredith's words. In reality, she attempted to listen in on a discussion between Manny and a few others standing at the communal point. She saw Manny at her, staring, though with no sign of tender feeling.

What was to be thought of her animated caricature?

She played with her phone to ratchet up popularity, showing him her best side.

Look at me! I'm not the harridan, Baba Yaga! Does Manny even like me? The way he looks at me I'm not sure if he just wanted a fuck, she thought. She again looked to a Manny now backing away.

Undress me you cunt! Lay me in your sepulchre!!

—Oh no, not again, not the rum thought-chatter, she thought against thought. To even think of the c-word shows I've been around Jim too long.

For acting such a way, I don't feel a naughtiness, nor a sense of shame, just a frozenness, just thoughts continued, continued her thoughts. I estimate I would feel worse about it if Jim was not such a douche.

Manny. It's the lust-look she gave him; it's his backhand winner down the line.

Martha's 'give a fuck' attitude, though appearing before seemed from somewhere else. Sailing on colossal waves is brinkmanship.

#

Another night, another debate:

'How easy it must be to be considered an upstanding member of the community and eat meat, time and again, without a moment's thought for any animal.'

'I only got the tail end of that. What's he prattling on about now?' Jim asked Dave on the quiet.

'I'm not sure, something about eating meat,' Dave replied in the communal area.

'O God, is he being moral again?'

Sage went on:

'One can eat so much meat so often that when it's placed in front of them, it just becomes an article of commerce. Like cracker bread, it becomes so easy to eat without any compunction as to its source. Life can be easy when you have little room for morals and your ignorance is top drawer. In time, you wise up, start questioning things more—a sign that your moral compass is orienteering. This is a natural occurrence, but it is then up to you to decide how much you want to change your life by how much you're willing to pay attention to the compass. Making your life harder in this regard has been so positive for so many.'

'Is *that* so. I don't see the point in not eating meat,' said Jim, motioning his chicken drumstick to the sky, taking a chunk out of it. 'I mean it's feckless isn't it.' Jim only knew that word because it sounded like fuck. 'Supermarkets don't give a shit if I don't buy their meat, with my one-man protest. The animal's already dead. In a box.'

Supermarkets are kindhearted enough to give animals coffins and epitaphs. The coffin Jim had opened read: '2 chicken drumsticks, 100% British chicken.'

'But you could say that about anything. Why vote then?' Martha asked.

'Exactly! Why vote!' said Jim.

'But that's a bit like saying why anything? Why live?' contributed Anjit.

'As a vegetarian I want to go the whole hog, pardon the pun,' said Martha. Jim's argument made about as much sense to her as The Buggery Act of 1533. As Martha said the basic parts of her contention, the more compounded parts revealed themselves to her. 'Like cats for example. I love cats probably more than any other pet, but I couldn't have one. It would be hypocritical. I would feel too bad for all the local wildlife they decimate. Local mice and bird populations fritter away in areas with lots of cats, and it's our human greed to have cute pets that is damaging our e…'—Martha realised how many people were now listening and began to flap a little—'ecosystems.' On hearing a tremulous version of her voice she became even more anxious—a skittle down at the bowling alley. She recovered. 'Not only that, but all the meat products we feed cats just add to the insensate meat market. No. I can't do it.'

'What's the rest of the hog? Anything else like?' asked Jim.

'Loads else. Like leather. I've seen vegetarians wear leather and I don't get it.'

'If you buy from supermarkets, dear Jim, you increase demand,' said Sage. 'Meat is a euphonious euphemism for dead animal flesh; food with a face. Humans have gone one better for the aim of profiteering by softening by telling cow eaters they are only eating beef, and if you give us more money there'll be steak for the posh cow eaters. After the wording comes form: limit blood content and entomb with nice packaging for the full distraction package. You see the moral world is invariably left with dilemmas, and so many regard with scorn the mass production of animals, and many that want to eat organically are priced out of it. Some of the worst offending supermarkets are throwing a third of their stock away a day. A third a day! And then about a third of the stock bought by customers is thrown away. Remember when you were young and grandma said to you: "don't waste water." Well kids, forget everything you learned.'

Jim was furious. Manny by himself was one thing, but he wasn't having his girl form any kind of union with that beardy shit—the oily-worded man of compassion!

Driven away by Sage, Jim shifted too fast one way, thinking he was supersonic. He veered back to get his head on Martha's shoulder.

She turns her head, the use of her sleek eyeballs galls him, for the eyeballs are in the main shadowing Sage's, switching between left and right to mirror the mystic's.

Smoke dawdling out his mouth, Jim remembered that Martha—whilst carousing one evening at a rabble-rousing anti-globalisation demonstration—told him how beards reminded her of sea foam. She told him she did not trust men with beards as they had something to hide.

'I sometimes wonder whether people don't do things just because the law says so rather than because of any moral convictions,' said Martha. 'No time for critical analysis in a soundbite society the media choke us with.'

'WhatsayIwer…' Sage dissected some ideas from his brain that scrimmaged with his lips in a word congestion. 'What I'm saying is as you get older, one hopes that what you lose in nihilism you make up for in wisdom. We have a problem in this society with labels, and this applies saliently in our chinwag. How we decide to eat, in an ethical context is based upon decisions of harm reduction. There's the omnivore who does not care how much and how often or from which source his meat comes in. There's the one who feels some guilt and tries to limit meat consumption to choice animals, makes sure eggs are free range and tries not to eat meat too often. Then there's the pescetarian, then the vegetarian. Then there's the vegan, and then you enter the world of people like fruitarians. Some of these people only eat fruit that has fallen as to pick the fruit is to essentially 'kill' it. But in such a diet, multifarious deficiencies can arise, and then there might be the need for unnatural-looking supplements. Essentially, somewhere down this long line we have to be selfish in some way if our interest is healthy survival. It is just a matter of where we individually draw the line.'

'What do they mean picking fruit is killing?' asked Jim.

'Our vegetal knowledge is always improving. There's growing evidence that vegetables, for example, feel pain, and are recurrently picked and eaten whilst still alive.'

'Cripes, that's extremely interesting,' said Martha. 'You're right, it's tough being vegetarian sometimes given that you're ridiculed by some meat masticators, and are even told by some vegans that vegetarianism isn't going far enough.'

'I agree with them actually,' said Meredith. 'Vegetarianism on its own isn't enough.' Martha could hear her stomach rumbling; the contents of which were suitable for vegetarians. In fact, it was bustling with vegetables and the rumbling was not for hunger but for anxiety.

Martha's inner voice rises like a beanstalk. Over it, Miracle-Gro is liberally poured. The inner voice just left the airport at Anxiety Land:

How can you?! My sidekick! My only female hope. To be unhinged, and yet you turn this back of yours on me. We must agree on everything! Don't do this. Not here. Not now. Not in front of all these people.

Thursday's bell practice begins for the eve, tolling the air, landing at where Martha seeks company. Meredith is all set to continue: 'I've been vegan ten years and I love it. Buying eggs still contributes to factory farming and free range hardly means jack. All the unwanted male chicks are slaughtered for no meat. And what the cows are subjected to during the milking process is torturous. All this for humans.'

'I love cheese way too much to go vegan, milk I'm not so bothered about,' said Jim.

What is this?! Martha's inner voice returns to ask. I am but a waif, hack down the shackles!

Martha's new head presents her a scene replete with greenness and vegans and sad-looking animals and daisy grubbers and poker sticks and pitchforks and hayforks pronging her.

She has that sinking feeling. She feels like a human drill. Vegan Baphomet, who looks like Baphomet but with a big green 'V' on his chest, is talking:

'I want to eat your smile, for it has touched the blood of four legged mammals. Always prating on about how noble you were when you bought free range eggs. You didn't think about that when you bought a quiche though did you?! You may not eat meat but you eat dairy, you little bitch. And anyway, even if they were free range eggs, you won't be buying them here because you're in vegan hell now.'

Meanwhile Paul and Manny were talking privately, both leaning against the frontal exterior of Manny's august hut. Paul stunk of enough beer to kill a frail old lady.

'So what we gonna do? I can't just have you here drinking all the time,' Manny said.

'I need help. I know I do. I want to get help.' Paul started to speak louder where other people were. 'I've had enough. I want to go and get help for my alcoholism.'

'Good for you,' Burt called out. Cathy heard too.

'You've got to stop that drinking, lad. Ya know, it's makin' ya look ugly,' she said with a light heart.

'You can talk bacon face, but I can't eat you because of my Jewness,' said Paul in retort with a laugh like a clap.

'Ach, so rude. Alright then fat bones.'

'More to love in't there, more to love. In't?—I'm even starting to sound like you.' Paul produced a new laugh to wake the dead.

'Anyway, what are you going to do?' asked Manny.

'OK, I'll try and stop…or at the least calm it down. But it'll take time. It won't be overnight.'

'Good chap.'

#

'There are those businessmen who run their organisations or companies to match their view of the world.' Martha had just begun a new chapter in the discussion that carried over the next day. Rain had called off last night's early, from which Jim had not since said a word. It was just Sage, Martha and Jim this time by *Shard*. 'Sage, I remember us talking about how we're taught at school to be competitive and out for ourselves, and how this is not in line with the laws of the universe. The laws of the universe dictate that no-one else's happiness is less important than our own, so why do schools, our parents, and so many in society push us into working towards the inverse? Such slaves to money. You hear some businesspeople say things like, "it's a brutal, dog eat dog world out there." With this excuse they will act in whatever way they want, lying through their teeth to get the job done—selfsame to how it was with my last two jobs, and I'm not going to tolerate it anymore. I simply won't roll over anymore.'

Martha thought herself a shit poem:

I am talking, you will listen, you will respect me,
Naff off assimilation,
I will not conform to your inaccurate ideals, I will not conform.

I say, what will it take? To be on the deathbed or in
the nursing home,
Before it's realised I am right,
Before we realise how little money is,
Oh how little it matters at the point of near death.
I will not conform, I will not conform…

…Well, maybe I will…just a bit, just in case.

—It's good to keep your options open, she thought.

Martha was not a Poe nor a poet, but she liked to fancify her words; crop circles please for the page.

And inheritance? she asked herself. 'I was thinking about how silly money is and how I'd rather live in a favela with a loving family than in a family at loggerheads, living plushly in a mansion. Still and all, maybe inheritance is a nice thing? Dying in the knowledge that money earned in your life will go on to support your loved ones?'

'So now your family's more important than everyone else's,' said Jim. Martha was just amazed Jim had been able to remain quiet so long.

Martha ignored her insightful boyfriend and was beginning to feel the day offering itself as a counsellor for simmering thoughts on the leash. Now boiled and frothy, she spared the word. All words. And so it was that no more words decided to happen.

Today Martha had primped her hair in a plat with a pink bowknot. She felt a hand against it. 'I couldn't help myself,' said a livelier Jim. The way the hand skulked and disturbed was as irritating as wasteful expense from unneeded air conditioning. Martha thought it out: Jim is a kind of pokey breeze in the neck.

She took the thought and wrung it before hanging it out on the line to dry. Jim was going to try again, but on seeing Martha's iron brow, thought better of it. She gave Jim the slip like a case of magnetic repellency. Only a perfect painter could capture the dreamy way of her turn. Her eyes were as red as beefsteak fungus. Jim had had about enough.

'Emotional nutcase,' he said looking at Martha, but far enough away that she was out of earshot. Sage could not hear as he had his headphones on, catching up with Radio 4's Woman's Hour. 'Martha's so sensitive, man. It's hard to get near her some days.' Jim's words were aimed at Dave, to whom he was speaking under a juiceless sky, later that afternoon by the vegetable patch. 'I really don't know what goes through that girl's head sometimes. You're always there Dave, cheers.'

'Well I can't exactly move fast in this fucking wheelchair.'

#

In an April springtime a coalition is crystallising. The setting: *Lake Horizon*.

Jim: 'I've always wanted to know how to run those old 90s DOS games.'

Burt: 'Come to my tent tomorrow, 11 a.m. I can show you how to run the DOS emulator then.'

So tomorrow Jim did. On entering, an agate wind chime Martha had made jangled impatiently. Burt had just upgraded a soldier on new strategy game,

'Important Battles IV.' Ten minutes prior he had been watching anime porn. In his tent, of a Native American style, Burt patted down his hair by a wood burner. Wig-warm. On one side of the tent was a life-size photograph of Dame Edna Everage whom Burt found attractive in a way we just cannot go into here. Inside the tent, one could tell a lot about Burt's mental posture. It looked desperate, decrepit, sorrowful, despairing. A down-at-heel piece-of-shit excuse for accommodation. Fred was out to lunch.

Following on from yesterday at *Horizon*:

'This is how you run it, mate,' said Burt, getting the DOS emulator installation under way. A DOS emulator allows you to run old DOS games of the 80s and 90s on modern computers that otherwise do not support their playability. Burt found this definition in Geeks Weekly Magazine.

Zombies and dragons and other common mythical creatures were splayed about the tent. When it came to games, burly Burt had it covered from 'FootieTeam Manager' to fantastical classics. Fun>long-term fulfilment. By computer games he played his life away, each a fluffy pink lullaby sending Burt to sleep from the workings of a normal world.

'Nice one, cheers man for showing me,' said Jim.

'Nah, it's good to have you here. Not much else to do as Manny won't let me have chickens.'

'Chickens?'

'Yeah, Manny's worried they'll shit everywhere and he doesn't want a pen either. He says they're a liability. Think he's worried about them escaping a pen or of Fred attacking them. Have always wanted my own chickens. He doesn't want to have to contribute money to a pen either. He'd rather spend the money elsewhere, even though I haven't asked him for any money. That guy gets on my tits.'

'Mine too,' said Jim.

'I'll bet.'

'And Sage, that hammy bastard.'

'Ay. Sage isn't afraid to stick the oar in when it suits him. That guy turns up like a bad penny.'

'Ha, "Sage." What a stupid name.'

There was a long pause as they both thought about the guy in white.

'Say, you can give my wheels a spin if you fancy sometime?' said Burt.

'What wheels?'

'I bought a motor the other day.'

'Whoa, really?'

'Yep. Old, old thing. Fifth-hand.'

'Cool man yeah sounds good.'

'I used to have me a caravan but not anymore. I might up sticks and drive back to live in that house I own. I can't see things getting any better here what with Manny controlling everything. What a liberty. The shit's gonna hit the fan and I don't think we'll have to wait long. Mark my words, as sure as I stand here today, something's gonna give.'

Jim wasn't sure what he meant, but there was a definite sickness about his voice, the likes of which he had not heard before.

Only a little later on, Jim took up Burt's offer. He had not driven a car for far too long. He entered the car to find his bygone self. But how could he be himself when he didn't know what he was? Ah no he did—a failure, that was right. Vroom vroom! said his head. Jim flapped around, twiddled the gearstick, drank some time, coughed a bit, sighed some, vented, fumed at the mouth. Spittle glided as he cursed the world, Burt's car, his luck. Became languid. Got depressed, asked why me? The fail box enclosed him, morphing from cardboard to titanium.

The failure alighted. Small-talked with Dave and Peter. Pretended nothing happened, it's better that way.

Paul went down the road and into town. A chugger caught his eye and asked him if he would talk. He said he couldn't but it expired he ably could, for he had to talk to tell her he couldn't, as he didn't have the time. He had time, it just chose to run out. With an unflinching gaze, a head vised from drink and the energy of a raucous fruiterer, hale Paul went to the bank with bagged monies and thence to the post office. He felt like a marauder, buccaneering on the Spanish Main. Carringdon on the whole was ordinary, Cherryblossom Street within it was alright. The post office was found on an adjoining street where it was easier to find run-down people and half-arsed shops. Lordy Lord, there were shadowy areas of business down those backstreets. Down the backstreets lived shame and lost riches, down the backstreets lived bookies and public houses whose patrons looked as though they'd lived there their whole lives— yet you never did see any fucker go in.

'Who's aboot?' Paul said, in a Geordie accent, ramming open the post office door like he was the third billy goat Gruff. 'Why aye lovely, how are yous?' he asked a female octogenarian, noticing others too.

'Oh hello,' she said, her unnaturally high pitch conceivably implied insecurity. One counterperson looked on as if she had the heebie-jeebies.

'Hello Cecil,' said another lady, abraded by time and outdoor exposure.

'Aha! Why aye pet. Megan isn't it?'

'Yes, you remembered.' She chuckled.

'I cannae forget a pretty face. How's Mavis getting on?'

'She's grand. The daughter's done ever so well, she's a doctor now. Shame her youngest went wrong, he's a dead loss. Do you like raisin wheats, Cecil? They've got buy one get one free this week at the corner shop. O you'll love 'em, just over in the corner. My grandson gets through them like there's no tomorrow. Get the raisin wheats while you can won't you, get them now. It's buy one get one free.'

'Take care now,' a counterperson said to a white-haired man, putting on his flat cap as he hit the road. You know you're getting on when you start saying 'take care' to people. People say back: 'oh you're looking well.' You know it's time for the retirement home when people start saying, 'mind how you go,' or 'would you like another cushion so you can prop yourself up?'

On his way back, Paul stopped off at one of the bookies. He played the virtual roulette wheel to lose ten pounds to remind himself what it felt like to know anger, to remind himself what it felt like to have something to fight for.

CHAPTER EIGHT

J azzy beats and genial burble permeating in nocturnal late April announced that the weather would surely only perk up from here on in. Plus it was Ed Balls Day. Near the communal area, there was batucada and house, and soon, Charleston time. Meredith danced with funkiness drinking one of the many strawberry beers Paul had bought and shared. Her mother used to dance that way. Her dress, that dress! Peg-top. Lashings of apricot jazzed like the music, spasmodic, acidic and rupturable, igniting to recycle. Sitting atop a beige background they nictated and growled with Meredith's every swing and stretch. An apricot rabid, molesting the beige, spilling out for air. Meredith looked like the most brilliant Christmas tree worm.

Astounded by the sight of the well-worked contours of her body the dress helped pronounce, Jim found an uncontrollable compulsion to corner her in his eye. There was just room enough to place her in that corner without having to worry that his eyes could dart back if necessary should Martha turn to see him star in his latest stage adaption of *Letchgate*. Melodious shadows of sound cushioned tensions and the sexy booze axed inhibition. Wanton thoughts were carved in Jim's mind over Meredith, until…

About-face! With a full-on glare at Meredith, he thought she looked a humpy prat. Faux person through the dress. The cellophane-coated skin! And Jim didn't like jazz, it was too pleased with itself. Rounding her delicious haunches, there a ran air of ostentation about Meredith as if to say: yeah, you better be looking at me as I drink my drink. I'm so out there, I'm a big deal. Look at the way I dance, at the way I coast, at the way I pout, at the way I…oh, you are looking, jolly good.

Though as a non-Brit she mightn't have said 'jolly.' Debonair. Light as candy floss. Meredith the grandstander couldn't care a flying fuck what anyone thought. It was through her and her alone that others remembered they too liked to dance. She danced away from the unwritten laws that govern all orders of men: of laying bare unripe—all the way up to—fully fledged senior moments concerning inadequate impulse control, that not all men wish to subjugate. Martha was in no mood for thoughts of this kind, blithe with the freedom bestowed on her by her eco bestie, and hops.

Dave was time-travelling. Enjoying the nascent show, he very carefully watched Meredith. She brought the 1950s to his version of 2022, rotating his mind, making him think he was her Gene Kelly. He noticed her castanets in hand. Dave was on the one hand frustrated by undersellers, on the other, lagging from the over-graduated, but when it came to dancing, Meredith's was like the middle bear's porridge, juuuuust right. Meandering whirlwind. Right on time.

Stepping on the note. But her form and her endings were flimsy and abrupt. Dave knew she was not a great dancer, but he loved the *way* she danced. Others clicked their heels, and as though they were opening automatic doors they let her pass as she moved to fill the spotlight.

Peter, originally frowning at proceedings noticed the indelicate attentions of Dave. Carried by this and the Charleston's cadence, Peter lunged into the dance pit. His feet took him places he was unaware he could go; he was spinning like a whirling dervish.

Jim loved to watch Martha. She danced like mucilaginous seagrass. The undulator. Ethereal riser and faller. She could not afford to fall much more. Her hair a gourmet of keratin, her boots on the ground like a fine rain, sprinkling the land with nourishment, whetting the curiosity of Jim's mind. A dance to remind Jim. A dance to remind him of untouchability; or was that balderdash? His untold desires, a life and self could unlace before a caramelised woman.

Tomorrow became.

'Did you see Meredith last night? I wouldn't say she's a vamp but she knows how to get in blokes' 'eads. Know what I mean?' quizzed Paul.

Hmm,' said Dave.

'Certainly knows how to get into'—nodding sidewise at Peter—(h)'is.' Paul gave a scream for raillery, swigging strawberry beer from a temporary table at the communal area, his heart pumping. Burt laughed and the others, for acknowledgment of joke-formation, gave skinny laughs to be polite. Peter tried to laugh. 'Yeah I've seen those two together. Like putty in her hands.' Burt and Paul laughed boisterously together with the others slightly ruder this time. 'Women in their late 30s worry me. If they're not after a sperm donor, it's a meal ticket. How about you Anjit? Haven't seen many of your lot round here,' Paul said laughing his usual way. 'Any nice Indian pussy about?' Paul the fribbler was laughing profusely, and only Burt kind of joined in. 'I wouldn't go near one. They don't even wash their hands properly *do* they.' Now there was definitely no-one laughing. No-one except the speaker. With each quip was a redder shine, telling the story of Paul's keenness for playfulness at any expense.

There was a silent boom. 'Hey Peter,' continued Paul, 'will you do me a favour and check Meredith's not in my tent warming up my sleeping bag again?' And again came a crashing cackle from Paul. A market of red shades. Big easy red.

'I haven't seen you with a bird,' said Jim, in a blasé manner, looking Paul's way.

'What did you say?'

'I said I haven't seen you with a bird,' Jim said, matter-of-factly. Paul drew himself up, and sharp.

'Say it again and see what happens, yeah?! See what happens cunt. Me and you are heading down a cul-de-sac, son, and the cul-de-sac's got my address on it so you'll wanna stop trespassing. Swivel on it, yeah. Are you trying to mug me off?!'

Cutlery bounded Jim's way as Paul levered the table to the ground like he was a shot-putter, saying as he did, 'take that you cunt, and when you take it, you're gonna take it like your mother would!'

Three of the dwellers had their restraining arms around Paul. Jim looked at the ground trying to look collected and current. 'Hey cunt, look me in the eye. I want to see how hard you are,' Paul said, and he was not sure Jim heard as Jim was being hustled away. 'Hey cunt! Cunt!!' Jim didn't look him in the eye, and shoved off towards his undistinguished tent. 'You wanna go?! You're like a chocolate flake, you crumbling bastard. You've got ideas above your station, you wanna head back to Greenwich mate.'

Solicitous faces looked on as Paul unshackled himself and stomped about delirious.

A temper so great it flares the street lights blue with sorrow. Walking back is cold in the vast.

The others formed a human wall, perhaps of love, perhaps to obstruct Paul from running after Jim. When it was right they folded like the night. Jim felt sick and his brain reminded him of a caution. When Burt marked his words with his eerie forerunner, was this what he meant, or was there more to come?

'What the actual fuck?' said Meredith at the communal area in the aftermath of the fracas the next morning. Zilch had been picked up from the night before.

'It was some of the stuff of nightmares,' said Peter, next to her. 'Did you hear what he said? He was incandescent. He was saying racist stuff about Indians and then as everybody left him to it and got to bed, he became more inebriated. "Oscillate black man!" he said. "Oscillate, I want you to oscillate!" The guy's just crackers on the sauce.'

'Which black man? Were there any here?'

'No, that's the point. He's like a powder keg.'

'What's with all the mess?'

'Jim said something and Paul went apeshit, hurling everything around. Paul didn't like it when the boot was on the other foot, then things were not so funny anymore.'

Martha sighed.

'It would be Jim,' she said.

'Funnily enough, on this occasion it was all Paul's fault. I've got to find Manny about this. He's got to go.'

'Does anyone actually enjoy fortune cookies?' the wandering Sage threw up into the atmosphere, just passing, finishing off a Chinese takeaway. 'Or do people just gnaw through them, ever hoping for the message that might bring hope to the dinner table, or that might unleash a bonanza or epiphany in their life or at least in some small way make it more tolerable?'

Someone said something but Sage was so happy with his question that he wasn't really listening to the answer. So he asked the same question again but in a different way. Sage quite liked how he asked that question, too. Someone replied something about getting hot under the collar about the concept of fortune cookies, and about how being hot under the collar related to the previous night. 'Intoxication—the much needed yet mendacious liberation!' said Sage. 'We must banish our anger but how? I know. We watch anger bubble and be mindful thereof, but do not react. The other way is to punch some cushions or a punch bag. Anger is an enemy of man. It compresses him into a sardine box when his potential is a cigar box.'

'Yeah very good, thanks Sage. How about not trying to act the sage for once?' said Meredith. Martha's smile of assentation was also a smile of respect for a confidence Martha unceasingly longed for. Sage looked bemused.

'No, I *am* The Sage, and Paul, you think threats and violence are hard? Try loving everyone, that's a lot harder.'

Paul was not there because he was in Manny's especial hut.

'People have said you were saying racist things. Is this true?' asked Manny. In front of him was the archetype of a man spent.

'Couldn't tell ya, I was off me nut. All I remember is Jim in my face, playing me like a fiddle.'

'Understood. Do you have a problem with blacks and Indians?'

'No. I mean not per se. I love everyone. I just don't like it when people come over here and take take take. It's a temperament thing too I find. They're not always the same as us Brits.'

'I'm Latino, what do you think of me?'

'You seem alright. Jim don't like the temperament of you people.'

'What? You know what, I don't want to hear any more. We have no black people here but that doesn't mean we can't be offended if they are not treated the same, and I want you to get on with Anjit and me. You shake hands with and apologise to Anjit and Jim. You subscribe to your opinions, but keep them close to your chest if they're going to cause conflict. That's not what we're about here, and I'd like to remind you of my kindness in letting you stay here in the first place. I don't want people coming to me telling me you're pissed again or have said something offensive. Do you understand? This is your last warning.'

'Fair dos.'

Paul's head shone brighter than his past as he went back to his tent in reflective vision to micromanage ill tempers. Nautical nomenclature came to the fore in his mind until it made way for a conversation he remembered initiating with an old gay friend:

'I want to go gay for a bit and I want you to be the one to open me up. You bring the poppers, I'll bring the cheese and wine.'

Paul sighed. He missed cottaging in the Cotswolds. When Paul set off for gay world, it was intended as a one-way ticket. He now knew he should have got an open return.

'You're not bisexual, you're just greedy,' his mum would say. He still liked girls. Sort of. He couldn't decide. There are girls, there are boys, there are toys; take your pick. Paul's mum still liked that he might like girls. He was her only son and she wanted grandchildren to play in her garden. One December she exhorted Paul should he be tempted to divulge his thoughts for men:

'Don't tell your dad, you'll ruin Chanukah.'

Paul harked back his mind with a momentary re-entry into the all-too-familiar world of the self-hating Jew:

Disgraceful Jewboy picking up his denims as the arrow twists. The skim and the skimmer of people. Did I just say 'fuck' one more time? Fuck fuck fuck fuck fuck fuck fuck. The line of fuck. Think it because I want to, say it because I can. Decimate anti-profaners.

Let's pick daisies and sing Kumbaya. Is that because I can because I'm such a cool Jew, pinching at the furrowed brow of my little Jew head. That's not even a Jewish song, Jew. We'll make an honest man of you yet, Jew. You've really Jewed it up this time, Jew. It always has to be about you, doesn't it, Jew, and you always have to mention the fact that you're a Jew. Jew Jew Jew Jew Jew Jew Jew Jew Jew Jew Jew…Jew. Give the Jew an inch he takes three miles. Let me negotiate that for you gentile.

Things all started to go wrong after the ghastily received bar mitzvah. Lionised in the process, several years later Paul would turn up in a calendar called 'Juicy Jews.' It was the eighties. In tribute to Ziggy Stardust and the Spiders from Mars, Paul formed a group called, Caramel Moonrock and the Pink Flavoured Stars. Their biggest hit was 'Pavement Coloured Ostriches Skiing Down a Funnel of Entropy.'

Paul started to remember the acid trips and the similarities to spirituality and the hallucinogenic path. He remembered the hallucinogenic take on geometry and its interest in the fractal. He remembered his love of the potential of medicinal properties in hallucinogenic plants for mental health. He remembered emptiness and ego death—it beat the numbing down from his daily microdosing of syrup-based children's paracetamol. Paul was tripping backwards:

You are expansive, aren't they? (All he could think.)

Paint stories, write art. Frame the walls, line them with madness. Paul's corniced rococo walls were no longer flabbergasted, unlike Jim's. If you could smell colours, how would they taste? Would red be of blood or raspberries? Bloodying raspberries? Don't let it bother you. If you never do drugs, you can never answer such questions, Paul said in his mind to the world. Into the slipstream. The psychoactive vaults and the abstruse relations between narcotics and mind. Would you not believe in something if it were true? My mind's made up, don't confuse me with facts, as the old saying goes. Would you be like some newspapers that look at facts and use the worst parts of those facts to make their facts a little more factual?

Jim thought back to when he grabbed his keys like he would a pair of bollocks. He was one fifth bisexual. If Jim had had a few, and a man exposed himself to him in a public toilet, Jim could not, with any degree of certainty, not go for the squeeze. In Jim's eyes, he was ninety-five percent straight, but, you know, you have to allow a bit of leeway for a cold rainy Monday on the Humber.

'I've thought about reforming "Moonrock," but I'd need new members,' Paul later told Anjit at the communal point, which had now all been cleared up by Paul in furtherance of making amends. 'People thought I was 'avin' a bubble when I told them. I am sorry about how I was with you. I didn't mean it. When I look at people I don't even see colour. I was so fucked I don't even remember what I said. It was only 'cause Peter told me that I know now.'

'It's OK,' said Anjit, looking unsure if it all really was. 'Anyway, you were saying about Moonrock…'

'Ah yeah. The former members I've lost contact with or lost them through death. It would be a big challenge to get it together again. Also, when you're young and people come to see you play, they're interested to see if you're any good.' Paul looked groundward at the mud. 'At my age they come to see if you've still got it.'

'And do you?' There was a brief pause. Paul looked up to Anjit.

'I don't know that I do.'

'Oh…'

'Well I guess you saw me work me magic on the old tea tin so you've already seen me perfect timing.' Paul gave a Paul laugh. 'I guess one day I could get the old thing going again. But I'm not sure how to deal with the watchers. I feel like they're scavengers, waiting for the old guy to fall.'

#

'Some self-involved cunt's stolen Martha's cheese,' Jim said in the kitchen to break in the first day of May.

'I don't even like cheese,' said Kristoff.

Martha managed a drizzling of unschooled tears after learning of the fate of her Sainsbury's Taste the Difference cranberry-encrusted Wensleydale. You really *could* taste the difference. A delicacy in an ecovillage, how unmistakable an item to have vanished! The tears got brighter; the power of crocodile tears! Such wasteful liquescence could not go unnoticed and Jim was feeling ruttish. Had he really this cross to bear?

Melodramatic squaw, Sage thought, eyeing from afar. Unlike most, Sage did not feel guilt about such thoughts as indeed some sages would. Rather, he was present for the thoughts and with childlike wonder was amazed how he could think such a thing.

What is it like at the 'sense stores' when a child goes into a fantastic sweet shop for the very first time? It was that same wonder Sage perennially sought for life. A work in progress.

A woman will never know the power she can have over a man, thought Jim. Jim challenged any woman to with one hundred percent wholeness know how the slightest act on her part can drive a man to frenzied toxic desire. Martha was not interested in cradling a desirous image of herself and she thought it unfair and unholy to be of that image.

'It was expensive, that cheese' she said through aging tears to Jim. 'It's not easy going through money like this.' Martha malevolently coiled dangling tresses from her head of caramel. It was malevolent because she knew not the power of hedonism it could agitate in a man; she knew not but for patterns of the subconscious. As effective as the little grubber kick in a rugby game.

'We'll get to the bottom of this,' Jim alleged.

Jim once thought Martha had the resolve of a hardy ship—oceangoing. That was before she disembarked at the ecovillage. A smidgen of him noticed her fakery, liked her more for it, reminded him of his version of femininity.

'Has it really come to this?' said Peter.

'What's that?' enquired Jim.

'We're going to have to start putting labels on food. This is sad.'

Jim left a carking note on the kitchen wall:

DO NOT EAT OTHER PEOPLES FOOD. LABEL YOUR ITEMS

Jim had no time for apostrophes. The note was appended just above Peter's which read:

TIDY UP AFTER URSELF

Peter, in a bid to be more like Meredith, found he had less time for full words.

Unknowingly results-driven, Martha's twirling hand twists really did the trick. What wasn't probity could fall away to tact. Jim's mind felt unscrewed. Chunks of text on paper felt fun. All such events played out in a dot of time in human history and less than a quarter of a dot in worldly history.

Yet it transpired, humans were there, people sounded off but loved to live. Acts from biological masses on an orbiting, spinning, terraqueous sphere, searching for meaning in a stupefyingly ample three-dimensional theatre.

In the same afternoon, Sage was adding shallots and red wine to a saucepan by some of his finest eco friends. Having remarked them, he was about to give his opinions. Then they would feel bad.

'Paul's right. Whoever created cheese and wine evenings ought to be the leader of the free world. Jim, you know in some ways you are really quite advanced in your spiritual peregrination.'

O God, thought Jim, more crap to come. 'Yet you do not even know you of this advancement,' Sage continued. 'Your self-confidence is very high. You are very at ease in yourself, and especially around Martha.

You can manage fine with most people. Indeed if I think back to myself in the early stages of my development, it might be hard to imagine now but I was very nervous. Where you need to improve is your awareness of both others and your milieu. You say things that people don't like, yet do not realise yourself why that is, or even that they have taken offence. This is the area where I would advise you focus your meditative attention.

'Now Manny, you are a man of great energy and ideas. The fuel of this ecovillage. But there is a monumental disparity between telling it how it is and telling it how you think it is. Some would regard you too pumped up, a blowhard, a princox, a man unknowing of his own energy. You have been appearing insensitive to others, telling tall tales, outdoing him, outdoing her…'

'What are you talking about?!' facetiously asked Manny.

'You're stepping on the toes of my words. Anyway, as a rule, you seem to mean well. Both you and Jim at times are on the cusp of arrogance. It is important to remember that arrogant people are often idiots who get found out without losing time. They paint a picture of you cursorily and think they know what you're going to say before you've said it. Arrogant people are often show offs, and show offs peel like losing scratch cards. Let me tell you about idiots.' Please don't, thought Jim. 'Idiots will always find a way to be idiots. The worst kind of idiot is the arrogant idiot. He thinks he knows everything but he can't do nowt.' Sage raised his head to ogle Cathy. 'Vociferously, the idiot will blither about how knowledgable he is about simple material things, with no thought to observe, learn or gain anything from anyone. Then there's the middling idiot. He's not arrogant enough to think he knows everything but is too happy in his witless ways to change them or to trouble himself with any new wrinkle. There's the genuine idiot otherwise known locally as the village idiot. Fundamentally stupid, he's not able to think outside the box, but he's bearable. If you'll pardon the expression, idiocy, on its own, can't be helped. Some people are just born that way; the lights on but no-one's home. But the less they try, the worser idiots they become.

'Watch the scene if you know what I mean—at a conference. At a conference, rest assured there'll be our uppity idiot there thinking he's a know-it-all as per usual. Only too happy to talk, but his words are unsubstantive drivel. He's the salesman with the counterfeit coat. He says what he needs to, to get over the line. There's the guy who *does* know everything or perhaps, a lot, but he gets talked over or is too nervous to articulate his thoughts properly. Then there's the standard guy knowing a standard amount. He says a few things to satisfy expected input. He keeps schtum the rest of the conference because he doesn't really care. All he thinks about is going home.'

Jim was hoping the talking idiot had just shut up.

He hadn't: 'I'm iconoclastic, not for the sake of being disruptive but to find absolute truth. Do not cave in to social influence or pressure.'

'I like to think I'm classy. Stay classy I always say,' said Meredith.

'Yea, and quite the lady you are too. You know I have studied the female. You hear a woman say "I love a bad boy," or the classic "I want a nice guy, but not too nice." This last example evinces that the woman has admirable intentions but that she ultimately cannot see past that time of the month where she seeks the dipstick.'

'No, some women just like dipsticks, it has zip to do with the time of the month.'

'You could well be right there, Mademoiselle Meredith. There is certainly something to say that tribal instincts play a part—where the woman looks for the aggressive man as it seems more credible that he could obtain the food to support her. It is the woman that can override these tribal instincts, and look for the bonhomous man, that is the best sort of woman. She realises what in this day and age are the truly important qualities in a man, and she has settled her volatile thoughts. Temperance in mind and action is irrefutably the way forward. The wise man looks at the fool and beats him over the head with wit.'

'I don't really know. I just look at it simply really. I just want a nice girl to treat me right. That is all I ask,' said Manny. Now Jim was really hoping the man in robes had become threadbare in his ideas for speech. Out came the needle.

'In basic terms, my message is: you go and get your bad boy, and when he starts hitting you or cheating on you, don't come back to me. The women like best the men that can forget they are in the company of women; the men that can be themselves as if with their male friends, without the less palatable parts of male banter of course. The modern woman seeks a certain type of balanced manliness. He must be quixotic but a realist, confident but not arrogant, emotionally intelligent but not a cry baby, strong but not violent, sexy over sweet…'

'Thanks Sage, what do I owe you for this advice? Huh?!' said Jim. Jim went kablooie. 'What makes you such a fucking expert?! Why is it you always think you know everything? You never ask, you always tell. We don't need your advice!'

Jim departed the picture. Sage turned to Martha, saying hushedly,

'Quite the bad boy it would seem, is that why you like him? Or is it his constant passive-aggressive attempt at machoism to make up for a lack of personality that rings your doorbell? Perhaps he is letting off steam from being the wrong end of Paul. I was just about to get on to talking about the female idiot; that is how you will turn out if you stay with him. Sometimes the most beautiful things have the most dangerous guises, and Jim isn't even beautiful. As for you, Martha, be a surgeon of your life. Draw where no-one has drawn before! Let me tell you one saving grace about your birdbrain, Jim. One day he'll realise what's really important in life. My only worry for him is that when that day comes, it may be too late.

Not long after, Martha found Jim by the entrance who had a present of words for her just waiting to be unwrapped:

'The next time Sage goes on like that, he'll be psychoanalysing my fist.'

Jim went back to his run-of-the-mill tent to be alone. Tucked away in the corner of Martha's corner of the tent was a pocket-sized browny-red book, before now unseen. Curiosity never killed anyone, said Jim's mind, and checking behind him that no-one was coming, he unveiled its contents. The writing was cut into paragraphs. It appeared to be a journal. Jim skimmed past its initial parts, and came across ready. He stopped near its back:

March 16th 2022

Jimbo just ignores me and makes me feel rotten.

… ignores my flirtations, oblivious to them. Perhaps he is being polite in acknowledging my having a partner. Either way, the more he ignores, the more of him I seek. Is it out of fear more than anything else? I wonder, when we hug for that extra moment longer than we should, if it means anything more to him.

Jimbo? She's never called me that in her life! thought Jim. Jim was benumbed by the affront to his ego. And who's this fucking dotdotdot character she so likes? Was it Manny, or someone else? Jim thought.

There was another passage Jim leafed through to. No date on it:

Why does he treat me this way? People say I should walk out on him. It's such a nice place and the people are so amiable, I can't leave. I'm tired, going to put this down now. I don't know. I just don't know anymore. I'm tired, I'm going to put this down.

It was time for Jim to put it down too, before it put *him* down.

#

'Just been to USA Nailstars,' said a young lady at the communal point, flashing her fleecy fingers.

'Where's that then?' questioned Meredith.

'Just off "Cherry" Street innit, then off Marple Street, then off Alton Close. Back up a bit and you go down a side road. Perry Drive I think it is. It's well cheap there. Good in all.'

'Oh Martha, I don't think you guys have met,' said Meredith. 'Let me introduce you. This is Hayley. She's a local resident, not far from where Sue lives. Hayley, this is our new friend here, Martha.'

Hayley, or 'the emotional bin bag' as some knew her, had been flung from street to street. She loved hanky pank and went many haunts to get it. It was more often than not at the hands of some douchebag. The douchebags loved that she was recyclable. They called her 'convenience store' because she was open 24/7. Her current status was: closed for refurbishment.

Deemed surplus to requirements, she has just left a ménage à trois in Spickswick.

Of this time, she pinned her memory. She fantasised her sighing could finish amongst a stack of bluebells, dandelions, forget-me-nots and daisies. Hayley couldn't help but be seen. There was so much orange about her as to be hard to tell what shade she naturally was. Chav— she wore that word like a badge of honour. Blusher, lipstick, eyeliner; she tried every trick in the book to paint the face with nothing behind it. Or was there? Somewhere behind the sunken eyes, new nails, masses of perfume, and chavtastic exterior as she liked to call it, lain something that many lacked or dismissed, that drove people to do some of the most brainless and beautiful acts: faith.

'Hi Martha, alright?' said Hayley, brushing off leftover nail dust on her sleeves from the manicure.

'I say she's new, but you've been here a while now haven't you,' said Meredith, turning to Martha.

'It's been over half a year now,' replied Martha.

'Has it really? Gosh, time *has* flown.'

'So anyway, I want it short, but not too short,' said Hayley. 'I mean last time she cut it the woman cut my hair too short. And she didn't cut it nice, you know what I mean? She wasn't all bad, she's been good before like, but it's money, you get me. I want it good for what I pay. I mean she's nice, we talk, but I want someone who can talk and cut good. Or just cut good, you feel me?'

'Yeah, when I next go I just want it medium-length, like last time, but I want to try purple highlights,' said Meredith.

'If everyone was hairless like me, barbers would be out of a job,' said Paul.

He was right, they probably would, thought Jim, which would make him even more of a tosser than he already was. To Jim, Hayley smelt of cheap lady. Acrid. But the world of ladies' perfumes and talcs is a world unknown to most men. Jim initially had thoughts to want to roger her, but then thought again of it lest he'd get too much of her on his pillow.

#

When the next day arrived, Jim knew he did not want to do it, but his thirst for information was inexorable. In the same corner of the tent, rummaging through Martha's pile, there it was. His inamorata had just plunged into a bowl of rolled oats in the kitchen. Jim could not face passing an eye over the rearmost parts of the journal again, and consequently fell back on the parts nearer the front:

December 20th 2021

I've gone past feeling depressed. I think I've suffered from depression without realising for a while now. I think this because every time a depressing thought is dismissed or diluted by reassurance, I'm only happy temporarily. By and by, another depressing thought comes along that my brain has searched high and low for, and replaces the old one. I feel like I'm stuck with this forever. I used to be happy all the time when I was a child :(I need to break the cycle. Help!

Peter was skimming rocks off *Horizon*. The lake was in places three fathoms deep. The priest that day at the local parish delivered a heterodox sermon, bifurcating opinion. Kind and caring, a man of good repute, the deeply pious priest had a dash of New Age about him. Hayley was present, as the priest, though not gay himself, relieved the precentor of his duties to allow for a collection of three gay or bi choir members to sing the focal section. One of the gays had to be fetched from a neighbouring townlet to make up the numbers. Hayley juggled her thoughts a tad and held her tongue. On present matters, her thoughts converged:

these people are ultimately going to hell but in the meantime, we don't judge. One of the singers was terribly off-key. Alternating like Birch Street's traffic lights were Hayley's thoughts: would you kindly think you could take your buggery elsewhere? Sodomites don't belong in the land of the living, certainly not in a church. Not in my church. Go back to Sodom. Gomorrah and gonorrhoea are linked for a reason.

On with the next reverberating hymn, and in harmony with the choir the other churchgoers sang, and in this case it was a mélange of faces somewhere between delighted and aghast…

All things bright and beautiful,
All creatures great and small…

The whole thing made as much sense to Hayley as shoplifting in a pound shop. No transgender people were present.

Christ the Redeemer! Deliver me from sin, she thought, and my forefathers from sin and these people from sin and please God find me a new church.

There was talk of the goings-on at the parish getting out to the local news. Of those congregated was a Malcolm Lithwaite. A doting ex-serviceman from Staffordshire, he was not averse to semi-clothing himself fortnightly like a tyrannosaurus rex. He made up his surname, just because. It hadn't occurred to Hayley, but she thought posher than her speech let on.

Anjit had been augmenting the decrease in natural ecosystems at the start of the church service, ripping out tree roots and plants near the vegetable patch, all the while assisting, in temporal history, the only virus to wear shoes.

'What are you doing?!' Jim asked, disconcerted.

'What?' replied Anjit, looking befuddled after a bit of screensaver mode.

'You can't just destroy the plants like that. What do you think the others would say if they saw you do that?'

'Trust you to give a shit. I didn't think you would care what they thought, *or* about the plants.' Jim knew Anjit's words were close to being a good point, but he toddled off to smoke a cigarette, happy with his good turn for the day.

Anjit was working on a few shade-tolerant yet half-hardy plants that looked more willing to sacrifice their subsistence. If starting to leaf they'd turn the other blade. With Anjit's digging, topsoil's mask slipped a teensy ants' nest.

'Meredith's on the mark. Sometimes instincts are the greatest teachers,' said Sage, surreptitiously surfacing, and who no-one knew was a big league entomologist, kneeling in admiration of his eusocial friends. Martha took after him. 'Be careful not to churn up the vegetation too much,' Sage continued. 'From a position of pain, we can transcend to a world of success. It's too easy to sit at home in a goodly armchair. This environment is difficult. It strives us on. Many successful people have overpassed extraordinary obstacles and started in difficult circumstances. Here, I want to make a success of myself, for once. How about you?'

Sage was careful not to make the fringes of his gooseberry-green overgarment unclean as he dug around to be useful.

'Define success…'

'Not right now Anjit, not right now.'

Jim was back in a flash. Incarcerating the skin he knew exquisite, like batter on cod he greasily clung on to his woman holding out by lilacs and lavenders in the sun.

At Jim, Martha held her gaze, steadfast, fair, asking. Martha was troubled. Her quandary this: Not quite at the first moment but soon after meeting Jim, and she didn't know why and what part of her it came from, but, it, that time, felt collectively better than all the dreams she ever had. An unawaked fantasia. If ever down, she'd only need think of him. Barry Supperquiz, though, has since gained ground in the dream stakes.

Like an appendix, Martha knew she was about but questioned her importance. Suffering the hour, she knew at least this: that she was to clamp down on upsetters.

Henceforth, people who made a king-size mistake with her were entitled to a second chance, but they sure as hell weren't given a third. She knew it a truth, just as the essence of fire is hunger. But there was one person for whom the rule was non-applicable—Jim; for love is a veil around reason.

Now she wanted to say how she felt. How the lover botched her contemplation. How he patronised and smothered her intelligence. How his social ineptitude and boorishness made her feel. How his bourgeoning belly and lack of care to change it repulsed her.

She wanted to, she could not. She loved him, and as with Chargergate she knew she would love him even more once he howled her down to unmask a cowering demoiselle.

A flock of pigeons were winging circularly and below there was worry a shit storm was on its way.

'I have to tend the vegetables,' the meditative artist said to the clinger.

#

Anjit later opened a bag of straw, strewing it over part of a soil bed. Martha cautiously plucked a carrot.

'Why do you use the straw?' asked Martha.

'The straw mulch keeps weeds out. I'm making holes in the straw for the bits I want to use. You could use paper too, like newspaper usually. All this straw also helps with water retention for the soil.'

'Cool.'

'The more we grow here, the less we'll have to rely on skipping.'

A sullen emerald wash from the still life of faraway hills adorned the vegetables in closer view. A tree breathed by the patch. Martha pulled up the left of her bobby socks. She watched the tree, how it crouched aground. In its lap was a nesting wren, newly deceased.

The trees by buildings and cars are looking much of a muchness, allied in nature with other English trees in a woodland glade, or the Sappanwoods of a Southeast Asian forest. The trees by buildings and cars are trying harder for their shot at bucolic mystery. The sun is prayerfully warming its fields of glory. The accouchement is over at long last. Aborning is a whatchamacallit, or possibly a thingamajig. Drops of water have started to feather over the ecovillage, and who knows whether by God and his shower, and whether His shower is a type of ablution, and whether He shepherded the incubation fragrant as honeysuckle. Revelation of her hour will not be bland.

Minds shaped by necessities given by the landscape, persistent weathers directing their outlook.

Saturday afternoon and the atmosphere has energy. Martha still has trees on her mind. Even though the upper part of the tree flails its arms, its base remains entrenched and uninterrupted by the weather or the passing of millions of cars.

Martha could see trees near at hand on hectic streets of London suburbia. Where are all these people going? Martha thought. She held a thought for each car that went by: maybe this girl's just come back from a brothel, maybe this guy's just come back from Turkey on holiday and is driving back from the airport, maybe this girl's just come back from a TED talk, maybe this guy's just a cunt and likes driving around for the sake of it. The truth was probably far less interesting. People were probably going to, or from, a job, or visiting friends, partners or relatives. But how can you ever really know?

'Why do they not teach gardening in every school? It could just be one lesson a week or month,' Martha said. With Anjit gone, Sage and Jim had joined her to break up thought.

'I wish children were taught to keep gardens in their hearts,' Sage said, 'watching love grow, chaining other gardens.'

Jim walked off.

'I can't take this guy anymore,' Jim said to Dave, walking past his wheelchair not far away. 'Someone please shoot Sage. From now on I'm just going to get away from him if he appears out from nowhere again.'

All Jim could think was Eric Soil. Mr Soil, as he was then known, was Jim's old headmaster. Soil had chapped lips and stunk of whisky. Wore twee jackets. Had humungous brown glasses and a zipped up forehead. He liked looking at the little boys and was far less cruel on the little lassies. On occasion, the never-assoiled Eric Soil could be seen at break times nodding off in his old banger listening to crooners.

Jim took a walk for fresher air. Kristoff was mounting a rock halfway between the brook and the Lilliputians, wanting to see if he could stand on its burred brims and not fall. Jim drew near him, arm-crossing, thinking of his lady in want, and how she drew better, and the meeting of their bodies this night.

'What you up to fella?' Jim asked Kristoff.

'Just balancing.'

'O yeah, 'cause that's normal for a fully grown man—balancing on a rock! Just joking with ya.'

'If I balance well, I believe life more balance.'

Over the next couple of days, news was soaking in. Somewhere in China a 131 mile per hour typhoon has slain hundreds of people, buggering up everything in sight.

In the land of politics, the front pages of British newspapers were giving an insight into a muckraking of the latest scandal in MP expenses.

'Have you heard those fucking Tories have pumped millions into non-renewable energy sources again?' said Manny, a whiff of ink greeting his nostrils. A jejune afternoon in early May, he was giving the once-over to the middle pages of a Leftist newspaper in the ramshackle kitchen.

'It's probably to help their business friends,' said Kristoff.

'And some more MPs, Tories in the large, have been thieving money again. With all this talk of new legislation supporting non-renewables, GreenNinjas have already started talk of a protest. Are you up for going if they do?' Kristoff screwed the lock on his money box, gazing archly ahead.

'I'm always ready.'

Hearsay spread like wildfire in the camp. About was a Leftist smog in thinking, that the Tory cabinet belonged in filing cabinets; that superintended cash cows had been injected with fat powder, grouped and bound on gravy trains to no placer. Manny shed a tear.

'A fine idea young moose!' exclaimed Sage in the kitchen once he heard. 'Upheaval is what is needed. Irrespective of what GreenNinjas do, let us expostulate and exercise our right to freedom of assembly!' The speaker really was in ebullient form. Teeth snappish, cheeks round and full.

Not a million miles away, Dave and Jim were confabulating through shared smoke.

'I think if Martha's not going then it would be good for me to go on this protest. Clear my head.'

'Mm-hmm,' said Dave.

'The thing is, we just haven't been the same since that argument.'

'Which one?'

'The big one.'

'K. Could do you some good then.'

'Yeah. I need space.'

The politicising gerrymandering centrist-searching psephologically-sucking filibustering fuckheads, thought no-one. Manny cooked liver and onions for dinner, and exasperated sighed for his thoughts. The onion: the vegetable with so much extra baggage. If it is not the layers you have to peel, it is the tears it makes you cry.

Earlier Manny read something on the GreenNinjas Website:

> *The Earth is 4.6 billion years old. Let's scale that to 46 years. We have been here for 4 hours. The Industrial Revolution began 1 minute ago. In that time we have destroyed more than 50% of the Earth's forests.*

CHAPTER NINE

M eredith and Martha's connection had advanced great guns, intertwisting. As Meredith tried hard to love, Jim spoke,

'I'm worried my missus is becoming a lezza, especially since the face painting and body painting between them has intensified.' Anjit and Dave owned the ears that Jim was arousing outside the compost toilet. 'Did I just say missus? Mrs Moyles, God that's a scary thought.' Best to leave that one on the backburner, thought Jim.

Before long, this spring everyone had been calling Martha and Meredith, 'M&M.'

The nametag created muddlement when Manny and Martha were in collaboration; another blossoming association.

Spring had come tardily this year. With snow falling 'til late March, an eruption of ornithological activity was currently, and would continuously deafen the community many mornings. The recent years had seen a liquidation in the manner of a piecemeal phasing out of wildlife; the ones that remained gingerly jutted out their homes. With delayed creature activity and unusual weather patterns, this year word had it, humans were to blame.

'Right then, when we get to central London, if it gets busy, we go single file,' said Manny at the communal point station to those that wanted to protest.

Single file? What is this, a school trip? thought Jim.

Parliament Square. Amassed were a roundup of stones almost as distinguished as cobble, and some early rainwater had them slidable. Now the water came no more. Eastward from here were a few vagabonds—two men and one woman, before whom Jim deftly bowed his head.

'Guys'—he began, and as he did so he realised he was about to state one of those things that you would really be quite uncomfortable about stating, yet commencement held sway for its completion—'we're trying to have a protest here.'

The woman and one of the men had a dual look of endurance that said they could outlive an ice age. The other man, liquor-eyed, had a bunchy body and a head the shape of a tangerine.

'Pardon?' said the first-described man, mystified.

'Yes yes I'm sorry, we have to do this here,' said Manny.

Jim felt like a human flyswatter. Just then, a pullulating loudness made sense. Spotted the GreenNinjas group coming from around the corner in their hundreds, maybe more.

'Why didn't we just join the GreenNinjas lot in the first place?' asked Jim. 'It would have saved us a lot of bother.'

'Never mind the past,' said Manny. 'Let us now combine forces.'

As the GreenNinjas detail arrived there was an almighty din.

Give us back our money
Give us back our land

Some of the placards had this wordage, and it was to be the main chant for the day.

'I can't hear myself think,' Anjit said.

'This is massive!' Cathy screamed. 'I could never 'ave expected this.'

Television crews and police got into the spirit of things.

'Where's Martha?' asked Peter.

'Oh, she didn't come,' said Jim. 'Said something about it being too loud or something. I don't know, I wasn't really listening.'

The hours ran, and with each hour that passed, the protesters became prideful and stately.

Nighttime and the others would be back soon, but not yet. Martha in hypervigilance whisked her figure in the strawberry air near soft-gloomed *Lake Horizon*. Up on a high from the spectral penumbra, a plane above winked in timely rhythm, aiding starlight. A hyena's call would not be heard amidst London's busyness, and to Martha such event could only pass in the trappings of a netherworld.

The begetter of independent union only sated in this moment by visions of faraway mountains is hiding from the voices of uniform minds. Chasséing while reacquainting herself with loss, the fire is lit and ascending are whispering embers from the first third of May.

#

'That fucking horse,' said Jim. 'If only she loved me as much as that fucking horse, none of this would have happened. Bucking, fucking Benji.'

Equine bastard.

'None of what would have happened?' asked Dave, an embryonic spring evening in May, in a no-man's land, perhaps, of ecovillage grass.

'Fucking hell. She couldn't even tell it to my face. Why does it always'—Jim looked up bearing teeth at the sky—'happen to me?!' Dave looked down to espy an envelope in Jim's hand. 'The fuck's wrong with her? Writing a letter. What are we in the 1920s for fuck sake?! What a splotchy mess! It looks like something out of the Dark Ages.'

With the use of a disobedient fountain pen, the face of the envelope was filled with ink and nerves. Jim managed to be thrown by his own actions in bothering to tuck the letter back into the envelope. Infuriated, he smacked it down and tramped away to safe ground. Anjit found Dave and retrieved the letter for him. The letter in Anjit's cupped hands passed to Dave's on this, the evening of the day after the protest. Wheeling his way towards his uncluttered tent, Dave opened the envelope. There was the candlelight, there was the letter. In his tent to himself, Dave puffed out his cheeks, burning the midnight oil to bury himself in hemp-based paper:

Dear Jim,

I wasn't sure how to start this. We both know things between us haven't been so great, particularly recently. It's simply not the same as when we first met. When you helped me up onto Benji, I looked into your eyes. All soppy I was by Benji's whinny. I'll never forget that moment. That we will find love here, it's written in the night - remember that poetic line I wrote you? We used to say I & U are pals before vowels.

You never listen to me anymore. It's all about you Jim.

You just ignore things. You have to be cold like polar icicles. You don't know why, you just have to be. I certainly don't know why, why you keep up the cold front.

I don't feel confident around you, so much so that I couldn't even say any of this to you face to face. We don't talk enough and I find it hard to. Recently if we do, we just disagree or argue.

The fact that you just went off on that protest knowing that I'd be left here only goes to show how different we are. You can just forget and carry on, and it makes me wonder what you think a relationship is. I think the wavelengths we're on are tragically different. I can't just forget, nor do I want to. Maybe I am too emotional but that's just me.

I'm owning my emotions better right now, but who knows how I'll be tomorrow. Since we've been here I've never really felt like you've wanted to be here.

You're so negative and it brings me down. This was just a start, Jim. I was hoping we could maybe go on to an eco smallholding or something like that in due time, but you never really bought into the whole experience and I can't just ignore and pretend things are all right anymore.

Jim, you do have good qualities, and I love you, but since we have been here you have changed. It's made me feel displaced, yet my heart wants to be here. I can't carry on like this. I'm sorry, but I think we should have a break. I know we're both here so I'm not sure how we're going to live together, but maybe we can find a way.

I'm sorry,
Martha

Martha wanted it succinct and not too newsy, and that was how she had it. She was feeling seraphic and couldn't help it. The mouth of her river less unclear, jets of water hopped to serenade shallows. Archangels, those supernal attendants of God, she felt, had granted her a lift to ballast. She figured that if Jim couldn't fill in the rest of the letter for her then it was his problem. It was one of the rare instances Martha had done something that turned out just how she planned.

Martha bewept as she remembered Benji, that day. The night of the day she met Jim she pictured pictured pictured: she was crying in love, in his melody streaming ten thousand seas of tears, at her knees exploding under the moon. She felt so unstable she could have died in love that night. The day after, with her,

Jim was unfeeling, and she wondered if he was worth her pain.

Recently they were cohabiting robots, fresh out of things to say and ideas to dream with. This is what Jim thought, though not in those words. Unzipping a little slower each time, they were *fucking* trimonthly, making love once a fortmonth. When games of hide the sausage between these animate beings took place, Martha felt like the racehorse with the blinkers on, hanging on grimly for the finish line. She had struggled with so many sighs to allow for the new Jim.

High time for a break. A fissure in a rocky union. A time to realise he was not her and she was not him.

Back one hundred minutes.

Martha was creeping towards her thin home. Tonight she will leave the earthly canvas and paint amidst the stars. What will it be like to leave someone, first, for the first time ever? The missive written, concertinaed, enveloped, sealed, wax-stamped to be sure. In her practical world, everything was just so. She had made a list of all the things she was going to say to him and another for all the things she was going to say behind his back. Depression just left her here. With a motionlessness the fiercest cup of coffee couldn't budge, like an attention seeker too anxious to receive attention, a lamenter too ratty for remedy, she simply wanted a hug. How dandy it would be for someone to drop by who could read her emotions just by seeing into her without Martha needing to say a jot. Sadly, like genetically modified men, mind readers that were consistently accurate didn't exist yet, and even if they did you'd have to pay the bastards.

Would jailbait portend emotional seppuku? At the coup de grâce, she wanted not a sole on hand.

Martha thought that however things were for her, they were worse for worse-for-wear Jim. She knew he'd take it badly; the question was just *how* bad.

Minutes quickstepped to the yawning part of evening, where it could be set.

A dragon's inferno. He loved, she loved, all of the same breath. Dragon got hosed.

Dave, having asked Anjit to leave his side for matters of privacy in his tent, would gawk at his old pal Jim for as long as required.

Jim had forgotten how to talk. It felt a lot different to when Paul couldn't to chuggers in the street. Jim could only squeak bordering on a meow. Dave pored over Jim. Neither man had a woman, both had pornography. Swarthier than usual given the time, looking like flagging bodyguards, Anjit was sluggishly sharing his shisha pipe with Cathy outside Dave's tent.

'I don't know,' said Jim, desperately cramming baccy into a cigarette paper. 'I just don't know what to do.' Devil's hair—Martha thought it—every clump of tobacco looked a shrivelled-up spider and Jim fucking hated spiders, especially the one Martha made him extract at 5 a.m.

Enter filter tip, clumsily lay down.

'I feel for yer,' said Dave the confidant.

'It didn't have to end this way. Not now. Not in the least. God, I wasn't expecting this.'

When Martha first found Jim, back in the day, Jim was just so amazed anyone wanted to go near his body parts. She had written 'of curse' instead of 'of course' while texting him about meeting up sometime. Whether it was an accident or a harbinger, Jim thought he better go and meet with her, and meet with her, he did, motoring to her side with imperishable gusto. The next text he read in his questionable life was from Martha. She just texted to say, 'I Love you xxx.' As he registered it, with each letter he passed, his heart felt closer to the hilt. Feelings preparatory to thought. The greatest power to defy logic, he couldn't be rid of it— love. It comforted every muscular twitch; tides of blood sweeping through his makeup. A Jim of new conformation and design. That she was made up too— no-one else could know unless they too had seen love's rhythms of change.

'I found her journal,' said Jim.

'Oh?'

'Yeah, not long back. There were one or two disturbing details in there but nothing I thought I needed to worry about; how wrong I was. It wouldn't surprise me if Manny has his dirty hands in all this.'

'Guess we'll never know.'

'No.'

The romance of day could never be simplistic, but they met a simple day. Martha had found him, but now she knew him. A nightmare on grass. A horror of horrors. Every cavern, cove, tunnel explored. Jim felt the nightmare in his paunch like a zap from the ray gun. His intentness took a deflection. 'Who are they for?' Jim asked, glancing at a box of prophylactics by Dave's bedside.

'Just in case.'

'Ah.' Jim gave a smile that relaxed the both of them.

'You wazzock!' they could hear Paul bark eighty metres away, accompanied by a choir of laughter. Jim felt like Paul was talking about him. Underserving and star-crossed by the Gods, Martha and now Jim had reckoned themselves.

'I'm done here, mate,' said Jim. 'Let's face it, I was only here 'cause Martha was anyway. I don't know, it's touch and go. It's good with *you* here and that, but I might just go back to Greenwich.'

'Give it time,' said Dave.

'Suppose. Bloody hell, she thinks I neglected her when we went on the protest. She seems to think that I moved on, that I didn't think about her. She hasn't given me a chance, man. It's like she hasn't even bothered talking about anything, any problems we've been having. She just writes me a letter, then…that's it.'

'Seems a bit rash.'

'Women all over for you, mate. They're just a big bag of hormones.'

'Hmm.'

'What a mess. I don't know what to do. What should I do with myself? Just want to fuck something up,' said Jim, rolling another.

'I've got a copy of *The Right is Right* I've been meaning to burn for a while. I was just looking for the right occasion. We could firebomb *that* if you like.'

'Firebomb—I like the sound of that. Good plan.'

Jim counted two flies schmoozing by candle-flame, and discharged despair in the form of a sigh. Jim too could fly but only on underwings. He remembered

Martha liked to sigh too. 'Maybe it just wasn't meant to be.'

'Maybe.'

'What do you think?'

Jim just had to ask, for where there was chance there was hope. Martha's reprieve would be, to Jim, like looking at bijoux reflecting discoloured iron pyrites.

'I'm not sure,' said Dave. 'I am less close to her now. For some reason.'

'Yeah, she's probably jealous of how I've gotten to know you better than she ever did.'

'A nice girl but she has seemed less happy…'

'Yes she has,' a mysterious voice said, seeping through the tent flaps. It lingered in the dark, it was soft and peachy. It was Peter. 'Pity really. Such a bright young thing,' he said, throwing back the mesh in so doing admitting nature's nose more room. Peter pawed a stein on the table. This done, he pointed his hand toward a bottle of cordial—'May I?'

Dave nodded him in.

In the meanwhile, in Meredith's bender Martha cuddled up to her host. She was a thought-severed sleepyhead.

'It seems so alien,' said Martha.

'What does, honey?'

'Not being with him. Singledom. The whole thing.'

'I hear you.'

'I have come to realise that there are those men I quite fancy, but I um and ah as to whether I really head-over-heels fancy them. These types of men can grow on you and you could end up having a great relationship with them, and love them, and they would love you back. But there is another batch, perhaps 0.2 percent of men that can send me head over heels right from the off. I could fall in love with them and stay that way for life. No qualms. To settle for anything less would be fibbing to myself.'

'Pay it no mind. You're tired. Don't try to make sense of it all now, sweetie.'

Meredith kneaded and scrunched Martha's wrigglers.

Martha bowed her head and squalled in an unshielded yet delicately artful way. A mortal ocean spray, Martha, only, could cry this way. After all, Jim was the one who introduced her to saag paneer, pizza toast, (and vegan spam by accident.)

'I feel lost,' said Martha.

'O honey,' replied Meredith, and she pulled Martha in a little tighter.

'I feel bad, I've just dumped someone.'

'You definitely did the right thing. He wasn't right for you.'

Feeling like the nuclear warhead for Martha's missiles, Meredith's grip became swampish. 'I'm here now. I'm here. I know it's difficult, but I think somewhere down the road, you'll know he wasn't for you. Why don't you rest your weary head and sleep here tonight.'

'Why couldn't he just say, "you're not mental, you're beautiful." Why could he never tell me I was beautiful?'

'I know hun, I know.'

The new dialectic in Martha's brain was about how there are in actuality thousands, possibly millions out there more suited to us, and yet love traps us into thinking there is only one. After crying, she felt the endorphins rise in her palette. She was nearly sick everywhere, crying so hard from the dispute in her mind. Love hurt when it went wrong. That's why Burt played 'FootieTeam Manager' so he didn't have to deal with all this shit.

Martha gyrated down the six-foot mattress. Meredith pulled the covers over the two of them, nuzzling attentively against Martha's occiput. 'You can stay here for as long as you want,' said Meredith. She bade Martha goodnight, and…what was that, that followed? Was it a tongue? Could Martha feel a tongue and an underlip with waterless grooves sensually playing with her teeny neck hairs? Surely, if so, it was all a bit too friendly to be friendly.

As this was going on, Peter, in his night-dark tailcoat was monopolising the tent of Dave.

'Were you there all that time? How long have you been outside the tent?' asked Jim.

'Not long. I have better things to do than play the eavesdropper.'

'That was creepy the way you did that.'

'Jim, I know you're suffering.' Peter reached in his upper coat pocket for his silky brown glasses cloth that reminded him of milk chocolate. 'I was sorry, truly, to hear about you and Martha. Please let me know if there's anything I can do,' he said, removing bits of day caught on glass.

'Thanks…it's hard. I don't know what anyone could say or do.'

'Dave has been good to you, I'm sure.'

Dave smiled.

'Of course,' Jim said.

'How is Martha?' asked Peter.

'I don't know.'

'I see. She has seemed sadder for some time, poor girl. What with her inner minefield, one wonders half the time if she is all compos mentis. Her height belies her little nature. Poor Martha. Such a sweet, sweet girl. Sweet things ought to be caressed.'

'Right,' said Jim.

There was an awkwardness in everything. 'I also haven't been great lately,' stated Jim.

'I feel for you, I do,' said Peter. 'Breaking up is a horrible business. But if I could impart a word of advice, and I have never known my advice to disserve its clients, it is that not everyone liked how you spoke about Martha, or even *to* Martha. It is wise to talk differently depending on whom you talk to. Goodnight.' Peter swung his coat away from the tent with a flourish like it was an adventurer's cape.

'Who's he think he is? Prick,' Jim with brusqueness said to Dave. Bifocaled twat thought Jim.

Burt was engaging in sexual congress with a young lady of the night. He was having a whale of a time. For her, it was like a chest of drawers falling on top of her with the key stuck in the lock. The whale however was reaching unsafe waters!

Christ, I cannot get it up, he thought. Maybe I am too fat?! The blood isn't flowing like it did! But I am too young. It must be nerves, but I'm not a nervous person. Come on penis, work! Guilt and shame are taking over. Come on you prick, I'm paying good money for this.

Burt had not taken into account that it may have been the female he was plugged into that diffused him. He settled for heavy petting.

'You smoke your reefa like a drug addict,' said Dave, back at his tent. 'You smoke it like you're desperate for that next toke and look worried when it's running down. People only have problems when they disrespect. You need to respect the drug, listen to its effects on your body. Don't give yourself to the drug like that, man, let it come to you.'

Dave had a bit less Dave about him. Add a bit of rosy, add a bit of green and Bob's your stoned uncle. Dave's parents would not have been impressed. Jim was not too impressed either—who is he to tell me?…but Jim put the joint to his lips and after a few puffs all was forgiven. They had a drug hug.

'There's something about living on the edge,' said Jim, and a certain Aerosmith song made waves in his head. The immediateness of aural jubilation he once knew in the song had since been terminated. He had heard that song seventy-nine times according to his music playlist and it was sure to be more. The first time is love at first sight; at the seventy-ninth lies a sliver of pain. To enmesh life's wonder again as a mid-thirty something, Jim discovered, was no mean feat. Maybe that's why people take up extreme sports, he thought. Dave liked to fill the kettle over the max line to keep things interesting. Never to be advised for reasons of safety, never to be the first of the gang to die. Jim wasn't sure. Shit all. Just to be at the commune symbolised a sidled step in life.

Everything was a bit too easygoing here for Jim, though. His muscles were aching for a ruckus. He wanted to be in, or preferably create something a little more 'ready.' Anarchism for the ungovernable—yes! He thought that up himself. 'I wanna fuck something up, create some chaos,' he said. 'Everyone and the government can do one.'

You devil you! replied his brain. Sage walked past, having seen and smelt the ganja.

'Self-discipline via restraint is one of the most important life skills a man can bring to bear,' he said before carrying on past them.

On Sage, Jim was beyond caring. Unbeknownst to Sage, behind those clothes after all, he did look a bit like Eric Soil.

Soil you mug, is that really you? thought Jim

'Dave, fetch me *The Right is Right*,' said Jim. 'Or tell me where it is and *I'll* get it. I don't want to involve anyone else. Too many knob'eads about.'

Burt and his woman seemed otherwise occupied in their one-sided love nest. An uncosseted Fred could no longer look Burt in the eye.

'Did you buy that?' Jim asked, *The Right is Right* now in Dave's lap.

'God no. Found it on a train.'

They burned the shit out of it. Trampling its charred remains underfoot, stamping out any right-wing messages, stoning it amid the stoned laughter, and who, and in what capacity, did he or she or they or it have the last laugh?

Jim was annoyed that all sorts of things you never think about buying or running out were running out, like vinegar and multivitamins. Pissed and broken, the dying ashes of the night snagged Jim's throat as he sunk a cigarette far too deep into his lips, inhaling and spinning, colliding with reality. All only served to make him more hopeless.

Dave was kind of right, Jim thought. That's the problem right there with smoking. You smoke the cigarette, get a bit of a head rush and a buzz, and then you're still left with all the same problems you had before you put the cursed thing in your mouth, only with added lung deposits.

Jim was so addicted by now that head rushes were a thing of distant memory; not that they ever were that great. Jim was a sacked town, a disowned clown, a giant red spot in an orbit of puss.

Jim thought back to when he helped Martha onto that steed of discontent. Jim was now a stowaway in Martha's upper pocket; she was now utter survival, disused, disarmed, landlocked, *his* Jesus Christ. He wasn't going to let her forget how he could make her smile.

An infiltration of one's own inner time: chills from a tawny owl's call and with the fact that discursive thought was stalling, that imageries were less palpable and mingling with greys, Jim knew he should probably get to sleep. An air bed was there by a resting Dave.

Sleep for a few hours, Jim—his greenhouse mind let slip—just for a few hours, when the tent fabrics will sprout new light.

Martha got to sleep that night in the peignoir she never wore. In the night, asleep, her friend wrapped around her like a matte black thread on a spool.

She awoke in the position Meredith kissed her in, frozen by indecision in what to say or do, believing the garment's rare appearance a mistake.

#

Jim palmed the snaking air, imagining it was a downdraught, and in there, somewhere, collected a thought for morning.

'Maybe I should take up men for a while,' he said to Dave. 'Then again, who's to say *they* will like me.' Traversing the width of Dave's tent outside it, Jim incipiently questioned his ideas of machoism. Mud was looking angry below. Jim could not think because his head had now completely separated from the rest of him. He looked like a Gugelhupf.

Now his body liked being carried by the flock, the follower without thought. It was like being pissed near exposed wires.

In cities, to Jim, people seemed to get on more with things but here people had more time for second looks. Those extra little glances of bits of persons, forming the sum of parts that made new loves. Jim gave extra, lurid stares to the women that reminded him of Martha. Even for the ladies that did not notice, those trips to the bank or the fast food joint would never be the same again.

'Imogen, how's things?' Martha said to her phone in the sunlit fields. Erring on the side of caution, her hand covered her mouth with the goal of making her think that she would less likely be heard. Seemingly however, no-one was near.

'O ya everything's amazeballs sweetheart, turns out my cousin's a total nutjob and tried to burn the kitchen down after that soirée, but anyhoo how are you?'

'Im…things have got really weird here. You know how upset I've been recently, and after the letter and everything? Crikey. As it stands I can barely even mutter Jim's name. Meredith was being really nice, consoling me. The next thing I know, she had her tongue all over my neck. I think I even heard her trying to sniff me. It got really, really weird, Imogen, I just don't need this shit right now.'

'Ya ya, that's sooo awks. My word, what is up with that girl?! I never trusted her from what you told me. Sorry not sorry. Too up herself, like, seriously, just because she used to be in fashion school. Hello?! She brags about her culture just 'cause she's changed her life around, and now she thinks she rules the roost or something, and what's with all her flanter? Whatevs. Are you thinking of coming home? That would be funarrific. We think you should, you absolute beaut, we miss you Martha.'

'I don't know. I want to stay here, it's just awkward now around Meredith, and Jim of course. I still love it here but find myself trying to eschew the two people I've been closest to.' Martha slunk. She had a new sigh. 'It's iffy with Manny too, we don't even bother talking anymore. I just want a bikini body and a guy who's not a twat. Anyway, I'm going to buy a new tent. A fresh start. The old tent Jim and I shared is just left like a forgotten memory. I can't go back there. I think he lives in Dave's tent now. It will be nice to have a space just for me.'

'Ya-*ya* ya ya. That sounds goo…an…leapin' lizards… but…tha…I'm g…'

'Im? Im you're breaking up.' The phone went dead. That made three people break up in a week.

#

Just another night post-Martha, Jim gave some time for his thoughts: I'm so alone I can't believe I'm not dead from rejection. Picking up my life with a rake, parts slip through to the sod. Sod, yes, that's what I am. And I can't afford a spade, well, not a decent one that wouldn't break after five minutes.

Recalling a trip to west Wales with Martha, he speculated now of the sight at that beach.

He is led out to see
the spumy waves as white as a wedding dress,
tonight the Irish Sea shall wave a little graver
her frost-white tips reach
a shoreline rubbed up by a pungent beauty.
Simple, melancholic dark. Unconscious,
Martha's dishevelled dreams to Jim's.

Sandy mucoid particles sprinkle to eye-cornered beaches…

Jim is lying awake in a bout of insomnia. You know *who* is on his mind. Her simulacrum pulls him under and the earth becomes him. The earth becomes Jim aside from his sense of self. He cannot fall asleep because he has to keep awake for the one he watches. He clothes her in his heart, her each and every cell. He tends to her like the mother robin her nest. There are keening calls within from her young, as well you might imagine: get a good visual picture.

'No. I don't want to. Don't tell me what to do,' say you.

The cure for Jim's parched lips he knows of is a cigarette, and he loved how David Bowie told him that time took it for him. The product for the chancer!

The goddamn cigarette packet bloodthirstily bewitches Jim from inside his coat pocket as an aeroplane whishes by. With not a moment's more thought, Jim pulls back the air bed covers. He gets to his feet with swift manoeuvre.

He finds himself in autopilot mode: to Jim, rolling a cigarette is like putting on a seatbelt.

The tobacco companies parade their chauffeurs. A ticker tape parade; actual ticker tape, and confetti. They watch Jim pack tight the cigarette in preparation. It was only right since nicotine asked him ever so nicely. There still could be no room for thought. Jim took the rolled prize to his lips and his face washed out in nighttide.

Out to opaque soundless fields. It was something that the land was drier than last night's. Jim lit up and anthropomorphised his cigarette for Martha. Knowing Martha didn't like cigarettes, the more he smoked the more she disintegrated in his earth. He became sore about previous immobilised thought.

O hang on, he was getting ahead of himself as there cantered a fresh thought. False alarm. A thought started but forgot itself before Jim could decipher it. His cigarette three-quarters done, in him deeply embedded Martha.

What Jim thought a lolloping hare was in fact something dancing in his far far vision. A westering grey pattern not slowing any. Just a honey grey. Deep deep greys coming out windswept as though a mini cyclone of deep grey dancing, stretching, mushrooming, polishing off terrain in its wake, paining, swooshing, all the while dancing. Hark! Felling grass, the dense grey bank of power monstrous-becoming, giving no quarter, claiming the land as far back as the hillside of Meredith and Martha's autumn talkfest. Rock 'n' rolling, manic trees guffawing, thumping in the breaking wind, so bold the wind…

Turn back Jim! Turn back, he thought he heard his mother's voice say. But he had to play the night watchman, for thought's sake.

You go back without me, thought Jim, I'll see you on the other side.

The picture in front of Jim is that from a painter doodling a picturesque artwork in a mental asylum. Wind. Steaming, terrorising the land, tearing up the fallen grass—the weather's martyrs. Curses! The wind is so hearty Jim's ears feel like they would in the high-up aeroplane: about to pop. Whistle of wind, punishing wind, anti-hopscotch wind. Jim is trying to snuff something different than the inundating freshness. It enters his palette like a million fans around him, drying his stupid tongue. Ablaze with paraesthesia, his hands are booby-trapped from the force of fury.

Turn back Jim!

He cannot move his legs for they are bulging with fright, submerged are they in a wizened face of mud. In the punchy wind, blowing hither and yon, Martha's energy has decamped. Jim mind has gone walkies. His eyes and nose are streaming. He looks ridiculous. And what was that, the irate wind said?! What does it say, Jim?!

A crusty tenor voice darker than Ivan the Terrible's insides rasped through the country lanes, forests, meadows, *Horizon*, up the fields, brook and rill:

'Back to your chamber Jim,' said the voice. 'Back to your chamber!!'

A long, long way away, there was what sounded like some kind of conveyor belt or a horizontal pulley scratching across the ground at breakneck speed. Jim was face down on the ground as if prostrating himself before the great unknown. Ping! Little tinkling bells in Jim's mind forewarned him of how he at first in mind risked sinking as though in dreaded quicksand! Wind's whip hand lassoed Jim's stringy head of hair, hefting him backwards toward the tent. He realised how tilted his thinking had been of late and how it all lay either adrift or in tatters from nature's way. He could move again. The noise was getting louder, rending the air. Bumbling backward, he scrabbled the ground amid the ear-piercing scratching sound, against the yowling wind, straight-standing once more, buckling once more, backwardly entering the tent by a secondary lasso and heave.

NOW HE WAS THINKING!!! Have I just seen the mysterious fog??? Am I going quite mad?!!

His hand quaking, Jim bit by bit, in jolted twists barely opens the water bottle and pours it on his hands, plashing the face replete with panic. He cannot get a taste like corked wine out of his mouth. It is the taste of mortality diluted with distress.

'Dave! Dave!! Wake up!'

'Banquet of flesh!' shouted Dave, mid dream.

After Dave's convulsive call out, Jim can hear the lunatical wind in his head yet he cannot hear a soul outside it. He feels what the English call rubbish, Americans, garbage, the band Suede, trash, and New Englanders, sculch.

Bleary Dave was coming to his senses. 'What? What's up?' he asked, feasting his eyes on Jim in carcass form.

'It's gone now! It's gone! But it was so powerful! So bloody powerful. I'm barely intact, Dave. I can still hear it ringing in my ears! You didn't see it? You didn't hear the wind?'

'I haven't heard anything, just you, waking me up.'

'Man that was insane. Either I'm going nuts or something lopsided's just happened. What Paul spoke about—the mysterious fog! I think I just saw it! I shit you not.'

'What? Come on.'

'I'm serious!'

'You woke me up because of *that*?'

'Dave, why will you not believe me?'

'This is ludicrous.'

'Dave!'

Dave closed his eyes on the pillow.

'Paul was winding us up while he was sozzled,' said Dave. 'I can't think any more about this. I'm off back to sleep. You should go to sleep too.'

Jim was milk on the turn. Miffed that Dave did not believe him, he worried about his sanity and whether The Gren had it in for him. And what was that voice? From where did it come? Paul never mentioned anything about a voice.

#

On grass outside Meredith's bender tent, as Martha set to crafting a wind chime it was as though her widening smile was encased in unbreakable glass. This effulgent day, Meredith was closing in on her.

'That's really nice,' said Meredith. Martha could not dismiss her belief that Meredith was very near the back of her shoulder.

'The last one I gave to Burt. I'd like to sell this and make some others to sell on an Etsy account, along with some artwork,' said Martha, turning lickety-split to Meredith, but a bite had been taken out from the former's wide mouth.

'That's lovely honey. I'm going to teach you how to crochet someday too.'

'Thanks, I appreciate it.'

'You are very welcome.'

Martha couldn't believe the conversation that just came about, and everything felt less uncomfortable the more dialogue there was. It was as though, between them, nothing had ever happened.

At times catachrestic, an unbound sketchiness used to colour Meredith's verbal style before the playground browbeating relented. It was at home where she gleaned the joyous escapism of knitting and crochet through her mother.

A hammer broke through the glass around Martha. It came to light, in her yo-yo mind, that her workings were incommensurable, and the clinking of the chime somehow mislaid the dignity of its expected tone.

'This will never sell,' said Martha. 'What a waste.' Her dolour was plain to see.

'It's A-OK. It happens. All part of the learning curve. I don't think it's that bad.'

Martha's mind was not about to go stale!

No Martha, I won't have it, she thought to herself. In the case of the wind chime, and indeed, in any event, if a human being has successfully done something before, it follows that I've a damn good chance too.

Martha sat happy with her new mantra. Fred the hound dashed about between the tents with fanaticism, but nobody saw why. What was it that so excited the quadruped?

Jim had nothing to give the world today in his head-fuck malaise. A stormy nightmare and its grey composition stayed over for the day at the base of Jim's skull, dragging like an anchor, sinking at the jowls. Jim had in front of him spine-weathered books that smelt of old people. Their covers were engraved with handwriting marks having been props for writing materials by his lost lover's hand. If he were to look very closely he would be able to see portions of old journal entries, but Jim was Jim so he never bothered. For the days and nights that followed, pizzas, Chinese takeaways, Indian takeaways and Old Fashioneds secured Jim outside of existing. He was buying party food with no party.

Cocktail sausages, chicken nuggets, vol-au-vents, mini pizzas, stupid little parcels of salmon, pork scratchings, beef jerky, mountains of cheesy puffs, scotch eggs, pistachios to remind him of his old mate, and fairy cakes as a last course. Padlocked with no person the key, was there anything in the story of karma that could emancipate his bondage? Jim, unsure had his body take him to doze.

In dreamville, Jim was back to his new favourite subject matter. He dreamt her a picture. In the picture were beautiful flowers Jim did not know the names of but had seen somewhere in a garden centre. Martha was painted lying naked. Her breasts looked in high spirits. Jim rearranged his trousers. That was better.

For the rest of the afternoon it was all hands to the pump. Jim was the archetypal wanker. The one-a-day wanker. There's always the quiet wanker; he wanks with the speed of the Japanese bullet train. No-one will ever know about the female wanker. Jim was back at the old tent he had shared with Martha to help him get in the feel of things. Moreover, it was dicey trying to find a private moment in the tent of Dave. It felt weird to be back. Almost ghostly.

In the olden days he could feel superhuman, for all it was worth, but how times have changed for irresolute Jim. He began looking forward to helping out Death scything crops in the world beyond. That was—wondered Jim—what Death used his scythe for, right?

As yet, Martha had managed to avoid her old flame but the avoiding game with Manny was over. The afternoon had one foot in the grave. Floundering in the kitchen, in searching for her pots and pans and cooking instruments and cutlery and crockery, Manny caught Martha, alone.

'I was truly sorry to hear about you and Jim. I never wanted that to happen.'

'Thanks,' replied Martha.

'I'm sorry I haven't spoken to you much in recent times. I've been preoccupied and forgot about the ideas that we talked about for trying to improve this place. If you feel up to it then let me know and we can start talking about it again.'

'Sure. I'm not thinking too straight at the minute.'

'It's OK, I know. Just let me know. I'll see you around.'

#

Days passed. Martha let them. One evening, Martha, while she hazarded a guess that she could never be accused of being a mindful woman peeped through a hole in Meredith's bender to make out Fred. He was curveting and running in circles hopped-up. Fred and Burt lived quite near Meredith. Meredith had gone to bring Martha some beans on toast from the kitchen, partially to bide Martha some time in her semi-hiding from Jim. Martha could just descry the Pomeranian from the backlight of Burt's laptop. Burt's gleaming mop of mustard hair introduced itself to the scene. Frolicsome Fred barked.

'Skedaddle you shit!' yelled Burt. In hushed ire the stout owner with ease of manner appeared to injure Fred before the pretty yelper could get away, delivering shadows against Martha's soul.

'Don't tell him that it was me that saw him,' Martha in her temporary accommodation later said, explaining developments to Meredith. 'I just saw Burt. There he was, the blockhead and do you know I think he kicked Fred, twice!'

'Oh my days. That's awful! Poor Fred. Did he definitely kick him?'

'Well, it was really dark. It could have been an air-shot but the intent seemed there.'

'We need to do something.'

'The thing is, I need him,' said Martha.

'What?'

'Even more so now with Jim out the picture, the thing is I might need Burt. I know this sounds terrible but he's the only one with a car around here and it's too useful not have him onside.'

'I hadn't even thought of that.'

'I know. That's not to say we shouldn't do something though. It's crazy the car situation even came into my mind. But what do you do in these circumstances? Call the RSPCA? The police?! Like I say, I'm not sure he made contact with Fred. I didn't see Fred limping when he ran away. It was so dark. I'll check on him in a bit.'

'Leave it for now. Leave it with me.'

What a kerfuffle. Something Martha didn't need at the end of the second third of May.

In one way, Jim had not anything to be depressed about the afternoon that followed the next morning. Be that as it may, in May, if he opened the book of his life on to the chapter just gone, on another day he had everything to be depressed about.

294

'I know Martha was depressed,' Jim told Dave on a walk. 'It said so in her journal. I hope it's not catching. Though I think I might have caught it the way I've been feeling.'

Jim had today taken over wheelchair duties from Anjit and was pushing Dave down town, setting his sights on getting something from the Chinese chip shop. Like Martha's hair, there were so many ups and downs, twists and curves. Like a pinball, unsure of his next direction was Jim, and he conceived of a vintage Martha just to be able to one more time taste her voice. Jim was no wine worshiper, and he certainly didn't know what good grape years were all about. He had forgotten what a good day was. Did it have a certain smell to it? What made a day go from average to quite good to good? Could you ever know once rudderless? Depression takes five years out of five minutes.

That nippy evening, nip nip nip, Martha, Peter and Meredith were sitting at *Shard*.

'It's refreshing to be outside with the weather noticeably warmer,' said Martha.

'That's what being at an ecovillage is all about,' added Peter. 'I think it's rather cold actually.' So does the narrator, he thought.

Big man Burt was on his way over.

'Bloody mongrel scratched me the other day,' he said once arrived. 'Stung like a paper cut.'

Martha nearly choked on her pasta. She wanted to go at him with a pickaxe specifically for the throat with the desired effect of putting the kibosh on noise from said area. Her beady eyes plunged daggers into his. Martha scudded away before any acts of regret could here befall. 'What's she got the 'ump about?' asked Burt. Peter simply shrugged and made a new dance with his eyes. 'Anyway, the old runt's gone now,' continued Burt. 'Can't find him anywhere.'

'Fred's gone?!' concernedly asked Meredith.

'Yep. Nowhere to be seen.'

'We'll have to do some missing posters and put them out in the morning.'

'Strictly speaking, he's not a mongrel,' said Peter.

Peter suddenly realised his proximity to Meredith. He was closer than he thought.

Please don't touch me with your sordid hands, she thought.

Peter was a sheepish blue. He had the last-minute look of a man rushing off to get flowers from a petrol station for the wife whose birthday he just forgot.

Ooh yeah Meredith, sang Peter's penis in his coconut. Peter was conducting experiments, x-rays, blood tests and gynaecological close-ups. He was a tapeworm wriggling around her, exploring every part of her physical geography.

Enough Peter! Enough you dirty old man, he in his coconut told himself, but Peter's peter wasn't listening: Go forth, said the penis, or I shall embrace your trousers.

No, not today Mr Penis! I win, thought Peter.

Meredith upped and left. It felt like she had spritzed Peter with pernicious eye drops.

Watch his pangs for her next showing!

Peter knew that Meredith could castrate him and yet he would not hate her.

'Your Majesty, I will be your eunuch!' declares Peter the Eunuch, guarding her from other leeches.

'I'm sorry I just couldn't sit there and listen to that,' voiced Martha, thinking about blockhead Burt. Meredith had joined her in the tent they shared. 'I so wanted to give him what for. We've got to do something, call up the RSPCA or…'

'Martha, Fred's gone.'

'What?! How do you mean?'

'He's missing. We need to start making some missing posters.'

'O my! Whatever next, I don't blame the little blighter.' Martha sighed an all-knowing sigh. 'Well we need to get to it then. This is horrendous. Oh, by the way I've got a new tent.'

'Oh really?' sounded Meredith, her voice with less power.

'Yeah. It's been really kind of you to have me here. Thanks so much. I had been saying to Imogen how I thought it would be best to get a new tent. It would resemble a fresh start. Sue was here and helped me pitch it. It's up near the brook, you know where I sometimes paint. I know it's a bit far but I think for now it will be gratifying having my own space somewhere quiet. To say thank you to Sue, I got her some beers but I'm not the least bit sure about them now. I don't know, wine? Do you think wine might have been a better choice? Because she's quite decorous, isn't she.'

'It's not like she's saved your life. I think the beers are very generous.'

'OK, ta. My mind's at rest now.'

Martha's thoughts took a wander: decorous? Why even use that in a conversation? Stop being so effing middle class about everything.

#

Over Martha the covers were pulled in her new tent as if by hands not hers. It was a queer phenomenon indeed, as odd as Captain Fuck himself, that Martha should find herself depressed. Her first major depression she bought from anxiety because anxiety was selling cheap.

If there's one thing about anxiety, it's that it reprimands you. It remonstrates with you about the pressingness of time, which is all you need if already crestfallen thanks to depression.

It made Martha nervous to know that the sky would continue to dreamily push cloud after cloud once she expired. Would nothing stop for her? Even the squirrels laughed at her, their eyes glinting as they beetled off with their acorns seemingly knowing something she did not. Bluish and abject, with her face under arrest, the second depression came from remembering being without Jim, and the third from being with him. Love and loveless. Constructs of each other? Was Jim playing no part and rather was she stewing in a vacuum of love? Any love and no bedfellow.

It came to Martha, this day, that thought— aesthetic thought of Meredith's construction—that Martha should plant some edible flowers she had been meaning to. Martha had enjoyed the setting for her new area of sleep but had not the sleep itself—joggling like a joystick, then like a key rattling in a lock through the night.

#

In glorious sunshine, Jim was trying to not stick out like the proverbial sore thumb the next morning behind summer foliage. His sense of self was snoring. A third of Martha in his eyeline, he looked with pinpoint observance as if possessedly obliged to by some spirit.

Sage, with his nose for people, watched Jim watching her whilst nibbling on a pomegranate. Martha done and gone, Jim looked in vain at the flowerbed and thought how Martha was once a flower to plant in bed. Gearstick in neutral. He had the lost expression of a manatee. By the vegetables, the angel had planted her apotropaic garden.

Things that once gave such simple moments of indulgent bliss like scarfing down gâteaux now meant sweet Fanny Adams to Jim the great extemporiser. His impromptu thoughts were multiplying. It could not be said that they were overly absorbing. Making quite sure Martha had gone, he pussyfooted over to where her hands had so carefully arranged what they had arranged.

'I saw you watching her bosom. I know why. They say it is the seat of emotion,' Sage said winsomely, as he padded up to Jim, placing a hand on his shoulder. 'You're a fair-weather man in a frozen land. She's as unjoyed as you are, she's just better at hiding it.'

To Jim's ears, Sage's voice was now some tinny kind of reverb, but he was too lackadaisical of mind to cross swords, too planted in her ground to vamoose.

'No I'm not sure you're right there,' said Jim. 'I've been so down. I think she was too mate, but she seems to be quite happy now especially when she's round Meredith.'

Not just a female, Jim thought, a lady. For you, milady I fall on my sword. God bless Martha Franks for giving me a place in myself where I could die.

And 'mate?' To Sage? What was Jim thinking? Bloody hell, things *were* bad. Unlike Sage, Martha could still hear what Jim was thinking. There was nothing funky about a funk. 'I've had problems with my innards,' continued Jim. 'I've been sucking on these sherbet-lemon flavoured antacids for a stomach complaint.' Jim presented the packet to Sage, angling almost for some kind of medical validation.

'As the Buddha once told me, in an audiobook, "let go with grace that which does not belong to you." The exact quote has run away from the home of my mind but it was words to that effect. Consternation, solemnity and doubt have ravaged your system, no doubt. Your skeletal love is disheartenment unbroken.'

He does talk some bollocks that Sage. That was Jim's latest view of his semi-friend, semi-enemy. A confidence reformed. Out from the brambles of his warped thinking, Jim, without let or hindrance, planted positive new thought-seeds in the garden of his mind. Any negative thoughts arising were weeds that needed to be yanked out.

Dust yourself down, saddle up, get back on the horse.

Jim saw the potential for turnaround from a rock-bottom state. Turn around? A certain Bonnie Tyler song came to mind and a sense of dismality returned.

Sage had already vacated, gratified from his soothing words of comfort, handing in his notice of compassion.

This is ridiculous, thought Jim. I can't hide forever like this.

He could see Martha in her new position by the water point. He reached into his breast pocket. With an Old Fashioned for Dutch courage, he was going in.

'Hi.' In all the days succeeding the letter, and with all the time therein to think of the words he could find leading up to this moment, 'hi' was how he began.

'Hi,' replied Martha in the pulsating exchange, somewhat startled but not as much as she had envisioned for this eventuality.

'Would you ever, at least consider going out with me again?'

'Um…'

'Just say yes, then I'll go.'

'Er…I'm sorry, I cannot say about this right now.'

He knew, at that first hesitation what it meant. Jim just had to get away. Wet eyes, dry mud.

Meet me in death row—there I'll know a prodigious meal and an end to toil.

Jim wasn't sure he'd ever been this bad. The other thing he wanted to, but failed to say was: whenever you feel down, just remember at least that cunt Jim thinks

I'm alright, except you wouldn't say 'cunt' because you're so beautiful.

In light of his dejectedness, Jim was surprised at how he had taken the time to prepare the Old Fashioned in a hipflask.

Martha used to feel like a change of water swashed against his forehead, making him feel he had more time left on this earth than he really did. His favourite tipple was the next best thing. 1987 was a good year for the vintage. Isn't that right Martha?

Jim has broken his own heart too.

Martha. She walks these fields puppetlike and guards the secret declared sacred. Shoving her forced smile into the world, with her two adventures into antidepressant land, was she now returning? And the secret? The secret is she'll never go back to Jim. Shh, don't tell anyone.

Martha's hair was like the uncut grass of Carringdon Ecovillage, her body was slim like a wakeboard and brittle as unleavened bread.

She waits for the trip switch in her mind to next tell her when to meditate. Mostly by Meredith, she distracts herself by dint of people the whole day through, and at night is left to her insecurities. Loneness.

Depression is a quiet city, maybe you are too.

CHAPTER TEN

Her eyes filled in by night's heartbeat, her day drained through a cheesecloth; a honey blue life, the bittersweet kind, hard-pressed poets remind you about.

'Is there anything we can do, Jim?' asked Anjit, robustly standing in Dave's tent, by Dave.

'Thanks. But it's OK.' All the energy of Jim's frown caught in a little vertical line between his eyes then up a little.

'We're off for our daily walk now.'

'Right you are, hope it's a good 'un.'

'OK Jimbo, see ya later.'

There's that name again. Jimbo. That's only the second time I've heard that, thought Jim.

On cinders the Lonely Gods had convinced Martha that she was culpable for her plight. They were an uncordial bunch.

Martha was staring off alone outside her tent and her easel was standing to attention. Her processes for the afternoon of her day represented the lifecycle of a hailstone: thudding, crumbling, wetting. She'd no plans to merely live life, she wanted to bend the throttle, breaking the ceiling in the land of no ceilings. Hungry to paint, but whilst there were better days than others there can be no highs in a monochrome of black. Any way she hoped, she could feel her tears dripping out of tomorrow.

A nice day in late May, Jim was inside, in Dave's tent, pacing. Hands behind his back, walking to and fro, this way and that. Bespangled by woman. He thought about her when he was washing up, when in the shower, when heaving weeds from the garden path. There was no garden. Only in his mind did he heave the weeds. He didn't know a shit about gardening. That book Martha gave him—he was never going to read that *now*. In every raindrop, every eyeball, every backlash, every turn of phrase he could perceive Martha. He felt her more than with her. Tears formed, and every time one smudged his vision it was like looking at her apparitions through hemihedral crystallinity. He remembered every part of her kiss, it lingered like a death march. End and destination were much the same. And the worst part? She could drive him crazy without doing a *damnnn* thing. Jim even started worrying about all the lines on his face he'd never met in his twenties. People say all that worrying will get you nowhere. Yes it will, he thought, to the cosmetic surgeon, that's where. Jim sighed as he remembered he had not the money for that. Fuck you lines!

How to deal with the break-up…some dream in over-chase. Others bleach blood stains, trying to forget as much as quickly as they possibly can. Jim just wanted to bury his head in the sand on the off chance he might find Blackbeard's treasure.

She whirled his pool, he loved louder than ever.

Jim had built up a modicum of confidence to emerge from his hidey-hole, as it were, and Paul was telling him a story in the communal area.

'Some years ago, I was at another ecovillage. I tried to emulate one of Charles Manson's famous tactics of giving a few people a far higher dose of acid than I'd dropped myself. Then, once high up in the clouds, I'd make the members watch as I wore Jesus-style robes. It was a cunning plan, a bit wicked really. Come to think of it, I looked a bit like Sage.' Paul held his stomach as he gave a great laugh. 'Anyway, the manipulation game failed. They called me "the commune clod" after that.' Out came another typically effusive laugh. 'I was fair game, I suppose. Yeah, never quite worked that one. Oh yeah, I have to say sorry about before, Jim. I get like that sometimes. It's just the drink. What was I saying? Oh yep, the green-eyed hippy sorts are too cynical. Very few of 'em have any time for Jesus, even if they would have believed my act.' Or maybe some of them had read about Manson, you mop, thought Jim. 'Yeah, I've mellowed out a bit now. Methinks people have started respecting me again,' said Paul.

Conversation took off its clothes. For a moment, only, the too shy duad couldn't talk. Jim was like a fridge—cold as fuck and every now and again you'd hear the odd rumble. 'You know, there is something else I do…'

'Oh yeah?' said Jim, barely bothering to open his mouth.

'Yeah, also a bit naughty. On trips to the post office, I pretend with the elderly customers that notice me that I'm actually me Geordie twin brother, Cecil.' Jim looked an eyeful of jarred-face at first, then smiled posthaste. 'Yeah mate, I go in all like, "why aye man," "what you talking aboot?" "Ha'way to the post office." ' Paul filled up with laughter and so did Jim flowing like a broken dam. It was the first time Jim laughed since the letter, that day.

#

Toasting vegan and non-vegan marshmallows for the evening in the rustic ambience were the settlers. There was a transportation of light and friendliness to the dark energy of evening: artificial light and moonlight were reflecting a landing of soulful paleness. As the night drew to a close, a curtain of dawn strained every nerve of light the sky knew how.

News came through the next morning.

Her forehead like that of the crease under a batsman on a double century, cracked by years of anxious frowns. Ninety-three years old, deeply afflicted by melanoma. The last rites were being read. It had been believed that the tumour was in situ, but had spread like a family tree from its localized position. All the lines in her face, Jesus saves. Angel of Death, take thy goblet and drink another last breath. Carried by her retinue of strong, handsome women, tootling on a palanquin, in the early hours of this day the good Lord took her up.

Cathy's mam had sought it. Only feeble signs left of the joys life can bring in clinical months of recent times.

Hopes dispersed one by one as wind to the dandelion. Nose-hairs like scorched grass.

Cathy's ghostlike disposition may as well have fallen to the mud dents below. To her favourite man, the one she calls 'little god,' unto him, in her head she heard her heart ask: by reason of spite and might, won't you permit me no light?

She thought of celebratory pastimes and listened to the now. She was bulldozing the future like bunged bodies for burial. The last of her immediate family to croak, her mam was a lady of simple pleasures: Corrie on the tele for 7:30, slippers on, mug of Horlicks and a Hobnob by a roasting fire, and she was *done*.

Sage wanted to say how sorry he was for her loss. He wanted to say it was OK, but that wouldn't do either. There were no words.

Time the great trickster, the more it goes on, the more it offers succour by shrinking the loved one to a remote memory, vitiating the blow of the traits that once prepossessed you. It creeps like a corn smut. The more it passes the more likely you are to get Alzheimer's and/or die, depleting memory to a debased cry, to nil.

''Ow did it all go so wrong?' Cathy cried. 'Me mam never would've wished this fer me. Her dyin' this young and me bein' without money fer starters. Everything is dead in the water now, all me 'opes an' dreams. Not just the ones I 'eld fer 'er but fer meself too. Say yer alright you,' she said, nodding at Sage. 'People 'ave their opinions 'bout ya, but I think yer alright me.' She waved her finger in his direction. 'A good listener, you.' Sage placed a consolatory hand on a highly strung shoulder. He was good at that.

'Salutations cupcake and many thanks,' said Sage. 'Requiescat in pace. For brave is the human that faces the dunnest night!'

Cathy watched the imago as she could hear the old other ways of her mother, imploring her to get her loins into gear for school, and to get down from that tree. It was like Cathy had her own mind's crackly film-reel.

The conversation was taking place in the middle of the ecovillage, it could be said, or 'social middle.' It was an area of grass halfway between the start of the dwellings and the end of them, if you did not include Martha's new home. 'How inner beauty differs from those externally viewing us,' Sage continued. 'We are wise to all our secret areas, our foibles and disgraces we've committed on ourselves over the years. Even so, if the person piping us does not know us intimately—how easily they can innocently fall in love.'

Sage's dad was a pretentious wanker, or such was the general consensus. He had said something similar to his son about relationships. Right up until his hospital death bed, he used the lines: 'I must go, for trouble is afoot. May the deep blue sea not stir and storms never near wherever you should set your sail. I bid you farewell and good tidings on your quest.'

His mum was fairly normal, and light to pick up.

'The reason I mentioned that about relationships?' asked Sage rhetorically. 'Because, as my yogi friends remind me, in the words of the late Osho, the minute you start accepting yourself, you become that bit more beautiful. In the morning when you wake, are you afeard of the world? Are you pushing yourself to the limit?'

'What?' said Cathy. 'What are ya talkin' about lovey? Takes a lot t'scare me, don't ya know, but aye, I could do more, but then we all could, couldn't we?' Cathy could feel her earsplitting tender-heartedness waning as she thought of life.

'I've studied you. You seem to lack care, to lack joie de vivre. Try this.'

Sage found from the underside of his robe an ornate oval bottle, tartan-blue, encrusted with crustaceans of the sea.

'*I'll* say! Is Mr Sage givin' me a potion?'

'Behold! Herein lies the ancient Indian herb of Ashwagandha. Take the bottle as a keepsake. Treat its contents as a toy and you will suffer, use in moderation and you will be aided.'

'Behold, 'erein, now there's some good old English words for ya!'

Sage acquired the mystic contents online from a chirpy health food store in Flintshire.

'The problem I've found is that women, particularly in their late thirties and forties tend to have more money than they did in their twenties and wherefore have a more extravagant list of activities they do and wish to do in their spare time,' said Sage. 'They'll happily talk for hours on end about the number of exotic holidays they've been on by the year, the extreme sport they've just taken up, the Zumba classes and the flower shows they've attended. I can't help feel along the way they've missed the point. They spend all their earned money and time seeking happiness by the external hand of the newest or most "amazing."

Cathy, you are beneficent. It however has come to my attention that your chin…'

'Yeah I know the type ya mean, Sage. Ya find a lot of women cut their barnet shorter as they get older too. I think they just do it 'cause it's easier t'manage. Not me. No siree. I 'aven't the shrapnel fer it these days.'

'Things generally get shorter as we age: mental capacity, fervour for life, centre of gravity.'

'Ooh Sage! Ya ain't no divvy. A funny one too aren't ya. You use your loaf. You've lifted me no end. I was thinking of gettin' a new tattoo done, and ooh, that reminds me, I do love a guy with ink.'

'Spiffing, I've biros aplenty.'

Cathy's face opened in less turmoil as she complimented the breeze with a relaxed laugh.

'Oh Sage. Go on, gimme some more sagely advice! I'll be up all night 'earin' yer pearls o' wisdom now won't I.'

'It would be my pleasure to impregnate you with knowledge. Here's one bit of advice to avail yourself of: do not forget wonder, for the older we get, the easier it is to lose. Uphold wonder, and as an aside, I should say that, as for pens, I'll soon be upgrading to the ballpoint.'

'Sage, would ya go vegetarian fer me?'

'I wouldn't put it past you, such is the power of a good woman. Dear Cathy, you have the most kissable cheeks in all Carringdon and its borders. Your hair is leathery…sorry, not the most veggie reference. You provide in me a mansuetude of heart. My dear, you have a regal air about you. When you sit beside me you convert this field to a green palace, the green of Brazzaville taxis. Your hair, from its colour, its texture, reminds me of the Greater Antillean Grackle. Its graduated tail, the rectrices from centre to outer shortening by gradations perfected in nature. The profiling empress towering o'er my shoulder. You bring me light just for being in my atmosphere and…'

'Manny!!!!' From a forested area deep in the eco-village, a scream of thunder that swallowed the sky belonged to Anjit. He was looking at the body of Kristoff, swinging with no resistance. The body parts went where the restful breeze moved them. Ligature at the neck. The eye splice teetered from a wilting oak. A grounding call of a wood pigeon ensued.

Everyone heard the scream and everyone gathered.

'There's a note,' said Meredith, with a sorry, sorry voice. She rubbed her eyes away from tears and read the note out loud:

"For my English I have translate:

It saddens me how in this lifetime I do not think we will see ideas of my hero, Jacque Fresco and his Venus Project put into place. Just to have it seriously explored would be something. Please edit it, expand it. It saddens me how as a society we've senselessly decided to make paper that we call money so important, all because of inability to defeat greed.

I cannot go on knowing that footballer is paid £500,000 a week yet boy in Nairobi works on scrap heap all day for 70p. I cannot go on knowing some medicines are able to cure yet are unaffordable. I cannot eat my next meal knowing that so many are starving. For this, I cannot go on anymore."

Kristoff's arms in the breeze swayed carelessly as if to convey to the quick just how much he had given up, even after life.

Upraised last night, a pair of shoes dangled from an electric cable seven streets from Cherryblossom.

By Kristoff, there fell, amidst a glacial unreality, a vibrant hush save the trees wherein life force hadn't altered in a heinous act of impiety—if they were adolescents they'd have ASBOs.

'His boy is just like him,' said Sage. 'It will be hideous for him to hear the news. Kristoff's mind met its demise long before his body. He was a good man. He just couldn't face the selfishness and deceitfulness of the moderne times we find ourselves in. A life at rest, he was an insociable soul to begin with, and a tortured soul to end with.'

Paul stepped in,

'He's not dead, he's just gone underground. He always wanted to be in the underground scene, now he fucking is, three cheers for Kristoff!' and Paul raised a can of strong beer.

It was the only time Anjit had seen a dead body. Transfixed, he perspired, dripping with terror. His lips formed the shape of a horseshoe. He like the others did not have the right energy to join Paul.

Manny cut away the noose and discarded it. With Meredith and Sage, he laid the body down on the ground and enrobed it in cloth.

Martha, silent like the gun that never fires, was one of the last to see what the commotion was all about. Her first reaction was to put her hands to her face and lean into the shoulder of Jim. They were together, alone, a short way back from the rest of the assemblage. Lo and behold, the old fridge was rumbling:

'I hadn't seen any sign of it,' said Jim, looking lousy.

'O Kristoff!' cried Martha. 'He must have been so low. Why didn't I do more?! Why, when I have a keen sense how he felt?

I may have been able to lay something on him. I feel it in my legs when I am mournful. They become so heavy. I feel it in my stomach when I am anxious. It gets so tight. You just feel invisible. You know you're not who you want to be, who you can be. You can apprehend why people do not see you. What can you do? I feel it in my eyes when I am happy. When you are truly happy, you smile with your eyes. I noticed something a couple of months back with Kristoff. There just wasn't any fight in him anymore. He'd lost his fight.'

I never thought to look, personally, thought Jim. But then I do have the attention span of a grapefruit.

Kristoff seemed such a drab man, but Jim, on this occasion, decided to keep things to himself. 'I could have done more,' reiterated Martha, before overcome with tears, going to her book by the brook. She was reading the hinder parts of 'The English & Their Sh*tty Rules:'

A few months ago I watched a rugby union match between us and England at the Vélez Sársfield stadium, Buenos Aires. You English guys are pathetic, pathetic! There was the unwritten rule amongst the English to neatly queue. The next minute you English slobs stank of beer and had your bellies out taking a sick interest in the sun. Some of the Argentine fans were looking at their phones for the football scores. Not even that bothered and we still beat you. You guys in England keep creating your silly little sports, and here in the Southern Hemisphere we'll keep dominating them.

Martha had only given heed to approximately two words in what she had read. How could she possibly concentrate? Then came a realisation about the marrow of fleetingness, and how Kristoff was time's unfortunate guinea pig. She turned to think of her oeuvre. Overcome by Japonisme, minimalism, Rayonism. Wanting florid, ornate, baroque! Adjectives>nouns!! Twist open the valves!!!

'What happens in this sort of situation? I've never been in anything like this.' said a flittering Meredith back at the scene. 'Do we call the police? Would they think it was any of us? And what about informing his next of kin or something?'

'No-one knows the contact details of Kristoff's boy or his other relatives, for he was a private man,' said Sage.

'Do we need to register 'is death?' asked Cathy.

'There is no register of death here,' Manny said. 'He was of the commune. We are outside the government's so-called register of death. They do not need to know our whereabouts. As far as I know, he had lost all contact with relatives. We were his only friends. Only we need to remember him, and we will mourn.'

'This is bonkers!' screeched Peter. 'Have you really swayed that much from reality?! I can only assume you are joking. You're power-mad and are trying for some dramatic sense of isolation. In fact, you are time after time seeking one-upmanship over any person you perceive to be a threat. Bonkers!'

'I have to agree,' said Sage. 'In acting this way you have transgressed your remit, and, as the common man would say, you have lost it. Do you even mind that your mind has gone?! I do not think you can be in charge any further.'

'Hear, hear,' said Dave.

'I agree too, and anyone with any sense will,' said Meredith. 'We will find out the best we can who his relatives and friends outside of here are, and do the right thing. I can't believe we're even having this conversation.'

You started the conversation, thought Manny. The protestations made Manny feel sleepy and berserk, like he was trying to officiate on a capsizing ship with God knows how many overboard.

'Fine,' Manny said, and with his volubility taking a pounding he turned his body to zero in on a domed canopy of ash trees.

'You alright Anj?' asked Meredith, assisting Dave's assistant with a well-built arm around him. Anjit had moved as much as a stick in the mud.

Jim had heard and seen enough too. He took a constitutional in the long grass. *Lake Horizon* looked different today. It wasn't just a place, it was an atmosphere. Dark watery shadows had pickpocketed the lake wherever they chose. Greying blue dents in its balance looked evilly englutting. When Jim returned, a few police cars had parked up.

Oink, oink, he thought, here they come. Jim couldn't help but think how hubristic they all looked.

The mares of the moon Galileo first thought were seas—dinginess settling, forthcoming: an approach of those foreboding seas. Police and police cars and a felo de se. Time got stopped up at the ecovillage. For upwards of three seconds, car doors closed. Dave put on some Pink Floyd. The dark side of the moon was coming.

#

'This area will be cordoned off and forensic experts will arrive,' said a perambulating policeman.

'Books are so long aren't they. How does anyone read a book? Tell me officer, if you get to a word in a book and don't know its meaning, do you look it up? I bloody don't. I stamp my feet and put on some rock music. I mean, I don't have the inclination. I despair, I'm offloading again, yeah I don't know why I even started this topic…'

'What are your intentions on this site?' said the lawman, replying to an intoxicated Paul trying to fight off maudlinism.

'What's it t'you, ya big bozos!' said Cathy. 'I thought you was 'ere fer Kristoff?! Shows 'ow gullible silly old Cathy was.'

'We have no intentions. This is common land. What do we need intentions for? Is this not the basic right of humans?' asked Meredith, unhopeful of any sought-after response.

'Madame, we're only paid to ask the questions,' said a rounder bobby with a flowery tongue. 'We need to ascertain a few particulars, that's all.'

'Shame on ya,' said Cathy. 'We're grieving fer our friend and that's all ya can think about.'

'Lunar regolith differs from the earth's for differing reasons, in all likelihood of picayune interest to most,' said Sage. 'You police and our community are like these dichotomous differentiations, of differing toxicities. And who is who?'

Burt chose to confront the whole day with silence.

The night coughed fragmented splutters of rain, the sun shut off in kaleidoscopic sweet potato colouring. Felled and booted to city slums manned by darkness were Martha's conceptions of a rural paradise;

how night disposes.

#

Jim flashbacked to when he was first shown round the camp by Kristoff.

Martha recalled the Siberian javelins of cold in November, a shivering Jim edging into view—that goose-pimple fuckface. She called to mind how his warm look for her eyes told her, how with her, he was in love, and that he wanted no change in the arrangement for the foreseeable future. In her tent now Martha thought of sacrifice, of the immolation of Thích Quảng Đức, and the celibate life sentences for monks and votaries alike.

May was done. Jim was still in bed. He did not think well of the supreme being if one indeed existed.

The whole thing with Kristoff, it really…really stuck in his craw. Kristoff had emotions and dreams the same way anyone else did, and for the first time Jim seemed awake to that.

'What time is it?' he asked Dave.

'Just gone ten. Time for a shower.'

Jim rerouted his attention toward his one-time best friend, living in a cupboard. The last time Jim saw him, the friend was in a post-binge state sat looking at the ceiling. Mouth agape, gob all over his face, hollowed out pistachio shells and dreams like Kristoff's scattered all around him. That guy just could not come to terms with letting go of what he had coined the 'sophisticated peanut.'

Jim started to realise that the most he and his old mucker ever had in common was a love of getting pissed and of having the occasional dalliance with coke, and not the kind of coke you wash a pistachio down with.

Jim stared with a sinister, dismantling look; aglow like a china doll. It took him six efforts to get out of bed thinking of lost souls before him. Souls that were close to him. Jim searched *his* soul but like the inside of a kettle it was best not to look.

People had to die. Suffering existed in the world and didn't look like desisting anytime soon. Jim realised thus that people in depressive states could catch a certain solace through others' worser miseries. In some measure, it could numb their own anguish for an hour or two to a manageable rate. Jim knew there was always Peter to look at.

In these lands, when sun and warmth forge a rare tag team and with the sentiments this stirs in an Englishman, that Jim could only stare at images of death this sunshiny day is how he knew he was in a rut. Locked in a house of nettles. He felt like an overused bollock.

'God I feel lower than a worm in landfill,' he said to Dave, who had finished his shower after Jim had finished thinking. Dave couldn't use the makeshift shower, so he had gone to the showers in the local gymnasium. 'I know the type I want—the defiled skag that only wants to be banged hard. Hayley is the nearest thing round here but she hasn't been about. An insertion here, a knobbing there, it's all the same to her. That's how I could take my anger out on someone. Yeah! I could take my anger and transform it into sexual energy for Hayley. That one doesn't save anything for the bedroom, she just lets it allll hang out.'

Dave just looked, at nowhere.

Jim went for a bite to eat. Meredith was sweeping the kitchen intelligently: fast with hardly a pinch of haste. It all was happening while she reminded herself of her soft spot for paradoxes and doublethink. Jim looked at Manny. He was there too. Manny was a doer. Jim felt that doing things impressed the ladies. If he did more things he'd end up doing more of *them*. He tucked his newfound philosophy into a lower jacket pocket next to a pocket watch given to him by his granduncle.

'Is any help needed for dinner tonight?!' he later shouted to Meredith, while seated perpendicular to the ground in the communal area, as in the kitchen she drew off a saturated green and white dishcloth. Meredith didn't answer at first.

'Ermm,' she said, at last. It stood to reason that there was a possibility she was flustered by his capability to ask such a thing. 'Nada, right now,' she continued, and broke into song the way morning does over tombstones.

Manny saw himself out.

Jim did so very much of nothing. He went to put some toast on. Taking it out, crumbs flew to where Meredith had just seen to. Jim decided put his hand precariously near the toaster's filaments. He figured the worst that could happen would be Meredith would have to perform mouth to mouth.

Just outside the kitchen, Sage was putting some wood into the storehouse as he touched base with Cathy.

'You would be joining me at a better time, dear Cathy, were it not for the fault of an expiring young morning aborting in conceiving afternoon.'

'I take it yer talking about Kristoff,' said Cathy.

'That I am.'

'It makes me sick to the stomach it does. So weird goin' past Kristoff's old tent now, what with 'im not bein' 'ere an' that.'

'Not half, pumpkin. It is most striking the way Kristoff's living quarters and all objects therein have now no-one to belong to.'

#

In the undeveloped evening, Meredith twatted herself against an outspoken tree, falling momently to one knee. She thought of how she still stretched for her ex. She thought of all the aspersions she received for *Quantum Cappuccino*, feeling them attritive to her root. *Why* it could have been the official magazine of planet Neptune.

A pair of vinaceous eyes looked down as she uncovered her baccy pouch to find it uninhabited. For the moment she had neither—each tip gets redder the more you try, and be it a cock or cigarette, she was used to having something in her mouth. What was this? International Fuck Meredith Day? Almost as red as the nose of Rudolph, she pounded her way to the communal area and there was not any living soul in particular she looked at as she spoke without caring who her words were for:

'I'm getting a bit fed up! Some of you aren't pulling your weight around here!!'

A blur of collected faces looked either downward or into the distance. Meredith would have gone on to specifics but no-one responded, so she parted in a pet with no known direction. Cathy went after her, feeling for her own baccy pouch in an effort to placate histrionics.

Meredith had hit the big time. A rags to riches—who does the dishes?—story, from small-scale drama queen to director of and headliner in her own full-scale production. It could have been *Hairspray* and baldy Paul wasn't invited to the premiere. Peter was still waiting to hear back from his audition for a cameo role. Don't tell anyone but Meredith still had a sheet of preplanned answers should she one day find herself on a sofa with Jonathan Ross.

'She's blatantly talking about the kitchen area,' said Anjit.

'OK,' said Dave, sneakily shucking corn on the cob under his zip-jacket.

'*That* and she's probably on the blob,' said Jim. 'Or maybe she's just wondering what it will be like to be a single woman in her forties? They tell you life begins at forty only to make you feel better. I'll be lucky to reach forty because I don't make enough right decisions, even though everyone keeps saying how intelligent I am.'

It was true. Jim had an eye for comedy and modesty—two British greats.

'Sometimes, though, what people say and what's really rattling them are two different matters altogether,' remarked Peter. 'I'm not sure she cares that much about the kitchen at all.' He leaned in. 'Last night, I heard her having an altercation. It was over lipstick or something.'

'Who with? Didn't you hear anything else?' asked Anjit.

'I'll tell you later, we should go. Martha's cooked a lovely stew.'

With hands outspread, Anjit walked towards Dave's wheelchair:

'Are you coming for dinner Dave?'

'Yeah.'

The stew, naturally vegetarian, was indeed lovely, and everyone agreed by the emptiness of what was left. Martha had made it piping hot in the hope that by some strange quirk of fate it would corrode testosterone and nullify Jim's acerbic dirk of a tongue. As she picked at her plate for leftover memories, a customary timidity was present for all to see. She was nervous for eating in front of others, she was nervous for anxiety that was a score of years her junior, and she was particularly nervous to please others from her repast.

'I was saying to Dave earlier how things really don't feel right without Kristoff here,' said Anjit.

'You an' us both, love,' said Cathy. 'I was saying the same thing to Sage earlier.' Everyone looked down and subdued. Like an airship, stationary in a hangar, a toboggan stationary in a chute, Martha was waiting for the cumbersome silence to evanesce.

The leafy plants jilt the moribund sun. So attentively their flowers listen as the early evening wind prances and falls, prances and falls.

For dessert, Meredith had made an Eton Mess, of a vegan sort. It panned out a bit wrong. Everyone tucked into their fruity car crashes and everyone looked petrified of Meredith, to wit, no-one whinged. Meredith was glad she had said what she had said, and went at her mess like it was the best fucking thing ever created. Martha didn't like Eton Mess and her ferruginous cheeks sat there hanging as though a couple of budgerigars had tucked cosily inside apiece. Looking moreish, Jim wanted to teeth them. What a pavlova.

Peter did most of the washing up. There were things he could leave for other people.

On a whim, Peter threw the drying cloth onto the plastic dish drainer like he was Scottie Pippin. Thereafter he saw Meredith smoking outside alone on a log never seen. It was a long way left of the kitchen and communal point.

Even if we do get together, he thought, how will I tell to her about the overactive bladder?

Peter adjusted his hair. He was going for the windswept look. Rubbing his eyeglasses clean, he noticed there were a couple of other logs at the foot of the first he saw, and catlike, he drew closer.

'What's occurring?' he embarrassedly asked.

'Um, yeah, I'm OK thanks.'

She wasn't really. She was a mixed bag. A bag of liquorice allsorts and she hated liquorice, and they had gelatine in anyway.

She surveyed her recently filed nails and there were a pair of chaffinches in a beech tree. She switched her eyes back and forth between the set of images. 'What's new?'

'Not much,' replied Peter. 'What's going on over here then?'

'Oh, Manny and I moved these logs yesterday to create something a bit different,' said Meredith. 'It's like a second, mini communal point really.'

'Is that so.'

Peter really was exceedingly nervous. 'I've…I've thought about you a lot recently,' he said. Meredith frowned caringly. Peter wasn't sure whether to press the point, but he did anyhow, because according to Peter, you only live once. 'I want to protect you and…'

'I don't need protecting, I'm a grown woman.'

That's true, Peter thought, she was. Right now Meredith thought she was on motherfucking stilts, but women liked hearing these things all the same, thought Peter.

'I was just…you know…just thinking how messed up this world is.'

'Well we all think that,' said Meredith, removing a Dalmatian-coloured shoe to shake free an unwanted little stone caught in it.

Peter found Meredith was so beautiful it was hard to look at her and listen to what she was saying at the same time, particularly as her fire made her sexier.

'Somewhere along the way, people forgot about love. I mean, eh, isn't that what this world is all…is all about?' asked Peter.

Meredith's sightliness in the sun melted poor Peter down to a gooey paste. She looked at him as though overpowered from the smell of a tangle of freshly fallen pine needles crunched against her sole. Peter looked inquisitively at her inexact gaze. It appeared he was about to put the pedal to the metal with his mouth: 'Love, sweet love,' he closed with.

The cheesiness of his words had gone from a mild cheddar to Canadian extra mature. It was a moot point as to whether it was shrewd to go all Canadian in front of an American. The way Meredith looked at him, he might as well have been a girl, or Beaker off *The Muppets*. Peter's vocal output tripped over Meredith's pococurante-ism. The shoe was back on.

Peter was on a wild-goose chase for his best line to take things to the next level:

'So Meredith, I hear you like crosswords. Fancy a game of "Boggle?" '

The coyest smile creased Meredith's face. She made an attempt, with some difficulty, not to laugh once she realised he was expecting an answer.

'Um, no thanks,' she said. 'I've got a heap of things to clean.'

'Rightio. Er…I mean…rad. I'll see if Anjit wants to play.'

How then for this appropriator of fantasies?! What was her part in the cosmos? Could Meredith only find the part for her role through someone lost?

Once Peter had left, Meredith realised that actually it served a twofold purpose—Peter's reverence of her: it very little alleviated the blow to memories of Jake, and reminded her that at least some guy liked her round here. It was easy to think of Peter this way while he was absent from view, but he'd only need approach again— that's when the stomach cramps set in.

To Meredith, Peter had overambitious cheeks, a plaque-coloured flop of unbrushed hair above Theodor Morell spectacles, and a body that disappeared into his jumper.

To Peter, Meredith put up a sluice gate for his flights of fancy; that lust witherer! The conjuror could practise her witchery any hour of day. Peter always thought her nose too aquiline anyway.

When Peter said he wanted to see if Anjit wanted to play, in geek world that was code for: I'm going back to my tent to wallow and rethink strategy. Though that his thinking, Peter and Anjit caught sight of each other as Peter inched towards to his hexi-tent.

'So what was that argument about earlier that Meredith had?' inquired Anjit.

'Ah, doesn't matter now. Or at least, I'm not in the mood for that now. Stop by my tent later. I might be in the mood then.' Peter was not in the mood because all he kept telling himself was how he was a waffler, a faffer and a flapper.

Getting some supplies on Cherryblossom Street, Jim was back to mooning about Martha. She still stirred in him wireless desires and he hated that she did. Even the local bins looked like Martha. So much of his life he now shared with her, and she didn't even know it. By Jove! Never had he known such power to put the pussy on the pedestal.

Around 8 p.m. Anjit approached Peter's hexi-tent. Above the faraway sound of two local men quarrelling like cats, a serious noise from within Peter's home impinged upon Anjit. Finding that most of his weight had reached the balls of his feet, Anjit scuffed his way in.

'From Stettin in the Baltic to Trieste in the Adriatic, an "Iron Curtain" has descended across the continent,' Churchill said to Peter from Peter's computer. Listening whilst messaging, Peter was online shopping for women. He had met so many of them from behind his computer screen.

One man was eyeballing the screen, the other in screensaver mode. Anjit's confidence was going to smithereens, and he was caught unawares how Peter was on the phone:

'Yeah well you need to up your game,' said Peter, lucidly. 'Now pay attention. I'm sick of the recent letdown in consistency of the dough balls for my malai kofta. In the last two orders, they really have been substandard. Similarly, the last time my Peshwari naan was burnt too. Now look, I've got Okey Dokey Curry Restaurant round the corner offering me two free papadums with every order—something you might like to think about, hmm? Goodbye.'

'Hi Peter,' Anjit said apprehensively. He followed Peter's beck.

The recipient of Peter's latest online message looked at Peter as if to say: on my profile I've only found the time to write one, albeit grammatically incorrect sentence—oh by the way here's my tits. A hand on the hips from a side-on view, she wore a low-cut tight top jailing her mammary glands. Anjit could not see what Peter was writing. The message read,

> *On first look I wldnt think it, don't know if others wld too lol but looking closer at ur photo I definitley think ud be an all rite fuck.*

Peter gave a maniacal cackle that pervaded the tent and beyond to what felt like a five-mile radius. He got on to another profile.

'This one likes speedway. What does that mean? Is that a thing?' asked Peter, as neatly as a colonnade of alpine trees.

'I'm not sure, but it sounds like something moving very quickly,' said Anjit.

Peter's expression altered.

'Before was just for play. This is where we do the business.' His eyes lighted on Anjit's. Softer eyes saw Peter write:

> *It says on your profile you're confident. You shouldn't be. You look petered out in that pic. Lolz only joking you look fine girl. Gotta love the bantz! I love confident women that know what they want.*

'Listen. Over the years, Anjit, I've felt like a perfume. Women just have me on the shelf. There as they want, to use when they want. They don't even like the perfume that much. It was the one they had politely received from grandma at Christmas. Although they prefer other perfumes, they know I'm the safe, reliable perfume that won't overpower them. Put me on then forget about me for a while. When they're down in the dumps a few months later, they think: ooh, now where did I put my Peter musk?

'I'm just a commodity to women, Anjit. It was the same at school. Girls just laughed and threw stones at me. But that was all before I found a certain something. Something I learned from a man named Benny. That man's like an unsleeping panther. I digress.

'Are you ready to be a businessman Anjit? You see in what I've written, you see how you push and pull them. At first you hit them hard right in the feels. It's always best if you can unearth what snags them, dent their confidence a little, have them taken aback. But then you bring them back with the compliments. They realise you're just joking around in the end, but in a sense it's too late. They read that first line and they thereupon think you're a numpty for saying that. But because they've been emotionally shaken up, and because you bring it back with the compliments they then think: ah, he's not so bad, he's just playing. He qualifies the parts of my appearance I dislike the most.

'Even if they think consciously find you nauseating, they've already had the powerful psychological hit which acts on their subconscious. They might feel subconsciously that they have to try extra hard with their appearance to impress you and they might look to your approval more than they would the next nice guy. You see what I mean, Anjit? The nice guy doesn't get the girl. You've got to get inside their heads. Ask Jim, he knows some of this. Forget all that crap about being a gentleman. Nice guys are *so* last century.'

'Oh…right, OK, ermm…thanks. First time I've been inside the hexi-tent…looks good.'

'Agreed. It is more a hexi-yurt, in point of fact. The walls are four by eight and the roof is half the four by eight. Plywood's the trick here sonny. This is half the cost of a tent, and a tent would only last you a year or so.' Peter rested his hand on one of the six sides. 'This baby can last five to ten years. Anyway, I can tell you were about to mention that Meredith altercation again. It was nothing, I'd much rather go back to what we were talking about.'

Peter, soused with confidence looked back at the monitor. 'Oh look Anj, here's one of your lot. Shall I ask her if she knows a good curry house round here?' He gave Anjit a little nudge with the elbow. 'Just kidding with you dude.' Peter pointed to the screen. His manner returned to militaristic. 'See all these lovelies here? They've been bookmarked. That's because they're on the rack. The Peter Rack. I'll come back to their profiles in earnest for the purpose of closer examination mañana. I'll see if I actually want to message them. See this sket here—minging bordering on butters—she is for when it gets desperate. For now, she goes to the back of the rack.'

'Cool, I'm going to have to jet. Laters.'

'Hold on a second, Anjit.' Peter said hesitating, in his only hesitation since Anjit had entered the tent…sorry, yurt. 'You haven't have you, by any chance heard of "Boggle?" '

'Er…no.'

'OK then, never mind. Oh, and one last thing before I forget to mention it. Have you ever seen the way Burt washes up? Next time he does, watch him and see how angry you get.'

#

'I've got to the stage where I'm looking on my friends' social media pages just to live a segment of their lives,' said Jim. He was back in Dave's tent after his small-time tour of the general store. 'I'm reading article after article on the BBC. I just read about a man who spent a whole year dressed up as a camel. I'm signing up to shit gardening magazines, Dave, just to make me feel important when the emails come through. Look at this.' Jim showed Dave his latest edition of *Gardening Addicts*. 'I don't even like gardening.'

'Shame. Sorry about that.'

Was this Jim's nadir?! A conviction handed out from the former partner in crime on the run, there was an unsung promise of coupled longevity.

Sentence: depression. How many years will Jim be put away? Mild depression blankets the day, but there are ramparts to be found for sure around the edges, and the path that leads to them decontaminates care. Jim's mind expanded like a heated solid.

Now Jim knew, with costly stridence, that melancholia is not a toy. Depression had him left a crying bag of bones. Not dying, just running out of life.

'I know, guys, that some of you don't want me to talk,' said Manny on the day that followed. 'Fear not, I won't be long.'

'Chance would be a fine thing,' whispered Sage to Cathy, who just about managed to withhold a giggle.

'Some things though do need to be said, whether it from me or someone else.' Manny had somehow managed to persuade everyone of the ecovillage to forgather in a circle on the grass. It was such a nice day by the communal area that everyone was sitting on the grass rather than on apparatus. 'Firstly, let me start off by saying that I have decided to go ahead with the water filtration system. Martha, I would appreciate if you could help with the design. Anyone else too can help and give ideas for development as I will only start with the basic design. Secondly, I have fixed the leak in the shower. Thirdly, in doing what's right and proper by Kristoff, we should lay a memorial stone at the point he passed on. Lastly, I have enormous ideas for the ecovillage. I think there's so much more we can do. We should advertise more and have more open days. We lounge around too much when we should be networking with the other communities. It would be satisfying to have more children with their families visit, and have more things available for senior citizens too. Maybe we could make a bowling green for them to play bowls on one of the open days? Does anyone have any questions or suggestions?'

Manny drew a blank, for all minds were a blank. 'Suit yourselves,' he continued. 'It's up to you, it's your ecovillage. If you ask me, I still think I am the best to lead here. You may not want me as your leader anymore but I think everyone should be able to have a say, no? Oh…I nearly forgot, Peter told me he has a few words he would like to share with you.'

Peter came forward, holding out several papers.

'Never have it said, that whilst differences have been felt, and shall remain, that I have not in some way respected each and every one of you. Indeed it is a mark of the esteem in which I hold you, that I have gathered you all before me today so that no-one is left in the dark.' Peter gulped. 'It pains me to say it, but there is a confession I need to make.' Peter had his glasses at the end of his nose. Both lenses had had an overdose of cleaning fluid. 'Everything is a lie. Everything you know about me, everything I've said. I would not be surprised if by the end of this talk, everything I have said within it you also suspect of being apocryphal.

'That whole story about my mum, my dear mother,' he said with tears yet to roll. Ideating her, with him, on a violet isle. 'That story was just a funny lie— disinformation to make me popular, to make you think I was resolute and could come back with humour from adversity. And so, I never lost her in the food court. She lost her battle with Alzheimer's. I couldn't take how she gradually and gradually lost any sense of me. She was all I had in the world. She was the only woman that loved me the same way I did her. Like the Colossus of Rhodes, she was gone, and she has fallen a million times in my mind and a million times more in my heart.

'In this place, this beautiful ecovillage, I have found the only manmade construction, if you can call it that, where I have felt at home. So if you take that knowledge and my forty-plus years of life, can you not see how all those pent up years of being an outcast have…and I…eh, yes. Now I am in a forward-thinking land.

'From a little boy, I have always wanted to be famous and right now I feel as famous as…as famous as I've ever known, yet with a heavy heart.

'I'm a bad person I know. The truth is, I never got over losing my mum, but that is no excuse. My life was so bad, and I always wanted to create mischief and magic.

'Dave,' said Peter, brushing his face with his arm, 'I was outside your tent for the whole while you were talking to Jim after his break-up with Martha.' Several gasps from the villagers punched the air. 'I knew everything of Martha's whereabouts whilst Jim was away because there was no man for her here, and I felt I had to watch over her.' There was catastrophe in Martha's giant gaze. She let it scrutinise Peter. A detonating dynamitic aftershock shuddered its way across the ground from Martha to Peter, up through his feet and calves. That was quite enough for his divergence.

'We are all human and we all make mistakes. Sometimes some of us are a bit too self-righteous round here. I am sure all of you have done something in your life you rue. In the history of the world, I, for one, do not think that what I have done is all that atrocious.' Anjit shook his head, having switched set modes to overdrive. 'And some of you also need to look at how you have been here and what you have done.' Peter looked at Martha with the leery suggestively paedophilic goggle of a school-wear shop owner bent by time, mental illness and its flux.

'I love someone who doesn't love me. This has given rise to a lot of emotional pain. The emotional pain intertwines with the way I have acted. Think of it as like paying a governmental tax except not in currency but dealing in emotion. It cannot help it, the way I have acted. It does not excuse it all, mark you, but then you have to add up the reasons.

'I…I…I conspired with Mary Beswick. That time she came here at the start of April—I knew before she came she was coming. Regarding our illegal activities on this site, I took the standpoint that everything they know, I will remind them of, and of everything they don't, I will inform them.

'I am nothing. If you want to hate me, hate me. I am the scum of the earth. All because I wanted to be something. Someone. Even if it just meant I was notorious in the confines of our ecovillage. Anything any of you has ever done is probably not as bad as what I have done. I realise now it was the wrong thing to do. I have sold you all down the river, and for that I am deeply sorry.

'If I should die here, do not listen to me any more from the grave than you did in life. My soul feels darker than you will ever know. Please, I urge you to find love in your heart to forgive me. I beseech you! Please understand, or try to. Then again, why should I seek such a thing, I who have caused such strife. I am nothing on any of you. I've had my moment of fame.'

Dave took a capful of Gaviscon Advance. No-one else did anything much. Nature gave some charm to the uncomfortable noiselessness. It tasted a whole minute.

'I've got a right mind to throttle you,' said Manny, incisors seeable. 'Give me one good reason why I shouldn't!'

'We're not going to get anywhere by doing that,' said Paul. 'Even if he *has* stitched us up like a kipper.'

'Yes, Peter has done wrong,' said Sage. 'But the more you love your enemies the less they become your enemies and the more they become people. Blame and rancour just breed one another.' Sage finished thinking aloud. Seeing a slyness in Peter's eyes, Sage became uncomfortably warm and fireballed him a look, giving a facial expression as if he had just sat on something he really shouldn't have. Parboiled, Sage was about to blow! 'You marine…gastropod!! Heel, what were you thinking?!'

'I'm sorry, I know,' said Peter.

'You be*gunking* gastropod!'

'Because you'd go to prison?' Jim said, looking at Manny, in belated reference.

'Keep your trapdoor shut,' said Manny.

Peter the pedant craved fizzy sweets. Any variety would do…

skiving to an off-license…sinnerman…catch the snoot, supercede the whom

it clothes.

It all felt akin to loving someone really hard when they couldn't give a shit.

'Peter is like Japanese knotweed. I ought to strike the God-awful pillock,' said Sage.

'Hey man don't talk like that,' said Paul. 'Let's not ruin the energy here. That's someone's brother, a father's son—what would *he* think to hear that?'

'If we follow the natural progression of logic, it would suggest his father is also a pillock.'

'Apparently his mum was last spotted at KFC,' Paul said, can in hand, half-pissed.

Burt was about to have *his* say:

'I remember him telling me about how he always liked the baddies, the villains of the piece in those old Western films, but I never expected *this*. He said it made him feel like a kid again when he watched those old films. Now the prick's found his starring role.'

'He might star in the follow-up to *Lawrence of Arabia*, yeah: *Prick on the Nile*,' said Paul.

'Bloody Beers,' said Cathy. 'I knew she were trouble. People'll only be too 'appy to fook you over if ya let 'em. Stupid old bat's well past 'er sell-by date.'

'Beers has played the ecovillage, not us her,' said Sage. 'The dried up bitch. She looks like battered onions. That she was party to all this, it doesn't matter now whether it was her or Peter that initiated deviousness for shared ends. But of Peter, our little friend, let us be clear. There is no beginning to his talents for manipulation and deceit!' Sage carried on, asserting with his left forefinger. 'He hath gudgeoned us, hath brought reproach on our beloved home! That boy can spin a yarn all right, sacré bleu, quite simply beyond the pale. No matter how verbose a supplication, that saboteur can forget forgiveness. If only I had not sold my tantō, I would decapitate the reprobate and copy Boisrond-Tonnerre's idea of using a skull for an inkwell. This I would do with the skull of Peter for use in writing my prophecies!'

'Alright lovey,' said Cathy, and she linked Sage's arm in a bid for calm.

'Now listen,' said Manny. 'Peter is a nonentity. He is no longer part of this project as far as I am concerned. But for the rest of you…some of you, if this all fails you can go back to live in your parents' middle-class habitations. I don't have that luxury. We're gonna pretend as if nothing's happened, keep going and try our damndest to make this work.'

Manny said all this never quite looking at you as he looked at you, like a misty-eyed visionary. He was a visionary, Jim felt, and Jim pined for his energy and prowess with the project. 'Eighty percent of the time, we need to be united,' continued Manny. 'The rest of the time, we need to be vigilant. Granted, we have a good generic ethos here but you can't be too careful these days. Trust no-one. Twenty percent eye for an eye, tooth for a tooth, every man for himself.'

'There you go again, what about the women?' asked Jim.

'Don't get clever Moylesy! From my perspective, as long as we get no winding-up order, there is no winding-up order.'

'You've used the wrong term, man of Mexico, but I know what you mean,' said Sage. 'It is the duty of all men, particularly those lacking in showable physical presence to strive for the heart of a lion; gold-maned. Parallel interests have intersected and a Pyrrhic victory scored. What Peter did was sacrilege. The rube masquerading as a knave. Punishment will no doubt be meted out in kind, and he won't have a leg to stand on. Despite the acrimony I feel inside, it simply would not be in keeping with how we do things here if we were to evict Peter like he has us. Let him feed from the love of this place, our love for it and for each other. Let him be garroted by love. His Anschluss with Beers will founder and his plans, like Albert Speer's, will never fully be realised. Let Peter and Beers fall on each other's sword; a Berlin in ruins. We have freedom and Peter has the freedom to be undermined. His health now is good but it won't always be, and when it starts seriously failing and he starts to worry, his conscience will be his undoing, for it will have a few questions to ask him.'

Peter took it as a good omen that he was to see his psychotherapist. If he had things to talk about, it meant his mind was suitably animated. Maybe if there was one week where he did not feel like going to the psychotherapist, perhaps things in life were easy, too easy to be piquant. A paucity of objects of life he could throw around his head would mean a mind dead like Kristoff's. 'Of those that threaten our village with extinction,' Sage continued, 'some of them might have to die in mysterious circumstances. I'll have you know there's more chance of that than of us eviction!'

'I can't believe this is happening,' said Anjit to Martha. His body began to stoop, his mouth to open. 'I remember seeing binoculars in Peter's tent. I never thought anything of it. Everything we've built is demolished.'

'No, don't say that,' said Martha. 'We haven't received an eviction notice yet, much less a chance to appeal. Let's keep positive.' Despite Martha's words, she no longer had the ecovillage registered as a 'safe place' on her phone.

'Dammit, I had been talking with Manny about sorting out the slug problem, particularly for the wetter months,' said Anjit. 'I was hoping to dig a pond to attract the ducks as they love slugs, and also the pond would've looked nice. Now what's the fucking point? Peter, what a…I'm sorry I know it's not with the spirit of this place, but seriously what a dickhead.'

'Yeah, he is a bit.'

CHAPTER ELEVEN

If you go down Monkton Street, seven streets off Cherryblossom, every Sunday afternoon around three o'clock, there sits a man on a chair drawing murals on the ground. His name is Felix Ham. His work resides on a pedestrianised walkway. Some will stop and stare as they pass, others do not see. Some have their eyes stuck in technology. Most, if not fully, will see a mural in the corner of an eye. Occasionally someone will walk on the murals by accident, having not seen them at all.

When Mr Ham closes his eyes, he sees images of women he has not met. A man of antediluvian distinction, or as a matter of choice not a man but a fellow of all souls, a gentleman and a scholar. Gentlemen do gentlemanly things, like keeping doors and options open for old ladies, puffing on dusted old pipes, and preening moustache hairs with undivided attention.

He was a close friend of Carringdon Tory councillor, Danni Stiletto and by happenstance a relative thrice removed from Eric Soil. Of noteworthy finery there was a strigil and diamond accoutrement atop his mantelpiece alongside feather-dusted figurines of Napoleonic soldiers in his antiquated, oaken cottage. He once had a lady from Spain. If she ever got out of line he'd remind her of the Armada. Then she jumped ship to leave him high and dry.

A hopeless romantic, as the monocle sits, dependably, in the orbit of his left eye, he writes letters to his subjects of heartbreak, so many times written before in his mind. You know he's reliable 'cause his kettle's always full. He used to lave his hands with lukewarm coffee and work at a hospital reminding everyone how he helped save people's lives every day. He's always thought pretzels quite the unnecessary snack.

Today Ham reads in the Carringdon Herald that an eviction order has been sent to Carringdon Ecovillage. Meredith holds it like the world in her hands:

NOTICE

UNLAWFUL OCCUPATION OF LAND ON THE EAST SIDE OF LEOPOLD CLOSE, CARRINGDON, LONDON

To: All those occupying land on the east side of Leopold Close, Carringdon, London

You are trespassing on land owned by Stalybridge Holdings Limited. The full extent of the land owned by Stalybridge Holdings Limited is shown edged black on the plan attached to this Notice.

You do not have permission or consent to remain on the land and you are trespassing.

We hereby give you notice that we have instructed solicitors to issue possession proceedings without further notice against you to remove you and your possessions from our land if you do not vacate the land by **9.00am on Thursday, 18 June 2022.**

Signed: **Roland Hines**
For and on behalf of Stalybridge Holdings
Dated: (17 June 2022)

'Peter, why were you such a prat?' said Meredith to Peter at the communal point, where there was an eight percent chance of precipitation that afternoon.

'Why can't you forgive?!' he answered. 'Why are you even talking to me? You spurner. You only talk to me when it suits you. Who would want to be with someone anyway who screws their face up like a fish? You don't like it, yeah?! Well you can stick your inhaler where the sun don't shine. And stop clogging the shower with your hot off the press, finicky frizz of hair. Oh, and another thing. Why don't you grow up already and stop using photo filters.'

A dotty butterfly paid a visit, black on orange, dots on background. Peter missed it for he had stomped away.

'Alright guys, come on now, it's not all buried in the sand,' said Paul. Martha put her hand on bony-bodied Meredith and loved how she was rangy like her, but deplored that she was not in the right.

'A shame we'll never get to build that polytunnel we always wanted,' said Dave.

Martha went to insert her AirPods and shilly-shallied about putting on some acid dinner jazz. No! she thought. I'll stick to Brahms. I know where I am with Brahms.

Sage took the document from Meredith to see it for himself.

'Ah yes, Stalybridge Holdings, a longtime associate of Beers,' he said.

'No doubt this'll be a construction site soon,' said Cathy. 'They'll be tryin' to expand their business interests, in't it.'

'Keep the glass half full for now,' said Sage. 'Onwards and upwards.'

Jim secretly liked that the unicorn had had a cardiac arrest as it meant it forced the option to put a step through the portal to his real world. Or did it do the opposite? The fact that he had come this far and that there wasn't that long to go could mean that it was one of the few doings of some rectitude in his life seen out to the end, and an easy one at that.

#

The oft well-shod Meredith decided to celebrate the first day of summer with a bespoke mauve cambric dress. The sick-yellow sun clamped her left cheek. By a greater margin than her previous clothing offence, Jim was repelled inasmuch as the dress engendered thoughts of offenses to globular affairs such as sewage, daytime detective shows, offal, fungal crumpets, the way youths use chill as an adjective, Eric Soil, what you will.

'We've been given a chance to represent our case in court,' said Sage outside his bender.

'So good of them,' said Meredith. 'I like the way they threaten to kick us out the day after we receive their eviction letter.'

'Yes, quite so Meredith. Their intimidation tactics will not work on us.'

'When is the court hearing?'

'Two days' time. The 22nd of June,' said Sage.

'They don't give us much time do they.'

'No, but we must carry on as normal. In this vein I have orchestrated an open day and invited woofers onto site, for their sins. It is that time of year.'

Woofers are volunteers that usually work on organic farms and often in more exotic places than England. Nevertheless, the dwellers will call the new people to arrive at the ecovillage 'woofers' as it is a much better word than 'volunteers.' First, there was the small matter of the court hearing.

All rise! There was a representative of Stalybridge Holdings present in court. All the dwellers had convened except Peter and Burt. A larger court room had to be prepared in place of the usual one so as to cater for the number of eco villagers. Cathy looked like she was having a real job trying not to blurt out something in the direction of the representative, as District Judge Graham presided over proceedings. Judge Graham pointed out that Stalybridge Holdings were seeking a possession order of the land on the grounds of trespassing. They wanted to use the land to build luxury flats. Judge Graham also took into account that the ecovillage community had made their stake to occupy the land.

It was the villagers' turn before the judge.

'We need more time,' said Sage. 'We simply need more time to present our defence, and, Your Honour, I would like to draw your attention to the European

Convention on Human Rights, as this provides us assistance in our case.'

Sage's parting words to the judge: 'I wish to invoke clause 39 of Magna Carta.'

Cathy and most definitely Anjit looked around with baffled expressions.

'What folly! A shower!' exclaimed Sage outside the courthouse as he took the mic. A modest gathering of local press had assembled. 'I had not told anyone else of the little trick up my sleeve,' Sage continued. 'In a short space of time, the judge declared the court adjourned. We have been granted a stay of execution, giving us a week to provide evidence in our defence for the next hearing expected in early July. Make no mistake we are the victors here.

'We know, the judge knows, and so do you that the whole thing stinks. Withal, I extend my gratitude for the court's decision. We have every right to the land that is rightfully ours. So to Stalybridge Holdings and all the other oppressors of free rein, I say stick that in your proverbial pipe and proverbially smoke it until your proverbially pass out. Remain vigilant! Remain steadfast! Keep digging!'

Paul held Sage's arm aloft in victory.

'Three cheers for Sage,' he said. 'Hip hip hooray!' Most of the dwellers, overjoyed with Sage, joined in. Good God! Some locals joined in too:

'Hip hip hooray! Hip hip hooray!'

Stalybridge Holdings were unavailable for comment.

#

After the back-patting, Sage felt like a new man back at the ecovillage.

Careful now, you're in danger of inflating your ego, thought Martha.

'Let us not roister,' said Sage. 'This is no time for a jamboree! There is work to be done and an appeal to lodge. The Magna Carta does prohibit the commons from being on someone else's land, but it might yet hold the key to saving us from expulsion.

'The Magna Carta, with the help of Archbishop Stephen Langton, was sealed in 1215 by King John of England. Originally drawn up to repress this unpopular King's relations with unruly barons, it protects denizens' rights in what is viewed by some as a façade of freedom. A façade because although regarded as an integral compartment in the evolution of the uncodified constitution of the United Kingdom, eight hundred years later it can simply be used or passed over to suit those in power. In practice symbolic, little more.

'The lesser known 1217 Charter of the Forest was sealed just after King John's death by a ten-year old, namely Henry III under the regency of William Marshall, 1st Earl of Pembroke. This gave freemen the right to harvest building materials and firewood. The Magna Carta in clause 39, the clause I used in court, affirms what appears to be a hopeful message of freedom until you get to the last fifteen words:

No free man shall be seized or imprisoned, or stripped of his rights or possessions, or outlawed or exiled, or deprived of his standing in any other way, nor will we proceed with force against him, or send others to do so,

*except by the lawful judgment of his equals or by the
law of the land'*

'I've just done some research on my iPad,' said
Meredith. 'What you mentioned there, the Charter of
the Forest, I read some information about that. I like
the part where it says, "if he has made forest of his own
wood, then it shall remain forest, saving the Common
of Herbage, and of other things in the same forest, to
them which before were accustomed to have the same."
The Common of Herbage means you can raise your
own livestock, specifically for commoners. The
sovereign cannot remove you. I think we need to
emphasise the human rights part of the case. We need
to research more on common law and natural law rights
to live on the land. There is also the European
Convention on Human Rights that you mentioned in
court, but thanks to Brexit I'm not sure it applies to us
anymore. But I guess the judge didn't say diddly-squat
about that.'

'Good work,' said Anjit.

'Indeed it is,' said Sage. 'Everyone, take a leaf out
of Meredith's book. No respite! Let us garner all the
information we can to corroborate our appeal. Let us
share on social media our struggle. Let us fly our
banners. Any way you see fit, as the mood takes you,
thwart the farce.'

'Right on!' said Meredith.

'Might I suggest that we make some sensible
decisions should the worst occur,' said Sage, uprightly,
proudly roving Carringdon Ecovillage with a straight
stick he had found and grabbed from the ground to use

like a cane. He slammed it to the hallowed mud with a thunk. 'We will appeal without doubt, but should our appeal lose we need to think of fitting ways to go about things before the bastard bailiffs come. First things first. Materials. We use the hazel from the benders so that we can take it with us should any of us wish to recycle it for future benders. We take all the free stuff given and donated and anything we don't want or need anymore, that is of use, to the Oxfam shop on Cherryblossom Street. I'll be damned to blazes if I can think of anything else for the moment, but there is a start.

'Tomorrow sees the arrival of the woofers. Let us welcome them the way we ourselves would wish to be welcomed.' There were a few cheers sealing approval. Sage turned to look at where Kristoff had died. For the time being, a single stick in the ground marked the spot. 'Let us too remember Kristoff, always, and go on for him, fighting in his honour, fighting the fight he could not.

'I have taken it upon myself to build a play area. I want to build it for Sue's children as a tribute to her and all the other locals that have helped so that their children too can enjoy our place on a broader scale. Additionally, it will be for any children that come to our open days and mini festivals, and it is to the children I now speak. Sail into Carringdon! We will create a river out of love.'

There were no children who could hear. Sage, from his robes, took out the eviction notice and nominated his left arm for gesticulation. 'Eviction knows no fear for us. Let us be defiant. At a good clip, we will keep digging for the future of our children, and this behest, this nitwitted piece of paper shall not deter us. Let us be optimistic about our appeal and pretend all the recent troubles that have come our way never happened. Dear friends, we do not need a symposium, nor will this be a playing field for paranoiacs and calumniators! Rather truth be our name. Remain vigilant! Remain steadfast! Keep digging!'

'Keep digging!' a few yelled back.

'Right then who's going to help me with the play area?' Sage got hold of a spade from the storehouse to dig in the dank wooded area of his speech. All the chums of the forest were present, even Burt. Everyone. Everyone but one. Using a thumbnail to pick the insides of a twig, watching the others, a head silently poked its way out from the side of a hut.

Manny. *Los cortesanos aduladores!* (*The fawning courtiers!*) he thought in Spanish. A rarer time was here. It was unlike Manny, since he had come to the ecovillage, to think in his mother tongue. Nearby cedars were still swooning from Sage's words.

#

'It's a temporary volunteering scheme for a two-week stint.'

The day of the woofers had arrived, and of those newcomers, a late thirty-something called Jeff had spoken. He was next to a young girl called Mel and a retired older man called David in the communal area.

'Do you mind if we call you Dave 2?' asked Paul of David. 'Only we'll get you mixed up with our Dave otherwise.'

'No problem,' said David, or Dave 2, as he was now known.

Jim wondered if the threesome were doggers as well as woofers. Once a dogger always a dogger. Jeff was an excellent handyman. Mel caused something of a stir among the lads. Sage and Jim were on quiet investigation in tandem.

'She's one of those green, yoga people,' said Sage. 'Her lineaments, lightly sculpted, in particular the skin around the eyes, give the observer directly but perhaps unfairly, the impression that her life up to this point has involved rare hard work. This assumption is confirmed by her soft scally hands. Either that or she uses expensive washing up liquid. Deep-set eyes. A nose squashed into its surroundings, almost feline.'

'I just think she's pretty in a really boring way,' said Jim. 'She's trying to liven herself up with that glass plug in her ear. I still would though.'

The trichroic plug was of teal, khaki green and peach.

The green world turns to Mel. From recycled floorboards she is clawing out a recycled nail, newly bent. In the foreground is Dave 2, holding everything in place. With every whop of the hammer, Mel is imagining the next nail is a former spouse who cheated on her.

It does not matter what they are building; you just need to know that they are building for the green world crawling out of asphyxiation.

'Do I hold it like this?' asked Dave 2.

'Yes,' said Mel.

Summer raised an eyebrow today so Jim decided to buy himself an ice cream. To earn some extra cash, he had recently signed on with no intention of finding a job. He used his latest payment to buy himself a deck chair and some sunglasses. Outside Dave's tent, he put down his ice cream and sweater that was tied around his waist, and slipped off slightly silted sandals. Coming back only three minutes later, the ice cream had gone.

'Who's eaten my fucking ice cream?!' he screamed. He had his suspicions as to the culprit. Apparently nobody saw Jim eating it nor anyone come near him. No-one saw anything. It was one thing if it was the regular sort, but the strawberry swirl one? That wasn't on.

There was a cooling off period in Jim's head, with no thanks to the missing ice cream. Easing himself deeper into the deck chair, Jim kicked back to fall in the arms of Morpheus.

Jim had a dream that he had an Eastern European friend with benefits called Tatiana who had just given birth to two of their babies. She was twenty-five years old and blonde. As calamitous as Jim found his situation, the most alarming part was that the newborn babies did not emerge as humans but omelettes.

On waking, Jim had an idea that the dream might be the subconscious guilt of his overuse of poultry products, showing itself in metaphorical dreamlike imagery.

Fronted in the main by Sage and Meredith, an appeal was duly lodged to court. Behind the scenes, phrenetical research had been carried out on charters and treaties and so forth, among them the Magna Carta and the European Convention on Human Rights.

In three days, witness statements have to be, and will be sent to court. The waiting game is almost here.

#

On the last day of June, Jeff was unerringly chopping wood.

'Do you know what you're going to do?' Peter asked him, putting his thumb up as he did so. They were deep in the wood, in fine fettle, not far from Sage's life-giving speech and Kristoff's end.

'I do,' said Jeff. 'I nattered with Manny about that. Wood framing and dry stone walling I think. He said he could do with a wall around this place.'

'Oh *did* he?'

'Yeah, I've got some experience of that sort of thing and I need to prepare for the open day tomorr…'

'Jolly well.'

'The voluntary scheme is joint, so after the two weeks we'll leave together.'

'As you wish.'

On the following day, the inelaborate open day was taking shape at Carringdon Ecovillage. Carmel Yap had heard about the event but she could not make it as it was ladies' night at 'The Flamenco' bar in town, and she needed to allow time beforehand to caper with her spirit animal.

Meredith and Martha were in charge of face painting for children and Sage. Paul used his ghetto blaster to tell the world about hardcore punk.

There were a few complaints from parents. Paul was also manning a stall which was half free and half unfree. It had decals and posters of cult heroes, timeworn clothes, newfangled bangles and other knickknacks on display. Sage had earlier given another of his guided meditations and Anjit had participated by giving a short talk about the carbon footprint. Dave was going around handing out leaflets designed by Sage and Martha that told people more about the ecovillage and its date with destiny. Mel and Dave 2 had paired off to present a talk about volunteering opportunities and give gardening demonstrations. In addition, Mel led a foraging expedition and forest clean-up of waste cast illegally. Sue was there too, responsible for food and refreshments. A hula hoop was available for those who wished to derestrict their lives by encircling themselves in restriction.

Jeff was about to give a presentation. He courteously waited for everyone to be in one place, and for parents to use leverage in quietening their children. One of the couchant children searched him with derision, wishing he could be at his Xbox. Most faces crackled.

'OK, is everyone ready please for the woodcarving display?'

All eyes on Jeff, gravel in his voice box. 'Thanks for coming today. My name is Jeff. I'm here from the volunteering programme, Green Go-Getters.

'Without further ado, I'd like to begin by talking about sycamore. Sycamore is readily available and widely regarded as an invasive species. For those reasons and others, it is good to use. It grows back fast, so it's very sustainable.' With ennui not present on any face,

Jeff in manner became staid and his voice orotund. 'A nice, clean, straight-grained wood; that's sycamore for you. It's non-toxic so it's good for kitchenware too. Not too hard, it's easy to carve. Wooding is tenably the most important activity for any ecovillage because this carbon-neutral fuel is the most important material here for us. A little steer for you: use an axe for the first part of the carving process because it gets a lot of wood chopped quickly. But then the shape needs to be refined, so it's best then to use knives, carving tools—that sort of thing—as I will demonstrate.'

Listen to the people as they clap clap clap, and unclamp nuisance once Jeff wraps things up. All things considered, the day went down an unruffled success.

#

'I like the weather like I like my food like I like my women, hot hot hot!'

Here were some words a few days later from the longish lips of Sage. It was a hard summer's day, a somnolent day in no hurry to get gone like the rest of us. People watched the sun lobbing itchy streaks of yellow. Steamy, it just kept on, and on, livelong, baking insects. Only yesterday snails and slugs quaffed on drenched concrete, today they rolled away to grey.

Poor pale Martha was a desert mannequin in a mirage looking to an oasis of yesterdays. Even with the hope that an oasis brings, thrust upon her, a woe undying.

'God this heat is insufferable,' Jim said to Burt at the charging point.

'Too hot to trot,' replied Burt.

The sunshine human flesh had been missing for days hit Jim like a philtre. He fell in love with Martha and was dumped all over again. As if strapped in a straightaway tunnel, the heat squeezed forward, smothering him, and only him, to him. Everyone else was in warmer apparel than Jim who was in a sleeveless shirt and yet had to go inside.

'It's my Nordic genes,' Jim said to Dave in the tent of Dave whilst unwinding with a hand fan. 'It's in my blood, I'm used to the cold. I can't take this heat. It's like I've been poked with a Viking atgeir, telling me I would be better off away. But if I were to go away completely, where would I go?'

'I don't know,' said Dave. Dave thought he heard a bird tweet but soon realised it was just an exhale from one of his slightly blocked nostrils.

Jim's void of love meant he had to win his fallen love back beginning with 'M.' Didn't he? Just to love something? Tarrying in ineluctable territory, freedom was a winless entity or so it seemed.

Like Dave, Jim didn't know. He didn't know anything for the rest of the day.

Surely Martha will not take me back, he surmised in the evening, by a gnat.

'When I was younger, in more oblique times, I used to stamp on ants as they legged it athwart the concrete,' said Sage. He was in the newer mini communal point. 'I liked to watch the buggers stop and expand once my foot had kissed them goodbye.' Present were some rather horrified looks coupled with a few laughs. 'My sadism became more ingenious when I built a little moat for them around their home. To my credit, a few I did save as they ran the water gauntlet. Most didn't make it. I would feel bad with myself if I intentionally tried to kill anything these days, but that ant scenario is how I see much of how society operates.' This time even Dave sighed. 'The ant workers' feelings are nugatory in the eyes of their big bosses. The bosses collect their money and have no care for anyone scotched along the way, as long as they can get away with it of course. Big people falling on smaller ones, rubbing against their will. Through so-called promotions you can climb the anthill. Mayhap you will get to the top. But you're still essentially an ant. And you're still susceptible to being squashed. I don't know about you guys, but I couldn't live in that society anymore. Even charities I have trouble with. When the head of a charity is on one hundred or one hundred and fifty grand, I wonder where the money has come from. If their salaries were halved to still very respectable amounts, think how much more could go towards the people we're trying to help. Philanthropy's a posh word for what people *should* do.'

Martha now thought of Sage as a plagiarist and copycat. Sage knew full-well most of those ants wouldn't make it. Sage had played the anteater in a game of survival of the fittest, though he was only eight. 'It is a fey evening,' Sage continued. 'A humid and brindled sky, why how my words sit cutely juxtaposed! The weather is hot yet short of satisfying; charities abound as institutions for the common good, but, I might ask, to what scale of purity?'

#

Time took a skip and a jump and landed on the morning of July 7th. With something catching his vision, Peter's eyes dropped down past his head for a look-see.

'Hey, our programme's up now' said Mel, to a Peter short of breath, having ran to catch up. 'Those two weeks have really *flown* by. We reminded Manny a few days ago and we just looked for him but we couldn't find h…

'Don't worry about that,' said Peter. 'Well thanks for coming, that was good help.' Peter had unshaven blonds on his chin and higgledy-piggledy head hair. 'I'll take care of things from here, and let Manny know it was me who saw you out. You've got my contact details so do get in touch if you are thinking of coming back.'

'It's now we go, is it?' asked Dave 2.

'Yes,' said Jeff.

'Thought it might be later. Ah right.'

Three days later and a crowd had surged to Sage this 10th of July.

'What does it say?' asked Cathy.

'Tell us,' said Paul.

Dave looked down to inspect his wheel lock.

'Is it really from them?' asked Anjit.

'Shh shh shh,' said Sage, as he laid claim to being the communal area letter opener:

Notice of Hearing

In the County Court at Staines	
Ref. Number	B00SN305
Date	10 July 2022

1) TAKE NOTICE that the Hearing will take place on 24 July 2022 at 9:30 AM
at the County Court at Guildford, The Law Courts, Mary Road, Guildford, Surrey GU1 4PS

When you should attend
2) The hearing scheduled for 28 July 2022 has been vacated.

Please Note: *This case may be released to another Judge, possibly at a different Court*

'Fiddlesticks. So the appeal is in two weeks,' said Sage. 'Typical. They said it would be in early July and it is in late July. That as it is, as the light omits my esprit, for those that judge we shall be ripe-ready.'

The document also listed names of one claimant and five defendants but we cannot show them for legal reasons.

Jim, hangry and exacerbated at the subpar cooking going on, plodded to Cherryblossom Street to feast his eyes on the menu for Sacramento Pizza. In a madcap pirouette of mind he was putting away pizza for nostalgia to remember a time when he could eat the bastard and not get fat.

You could tell Jim had been away from himself too long: rambling past the shops, minding his own business, and then, oh, that feeling you get when you think someone in the window is very stilly staring at you, only to realise it's a shop mannequin.

Jim passed the local bakehouse.

After manifold jobs, the now owner has renovated a highly successful independent bakery in the town. A true perfectionist, except for the time he deduced that his daughter was being spit-roasted by the local coke dealers—the bread was particularly burned that day.

#

How far do you travel with scruples involving living beings? People leave lamps by open windows in summer knowing that flies will die by the lamp. Except many don't know because it's not something many think about. They know once it's too late for the fly and his flying associates by the litter of smudged black dots on the windowsill. It is forgotten about two minutes later.

Do you not go outside on the grass with the knowledge that if you do, you might step on and kill a slug, a worm or a snail? God forbid an earwig. Not to mention all the microorganisms that could be harmed. The Jains think about this. Are they right to? Bakers commit genocide on microorganisms on a daily basis. What is anyway acceptable? Who invented the word acceptable? Find them!

'I can't deal with this whining,' Manny said to Martha, as he washed up unhurriedly in the kitchen that evening. A skinful of the finest, cheesiest marijuana one could find in the county sat on the sidepiece as a reward once he finished. 'People don't know how lucky they have it here. If I hear another person complain about the soup or the stews that are made with labour and love, I'm going to put my fist through this wall.'

Manny's history was from a people that did not seek honour nor respect but a meal a day. Jim overheard the conversation, having returned from his liaison with food. In his mind, there was no getting away from how Manny was the quintessence of how people of Hispanic derivation are ruled by their emotions, with their arms subsequently thrashing about like those trees from Sage's words. Germans, now say what you like about Germans but at least with them you know where you stand, thought Jim.

#

'Ahem,' Peter said another misunderstood evening, banging his rubbed spoon against a Honduran pitcher to draw everyone's attention. 'Everyone in the communal area, would you come to the kitchen please?' He waited for the waddling of feet, and then: 'Let me start to make it up to everyone. A maiden voyage on my way to atonement. Tonight, I will cook for you a lamb dinner…'

'Even though the majority of us don't eat meat?' said Anjit.

'I was just coming to that. Thank you, Anjit.' His thanks were unambiguously sarcastic. 'Of course I have proposed a vegan version too of the same dish. Let me cook for everybody tonight. It will be a tiny way I can help repair the damage. A stepping stone, if you will.'

A gargantuan silence lasted a good eleven seconds. 'Please?' asked Peter, almost in tears. 'Please!'

'Fine,' said Sage. 'Just make the thing and let's not hear more of it.'

What a miserable bunch, thought Jim. They looked as miserable as impresari lodging with nothing but their own importance and a compost can, forcing it upon themselves to live in a ghost town.

'I know I've been here a while, but I still can't get over how you guys call these "chips," that's too funny,' Meredith said later, looking at the fries on her plate. She had soya instead of lamb in like manner to the other non-meat eaters at the communal area overrun with sunniness.

'Is the soya good?' asked Jim, in a way that inferred he already knew the answer.

'Yeah, tiptop,' said Meredith, suddenly feeling very British.

'I tried that stuff once. Never again,' said Jim.

'Oh for heaven's sake! This tastes good and it's ethical. Sheep have feelings too, you know.'

'Not this one it's dead,' said Jim.

'This is good shit,' said Anjit, in a complex world of his own.

Well he certainly got the *shit* part right, thought Jim.

A stray black long-haired moggy with golden eyes that Paul had named 'Buttons' had been frequenting the ecovillage the last four days. Buttons circled around, waiting for morsels of food to drop to the unfixed ground, soon realising there was not a dicky bird to his liking. Jim felt more warmth for the cat than anyone else around. It felt like Buttons was the only living being who understood Jim's pain. Probably didn't share Jim's pain, though, as Jim would have thought human pain was bigger than cat pain.

Of the three opposite her—Paul, Anjit and Burt— if a contest were to ever arise to see who could finish eating themselves first, Martha thought Paul would be a shoo-in to win. Burt would surely take too long to eat his mass and Anjit would be too cautious, whereas Paul would just fucking have it.

#

On the day of the appeal, Martha didn't show. Seen too much, read too much. Others' experiences in analogous circumstances troubled her so. At the communal point, Martha heard what she had feared from the pack's collective body language as they lumbered back from court.

'Our appeal was quashed. Pathetic,' said Paul, in the mild afternoon light.

'Treason was upheld as their basis in law,' said Meredith. 'Most of our arguments made were not listened to. Due process of law was never applied, I'm so cross right now.'

'The judge said there was no'—Anjit stopped to hand-signal quotation marks—' "compelling argument." She said she had to put emotions to one side and was just "applying the law." '

'The judge said it ultimately came down to whether Stalybridge Holdings had private law rights over the land,' Meredith said. 'The basis of our appeal was thrown out because of that, and the bitch had the audacity to mention that we had already been here for over two years and were well aware of the risks in staying somewhere like this. It doesn't matter that we brought up, for example, the fucking Human Rights Act. In Article 8 there is the right to a private life and family life and in Article 10, the freedom of expression. But none of this mattered because they didn't give a hoot.'

'Forsooth,' said Sage. 'All the representative for Stalybridge Holdings needed to say was that the land is privately owned by the claimant. That really was all she needed to say.'

'It was just drawn-out talking in riddles,' said Meredith. 'Plus they didn't seem to take into account all of the testimonials and messages of support we have received from locals and people who have visited. It was a travesty.'

'We're the war on drugs they kept telling us about,' said Paul. 'Like internet piracy file share or livestreaming sites, they shut one down and another pops up. They can't massacre an idea, there will always be ecovillages.'

'It's an ongoing fight 'til the death,' said Anjit.

'Papers are due to be served here within the next forty-eight hours,' said Meredith. 'We are looking at anything from two to four weeks until the bailiffs, I mean, bastards, come.'

'The resistance begins!' said Anjit. 'Meredith was our star. She knew so much about the legal processes and we've a lot to thank her for; a real trouper.'

'Bravo!' said Paul and many clapped.

Puzzle out the ones that didn't.

'I have no ego but I was a star too,' said Sage. 'Just saying, in the interests of accuracy.'

'Tell yer friends an' loved ones,' said Cathy. 'Tell them to tell their friends an' loved ones. We need diggers!'

The word too was out on the ecovillage's social media and website pages. The injunction on them made, the County Court writ for the possession order granted. Nothing enforced without a jostle.

'What should we do with our materials and all our stuff?' asked Anjit behind Dave, his nails scrawling indentations on the rubber of Dave's wheelchair handgrips.

'Yes, Anjit highlights a hot potato,' said Sage. 'I will set off with the necessary items to the charity shop tomorrow morning, dead on ten o'clock. Anyone wishing to help me collect items before then would be very welcome. Pray join me tomorrow to help bring it all. As mentioned before, any unneeded hazel should now be collected for recycling. When the bastards come, remember not to waste the hazel from benders when taking them down. This is all…very…flipping annoying!'

As Sage looked at Dave he was reminded of the affinity he had for him. 'After founding this place a few years ago, why did you not want to be the leader of it, as such?' he asked him. Dave took a cigarette from his lips.

He thought about mentioning the trials of his mental and physical life, how a lack of mobility crimped peace of mind, how his love of anarchy did not fit in with the concept of a leader…

'To tell you the truth I couldn't be bothered.'

By closing doors of day was a laid up ecovillage tapering off. A woman with a handkerchief was scowling and squinting as she jogged nigher.

'Sue. It's good to see you,' said Meredith at the communal point.

'I just saw Martha's text,' said Sue, getting her minty breath back. 'I had to get here. I just can't believe it. They're doing it. They're actually doing it. None of the locals I've spoken to want this. The new development isn't going to help any of us out.'

'More money to the corporations,' said Cathy. 'Money wins against our voices and the community's.'

Sunset caught a tumbling tear from Sue's right eye, twinkling.

'I remember when you first came to camp,' Sue said. 'All us locals came here to see what the fuss was about. We saw how you hugged and held hands in a circle. It didn't take most us long to realise you were doing good.'

Jim had not recovered mentally from feeling a little queasy after the lamb dinner. Though acting identically to the adult female he used to romance in not going to court, he had kept clear of her. Martha, reunited with the group, managed to look lorn. Downcast and shaggy, she had only noticed Sue's tear once it claimed a cheek. She had read a bit more of Kyle James. James, to Martha's annoyance, gave roman numerals to his chapters.

Why have the first chapter look like a capital 'i' and the second like the start of the peristyle Second Temple of Hera? she thought.

'O Meredith, I agree with what you said on the hill,' Martha said. 'I didn't then but I do now—that I don't think I could try my hand at the life I had before. Just to even be in some way more involved with people with such dissimilar ideals as me seems too much. Too many normal stupid people. The idea of life is to develop your mind and body and immerse yourself in world culture. That should be the norm. The actual norm: distract yourself as much as possible with materialism and low-grade meat. Quick, cheap and easy; and not necessarily cheap in the financial sense.' Martha was on the last chapter of James' bad-boy book:

> *Whenever I get a problem in life and need someone to turn to, I think, what would Jeremy Kyle do? The name like mine, the look like mine. When will they give me a TV show like his?*

> Around my neck
> the crucifix, the point at which
> my life took new meaning…

> *What on earth was she on about when Jilly Wright wrote this? Any Jilly Wright fans put this book down now! I hate religion and most of all I hate you.*

> *Religion gives people comfort, so does Marks & Spencer's. The English with their shitty rules. Why do we continue to churn out ponce after English ponce to uphold the rules of previous ponces.*

'I know of a friend whose ecovillage in Birmingham won the case to go to appeal at the royal courts, and they got a second stay of execution.' said Sage. 'All it really did was buy them more time. When it eventually went to the royal courts, it was defeated and they were evicted without the judge batting an eyelid. They were given two and a half hours to have their case heard but the judge said there was no good reason for them to stay, even though the case was backed by constitutional experts and even though there were families with kids staying there.'

'So are you saying we shouldn't take this to the Royal Courts of Justice to further appeal?' Anjit asked.

'Not only were there kids staying there, the grounds were also important because they held historical significance. We don't have either of those. So if the judge threw their case out, what chance have we got? They threw everything at the judge but the kitchen sink. The Royal Courts of *Injustice* more like. It is a must that the judge is able to find that we have absolutely exceptional circumstances to live specifically in *this* area of land, to make our living here justifiable in their eyes against the landowners. That is the only way our case can be, as they put it, "arguable." As Meredith said, it's a minimum of at least two weeks yet until the bailiffs appear. I'm not in my right mind to think. Artlessly, I am at my wit's end. I must withdraw from thought and take a recess from this weary, weary mind. Let me sleep on it.'

The Sage slept on it for three days.

#

'They're coming!' cried Burt.

'Come again?' said Peter.

'The basssterds!' said Cathy. 'Get me the chains! The chains!'

'They're coming along a wide front,' said Sage. 'Set the barricades! Mobilise! Hold fast!'

'Bastards!' said Burt. 'Meredith get the recording equipment. We're going to tell the world everything the bastards say and do. They said it would be at least two weeks before they came for us, it's only been three days!'

'And no paperwork's been sent! They've come unannounced!!' said Sage.

'I've got the ropes, the climbing equipment and chains!' cried Peter. Martha had begun in her mind, with arrows, bow and buckler, saying everything she wanted to say to the police, orating like Caesar himself. Anjit and to an extent Burt lugged the materials for the barricade into position. The barricade looked indecisive at best. God, why—Martha asked in her mind looking skyward, essaying a little her ego—are you letting this happen? Checking no-one was watching, she gently put her palms together and closed her eyes, saying, pacifically, with a little nod to the Holy Ghost,

'Dear God, if you exist, or if the creative force, for which I haven't a name, exists,

I know I haven't turned to you much in recent times but please save us from this ruddy end. And, if I may be so selfish, may I still yet be saved? Amen.'

In her body Martha noticed nothing but a furry hum, a dissipated sense of vengeance and, ostensibly, a tingle at the tragus of her left ear. Gurgling before it sinks, the brook is nowhere to be heard. The brook flows thoughts for Martha, for whom piety at church and at home are one and the same.

Time stopped the way the world stops for Messi and Cantona, writing poetry with their feet.

I'm not fookin' leavin' I'm not fookin' leavin' I'm not fookin' leavin,' thought Cathy in chains. Imbibing Paul's Jack Daniels, she was frenetically swigging as much as her gut would allow whilst tied to a kitchen mast. And done with that,

'Paul you 'ad the wine the last time didn't ya. Merlot wasn't it?! Merlot! Pass me the fookin' merlot.'

'I can't I'm tied to a tree.'

Come on love you've still got the Blue Nun, it's not all doom and gloom.

Burt looked purposeful, like hapless windrows on side streets. An unforgiving sun helped him glimmer like cobwebs warming in undersoil heaters. Martha was nothing and everything you wanted her to be. One minute scared by clamour and change, the next exhilarated by their efforts on her adrenal glands. In her mind are reminiscences as a five-year old, her garden in a sunset zephyr. Hyacinths wandering as if walking away with the daylight. Shadowed against sun-crest, feeling at one in her newer mother's arms, a flushed cheek pressed against a stomach inside a fuzzy green roll-neck top; the freeness of the sure.

Martha's galleries of responsiveness were jiving. Her mind like a heavy tome, Jim's more a picture book. A set of constellated ideas presented themselves all at once yet he could not pinpoint any of them. Jim was nothing and nothing, unintelligible and ambivalent, usurped by Sól's lazy rays.

'We are peacefully resisting!' Paul said up on the treetop.

He thinks of love. He thinks of how Martha must be attracted to Jim's low level of cortisol, and then Paul ducks to dive down ducts of the underground. Noses everywhere.

Security officers were gaining on the forest with no wooden latchkey.

'We are not breaching the peace, only you are my friends,' said Sage. 'We love you but not what you are doing.'

'We just want the plants fer the children so they can 'ave their own green space!' cried Cathy. 'Fer the children, t'show them a better way! Leave us alone! Ya take our kindness fer weakness at yer peril you do! We just want our plants!'

She cried until she could cry no more and breath could stop if necessary. 'You've turned on me waterworks, I'm fookin' fumin' now.'

'Yes, you try to uproot us, but we are rooted here like the plants!' said Sage, assuaging Cathy with a healing hand on her back.

It occasioned Martha some comfort to know, especially at these times most trying, that the men may never find the brook. These beings were as though from another dimension, out of tune, out of sync with the feeling of the forest. Do they not know its materials could unite to form an indivisible impassable wall of conflagration!

Amidst the mugginess, twelve men, some in sheeny yellow jackets, advanced. The jackets had blue rectangles on their backs with white writing saying 'police.'

The others were dressed in black, each with white writing saying 'enforcement officer.' Twelve paces more twelve men at the barricade.

'Fellas, ladies, we can do this the easy way or the hard way,' one of them called out.

Mascarpone-coloured eyes. Mascarpone man! thought Martha, outmatching the speaker's gaze.

What else could she do to bedevil the faithless? She wished it was Thursday for to hear the amenity of church bells. The stifling swelter seemed to oppress everyone but the police. Perhaps they had been given by their superiors an air-conditioning system in their underclothing. The first cock a snook, the off-you-trot sign, the first glimpse of the hard way:

Burt feels like he is sashaying like a hawk. He is in fact being led away, a chair leg for each policeman from the chair Burt has refused to detach himself from. They are aiming to get him past the borderline on the plan edged in the eviction notice. They have not enough collective brawn and they need to take a pit stop for a breather not far from the border.

Burt was proud of his efforts. His two-football stomach proved a fabulous ploy for the army of diggers. The police needed a new spade for the immovable, Brobdingnagian Burt. The brook was spurting and there were no more Lilliputians. Peter had one arm free with which to drink and brush against his face. Scraping a locally made birdbath was the beak of an erratic finch near Burt's new position.

'We're just doing our job people. Just doing our job,' said an officer. Like the armature of a magnet, the officer had no particularly strong ideas on anything,

'Unhand Burt!' yelled Sage. 'Your truths are pliable. Your spoils are money, and our scuppered work! Brutes in suits, awful lawful toughs, off our land you city crusts of grime! Don't pass this off as your only possible job, there are others you can do. Bargain Borstal are hiring.'

Paul was at the outside edge of his thinking box, desperate for a candy return. Like prey in the claws of a viewless predator, a tuneful folk melody from a bass singing voice doggedly drove the not-so-airy air. Burt's was the voice, his delivery exemplary:

> *'The trees grow high*
> *On yonder hill*
> *The battle cry*
> *It echoes still*
> *The die is cast*
> *They close the door*
> *On highland men*
> *Who are no more'*

All the while people doing their job marched on.

Some eco dwellers would have joined in had they'd known the words and not been rocked into silence for reasons galore.

'Come down from there,' said a policeman's shivery voice aimed at Paul in the tree. Jim could still not be certain of being able to identify any tree type. Burt took a deep breath to arrive at the next part of the song, and remembered how the cycle of life fatigued him: a death, a funeral, someone's wedding, a christening, a baby shower, a car bomb on the news, the annual fumbling around the attic to organise the crap.

Burt felt as though he'd seen and done it all a thousand times before. Insipidness turned to enmity on the exhale, oh yeah, and there was the eviction to be angry about too:

> *'The wind is blowing through the trees*
> *And down through the glen,*
> *The streams, they are all running with*
> *The blood of highland men!'*

It was a traditional folk song Burt had committed to memory from an author unknown. A pair of handcuffs were closed around the actionable upper parts of Cathy after she called one of the officers a fucking prick. Incidentally, like everyone at an ecovillage, Cathy was under the weather. With a head cold she was throatily elucidating how she could not blow her own nose with her hands tied.

'What are ya tyin' me up fer? Ya into sado-masochism? Ya dirty fooks.'

A thread, red, from Martha's dress fell to the ground. Martha vacillated about doing some last minute eviction washing up to deal with tenseness and as a way of carrying on as normal in defiance.

What am I saying to myself?! she asked inside. I don't want to do the dishes, I'm too busy thinking about space exploration.

All events played out in a dot of time in human history, arguably below the belt of fortune's tight-fitting trousers.

'Where's Jim?' asked Peter, looking around, hot-headed.

Jim had walked the plank. So bored. Of everything. And above all, of anything to do with the ecovillage. As soon as the bailiffs had arrived, Jim had sallied into town unseen. On his way out a poster:

Woodchip for sale, fresh or mature, mulch, chicken runs, essential oils etc.
Going cheap. Call Idriss for more info

The fresh energy of matutinal traffic; a resounding hum of sable waves through 'til late evening where energies tire and drown. Thinking of how he has lost his gaucheness, in his mind Jim doubles up and is also like a reverent handshake for the witchdoctor who's voodoo he does not understand, nor not fear, and as he sits to be called, there is a rainbow through the shutters of God's waiting room.

Jim had some bun from one of those multinational chain bakery stores in town. He didn't know what bun it was, just pointed at it and asked for one of those please. Sugar and ice in a zigzagged pact formed the top with straight lines of milk chocolate on top of that. With a chunky, menacing pastry below both those, it looked naughty and tasted even naughtier. Snatched with noisy gnashers, shimmering caramel hosed the back of his throat, glazing insides as it sank—you could feel the calories in a bite.

He grew outward and saw the town library, walking thither in doing so turning back on certain women he passed. Lascivious, lecherous, lurking Jim. Ooh he had a good look, don't worry about that. Had a good, good look. Look but you can't touch, look look look!

said his conk. Grappling, groping, biting rumps, breasts, teething protruding lady spots to remove them for them. He knew he was getting older because the girls he now looked at came with the automatic check for the wedding ring finger. And who was Jacque Fresco anyway? he thought.

To go to the library was to go to the second floor. Everyone else took the lift, Jim walked the stairs. Everyone was so fucking impassive in this place. Jim had not realised there was a lift. Once arrived, Jim looked around for a bit, forgot what it was he was looking for and got the hell out of there. The librarian was ringing the bell anyhow to signal closing time because everything had to be quick and it saved having to talk to anyone. No time to stop for a disunited mind, no time to study the unstudied. It was a day where the library was only open for the first half of the day due to financial cuts.

The newsagent afterwards was more interested in exchange than Jim's vague attempt at small talk. Next, it was to the convenience store. Much to Jim's excitement the store had the same old crap you'd find in any store similar. Necessary as it was earthbound, the store the runner, the people the furniture, Jim stood bewildered there was no milk left, at least not the size or type he wanted—small and semi-skimmed to be precise. Available were only dairy-free alternatives, and goat's milk. Jim had a face like a fried arse.

A Namibian lady employee with a ringleted hairdo had a smile as radiant, pulchritudinous and labyrinthine as the opening of a cowry shell from Walvis Bay at summer noontime.

Thoughts scooting. Checking his pockets. Twenty pounds to the good.

'Where's the normal milk?' he asked the worker.

'Sorry, we sold it.'

'Can I get any milk out back?' Jim suspected she was pregnant and so was hoping she'd take it the wrong way.

'I will check for you.' She draped her arms after laying down juice drinks she had been schlepping.

Out back was where there had been rumoured sightings of a revenant. It was believed to be of a man who worked the store a long-lived time before dying on the job. Derek Ford, fifty years man and boy, a product of the store. 'Sorry, no milk,' the woman said on return, whose demented, ambidextrous, incoherent piano tuner also happened to be Ella Sponge—

Delora's great-aunt.

'Sorry the tap's not working, you'll 'ave to pop your card in,' said the jocund checkout lady, concealing her midlife crisis. O God, thought Jim, that means I'll have to speak to you for another twenty seconds for the items I didn't want anyway.

Jim's annoyance forced him to get the bus instead of walking the short journey home. He sat at the front of the top deck of a double-decker facing the immense window. It was like a really shit rollercoaster ride.

All of this was such a waste of time. All of everything was such a waste of time. These were the final thoughts of Jim, for now, as a maleficent wind, frightful and stabbing, locked onto all it encompassed.

#

'We've learned so much from the other off-grid, DIY communities,' said Sage. 'Though our pickings be slim with the options that are obvious, I suggest we go up the old Commonsworth Hill. Cathy, Dave and Meredith would vouch for me here. It is a meritorious community.'

'Yep,' said Dave.

'Better than Camden or Hackney?' asked Burt.

'I am led to believe so, yes' said Sage. 'It is better established and has more opportunities for networking.'

'Better than Basildon Bohemians?'

'Hook, line, and sinker,' said Sage.

'It sounds more institutional than the others,' said Burt. 'Isn't that what we're trying to get away from?' Sage held his thinking face for a while…

'No.'

Unused as a couple for so long, Jim and Martha's end-of-the-road tent is the last thing bailiffs take down. Out of the salvage comes sass, and Meredith, on concrete with a crossword on her lap remembering her Janeness, is once again reunited with pain. She cannot bear the loss of the ecovillage. She is pain manifest.

Pain was, of its inherent constituents, one of those necessary negatives for Meredith that could be rented out from time to time.

Sage's spavined guitar was by now disabled on the Cherryblossom Street bridge. Like an elastic band stretched to its maximum, the rigours on her strings from being thumbed and fingered by the fires at night, to standing by the cold of mornings in clotted mud meant two of them had snapped. Even the most roguish smile of Sage could not make her gush sound any better.

For a long time Anjit's soles had courted the grass. Never humdrum, a sabbatical had taken place in his mind. Drowsy does it. His slowness more noticeable; like an unceasing rivulet, he now unknowingly had the ability to stare through you as if you weren't there. Max Linder knew too. Anjit had learned from the weeds, the suicide, the notice of eviction, the appeal and eviction. An unassumingness had crept up on him. He had a pain in the small of his back. It was an ex kicking up a fuss. He had taken an arced swipe at the world and not connected. He punched walls, punched himself, punched cushions, punched his tent—how could he be so late to notice Kristoff?! Enfolded by sunburn there were grumbles in his mind. His feet were to have more intimate relations with slabbed, tiled and carpeted ground.

Through shredded words Anjit said what needed to be said to those he cared for most, and the hours went by, for every tick a tock, for every hour a sun diminishing. The town belfry morosely played its part. Its 4pm reminder right there for a backpack on and a bagged up tent. Just to break, surely that was all that was intended.

'If we examine the protuberance of light, there comes a time to fall and roll face first in its miracles,' triumphantly began Sage. He was in receipt of a glower or two. 'Anjit has given a grievous goodbye. It was for me personally, I cannot speak for everyone. But you know, we are all victims of time, and the time we live in. What may seem stupendous today in one hundred years may seem feeble and fragile. How thoughtfully surreal, foxy, moving, sledgehammer and burning time is. We shall be back!

'I wished dear Anjit Godspeed, and that was that. O to take the head out of oneself! I hope to goodness that we have learnt whilst here with all our energies to see the greater macrocosm, to know balance, to sample the commanding ripples of revolt; to know less of no and more of know. I may see before me a fog bow or Brocken spectre. Carringdon Ecovillage was just an appetizer. On to the next course, I can see forever!'

The rolling began. Sage was champing a bread roll. A roll. A fucking roll. To call it a bap might seem excessive but to Sage, its title on the packaging of 'barm cake' just seemed unnecessarily adventurous. Appeared had the heavenly herbivore. In close view, Sage tuned in to Martha. 'Lend me an ear,' began Sage, bits of white about the mouth amidst a furious raid on the bap. 'I don't know if Jim ever told you, but you have the most magnificent neck. Would you mind I take a picture for my band of esoteric subordinates? Squiffy the Gent wishes to analyse the data in the laboratory.'

'Erm…OK…I've never met someone like you before Sage.'

'Quite. I'm not the beardy weirdy you first thought you had met, I imagine.'

Feel the worker! Feel the worker! Not literally, you'd be in the dock. Watch the tears crash and stream down the worker who is sick of work. Feel that we too cannot be of this worker! The worker is a poet after all. He writes his life out on a blank cheque; she does the same not uncommonly for less. In return…who returns? I return? You return? The genderfluid person has recognition, not always. Perhaps the new worker, the one revitalised can spare a thought for Martha's thoughts.

She was whiling away the hours thanks to thinking—Martha thought of thought and how sometimes what is not said reveals so much more than what is. She strived to think of each beginning as a primrose more beautiful than the last. Mother earth can recreate plants like the evening primrose by giving them many seeds that will be their legacy when they die. The seeds disseminate in the wind and with time sow into earth's soul to repeat the cycle of growth. Syllogistic agriculture is the philosophy that humans can facilitate plant progress by planting crops in such a way that they can maximise the way in which the plants can repeat themselves, with the least possible maintenance. Martha knew she could learn a thing or two from the autonomous self-seeding evening primrose.

Martha lambasted herself: Too fast on the cup, you've burnt your tongue again you silly moo. Wash it down with juice of kryptonite to defend against the one who once believed he was Superman.

Gazelle eyes, sandpapered soul. Martha's namesake, Ms Wainwright's 'Bloody Mother Fucking Asshole' equals the soundtrack. Martha's soundtrack. Hits the world like a thunderclap. Her art has developed. Never will there be enough to see it, nor indeed all the people she wishes to see it will ever be enough. There is hope, however, that in spirit it will touch them in some supernatural way. Martha Franks often thought how nice it felt to be part of something in a bigger something. Sage's appetizer, Carringdon Ecovillage was just one rabbet for the weatherboarded beach hut.

Sad about time.

Martha was a blue pin. She took on time and she asked for an extension on deadline day. Peter wore her extenuating circumstances like a crown. Like time Martha is. Time was Ian Brown's everything—no time for spilt seconds.

Money has tied the hands of the forest. Its roots and branches lie tangled and forlorn. The CEO of time remains unknown.

Standing redoubtably, Martha didn't have to be sad but wanted to be, to remind herself fully what sad felt like. There is a lagging of footsteps on the broken field.

Think less

Emotion less

'Are you going Martha?' Jim asked in an infrequent exchange with the former adorer. She set a gaze at him that answered nothing. It is the first time in his life Jim is abashed. Burt looked like a Spanish omelette, frying in the midday sun. A sun that had hobbled away, to life, from ephemeral cloudage. Because he was an adult by time not choice, Burt was currently renewing vows with his laptop—I do!

Sage is here. He is meditating for a ride to spiritual Disneyland. The thinking Sage, with the stare of an infirm speckled fish. The lost loves of Sage: it didn't matter that they were quite a way older than him, it just meant they had more experience breathing. They all were lent Meredith's pet crocodiles, Martha's drawbridges and Sage's moats on their palace islets.

Sage thought inward: *They* stem from a world colder than mine, from a compound suffocation greater than I. *They* get on the bus and there are smells of marijuana, fried chicken in breadcrumbs, and middle-age lady perfume. I know this. It is not some oracular vision. It is just life itself.

'What do you reckon Martha?' Sage asked her. 'What is your bidding? In considering risk-creating opportunities, in sum, of the Commonsworth Hill… well, is it for you?'

Her lips were on holiday. There were one or two insects on the grass. Martha decided to look at them instead. She cogitated whether God had had a miscarriage on the field. I will let the natural world answer, she is thinking.

There remains a feral fire leaping through the supple, fertile engine room of Martha's mind. Heaven help us if one day we will be able to hear each other's thoughts, Martha thought. Martha thoughtlessed.

Martha continues to live her life like a work of art. Herself an artwork, so many colours of change, hidden and revealed on different days on different takes. Jim saw Martha in Carringdon one last time. She is a horrible wound that won't close up. Perhaps to him she is less a person and more the materialisation of the dark side of his soul.

Have you not lost enough time from anxiety and depression already?! Martha taught herself to ask.

She, the author of my heart, my rhapsody falling out the charts, thought Jim. Maybe a good thing considering the modern pop scene, he thought again.

Martha was there, at his demise, every painstaking second, in her drawing room full of broken pillars. He is wearing her insides for her. Of his contusioned body, those vital ill organs just keep ticking over. His jacket carries her scent everlastingly.

Martha hoped that Benji was currently pissing all over a picture of Jim. As it was, he was by his trough, about to take a drink, just being a horse. His hooves had caused divots in the ground but he was near seven now and those hind legs were not what they used to be.

A cigarette is smoking itself to death on the prison yard. Overnight in the cell, Cathy feels every inch her tortured features.

Mrs McCall spends all her life waiting for the kettle to boil. She has just heard on the local radio about the end of the ecovillage and wonders whether fate is just a science we don't yet fully understand.

Felix Ham was the other spit-roaster.

Fred has found the arms of a loving kennel.

When Peter stares it is no longer redly. Today Martha has observed him staring in dumbfounderment. His mind has left the exosphere. The stars prick up on visitation and as they do, they really feel a bond. Peter has on his EVA suit. He is in the command module thinking he is Michael Collins, flying to the moon. Adrift ideas all became.

Paul and his mind continue lost in destination.

Dave found no successor to wheel him. Who could Dave confide in now that Anjit was gone, now that Jim was always dead.

The sky is parched breached by dark, the path lined with boulders and heartache. From the fiacre, she is crammed in a woodworm-chewed pushcart, perhaps a tumbril? Yokeless yet due for embarkation, Meredith has no-one to wheel her. Snare of hers set loose at the catch. Her mind puzzled, a riddle of seahorses is slung to the seashore. She stands smoking near Martha and Martha stands smoking from Meredith. Fancier of fitness and the best pelvic floor muscles in London, Meredith's temerity is prodded but hatched years ago. Still she turns confidence on and off like a faucet.

Manny is peckish, starkers cow for dinner.

The forgetful ecovillage. The grass and the insects had no-one more to walk on them, for now. Only fauna use the unfinished play area. The dwellers did not have a chance to eat all the vegetables grown, and fauna liked this fact the more.

Meanwhile the rest of the UK had a million empty properties and a million homeless persons. The sun of reason exploded.

…Well, maybe not, but that line sounded alright, did it not?

To certain fellows it seemed unnatural to spend so much time of human life enclosed by manmade floors, ceilings and walls of four. Womanmade is on hold 'til worthy of wordiness in the English dictionary. At Cherryblossom Street bridge, if you listen carefully you can hear the ecovillage swan-song play:

so it is, the final summons,

the feeling continued, the path was new; some were out, some were in.

If you enjoyed this book
&
want to be informed about Joel's latest books
then…

Sign up for updates on the homepage using
the link below:

www.joelschueler.com

Reviews on Amazon/Goodreads are helpful
and much appreciated

ACKNOWLEDGEMENTS

Special thanks to family and friends, and for the help I have received from ecovillage friends such as: Abdi, Vinny Edmunds, Peter Phoenix, Charlotte Summers, Simon Moore, Lammas Ecovillage, Kew Bridge Ecovillage and Runnymede Ecovillage. Apologies if I have missed anyone out.

Many thanks to the following people who kindly granted permission to let me use their work:

(Morgue joke) - Dave Fulton - 'If Katie Hopkins Ruled the World' www.davidfulton.com

(The amygdala game) - Neil Slade www.BrainRadar.com and Amygdala video: www.youtube.com/watch?v=WqOpZByFi_A

(Supernova information) - Lawrence Krauss www.lawrencemkrauss.com

About Joel Schueler

Joel is from London and has a BA(Hons) in English Literature & Creative Writing from the University of Wales, Aberystwyth. His works have been accepted across nine different countries in over thirty publications including Pennsylvania Literary Journal, The Bangalore Review & The Brasilia Review. He is a zealous writer of music, lyrics, comedy & more.

CONNECT WITH JOEL

Website:
www.joelschueler.com

Twitter:
www.twitter.com/JoelSchueler?lang=en

Instagram:
www.instagram.com/joelschueler_writer

Facebook:
www.facebook.com/authorjoelschueler

YouTube:
www.youtube.com/channel/UCwrenJpKQXd4s
YInXNPbcFA/

ALSO BY JOEL SCHUELER

NONFICTION

LOVE YOUR FEAR:
A QUICK SELF-HELP GUIDE TO MANAGING ANXIETY

http://viewbook.at/loveyourfear

Printed in Great Britain
by Amazon